CAT in an
ALPHABET ENDGAME

Carole Nelson Douglas
and the Midnight Louie feline PI series

"Midnight Louie's contributions are insightful, humorous, and imaginative... Along with all these wonderful offbeat characters, Douglas has an interesting plot, good story, and an intriguing mystery."
—*Affaire de Coeur* on *Cat in an Alphabet Soup*

"...just about everything you might want in a mystery: glitzy Las Vegas, real characters, suspense, a tough puzzle. Plus, a fine sense of humor and some illuminating social commentary."
—*The Prime Suspect* on *Cat in an Aqua Storm*

"a dazzling blend of witty prose, clever plotting. No wonder Midnight Louie is everyone's cat's meow"
—*RT Book Reviews* on *Cat in a Flamingo Fedora*

"Feline PI Midnight Louie prowls the alleys of Las Vegas, solving crimes and romancing runaways like a furry Sam Spade. This time out, the always engaging Louie stalks a serial killer."
—*People* magazine on *Cat in an Indigo Mood*

"fun, frothy, and charming."
—*Publishers Weekly* on *Cat in a Yellow Spotlight*

ALSO BY CAROLE NELSON DOUGLAS

IRENE ADLER SHERLOCKIAN SUSPENSE

Good Night, Mr. Holmes
The Adventuress (formerly *Good Morning, Irene*)
A Soul of Steel (formerly *Irene at Large*)
Another Scandal in Bohemia (formerly *Irene's Last Waltz*)
Chapel Noir and *Castle Rouge* (Jack the Ripper duology)
Femme Fatale
Spider Dance

CAT in an
ALPHABET ENDGAME

The Twenty-eighth Midnight Louie Mystery

by Carole Nelson Douglas

"Snaps and glitters like the town that inspired it."
—*NORA ROBERTS*

WISHLIST BOOKS

CAT IN AN ALPHABET ENDGAME:
A MIDNIGHT LOUIE MYSTERY
Copyright 2016 © Carole Nelson Douglas.

Published in the United States by Wishlist Publishing

Copy Editor: Mary Moran

Formatting by Dan Keilen

Images Copyright © iStock.com

Author photo Copyright © Sam Douglas

Cover and book interior design © by Carole Nelson Douglas

Printed in the United States of America

Library/retail trade paperback edition ISBN 978-1-1943175-05-5

Digital ISBN 978-1-943175-07-9

Audio book ISBN 9781520018065

www.wishlistpublishing.com

FIRST EDITION

This book and series are dedicated to all our wonderful and loyal readers and their feline friends who've joined Midnight Louie and me on this incredible journey

Acknowledgments

We've loved and kept your cards and letters and now emails, and appreciate the thousands of stamps you've sent to help snail-mail the annual newsletter, and those of you who've bought the books and T-shirts. We're amazed you always say you know how busy we are. How do you know? We try not to whine, because we are so privileged to be doing what we're doing. Yes, a writing career is 12/7. I'm often surprised it's a national holiday. I'm always wishing I could answer you more, but deadlines never die! Those of you I've been in contact with have been delightful and so inspiring and understanding.

Writing a series as long as this, over 25 years, means we've written more than three million words in this series alone. We started out sure we'd remember everything that had been done, and somewhere along the way realized we were not human computers. Books are proofread and edited many times, but errors still slip through because most of us read what we expect to see. Some imperfections can't be fixed right now, because control of the books are in other hands. There are dozens of people (and cats) to thank, but two brave readers have volunteered to read the entire series over for errors and typos, and they deserve our heartfelt thanks for helping make us as perfect as we can be for ourselves and our readers.

They are the indefatigable **Ken Green** and **Denise Thompson**.

Indefatigable is a funny-sounding word for tireless, determined, and dedicated.

Another long-distance runner for 21 years in supporting Midnight Louie's saga is my former student assistant, now an author on her own as Diane Castle, **Jennifer Null**.

These folks are beyond generous and have our whole-hearted gratitude, as do all of you.

Carole Nelson Douglas & Midnight Louie, Esq.

Previously in Midnight Louie's Lives and Times...

A cat *is* said to have nine lives.

Where I live, on and off the Strip, the odds are your average hip but homeless street cat will be Las Vegas lucky to live three lives.

(I prefer "homeless" to mean "free to be me", and I did quite well as a self-employed individual, finally becoming unofficial house detective at the Crystal Phoenix hotel-casino.).

One thing led to another, and now I reside at a cool condominium off the Strip, and volunteer as full-time bodyguard to Miss Temple Barr.

She is quite the fearless and feisty little doll, who has the advantage of looking as cute as a Yorkshire terrier that has just chewed your Christmas slippers to Kingdom Come while possessing the incisive insight of Miss Marple on speed.

We are quite the crime-fighting team, both of us being underestimated, which is annoying in my case because I am large and muscular for my breed, have all my hair follicles operating on full power, move with leopard-like grace, carry more razor-sharp blades than an infomercial Ginsu knife pitchman and, on top of that, am quite the dude with the ladies.

So you would think I am a pretty keen keeper of my own nine lives.

Hah!

Since I became an undercover private investigator dedicated to assisting a few of my closest human associates, I have been running through lives willy-nilly. Right now, not only are the next three in doubt, but if life were a craps table—where it is for many who only visit here—I would need to be rolling "boxcars", with sixes face up on both dice. That roll is otherwise called (after me, doubtless) rolling "midnight". To the individual not knowledgeable about gambling, that would add up to the number twelve.

To put all my cards on the table here, my circle of protectees has outperformed their growth potential, and I do not have lives enough to sacrifice for the looming trouble I see brewing for each and every one of them.

Miss Temple Barr has no idea the man she has put all her money on in the romance stakes is now risking his paltry single life investigating some more than just shady Las Vegas mob history.

Or that the man to whom she first lost her heart has made a dangerous deal with vengeful terrorists to betray the cause she and both of her main men have been pursuing for so long.

Or that sundry other people she trusted and considered honest are secretly at odds with those who should be their allies, keeping each other in the dark, and my Miss Temple most of all.

It is to shudder. And perhaps too much for even my capable shivs to sort out.

Here I should formally introduce myself as founder and CEO of Midnight Investigations, Inc. I plied the mean streets of Las Vegas for many years as a bachelor about town, and then moved into PI work. I now room with Titian-haired, live-in gal pal and amateur detective, Miss Temple Barr.

She may not be a Miss much longer, alas, if she weds Mr. Matt Devine as planned. Our cozy condo does not need interlopers, especially on the California king-size bed, which is perfect for the two of us right now, with my curl-upable twenty pounds and Miss Temple's one hundred.

Yes, she is a tiny thing as humans go, but as I said, she has the heart of a mountain lion and the relentless investigative instincts of a bloodhound. Actually, she is much more attractive in human terms than this characterization sounds.

For a Vegas institution, I have always kept a low profile. I like my nightlife shaken, not stirred. Being short, dark, and handsome... really short...makes me your perfect undercover guy. Miss Temple Barr and I are ideal roomies.

We share a well-honed sense of justice and long, sharp fingernails and have cracked some cases too tough for the local fuzz. She is, after all, a freelance public relations specialist, and Las Vegas is full of public and private relations of all stripes and legalities.

So, there is much private investigative work left for me to do, as usual.

Then you get into the area of private lives. I say *you* get into that area. I do not.

Since Las Vegas is littered with guidebooks as well as bodies, I here provide a rundown of the local landmarks on my particular map of the world. A cast of characters, so to speak.

To wit, I present the current status of who we are and where we are all at:

MIDNIGHT LOUIE, PI

None can deny that the Las Vegas crime scene is big time, and I have been treading these mean neon streets for twenty-eight books now. I am an "alpha cat". Since my foundation volume, *Cat in an Alphabet Soup* (formerly *Catnap*) debuted, the title sequence features an alphabetical "color" word from A to Z. So, *Cat in an Aqua Storm* (formerly *Pussyfoot*) comes next, followed by *Cat on a Blue Monday* and *Cat in a Crimson Haze*, etc. until we reach the, ahem, current volume, *Cat in an Alphabet Endgame*. I assure you that this is indeed the end of the Alphabet series, books A to Z sandwiched between two novels with "Alphabet" in the title. That is it. *Finis,* as the French say. Or is that *fin*? Or *finito*? Whatever, I can advise that it would not be wise to overlook anybody's multiple-lives factor for the near future.

MISS TEMPLE BARR, PR

A freelance public relations ace, my lovely roommate is Miss Nancy Drew all grown up and wearing killer spikes. She had come to Las Vegas with her soon-to-be elusive ex-significant other…

MR. MAX KINSELLA, a.k.a. The Mystifying Max

They were a marriage-minded couple until he disappeared without a word to Miss Temple shortly after the Vegas move. This sometimes missing-in-action magician has good reason for invisibility. After his cousin Sean died in an Irish Republican Army bomb attack during a post-high school jaunt to Ireland, Mr. Max joined the man who became his mentor, Garry Randolph, a.k.a. magician Gandolph the Great, in undercover counterterrorism work all over Europe.

Now however, those events have been turned inside out. Mr. Max, during his latest Ireland visit, has made a dark bargain—with what is left of the Irish Republican Army after the Northern Ireland peace agreement—to save a life. And he still remains under suspicion of murder, no less—by a hard-nosed dame…

LIEUTENANT C. R. MOLINA

This tough Las Vegas homicide detective and single mother of teenage Mariah is also the good friend of Miss Temple's freshly minted new fiancé…

MR. MATT DEVINE

Mr. Matt, a.k.a., Mr. Midnight, is a radio talk show shrink on *The Midnight Hour*. The former Roman Catholic priest came to Vegas to track down his abusive stepfather and ended up a syndicated celebrity in line for hosting a national TV talk show. Now Miss Temple's wellbeing may be protected only by Mr. Matt sacrificing his own.

MR. RAFI NADIR

After blowing his career at the LAPD when his live-in lady, not yet Miss Lt. C. R. Molina, mysteriously left him, has been for years the unsuspecting father of Mariah. Miss Lieutenant Carmen Regina Molina is not thrilled that her former flame now knows what is what and who is whose…since she told Mariah years ago that her dad was a dead hero-cop. There are soon going to be no hero-cops in this secret and shattered family.

MISS KATHLEEN O'CONNOR

Deservedly nicknamed "Kitty the Cutter" by my Miss Temple, she is the local lass that Max and his cousin Sean boyishly competed for in long-ago Northern Ireland, who turned embittered stalker. Finding Mr. Max as impossible to trace as Lieutenant Molina has, Kitty the C settled for harassing with tooth and claw the nearest innocent bystander, primarily Mr. Matt Devine.

Miss Kathleen O'Connor's popping up again like Jill the Ripper has been raising hell for we who reside at a vintage round apartment building called the Circle Ritz, owned by seventy-something free spirit, Miss Electra Lark.

Now reunited with her long-ago IRA associates, Miss Kathleen knows a life is at stake unless the man she has tormented for the past two years betrays an associate of his she stalked.

Someone (Miss Kathleen?) arranged for Mr. Max Kinsella to hit the wall of the Neon Nightmare club with lethal impact while undercover. His enduring traumatic memory loss means he knows he and my roommate were once a committed couple, but he recalls none of the emotional and, ahem, spicy details. So far. And now he returns as a secret agent again.

All this human conniving and canoodling and sex and violence makes me glad that I have a simpler social life, such as just trying to get along with my unacknowledged daughter...

MISS MIDNIGHT LOUISE

This streetwise minx insinuated herself into my cases until I was forced to set up shop with her as Midnight Investigations, Inc. She alleges that I am her deadbeat dad, but I will never cop to that charge.

MA BARKER

My long-lost mama who gave me a last tummy-lick and prodded my rear out of our humble abode next to the Bellagio Dumpsters. (Even high-end hotels need down-to-earth garbage control.) I elected to continue on my own, though Ma now runs the toughest feline street gang in Vegas. She is not pretty, but she *is* pretty effective. I have never quite banished a quiver at the memory of a four shiv-tip disciplinary slap-down from Mommy Dearest.

So that is how things stand today, even more full of danger, angst, and criminal pursuits. However, things are seldom what they seem, and almost never that way in Las Vegas. So any surprising developments do not surprise me. Everything in Sin City is always up for grabs 24/7—guilt, innocence, money, power, love, loss, death, and significant others.

I comfort myself that my ordeals may soon end and I can pull the covers up over my thick blanket of pages and catch some beauty sleep for a decade or two. But wait...

Like Las Vegas, the City That Never Sleeps, Midnight Louie, private eye, also has a sobriquet: the Kitty That Never Sleeps.

With this crew, who could?

1
Five-Alarm Fire Power

The onrushing yodel of a police car siren cut through Temple's dreams like a hot knife through custard pudding. Instead of fading, like a nightmare, the nagging alternating yowls frayed and snapped her nerves.

She was on her feet by the bed, hands to ears, watching her peaceful arched white ceiling become rinsed by lurid forms of red and blue as if as awash in patriotic stingrays.

The red LED lights on her bedside clock read 1:09 a.m. Matt wouldn't be off the air until 2 a.m. She was on her own. At least no intruder had broken into her unit, not the case ten days ago.

Her sleep T-shirt was short, her feet were bare and she needed to get outside to see what was happening.

Even as another siren came bowling toward the usually grave-silent Circle Ritz apartment and condominium building, she saw Midnight Louie's black silhouette stretching up to reach and pull down the French doors' levered handles to the small balcony outside.

"So that's how you make your escape," she muttered, burrowing into the "winter" side of her closet for a velvety micro-fleece jogging suit she slept in on cold desert nights. She'd have awakened an icicle wearing them in her native Minnesota, but in a Las Vegas July they were more of a sweat suit.

Temple didn't own a flip-flop—cursed backdrop for hammertoes and other unlovely foot maladies—but she did have a pair of fuzzy skunk slippers, child size. She stuffed her size-five feet in them and opened a door to follow the big black cat, now balancing on the railing, out into warm, noisy night. Below, other owners and tenants were milling, half dressed, around the slice of parking lot and pool visible from her second-floor perch.

She craned her neck to the balcony above, Matt's place, but it wasn't an object of police interest either.

Time to go down and see what the neighbors knew. Louie had opted to go up, his sharp nails snagging the bark of the single venerable palm tree that overarched the five-story building.

Skunk slippers don't climb well, so Temple grabbed her cell phone and unit key and headed for the seventy-year-old elevator. Since the fifties-era Circle Ritz was actually round, she had to trot halfway around the central mechanical core to wait for the car.

The small lobby was abuzz with people as hastily (if not as absurdly) attired as she. Outside, more of the same awaited her.

Some words from the murmuring neighbors hung like audible billboards far above the rest. "Burglar... Shot... Three squad cars... Ambulance... Taken away."

Obviously the stir centered around the farther part of the building, which overlooked the pool house pavilion. Temple edged through the neighbors, nodding at some she knew. Then she heard someone behind her say, "No, not Max Kinsella. He moved out a couple years ago, but, yeah, he used to be a famous magician..."

This bit of discussion coincided with her sighting a tall, dark man talking with a police officer who was shaking his head "No", even as he took notes.

Yes, it was "No". Mr. Tall, Dark and Confident was not Temple's former significant other. The Milan-styled beige summer suit he wore, now also wearing the strafes of red and blue lights that bathed everybody out here, was one of an uncommon but plural Vegas Genus of Gentleman Gangster, a Fontana brother.

How somebody as squat and chubby as Macho Maria Fontana had ten nephews as sleek and politely formidable as the Berettas they carried under their thirteen-hundred-dollar suit coats, Temple would never know. And only two of them married yet, the youngest and the eldest.

If she ever had time to write a blockbuster novel, the lives, loves, and deeds of Clan Fontana was a natural subject.

Identifying individual Fontana brothers was an art form, even for Temple, who worked for the white sheep of the family. Married Nicky Fontana owned the Crystal Phoenix Hotel and Casino and carried an impeccably honest reputation. Of the current bachelor Fontana crew, one wore a Roman glass ring. One an earring.

"Officer," probably Ernesto was saying, "it is obviously an instance of self-defense."

"Well, Mr. Fontana, then you can *obviously* hire a lawyer to prove that."

Ernesto was under arrest? Perish the thought that the gelato-pale, Italian summer-weight wool suit should pass a night in the slammer.

"Maybe, Officer…" Temple butted in. Being young and petite, no one listened to her unless she took action. "You might want to notify Lieutenant Molina about this incident."

The uniformed policeman wasn't Fontana-tall, but he could certainly look down on her. "Who voted you old enough to vote?"

"My driver's license." She was going to tell him right out that homicide Lt. C.R. Molina was currently seeing Julio Fontana. Or so it seemed. It was hard to tell what was what with the deadpan lady lieutenant.

"The lieutenant is off this shift," the officer said. "Besides, it's all over. The vic is in an ambulance heading to the ER and the shooter is going in for questioning." He nodded to the squad car and someone with red-white-and-blue hair in rollers was peering out the backseat window.

"That's our landlady!" Temple said. "Our elderly landlady."

"So they tell me." The officer nodded at the crowd of tenants who'd followed her to the scene.

"What is she charged with?"

"None of your business, Miss. Read about it in the paper tomorrow. Or you can inquire at headquarters in the morning. Or wake up Lieutenant Molina if you want to risk losing an inch or two of height, which it doesn't look like you can spare. Hey, Dan, let's get rolling."

As he hopped into the squad car's passenger seat the headache band lights went off. Electra Lark was a passing flash of plain white hair and a paper-white face in the back window as the vehicle slowly pulled away from the frowning crowd. Murmurs of dismay ebbed into departing shuffles.

"Don't worry," Ernesto told Temple. "I passed her some legal advice before they swept her away."

"Legal advice?"

"Say nothing until the Fontana Family lawyer gets her out in the morning. She's only being held for questioning. So far."

"Questioning for what?"

Ernesto shrugged a well-padded shoulder. Whether it was the fine tailoring or a gun holster or just awesome muscle, Temple didn't know. Now that she was an official fiancée she chose not to speculate further.

"My dear lady," Ernesto said. "The dude trundled away in the ambulance was a common burglar. Miss Electra found him in her penthouse quarters. What would you do? She approached the alarming sounds with her trusty semiautomatic and took a shot in the dark. Well, several. He fell out of the French doors to the balcony and had the ill luck to fall even farther over the railing to the ground."

Ernesto led her to a crushed landscape of Hedgehog, Prickly Pear and hooked spine Cat Claw cactus.

"*Ouch.* No bed of roses. Five stories, and he's alive?"

"So far."

"I can't believe Electra shot at him more than once," Temple said.

"You are not an older lady who lives alone."

"I'm thinking any jury, including grand ones, would be sympathetic to that factor."

"Sympathetic, yes indeed. However." Ernesto folded his slender hands prayerfully. "In Miss Electra's case she has already been that targeted 'person of interest' in a previous death. A very recent and intimate previous death. Police procedure is not always precise, but they can hardly fail to notice that. Once may be understandable. Twice might look excessive."

"So, what really happened here?"

"I'm inclined to believe that even the police don't know yet. That's when they get their most official and clam up."

Temple nodded glumly.

"I'm also inclined to believe that this was no ordinary second-story man, given your own recent home invasion also. If you want my opinion, you had better assemble what allies of whatever ilk you have to stop more 'senseless' assaults that may in reality be quite specific."

Temple narrowed her eyes. How much did Fontana, Inc. know about the amassed IRA donations gathered for years internationally, that were rumored to be so valuable and hidden somewhere in Vegas?

"Rest assured, Miss Temple," Ernesto said. "We at Gangsters hotel-casino and vehicle rental service will always be available to help in any small, or large, amusing way."

"Thank you, Ernesto," she answered as formally. "Rest assured, we appreciate your skill and finesse in certain areas and will always be grateful."

A rustle in the palm fronds high above shook the papery spikes like a small tornado.

Ernesto looked up. "All your allies of whatever ilk."

"I totally agree."

2
Three-Cat Night

From the faint, first siren call of the police cruisers, I knew that my role was not to remain on the ground among the powerless gawkers. I eyed the limp victim being lifted onto a gurney for a rough ride in an ambulance that may finish him off for good and immediately hit the Palm Tree Trail up to the penthouse balcony from whence he had come.

I regret to say my Miss Temple is as bloodthirsty as any one of these eight-to-eighty-year-old onlookers treated to a crime scene in their midst. Besides, she has the able support of a Fontana brother who is far too fastidious to allow any random blood drop to decorate his lapel. He will restrain her from giving too many pieces of her mind to the local police, given her worry about Miss Electra Lark's brush with a soon-to-be-dead guy.

I am not a sentimentalist, though, and wonder if our free-spirited landlady has flipped her lid. Not that she wears hats. She prefers to use her snow-white hair as a canvas for bright temporary colors. I fear that I have seen a few white Persian cats and poodle dogs so styled, and it is the height of silliness, but at least Miss Electra has free will in the matter.

Now she has no freedom at all. I did not exert all my efforts to save her so recently to give up now. Even if I must encounter her "psychic" Birman cat, Karma, here in the penthouse. Karma is by nature reclusive and I expect she is hiding by the back wall under the couch after the hullabaloo of a burglar turned falling missive.

I complete a leap from a limber palm frond onto the balcony without the sound of even a pad landing. (I am the strong, silent type.)

A flurry of feline boxing punches, shivs out, and a panther-level battle cry from another cat greet my subtle approach.

Meeowwwgrlllphtttt!

Could my would-be daughter, Miss Midnight Louise, be up here, cussing me out? She can be snarky, and considers me a deadbeat dad, but I have allowed her to help out in my Midnight Investigations, Inc. business. Also, I outweigh her by twelve pounds so it is impossible that she could give me a shellacking.

Backackackdowwwn-invading-vermin is spat at me in fluent alley cat. Louise may be a lot of things, but she rarely swears.

"Karma," I plead, while blocking a continuous sharp-clawed pummeling with my front mitts. "Tell me you are not channeling a performing Big Cat black leopard from a Strip magic show."

I am convinced my foe *cannot* be the wimpy Karma, a fluffy buff-colored lady with pretensions to calm Eastern mysticism, unless she has shape-shifted. We contenders here are both a part of the night's darkness, black of coat and born to be bad to the bone if we have to.

The frequent blows pause. "Grasshopper?" a raw voice questions.

I am too aghast to answer, but back off, dodging a finishing swat.

"Ma?" My voice trembles, but not from emotion. I am still mad about those double-paw smackdowns she gave us kits when we did not obey, even if she was right.

"You are already short of wind," Ma is muttering, as I see her pink tongue in the moonlight, wiping off a bloody claw. "Too many gourmet meals from a can."

"What is with the head wounds?" I counter. "I could have been an innocent bystander."

"A crime has been committed here. There are no innocent bystanders."

I search for a comeback while licking my own wound. Single. She got me only once.

Another voice interrupts. "*I* am the innocent bystander."

We both turn to the open balcony door. Framed by moon-silvered white-painted wood, Karma sits as calm as a show cat on a photographer's background. Her Serene Highness has tucked her white-gloved paws under her soft, long coat like a monk's hands into his sleeves. Not a hair on her pale head is mussed, and by night her heavenly blue eyes are mere sapphire rings around her enlarged black pupils.

I am struck dumb.

But, then, Karma would say I had been born that way.

The Sacred Cat of Burma seems to radiate light, and in that glow I see Ma Barker clearly, her scruffy, raccoon-ravaged, rusty-black best coat, her half-mast left eye and moth-eaten ear edges, her scarred muzzle.

That is what one gets for nine years of running the biggest, toughest feral cat clowder in Vegas. She is one awesome dame.

"Sorry, Ma," I mutter under my tongue as I smooth a ruffled jet-black front spat. "I did not expect to see you here. Must be major clowder business to bring you from the police substation."

Karma emits an almost inaudible spurt of purring, always happy to hear me eat crow. Or that abominable health food, Free-to-Be Feline, Miss Temple lavishes on me. Luckily, the clowder loves the stuff and I see they get all they can eat. I am quite the philanthropist when it suits me.

"This is most convenient, Louie," Ma says, settling into her bony haunches like a granny into a rocking chair.

I am sure that she would like grandkits from my superior line of her younger genes, but Miss Midnight Louise, if she *is* my daughter, is "fixed" and proud of it. And I suffered a certain neutering procedure, not usual, that disabled my ability to reproduce, but left all my working parts intact, known among people as a vasectomy. (For graphic details on how I managed to get what I call "a license to thrill" for life, you will have to consult an earlier volume of my adventures, *Cat in a Flamingo Fedora*. Yes, there was a flamingo-pink fedora involved that I momentarily was forced to wear. Every freedom has its price.)

"So why are you here at the Circle Ritz penthouse, Ma?" I inquire casually, working a torn sheath off a rear toenail.

"Karma called."

"She has a cell phone? You do too?"

"Do not be silly. You know she is the best psychic hotline in Las Vegas."

I turn a suspicious green peeper on Miss Serenity. "So what is the message, sweetheart?" I ask in my best Bogart.

"It is all too intuitive and revolving around celestial spheres for the likes of you, Louie," Karma says. "That is why I called on your more sensitive mother."

Ma Barker? Sensitive? She would have half of my second-most valuable member if I called her that.

Ma modestly tucks her chin into her ratty neck ruff. "I do think I am sensitive to certain vibes, such as danger and evil-doing."

Well, sure, that is her job. One does not need an advanced degree in Psych 101 to know that.

She leaps to the balcony rail and down the palm tree to the parking lot with practiced ease as I follow.

I escort Ma to the oleander bushes that ring the Circle Ritz parking lot. "I agree that something wicked this way comes."

"What is 'this way comes'? Did I not teach you proper grammar? It is 'comes this way'."

"Seriously, Ma. What brings you away from the clowder? Do you want to extend your territory, is that it?"

She sits and massages her muzzle with a forepaw. "My territory *has* been enlarged, Louie. I now see the big picture."

"How big."

Her head gestures up to the starry Nevada night sky, which is not very starry because all the lights on the Strip outshine real star power.

"I have been…up there. Higher than high. Higher than a security fence."

"Up…to the top of the Stratosphere Hotel?"

I did introduce Ma to stairs recently when I had to smuggle her into the rooftop suite of the Crystal Phoenix to consult on a case. That was only twelve stories but one humungous giant step for her.

Think about it. She has been a feral urban cat all her life in a desert city. Why would she have to climb service stairs in a hotel, or even four or five steps, when all those acres had been spreading outward since before Howard Hughes bought them? And she would avoid the hurly burly of the Strip except for ground-level Dumpsters for quick raids.

"So, Ma. You dreamed you went to the stars." She is getting loopy in her old age.

"Not the stars, son! I would never breathe a word to the gang, but the aliens got me. Their hovering craft landed and sat there camouflaged until I was enticed inside by Free-to-be Feline over Sardines Almandine, and I was whisked up into their alien mother ship."

"No!" I say, quite sincerely.

"I am sorry, son, but it was your introducing us to that succulent Free-to-Be-Feline that enslaved us."

"'Enslaved' is a harsh word."

"Oh, one or two clowder mates here and there have been kidnapped before. They return sleepy, having lost interest in, you know, what he's and she's do. I assume you know the facts of life by now without me telling you."

"Ma…! For Bast's sake."

"Anyway." She leans near enough to lick the inside of my ear, which was very pleasant when I was a kit and remains so. I lean away as she resumes her tale. "I have undergone the swift abduction into a suddenly hovering alien vessel, strange bright lights in my eyes, the needle in the naval, the entire alien operation."

"You do not say."

"I do. And I have the scar to prove it. And now, well, let us just say that I am not as much in demand among the youthful swinging set as I used to be. There will be no more Midnight Louies," she adds mournfully.

"Thank Bast!"

She gives me the eyebrow whiskers-raised look of imminent wrath.

"I mean, thank Bast you were returned and remain healthy."

"Well, my right hip has a hitch in it still…"

"Relatively healthy."

"And I did get a tummy tuck, which you got from your abduction."

I remember Ma Barker desiring such an alteration. I suspect it is a natural side effect of the neutering process and not an "extra" thrown in, as in my case.

"I was not abducted by aliens, Ma, but by something even scarier."

"What?"

"A hair product-addled D-list starlet who ordered her plastic surgeon to make it so I cannot father kits. She mistakenly believed her Persian and I had gotten together, but when the kits all came out yellow-striped…"

"So that mincing, yellow-bellied house cat, Maurice, your rival for the cat food commercial assignment, did the dirty deed with the purebred who is now no longer so pure."

"I will not hear a bad murmur against the Divine Yvette. It is not her fault she was in the throes of a hormonal condition."

"*Hmm.*" Ma purrs thoughtfully while cleaning between her toe pads. "It is not like you to miss such an excellent opportunity. Nevertheless, you did our coat color proud."

"I am touched, Ma. When would you, in your vagabond life on the streets, chance upon a television set on which to see your son make good?"

"*Phtttt!* You split for the neon-lit twenty-four-hour air-conditioned areas as soon as you could hold your tail, and other things, straight up. You settled for a diet of fast food in tissue wrappers, but I have lived on really fast food in wrappers of—"

I cut her off quick, before she can get to the gory part. I myself prefer to lead an eco-friendly, green life with people food that is supervised by government agencies to be wholesome. Mostly.

"Ma, I know the urban diet is lacking compared to free-range vittles. How does that mean you can glimpse a TV set when you and the clowder are on the move?"

"Through windows, clodhopper."

(Clodhopper is my pet name when she is annoyed with me and "grasshopper" is too affectionate for her current mood.)

The purring behind us has been strengthening and now it is a full-bodied *Oooom*, which is a common syllable used in Eastern-style human meditation.

Except now it alternates with the one-syllable word *Dooom*.

Which is not an encouraging word in any context.

I lower my vocal timbre to put a flea in Ma's ear. "What are you doing consorting with a penthouse pussyfoot whose pads have only touched walnut wood parquet, marble tile, and patches of carpeting her entire life?

"Karma was doing my horoscope."

"What!" I can barely keep my voice a raw whisper. "You put any stock in what this pseudo-psychic *house pet* whose pampered pads have never touched hot asphalt might say?"

"You seem a bit obsessed with manufactured floor and ground coverings, Louie," Ma observes. "I am the natural, organic type. And I will have you know I have been inside this penthouse, and any carpeting is one-hundred percent virgin wool. Karma's faculties best operate in an unadulterated environment."

"'Unadulterated environment', that is hogwash. Karma is an unabashed member of the one percent and we are street folks."

"You have profited from her prescient advice a time or two."

"She has volunteered her prescient advice more times than I can remember, but we make our own futures, and our own decisions."

Ma fruitlessly washes her crumpled vibrissae—whiskers to you. She is sensitive about them being called "whiskers" now that she is older.

"Well, I have some prescient advice for you, sonny. You know that some of my police substation clowder also monitor your Circle Ritz parking lot gratis."

"Not exactly gratis, Ma. They come for the delicious Free-to-Be Feline health kibble I provide."

"After you refuse to eat it. I know your game, Louie." She may be winking at me or it just may be her battle-worn eyelid twitching. She lowers her voice to barely above a purr. "You should know that the gangster clowders on the rough side of town have reported seeing recent suspicious back-and-forths between your precious human associates around here with some of the known criminals and cat-kickers on their turf. They watch those bad guys around the clock and know what is fishy.

"I have had them do freelance surveillance on this site since I heard that, and the guy who broke in here tonight is one of their 'Most Wanted to Catch a Case of Cat-Scratch Fever'.

"Not only that, when I interrogated them, they reported vehicles and persons of interest at the Circle Ritz are now frequenters of their turf."

"So who from here is taking a walk on the wild side?"

"Descriptions vary. They have followed some tall, dark-coated men back to this area."

Mr. Max Kinsella comes immediately to mind, but also my Miss Temple's acquaintance, Mr. Rafi Nadir.

"And most recently, another one. Yellow coat. I believe your favorite ginger-haired roommate has something to do with a yellow-blond someone who is always out nights and free to go slumming on the dark side."

"Not Mr. Matt!"

Ma shrugs. "You might want to keep a sharper eye on your Miss Temple Barr and her latest mate so he is not her last mate."

Ma has a point, which she drives home by bestowing a fond four-shiv tap on my shoulder before she makes like an oleander bush and leaves.

I choose to think the gesture is fond.

3
Midnight Stalkers

"Matt, my man!" Letitia enfolded him in her cocoon of warmth and bright silky color and soft, generous flesh the moment he entered the tiny radio studio.

They were both bumping the desk and equipment, but Letitia would not allow herself to be contained, in any way. In every way, including temperament, they were utter opposites, and he envied her for it.

He immediately checked the clock high on the wall. 11:50.

"I'm closing the show with a medley of most-requested songs, Matt," she said, catching his gesture. "Relax. We have a few precious minutes to ourselves."

And the days dwindle down to a *precious few*.

He could hear the muted lyrics of regret and longing expressed in "September Song", now massaging the airwaves in the dark Nevada almost-midnight.

"You always read me from ten miles away, I swear, Letitia."

"I'm psychic, didn't you know? It takes a worried man to sing a somber song. Now you sit your handsome, worried self down in the soft swivel chair, all its joints oiled and cushy smooth, and unfret that telegenic brow and tell me all about it."

He couldn't help laughing as her strong black fingers with the inch-long French manicure false nails shaped themselves around an invisible crystal ball.

"You're the one who should get her own television talk show," he said.

As "Ambrosia" she dominated the late-night radio audience, playing just the right song to comfort the lost, the lonely listeners who'd tell their sad stories and be encouraged to move on past their woes.

"No, no. No! No TV." She waggled those Chinese Empress false fingernails at Matt. "I must be mysterious. I must just be a Voice. I *must* possibly be assumed to weigh a hundred-and-twenty pounds."

She was a voice. A seductive, velvet voice, but she weighed maybe three times that imagined weight. Matt worried about that. He worried about diabetes. He worried about cardiac issues. Yet Letitia was the most comfortable-in-her-own-skin person he knew. His boss, the mysterious, the intuitive, the amazing Ambrosia.

He *had* been brooding driving into the station for his *Midnight Hour* two-hour counseling stint. Somehow she'd plucked that out of the air with her magician's fingers and bushwhacked him with ten free minutes of talk therapy, and all before he had to go forth live and do likewise.

"You're always recreating yourself. That's better than being packaged and marketed as an attractive product," he agreed.

"Hey, honey-haired boy! I sure do that. I package and market myself." She shimmied her ample shoulders. "My Ambrosia self. You've done the same, as an 'understanding' product too. You just happen to have some looks to go with it. I made me. You made you. God made the both of us first. And we keep it that way."

"I know I'm a good counselor. I do help people."

"But do you have fun? You gotta have *fun*. You gotta laugh at your own mojo, man. We can change lives, but we gotta start with accepting ourselves. Accenting ourselves. Take the bad of the past and BE-spell it into the good, for everyone."

He had no answer to that. Her unhappy childhood, was (her amazing) hands down worse than his.

"So why are we so pouty tonight?" she asked. "For me, I know it makes my Orange Tango lips look *gooood,* and I know that they come in contact with nothing but the radio mic, but guys ain't got no reason to gloat over cosmetics."

When Letitia got folksy he knew he was being mocked. "You're right, Letitia. I'm being an ass. An angsty ass. I would counsel myself to solicit a good kick in the pants. The ghost of the Mystifying Max in Temple's past seems to be banishment-proof. He keeps popping up like a skeleton out of the grave."

"That man do have some serious mojo, but that kind of thing can wear a woman out. And not in a good way. Keep that in mind."

Her upfront fashion style, her vibrant optimism, the way she morphed into Ambrosia, both slinky and comforting, kept Matt shaking his head as he settled into his combination chair and magic carpet navigating the entire country.

"Letitia, you've got my number. I do fixate on family skeletons and ghosts from the past. It's crazy to do that with all the great things I've got going. Who cares why my nasty stepfather, Cliff Effinger, was killed and who did it? Not anybody, really."

"Right. And if you keep on gnawing at an unsolved murder, you might dig up someone who doesn't want that solved going and putting a rattlesnake in your mailbox."

"So. Trying to keep up the tradition and 'protect' Temple as Max Kinsella always did, I might get the opposite outcome?"

Letitia nodded solemnly. "That's why I very, very reluctantly advise you to leave Las Vegas for the Chicago talk show offer. It's the only course that makes sense."

"I'd sure like to cut Temple and me loose from a lot of bad memories. I'd work days too."

"That's right. No Magical Max to wonder where he is at. And, hey, follow the money."

"Maybe I've dithered too long. The network people have been silent."

"After all those lavish efforts to woo you, sweetie? I bet my old seventies Plymouth against your fancy Jaguar gift car they'll get back to you. I expect to see you on my home TV any month now, where I'll be toasting you with a McDonald's chocolate shake. Then I'll stand right up and *do* a chocolate shake."

"Letitia, you always make me laugh."

"Then my work here is done," she said, patting him on the cheek and dancing light-footed out the studio door.

That reminded Matt of the crazy TV cat food advertising opportunity that *had* come in for Temple and her Wonder Cat. Would Midnight Louie have to do the Bunny Hop to earn his lettuce? What a mental picture. Could it be Matt had lost out to his own fiancée?

Did he want to throw away a career to catch the murderer of a man nobody liked?

He had to quit this Hamlet act before somebody really got hurt. Time to slip into the deep space of Radioworld.

The minute Matt put on the headphones, he saw himself as an astronaut or a diver, somebody who floated like an infant tethered to an umbilical cord, a person abnormally high or below ordinary reality. For him, connecting with call-ins, voices in the night with an endless element of surprise, let him utterly forget himself. The first caller could sound distraught, the next hesitant, or ranting, weeping, nervous, self-justifying, shy, egocentric—his two hours on the air had come to feel like emotional Russian roulette crossed with impromptu meditation.

Still, always in the back of his mind, his own doubts and worries murmured nowadays, soaking up his own advice and often critiquing it.

Only tonight what threaded through the routine was a faint filament of panic he couldn't lose, not even in a laugh with Letitia. Practicing the kind of intense investigative moves that Max Kinsella did could wear a man out all right, and maybe get him taken right off the planet.

The first line lit up. Matt nodded at Dave, the engineer, and sat back without a creak in the chair. They used a brief delay to "dump" a joke caller or cut bad language. Not all the touchy callers, though. Listeners liked Matt's adept way of derailing the difficult ones.

"Gee, Ambrosia was kinda a downer tonight," a bored girlish voice said. "What does signing off with all that 'September Song' stuff mean? It sounds like it was written in the olden days, girls with twirling curls and all."

"It was," Matt answered. "Mid-last century. It's about lost chances. That must not be what you worry about."

"'September Song' reminded me about having to go back to school soon. That's a downer too."

"High school?" he guessed.

"Same mean witchy cliques as junior high, only with bigger allowances. And *they* have all those jocks to date and wave under everybody else's noses."

"What's your name?"

A long pause, probably for a couple reasons. One was committing to a radio conversation, the other was teenage discontent.

"Jessica." Said with a wrinkled nose.

"Well, Jessica, that name has a certain gravitas."

"Huh?"

"Gravitas is when people take you seriously. I'd take a Jessica totally seriously."

"Really?" There came the edge of hope and vanity, when a young girl thought she might be Someone to Someone on the Radio. Or the Internet.

Dangerous.

Matt felt he was about to commit an Ann Landers. "All that high school stuff is not what's really bothering you. You were smart enough to know that was coming."

"Yeah?" She sort of liked being thought "smart". "So tell me what my issues are."

"Do your parents know you hate the high school vibe?"

"They say 'get good grades, forget about all that social media stuff'. And they're just... Me-dee-evil. Watch my phone and computer like I'm some baby."

"You are."

"Whaaat?"

"What classes are you looking forward to, what activities? What do you want to *be*?"

"Miley Cyrus?" She giggled. "That would send the parents up the fire pole in reverse. 'Classes, activities', that is so uncool, Mr. Midnight. So parent-y. I used to think you sounded sexy."

"Well, now we know what you really want. I can get to the next caller so you can sit there and listen, or you can come up with a reason for me to talk to you."

"No, wait. I want to work on the school paper, but that's so nerdy and the nerdy boys own doing all the jobs on that."

"Drop the labels. Nobody 'owns' anything in high school, except finding out what they want to be. And not everyone is going to like that, or like it if you're good at it. That's the real world. Now, you want to write for a dying media, print news. There are people old enough to be your grandparents who've lost their jobs and livelihoods doing that. What do you think they'd be saying if they were calling in? Would they be worrying about what some kids you'll never see after four years think of them? Wouldn't they do just anything to get on a crummy school paper? Maybe not. But maybe they'd wish they could go back to those days. And you can do it. And find out if you like it."

"Uh, but maybe nobody will let me on. Or let me on only to make me wish I wasn't."

"You must have something you really want to write, or you wouldn't freak out at trying."

"Well, maybe something on…bullying. Not me. Not big-time bullying, but little stuff that gets really mean."

"Okay. I have an assignment for you."

"You're not my teacher."

"I'm better than that. I'm sexy. You gonna listen to me?"

"Always." Said with adoration. Jessica was getting a lot of time with Mr. Midnight.

"You write something you feel strongly about. You write an essay. Not like an assignment, like what you really feel and you're not afraid of feeling."

Silence.

"And then you show it to your parents. Yes, you do. Because it will be good."

"Oh, I can't. I can't. I can't have them going to the principal, outing me. It would be horrible."

"Yes. But they're not going to do that. You're going to tell them you want to submit the piece to the Huffington Post."

"Get outa here."

"Did you know anyone can ask to submit a piece?"

"No! No way. No way they'd accept anything I wrote."

"Why not? You're a 'Young Person'. The media world wants to hear from Young Persons nowadays. Your experience and hopes are as valid as those of any adults. Don't abuse that chance on crazy, 'sexy', show-offing. Have gravitas, Jessica. I know you have it already."

"You think?"

"Everyone your age does, you just get distracted from showing it. What have you got to lose? A rejection? But you will have been considered, and you can try it again."

"It could backfire on me."

"It could. That's why your parents have to read it. Where do you want to make an impact? In high school? Or in the future?"

"I'll think about it," she said, gravely.

She thought about something else during ten beats of radio silence.

"Gosh, Mr. Midnight, you're way better than sexy."

Matt smiled. "Thank you, Jessica. Thank you very much."

The next voice was a world away from soft teenage girl doubt. It was deep, hoarse, male, and there was no doubt about it.

"Hi, there, Mr. Midnight. I've been around the block. I'm usually giving advice, not asking for it."

Matt felt his throat tighten. No doubt, this was Woodrow Wetherly, the Molina-referred retired cop now turned creepy.

"And I'm usually not up this late, Mr. Midnight. Gotta admit I'd never tuned in your show until lately. My, those sweet little female fans you draw…nice work if you can get it."

"You say you're asking for advice—?" Matt waited for the name.

"Call me Old Bill. Old Bill come due. *Heh-heh-heh-heh.*" That long wheezing high-pitched laugh was more sinister than the man's usual low rumbling voice.

"Bill will do," Matt said. "We don't need to age ourselves before our time."

"*You* may not, but I am just darn old. You don't sound that way. You sound young, sonny. Too young to be handing out advice."

"You don't have to take it. In fact, we've got a line-up of calls waiting, if you don't—"

"Oh, no. No kiss-off. You gave that pretty little thing plenty of time. Just because I ain't a fan is no reason to cut me off."

"You need to state your problem, sir, or the moving finger of fate moves on in talk radio."

"All right, all right. Keep your pants on. Or I guess you don't have to since you're on the radio." Another wheezing laugh.

Dave was about to cut Woody off, when Matt shook his head "No" and the old man complied simultaneously.

"My problem is a lie, Mr. Midnight. Call me old-fashioned, and I already told you to call me Old Bill. What happens when someone you don't know from Adam introduces himself nice and proper, comes with recommendations even, and you find out he's a liar, and he's got a whole lot more in mind than you know."

"Are you talking about someone out to defraud you, sell you an insurance plan you don't need? I can direct you to the Better Business Bureau or the Senior Services division of your local government..."

"Darn it! I want to know what *you* would say. If you were in my shoes."

"I'd want to be sure he'd told me a lie. And then I'd ask him why."

"Yeah, I could do that. But I only have his work number and I'm old-school, as I said. It's not right to call someone up at his work number and hassle him. And if I found his home number and called him there, it might upset the family. Maybe they don't know what he's gotten himself into."

"Bill—"

"No, wait. I got it now. Thanks. I'll find another way to send him a message."

"Old Bill come due" hung up and a woman's voice wafted into Matt's ears.

"Oh, Mr. Midnight, I'm so glad I got through..."

Matt looked at his watch. Like Temple, he liked the assurance of the time right there with second hands, but the multi-device wrist was here.

Stuck here for an hour and a half more, Woody's threats running like rats on the treadmill of his mind. Stuck here trying to catch the caller's problem. He pulled out his cell phone to dial Temple. It went to message. She always had her phone on. She was always in the condo at this hour. Had there been another intruder? Should he cut and run? Or had he let Woodrow Wetherly spook him?

"Yes," he heard himself encouraging the caller to talk herself out while he figured what to do. What he could do.

Luckily, it was the usual lonely hearts call, and Matt could advise her by rote. He hated his own glibness, but she ate up every self-help cliché and hung up gushing thanks.

Dave's bushy eyebrows raised along with his right forefinger. Signals that meant, *Wow. A hot one incoming.*

Matt sat up straighter, more than ready to hear the next caller. The show was dying.

It was another male caller, with a pleasant, deep, drawling voice.

"Mr. Midnight, I like what you said to that little girl. She needs to know she counts. She needs to know she's treasured. I grew up with that, and it made all the difference. You are our Las Vegas midnight hero, local boy gone syndicated. Your voice has the right pitch to make the mic go and fall right in love with it."

Matt felt a chill up the back of his head. "Did you grow up in Vegas, sir?"

"'Sir.' I like that. Real polite. You can never be too polite. Did I grow up in Vegas?" A deep rolling chuckle let the mic have its way with it. "You could say that, though I've been away for forty years. Hardly seems it. Forty years. On the other hand, you could say I did not grow up at all in my early Vegas moments, if you know what I mean."

Dave signaled Matt frantically through the studio glass window, circling his forefingers to "keep going". Matt got it. FBI guy and ex-priest Frank Bucek would signal the same thing if he were here. And Matt's former seminary mentor just might be somewhere in Vegas. Matt had thought he'd glimpsed him once. Not in a good place. Outside the nudie bar where Wetherly had taken him in the name of research into Cliff Effinger.

Dave was tapping on the studio glass, frowning and waving.

Matt shook off that memory and saw all the phone lines were lit up.

"You 'didn't grow up in Vegas'?" He fought for time to adjust to a voice that seemed so familiar…to everyone. "What do you mean?"

"Aw, I was so young, wanted every toy I'd never gotten, every girl. So I did what they wanted and let 'em 'market me.'" He dropped into an eerily spot-on Marlon Brando voice saying an iconic line. "I coulda been a contender. Done real movies instead of sappy stuff. I had every line in every part of my first movie memorized when I got to Hollywood. Man, if I hadn't have let Colonel Parker demand first billing over Barbra Streisand on that *A Star is Born* remake… She had a heck of a voice and was a producer to boot. That would have been an A-1 acting job. I shoulda taken some heavy non-singing roles, like Frank."

"Frank?" The name of Matt's mentor-turned agent from seminary again. "Oh, you mean Frank *Sinatra*."

"Yeah. *The* Frank. He owned Vegas, but I overtook him, after all."

"You could have overruled Colonel Parker on the Streisand film. He was just your manager."

"Oh, no, sir. He did so much for me, and my mama was gone and there was only him to guide me."

"He became notorious for mismanaging you and your money."

The drawn-out sigh could have auditioned to be an aria. "I won't say folks didn't lead me astray. Things look different from a different place, a different time. But I can't leave Vegas. This is where I laid it all down, every night. For my fans, my audience. Anyway, I have some tips for you."

"Me?"

"Yeah. The billboards show you're a blond guy. I hear you're going TV."

Matt cringed to hear that going out over the radio. The opportunity was hush-hush and very uncertain. Only four people in Vegas knew that. How—?

"Anyway, why I'm calling is I have some career advice. I was born blond. A natural blond. Not good. I noticed when I was real young dark-haired guys did better on the screen. Tony Curtis. Robert

Taylor. I decided right then I needed to be dark-haired onstage…
only those film actors didn't have to sweat the rock and roll until the
hair dye ran down into their eyes. And I did. That stung, and worse.

"But I don't see your new talk gig involving a lot of sweat. So
ditch the blond hair."

"Thanks. I'll consider it. Anyway, it's good to hear from you.
Again."

"I'm a performer. Gotta stay *up* to wind *down* after my shows."

"And you're back at the International causing a sensation," Matt
pointed out.

"So they say." The voice turned wistful, younger. "I'd like to try
something new, but everyone wants the same old, same old. I finally
was jus' about to die of boredom, you know what I mean?"

"Well, hey, you gotta love your new Vegas digs. It's a shrine,
really."

"Yeah. Classy. Everything I loved once is there now as well as
in Graceland. My wheels, my wardrobe. Even Priscilla sometimes.
Big change from my first gig in Vegas, that they said the usual gray-
hairs in the audience didn't get and wasn't successful. It was, my
man. They just didn't know how. How I got some new tricks off the
stage."

"You know how back as a kid in Tupelo, Mississippi, I'd go to
black clubs to hear the blues, and anywhere I'd go to black churches
to listen to Gospel?"

"I know you loved blues and Gospel," Matt said with a smile in
his voice. "I do too. Especially Gospel. I went to black churches to
hear it myself." Matt didn't mention he'd been a Catholic priest at
the time.

Dave was smiling on the other side of the glass and every phone
line had gone dead. People were just listening to that slow, musing
voice.

Whether this was one of hundreds of Elvis tribute performers
and wanna-bes, an obsessed fan, a deranged actor, a ghost, or a
mass hallucination, it was ratings gold. And, Matt believed, the
King might be feeling lonely tonight, but he had a message for Matt.

"You have a good show there, Mr. Midnight. Cool handle. You offer good advice, like to that little girl who doesn't quite know where she's going, or can go. I seen lots of little girls like that."

"Thank you." Matt quashed an impulse to add: "Thank you very much."

"Nice and polite, but nobody's fool. Now that 'old Bill' guy who called in. I don't have a good feeling about him. There is something 'off' there. Reminds me a bit of the Colonel. Yeah, I know now he was bad for me in the end, but he tried real hard at the beginning, and I don't have to see or hear or think about him anymore. We aren't in the same place now, if you get what I mean?"

"I do", Matt said. "And am glad to hear that."

"I don't wish anybody ill. We all are just all doin' the best that we can, from where we come from and where we're going."

"You know, maybe I should turn this show over to you."

The laugh was long and musical. "No, but you should get that black dye job." The voice grew fainter and reminiscent.

"Jumpin' Jack Robinson. Black cat. Wore a black-and-white, pin-striped zoot suit. He was like a fistful of jumpin' jacks, all right. Man, he could make those zoot suit pantaloons and that long, long steel cat chain at the side shake, rattle and roll. Proud that chain came off a toilet. Makin' do and makin' do well enough to own his own club. Down some rickety stairs to a basement like in speakeasy days. Way off from where the New Frontier was on highway US-91.

"When I got married at the Aladdin in sixty-seven, Howard Hughes was buying the New Frontier and some guy named Steve Wynn had a small interest in it. I remember seein' that in the paper and remembering my first Vegas gig. The New Frontier had a big cut-out image of me at the curb, grinnin' with my guitar like I was a 'Welcome to Las Vegas' sign. The city was not very welcomin' that first time, until the Colonel got some teenagers in on the weekend.

"Anyway, after our performances, me and my three band boys didn't go for gamblin' casinos. We visited other acts. They were all white in those days, but we heard about this weird little place."

Matt's heart almost stopped. He knew what was coming.

"The Zoot Suit Choo-Choo Club. Learned some moves off that cat I never did in Memphis. Killed, though. He was hung by that make-shift cat chain. Not long after I left town.

"Nobody much noticed me, until I had my TV comeback Special and came back to Vegas in sixty-nine. Whole different Vegas then. The Rat Pack with Frank Sinatra, Dean Martin, Peter Lawford, Joey Bishop, and Sammy Davis, Jr. Two crooners, an actor-in-law to President Kennedy, a comic and a singin', dancin' dude like two Jumpin' Jack Robinsons, all on the main stage of the big hotel-casinos. Like I was. The Zoot Suit Choo-Choo Club wasn't even history. No surprise. I was almost history before my comeback. Then the Rat Pack soon became history and Vegas was mine. For a time, Mr. Midnight. I think you know that. For a time. A time is all anybody gets and we need to make the most of it."

Matt's feelings and intellect suspended. Elvis at eighty, had he lived, back on the radio? Might as well be with half of Graceland a Vegas attraction now. A smart business decision. The "Memphis cat" and his heartland house and legend needed more tourist exposure.

What next? A Disney cruise? Elvis would love his Vegas shrine. He could relive his earliest days, when he used to sneak nights into the Zoot Suit Choo-Choo Club along with other performers around the dark side of the Strip.

"You still with me?" Elvis's voice took Matt's mind off of Jumping Jack Robinson's murder, not suicide.

"So, Mr. Midnight. You should live up to your name. You wanna do some ebony black hair, so dark it gets blue highlightenin'. Blue Lightning. And don't knock sweat. I don't think a talker like you will sweat enough. A rocker will. That's what they loved me for. I sweated my heart out for them. Once they don't see you sweat, they don't love you anymore. You've got to let it pour out."

Dave was signaling something as the caller's voice faded and stopped.

Pore out, Matt thought. Right. *It's all right, Mama.* No, it wasn't. Not after Mama died. What do you do when you've got everything in the world except the one who loves you?

Dave had queued up his closing song. "Are You Lonesome Tonight?"

Matt sat in the WCOO parking lot, his silver Jaguar from the Chicago producers the last car left, sitting under a glaring light, for security against theft. Two thirty a.m. and even the engineer had left. WCOO would broadcast canned music until dawn. It was a small station, lucky to have two syndicated shows.

The greenish lamp above highlighted his white-knuckled grip on the leather steering wheel. Visibility was now not a haven, but a liability. He finally started the car and moved it, purring contentedly, to the darkest side of the lot, overshadowed by a high wall of Photinia bushes. Cars were made to run, but maybe ex-priest amateur detectives should consider it too.

Maybe he and the car they gave him should run right to the network TV executives who'd offered him a juicy talk show gig in Chicago, with Temple riding shotgun, literally. The Bonnie and Clyde of the Circle Ritz.

Matt laughed aloud, softly, at his self-mocking scenario. That was something Temple would dream up.

He eyed the dashboard clock. He couldn't sit and think long now that he and Temple were sleeping at her place. That made his clandestine investigations harder to conceal. The whole point of sleeping together had been to avoid hypocrisy before they married...well, other benefits were the real draw.

He knew a threat when he heard one. Now that Woodrow Weatherly was joining Elvis in stalking him on *The Midnight Hour*, his quest to unravel his stepfather's grisly murder was even more dangerous. Trouble was, something just as sinister seemed to haunt the Circle Ritz vicinity, or inhabitants.

He let the idling car off its leash and headed onto the randomly lit two-lane road that led through a flatland of deserted industrial park buildings. Radio stations were built on urban fringes. The Strip's ever more towering Babel of new hotel-condominiums around the iconic brands of the Caesars Entertainment and MGM

Mirage consortiums made the distant horizon glare look like a sunrise was imminent.

Not for him.

He couldn't feed his need-to-brood mood any longer.

A bright yellow headlight appeared behind him, far and small, but incoming.

The mysterious motorcyclist who had followed him months ago was back. Along with Elvis. Or...Elvis himself?

Matt blinked and saw the oncoming light glaring on his inner eyelids.

The usual suspects burned a similar single-minded path through his brain.

Vengeful psychopath Kathleen O'Connor had left the country for Ireland. Probably traveling with Max Kinsella, the chief object of her homicidal obsession, who was drawing her away from Temple and himself. Also a motorcycle lover.

That left, most whimsically, the King. Elvis, obsessed with anything that had an engine. Cars. Big buses he personally drove to Las Vegas. A private jet. And motorcycles.

And Matt himself, who'd used Max's 'cycle for a time and had probably drawn an even uglier antagonist down on them all.

Matt glanced at the single headlight.

"Padiddle," he said under his breath. It was a road game. Call out that word when you spot a car with a single headlight or remove on article of clothing if you don't.

But this was not a car and he wasn't into strip poker of any type. So, like Elvis, he needed to discover what kind of engine it had. Had to know if it was Max's vintage Hesketh Vampire Brit motorcycle he'd left stored in Circle Ritz landlady Electra Lark's shed.

Only one way to find out. The Hesketh earned its name from the otherworldly scream the motor let out at high speeds.

He had a straightaway to the main highway and a car that did zero to sixty miles an hour in four seconds. He'd never stretched it much over the legal limit. He did now, even though he was doing forty. With spine-numbing speed, he was slammed back in the seat. The Jag leaped ahead, smooth as a steel arrow, a racehorse from the gate, like the famous leaping chrome jaguar hood ornament, already charging.

Matt was surprised by an adrenaline kick of pure escapist joy followed by a grim satisfaction that nothing could catch him unless he wanted it to.

The pinprick of light in the dark of the rearview mirror grew larger, but lagged and seemed to stop.

No wonder. *Holy St. Sepulveda.* The entry lane to Highway 91 was right…here. Hard, hard right. The car squealed genteel protest at rough handling, but smoothly entered the highway, unclogged by heavy traffic at this wee hour of the night.

Matt tried to spot a motorcycle following along on the access road, but found no sign of a light.

He continued on into Las Vegas proper (if one could ever say that about Vegas) via the notorious "Spaghetti Bowl" interchange at a mannerly and legal sixty-five miles an hour.

That successful maneuver had reminded him of another big cat, this one domestic.

Midnight Louie never hesitated to leap into action against foes bigger than he. He'd lunged for the intruder in Temple's bedroom and forced him onto the balcony for Matt to attack from the floor above.

Matt shook his head to shake thoughts of his second Elvis audio experience. There would be buzz about that on the social networks, but if you don't go there, you don't have to answer for anything.

4
Home Evasions

"And the squad car drove off with Electra in the backseat?" Matt asked six neighbors standing by an outdoor table with an overhead umbrella useless at night.

The scene was surreal.

Matt felt he had driven from one end of the *Twilight Zone* to the other since leaving *WCOO* thirty minutes ago. First the reappearance of the mysterious motorcycle rider, now a rerun of Electra Lark being a suspect for a death.

"Drove right off with her, yes," a balding guy wearing a checked shirt answered.

Matt had exchanged chitchat before with Jim Jordan and his wife, Jan, from the third floor, in the entryway and parking lot. Now they were all part of a buzzing cluster of tenants just outside the Crime Scene tape, watching a forensics crew operate under floodlights in the shrubbery bridging the Circle Ritz's white marble façade and the pool house decking.

The thirtyish couple was just star-struck enough to stay up into the wee hours to watch the real-life true crime show.

"It was just like on TV," Jan said, eager to share.

"The shot guy," Jim added, "fell right in front of Bill Hays' first-floor patio doors. The whole side of the building was lit up by squad car headlights and those red and blue flashing lights. Inside there, Bill must have passed a pachyderm."

"It was like one of those 'Blue Light Special' lights flashing at K-Mart," Jan added. "Then the ambulance came screeching and screaming up."

"What about Temple?" Matt had been scanning onlookers for a glimpse of shoulder-high red hair. She was easy to lose in a crowd, especially without her three-inch heels on.

"Oh, she was here before we were, walked right up and talked to the guy in the unmarked car that came last," Jim said.

"I wouldn't have wanted to approach anybody official, like a detective, on a murder scene," Jan said with a faux shudder. "Draw attention to myself."

The chills had to be for effect because the temperature at the station had read seventy-two.

Matt pulled out his cell phone and saw he'd missed a recent call. Temple's.

He muttered "Thanks" at the couple and sprinted around the building to the parking lot door.

Inside the small lobby, he didn't wait for the quaint elevator but headed for the nearby stairs and galloped up them two at a time as quietly as he could.

All the units had a short private entry hall with a big front door and doorbell. Matt slapped the flat of his hand on the wood. The doorbell's gong chimed for about five seconds.

Then the door flew open as if Temple had been waiting right there. "Matt! Thank God! It's been insane here. I called your cell when you were on the road."

She jumped into his arms and he made a circle at the same moment that brought them both pressed against the inside of the shut front door and securely inside home, sweet home. She was wearing her favorite fifties-vintage, red chiffon, baby doll pajamas. His favorite too.

Matt shut his eyes. "I could kick myself into next week. I had my cell phone turned off. After a dozen weird call-ins tonight, I didn't want to hear another disembodied voice, not even phone spam. I never dreamed you'd call. You make a point of not doing it."

"I never dreamed I'd have to. I know you need your cool-down drive-time coming home."

He felt a reflexive pang. Temple knew from living with a magician who had done two evening shows that night gigs were hard to come down from.

Matt pushed away the past. "Electra is under suspicion of something again? How many crimes can an over-seventy grandmother commit in a month or two?"

"Ernesto said residents heard shots, Matt. It has to be self-defense, but that shady attempt to rob Electra of her ex-husband's property is a closed case. I can't see what anybody would gain by continuing to harass her at her own home and an established property like the Circle Ritz."

"Well, those 'shady characters' trying to cheat her out of a building that held a valuable gambling license likely had mob ties."

"But there's nothing left of the mob except for a certain sleazy entertainment value."

"I don't know about that," Matt said fervently. "And speaking of which, wasn't there a Fontana brother or two sleeping gratis on the property after the damage last month?"

"Fontana brothers don't come home until three in the morning. They have their hotel and custom limo service to run, as well as lady friends to entertain."

"And what about our missing landlady?" Matt fretted. "She's in the slammer overnight. That's outrageous, Temple."

"There's nothing anybody can do before morning. Which is coming fast. The bros are getting their lawyer up right now. And you were tired from counseling lost Las Vegas souls," she added. "I wanted to get you tucked into bed first."

She led him into the bedroom and patted the new high-thread-count sheets, invitingly turned back. "Get undressed and make tracks for some exciting catch-up sleeping before we go to bail Electra out in a few hours."

It didn't take long for him to do as she suggested and forget the undercover work he was hiding from her for the undercover coziness of lying with heads propped up on pillows and the night's events to discuss. The events at the Circle Ritz, not those at *WCOO*. Electra's home invasion had kept Temple from getting an impulse to tune in and hear "Elvis" on the air again. And Woody's crude threats. Matt was relieved.

"At least I'm sleeping at your place now," Matt said, "so I know *you*'re not the person who took a fatal dive off the balcony."

"I do think *you* should visit Metro Police headquarters first thing and charm the details from Molina. She's getting tired of my smiling, mug-shot-ready face."

"At least that gives me an assignment that will explain why our elderly landlady is Suspect of the Week with the LVMPD."

Matt sat up against the upholstered headboard, worried as he had been lately, but tucked in and ready to talk. Temple laid her cheek on his bare shoulder to snuggle. She was more upset about the recent hullaballoo than she'd let him see.

Matt glanced at the soft white globe of a modern nightstand lamp. "I like what you've done with the place lately."

"Thanks." Temple smiled. She'd been slowly redoing the room, from the upholstered headboard to the bedside lamps on dimmers, changing it over from everything "Max".

"And..." Temple furrowed her smooth brow for the first time, "Louie is not napping in tonight. He so loves to growl and glower when you come home to bed and evict him. I'm a bit worried."

"So you think my presence has added to your cat's domestic drama? That's a PR woman for you, putting an optimistic spin on a man-cat duel over her. Which one is going to the mat? Spelled with a small 'm' and one 't'."

"Not the man. Louie will have to adapt and sleep in his zebra-print carrier if he's miffed."

Matt found that a cue to sweep her into his arms.

"So where do you think His Majesty is?" Matt frowned at the vacant foot of the zebra-pattern coverlet.

There were two things Temple couldn't change. Midnight Louie's *droit de seignior* claim to the bed and especially that coverlet he loved to sprawl on so artistically. Cats' color vision was shaky on the reds, but every one of them infallibly chose the most flattering color background for sitting and reclining on. Zebra-stripe with crimson piping made Louie a handsome pin-up boy.

"Yes, that is odd. Louie disappeared after the squad cars came. He hasn't been that spooked before," Temple said.

"Spooked? Louie?" Matt laughed. "Pigs would fly first and he'd probably soon have them hitched to a cat sleigh in the sky. Or maybe his own private passenger drone."

"I'm so glad you've come to terms with cattitude. Seriously, I'm thinking of putting a rather expensive but cool zebra-stripe cat bed near the television chest."

"Temple, he'll never use it any more than he will the zebra-stripe carrier you bought him. Face it. We'll have to take this coverlet to Chicago, but maybe ship him by stork."

"Chicago? Really, Matt?" She sat up, accidentally knocking her *Elle Decor* magazine off the nightstand. "You've seemed so torn about that move lately."

"I am torn. My memories of Chicago aren't the greatest. You know the family situation is even more awkward now. And I don't like keeping things from people I care for. It's a strain on me, and my mother, knowing I'm her new husband's brother's secret son. You can't even say that without wondering where to the put the apostrophes. And then, me being the celebrity in the family." Matt shook his head.

"Hey, Matt. That's a classic part of the celebrity backstory. Family secrets. You come with yours built-in. And forgotten decades ago. Besides, you wouldn't be committed forever. Those contracts are short, especially for a new project."

"Sure, remind me I'm on trial approval."

"Not with me." Temple's warm palm on his forearm, the warmth in her gray-blue eyes...he drowned in a wave of love followed by a strong current of nasty undertow. He had to keep secrets here, in Vegas, too. Even more so now that the violent death tonight echoed the break-in on Temple here a couple weeks ago.

Damn Effinger, Matt thought. Not letting him die and rot was the worst mistake he'd ever made. And now he really couldn't let it go, until he'd proved to himself that Temple wasn't the target all along. Her and maybe the ingenious map she'd made of an elaborate scheme written in the stars and somehow living long after him.

"Lighten up." Temple was leaning in to kiss his cheek. "All these choices we have to make are good. I'm okay with Chicago too."

"Practically speaking," he said. "I don't know what you'd do there career-wise. Or how Louie'd take to high-rise life. I suppose the À La Cat food ad sequence can be filmed anywhere. You're from Minnesota, so you know the winter snow up that way can make Antarctica seem a breeze. And…doing something in the daytime that's more interactive is sounding pretty attractive."

"Don't worry. I'll keep you warm. I'm glad we talked about this, Matt! I didn't want to push you, but we need to make plans. Now that Evil Kitty is out of the picture we can finally commit to our dreams and lives."

"If Evil Kitty didn't come back to push that man you saw taken away off the balcony. That'd be more likely than Electra doing it."

Temple sat up. "Don't even think that! But that reminds me of something else we need to clear up after you go first thing in the morning to spring Electra."

"I can hear that 'Something Else' has capital letters in it."

Temple sighed. Heavily.

"Spit it out. You'll never catch me in a better, more penitent mood, coming home to pandemonium and knowing I'd closed down your call."

"Okay." She wiggled to sit up against the headboard too.

"Look, Temple, I'll make a wild guess that this involves the Mystifying Max." Using the guy's stage name made it easier to say.

"You know Evil Kitty led him to his cousin Sean in Ireland. Alive."

"Alive and mostly recovered from that IRA bomb years ago."

"Sean had sustained some bad injuries and PSD and memory loss. His DNA was found in the ruins of the bombing site so everybody assumed he was dead. And you know Max went—"

"Yes, yes. Sean's a poor soul and a saint miraculously recovered. I'm waiting for the streaming Amazon video to come out."

Temple gave him a Look before continuing. "So teenage Max—Michael then—went home alone to Wisconsin, where he found cousin Sean's family suspicious that he'd escaped damage, at least physical damage, but not Sean. And the mothers, sisters, couldn't get over that, so the Kellys and the Kinsellas were equally wounded and broken."

"That's almost predictable, Temple. And…'Michael' had to cover up the stupid girl-chasing that had separated the boys. He was not Max yet, Max the magician. The parents would detect that awkwardness, the lies, the unsaid Something More." Matt leaned forward, alert.

"What?

He embraced and kissed her.

"Nice but… What?"

"You're a very healing person, you know that?"

"Not my most lavish compliment."

"It's worth more than rubies." He glanced at his engagement ring on her finger. A vintage piece. She so loved Art Deco. Bought on time with his first big-time radio station money. The pear-shaped diamonds and rubies shining like blood and tear drops, something he'd never noticed before.

That had done it. Temple pointing out, painting an emotional moment in his analyst's brain that he could identify with: a boy so guilty that he couldn't stop something bad from happening—*whack!,* the crack of Effinger's hand across his mother's face. Him behind some soft chain-link fence of string bawling. He must have been a toddler in a playpen. "*And* you *next—*"

Matt resumed full counseling mode. "So Michael made himself the Prodigal Son, went all vengeful and returned to Ireland to take on the IRA and became Max. Michael. Aloysius. Xavier. Kinsella. He used his baptismal middle and confirmation names to remake himself."

"I never knew about those unpronounceable middle names until later," she admitted.

"Survivor's guilt is a horrible state, Temple, because you can't do anything about it. And you couldn't have done anything about Max's obsession at the time or in those circumstances."

"I wanted a partner, not a guilt complex."

"We've all got those, even you, because you can't cut loose from Max."

"That's not true. I have."

"Have you? That's what you think, but… Okay. Now *they're* reunited, though. The cousins. Sean at least has a happy life in Ireland and Max still wants something from you even though he persuaded you to go to Vegas with him and left you flat in six months."

"Nine months."

"I was hoping you were delivered from that demon baby."

"Not fair! Max was protecting me from IRA guys who thought he had a hoard of American donations to the IRA, even then, that hadn't been delivered in years."

"I've concluded that hoard is a mythical beast," Matt said. "The supposed IRA guys who attacked you in the parking garage may also be. Did they have Irish accents?"

"Like I'd listen for that while I'm being pummeled? You're probably right, but back then everybody wanted to know where Max was, from Molina to nameless thugs. That's old business. New business? Sean and Max owe some heavy explanations to their poor families back in Wisconsin."

"Like we recently gave your poor family back in Minnesota." Matt couldn't help smiling at characterizing the robust, sports-loving Barrs that way. He narrowed his eyes. "Families are the last to know, but *we* don't have to be."

Temple took a breath and delivered a long, and probably unwelcome sentence, fast. "Max wants me to accompany him and Sean back to their families in Racine, Wisconsin, as a buffer, I guess, but mainly because I would know more about any holes in his memory since his bungee cord fall."

"And only you." Matt couldn't keep a tinge of bitterness from his tone.

"Not necessarily. You're the counselor. You know everything I know because you heard it from either Max or me at one time or another. So I volunteered you."

"What? I'm supposed to come in cold on a situation with two totally confused sets of parents, one pair seeing their long-thought-dead son back, but maimed from bomb blast injuries, the other son probably written off as a bad seed when all he was trying to do was protect them from their inability to handle a tragic situation for fifteen-some years."

"See, that's why you're so good at these human thorn-bush issues that a TV network wants you to do a show."

"That's just it. This emotional booby-trap stuff is not 'a show'. I should never have considered doing it."

"No. No, Matt. That's the last thing I want. Is that why you've iced the network? You think going live with counseling is immoral?"

If only he were so noble, Matt thought. He was as capable of being flattered, or seeing value in what he did, and the big bucks as anyone. No, it was the danger he sensed hanging over Temple that gave him cold feet.

Cold feet. Warm heart.

She looked so troubled and torn. Temple could *not* not help someone. Like Electra tomorrow morning. Like someone she'd never met before the other day, or the next day. She called it PR, public relations, making everything run smoothly, but it was insight and empathy and heart and he loved her to death for it.

And, trying to protect her, he had become as toxic for her as Max Kinsella had ever been.

"No," he said. "I've decided that a change of place, and of medium, would be good for me. You. Us. But I have a few loose ends to tie up with the radio station. And Letitia."

She nodded sympathetically.

"And then I'll deal with the 'Days in the Lives of Michael-slash-Max Kinsella.'"

"That's wonderful! And I've made a decision too."

He waited. Afraid.

"I know where we should be married."

"Let me see. It's either religious or civil, either there or here. The Polish cathedral in Chicago where my family are, and you can have a Princess Diana-long train on your wedding dress, or the Crystal Phoenix wedding chapel here in Las Vegas, where you can have a Princess Diana-long train on your wedding dress."

"You!" She slapped his shoulder in play. "You so understand my need for stature. Close, but wrong! It's at Our Lady of Guadalupe here in Las Vegas where I can have a Princess-Diana-long train *and* wear the Midnight Louie Austrian crystal shoes without worrying about them being ripped off during travel."

"Here? At OLG? A small Catholic Church. You don't have to."

"I want to. I think it would make Father Hernandez very happy. And more importantly, I think it would make you very happy."

"It's crazy, but genius," Matt said.

And it was. Both families on uncommon ground, the formal Catholic ceremony satisfying his mother's conventional dreams, and Temple's more liberal family loving the sweet ethnic simplicity. OLG, as the church was so inelegantly initialized. Where Temple had accompanied him to her first Mass.

"I hate to crush your diplomatic-level wedding ceremony dreams," he said, "but you do remember that's Lieutenant Molina's parish?"

"So? Let her help with the Flower Committee. I might even let her whistle a happy tune."

Matt laughed. "That's an image to bring nightmares."

"Here we are, talking and making compromises like an old married couple," she said happily.

"Uh, yeaaah," he drawled, "I was beginning to think the same thing." He pulled the slipping nightgown spaghetti strap off her shoulder. "We need to do a lot more living in sin fast if the wedding is looking so logical and so soon."

So they did something about that.

"You're a hell of a negotiator, you know that," Matt said when all had been said and done. "All I have to do to win the princess is to storm black-ice mountain of Max Kinsella's family past."

"I'm a public relations expert. Why wouldn't I be great at private relations too."

"Oh, you are, baby doll. You really are."

Reassured, Temple fell asleep with her small but firm fist curled in his, pressed against the middle of his chest above his heart.

Max bloody Kinsella was the least of Matt's problems. The faces of Effinger, Woody, the soul-patch man with the jackhammer in the junker trunk, Rafi, and even Molina, floated past his closed eyelids like a montage from an old black-and-white film.

Some would take what had happened at the Circle Ritz tonight as another colorful episode in its seventy years of solid Las Vegas history.

He was wondering if it would solve everyone's problems but his own.

Woody Wetherly and his veiled threats hung over him like the ghost of Cliff Effinger getting his own twisted revenge on him and Temple from beyond the grave.

5
The Wrong Arm of the Law

"So you think you can breeze into headquarters like Miss Temple Barr, P.R., on a tear and get a warm welcome from a homicide lieutenant?"

Matt found his welcome with local law enforcement much cooler and more skeptical than Temple had envisioned.

Lieutenant C. R. Molina was wearing one of her high-summer khaki pantsuits which were the same wrinkle-resistant fabric as her winter navy-blue and black twill pantsuits. Her office at the new headquarters building had fancier modern chairs and computers, but was still the same narrow dimensions.

She leaned her impressive height against the front of her desk, arms folded over her plain blazer and her mannish black loafers on full view. You would never imagine her in blood-scarlet nineteen-forties silk velvet crooning torch songs at the Blue Dahlia nightclub, and, sadly, she hadn't been taking that Carmen persona out for a bluesy walk for some time.

Matt shrugged mentally.

He wasn't going to remind the all-business homicide lieutenant of her kinder, gentler side. Seeing Molina about this matter might lead to awkward questions, but Temple felt he was more likely to find out why the Circle Ritz landlady was in custody. She was clearly the homeowner. She'd shot at an intruder already in her fifth-floor penthouse. At night. Alone in her residence. He didn't see why she'd been taken away for questioning.

Unless they had evidence of a relationship between Electra and the intruder, which was ridiculous.

"All we Circle Ritz residents are understandably worried about last night's intrusion", he began.

"I imagine that 'we' is principally your fiancée, Miss Temple Barr."

Matt smiled. "She thought she'd spare you the sight of her inquisitive face."

"Detectives are surveying residents even now. So, no worry. Her doorbell will soon be ringing and she'll be able to give her no doubt breathless account quite soon. I thought I would spare her the sight of *my* inquisitive face.

"And where were you at one a.m. this morning?" Molina pulled her cell phone out of her side pocket and started tapping.

"You know I'm covered, Lieutenant. On the air at WCOO-AM radio, doing my call-in counseling show, *The Midnight Hour*."

"And it doesn't bother you that *The Midnight Hour* is now actually two hours?"

"When the show became popular they upped the hours, but the title was unique, and syndicated."

"*Hmm*," she muttered at her cell phone, tapping away so fast she might have been Fred Astaire. "I assume the engineer can attest to your presence."

"Yes, he was there. It's a live show. Somebody has to program the canned music until six a.m. after I leave at two a.m."

"And by two thirty you weren't home yet? The resident Circle Ritz amateur detective didn't call you the minute the shots were fired?"

Matt hesitated. "Midnight Louie is good, but his claws are murder on cell phone screens."

"Oh, you kidder," Molina said in a flat tone. "That was an evasion. Why?"

"Temple did call, but I had my cell phone off."

"Is that usual?"

"It has to be off during broadcast, of course."

"But leaving and driving home?"

"I work nights, Lieutenant. Temple doesn't."

"The drive would take, what? Almost half an hour. No two twenty-five in the morning 'welcome home' surprises? You're only a floor apart."

"Are you trying to prove we're co-habiting, Lieutenant?"

"She's the nosy one. I'm trying to determine if you have an alibi for the Circle Ritz death."

"Death? The man has died? Me? Why would I be a suspect?"

"Not so far-fetched. After all, I hear you tossed a man off your fiancée's balcony recently."

"He was attacking Temple in her bedroom and she yelled 'Fire!'"

"Smart of her."

"By then he'd retreated to the balcony. I jumped down atop him from my balcony. It was a fierce, quick struggle. No one could see well in the dark bedroom or the dark night beyond. He broke my hold and scrambled or fell over the railing. I didn't 'toss' anyone. We reported the incident to the police."

"Did they find a prowler?"

"I don't know. Last we saw, and heard, he staggered away to the fringes of the parking lot and encountered the neighborhood feral cat pack. They seemed to do more damage than I did. How does anybody know what happened to him?"

"Your starry-eyed bride-to-be described the scene and your role as a WWF smack-down hero to Mrs. Lark when she arrived to help."

"You can see why Electra might overreact to another home invasion."

"*Hmm.* The same M.O. at the same place begins to sound like an appointment rather than serial mayhem."

"Oh, my God. You think I could practically kill someone and deny it?"

"We certainly know you are fit enough, not only to fight, but to climb those balconies like a Malayan flying lemur."

"What on earth is that?"

"A kind of pre-primate. On the brink of extinction, of course."

"Do I get the idea I'm on the brink too?"

"You came here, so you saved Detective Alch a trip. This will be an exchange of prisoners."

"Bail, you mean. So Electra's homeward bound?" Matt asked. "If it has to be that formal."

Molina straightened. "It has to be that formal. We are talking D.B., approximately five-nine, two-hundred and forty pounds."

"Dead body built like a bowling ball. Not the man I encountered on Temple's balcony."

"Say *you*. It makes a colorful comparison. Stuck by a bullet in the shoulder and falling forty feet backwards, four stories, with impact on the back of the skull. Head trauma likely killed him. He died in the ambulance, so until the coroner rules whether the bullet or the fall killed him, we have to treat your landlady as a suspect."

"So only one of Electra's shots hit him?"

"One could be enough. Same gun she kept in her place the last time she was under suspicion of murder."

"This must be different. The victim isn't another of her ex-husbands, is he?" Matt thought for a moment. "She's had several."

Molina turned to pick up a file folder from her desk. "Not unless an ex-husband of hers spent two-to-six for felony assault in High Desert State Prison."

"A burglar, obviously."

"Obviously, but was he known to someone else who resided at the Circle Ritz?"

Matt didn't like the sound of that. "Temple says most of the residents came down to ground level as soon as shots were heard."

"Since our Miss Temple had an intruder in her second-floor unit two weeks ago, I'm not surprised she was among the first on the scene."

"But this was farther at the back of the property."

"Can a round building be said to have a back?"

"Of course. Where the ground-level deck connects to the pool and pool house."

"All right. I must admit the dead man does not seem to have any obvious connection to the Circle Ritz."

"Not a hiree, not a pool or yard man?"

"At that hour? No. The dead man was burly, but not HDTV-inclined."

Matt was getting a bad feeling. Molina sardonic was a Molina to beware of.

"And Electra had to be taken away in handcuffs?"

"Charges aren't likely, but her story has to be taken down and investigated fully."

"'Story'?"

"And yours, considering you recently confronted an intruder at the same address that resulted in the man falling."

"I was driving home from WCOO when the man fell."

"Cell phone off. Seems odd. That's when you'd most get messages after being unavailable on the air."

"Not all of us are attached to AT&T or Verizon at the hip."

Molina smiled. "Got a little behind on social media in the priesthood, did we?"

"Got a little behind on a lot," Matt said.

Molina leaned forward so the full effect of her electric-blue eyes filled his range of vision. There was no quarter in them. "Even *you* would not dreamily drive home from a middle-of-the-night job without checking your phone after almost three hours of literal 'radio silence', ex-Father Matt. Or did she call in?"

"No!" He did *not* want to bring up Elvis.

"Touchy. Are you trying to be noble and hide the fact that you're now sleeping with Miss Barr in her own rooms? Trust me, it would be more suspicious if you weren't."

"Do I owe your certainty to a gossiping Fontana brother, ex-torch singer Carmen? Like Julio. Would you stoop that low, romancing one of Las Vegas's finest bachelor brothers to get eyes inside the Circle Ritz and our lives? You have a pattern of recruiting male civilians as your private confidential informants. Since you're married to the Metro PD force, maybe they're your surrogate boys club."

She recoiled as if he had snapped a whip. "You are definitely past the 'too good to be true' stage."

Matt was horrified by what she'd pushed him to say. There was much truth that the act of recruiting or coercing men to be her secret agents could substitute for a real relationship, leaving her single working mother status unthreatened. Max had been such a one, certainly. Dirty Larry, long gone and almost forgotten. Rafi. Now Julio Fontana?

"I'm sorry," he said. "You goaded me."

"That's my job. Never apologize. It's never good for an officer of the law to cross lines and have personal links, no matter how feeble, to a confidential informant or anyone."

"Do you hear yourself?"

"Do you hear *yourself*? You probably don't use your phone's GPS, Mr. High-tech Dinosaur. That buys you a precious forty minutes when you could have arrived at the Circle Ritz. Heard the shots. Climbed the balconies that form a step pyramid, and 'tossed' the guy off the balcony to his death."

"No. I was not there. Residents were gathered around the crime scene when I arrived and they told me what had happened."

"There's *something* you're hiding about your cell phone being off when you left work. Don't snow me. Maybe you can psychoanalyze me, but I can read a suspect. And there's something you don't want anyone to know."

Matt let his shoulders relax, willing anxiety and anger away. "You're right." About a lot of somethings he concealed. He'd throw her a small one. "Okay."

She hissed out a long-held breath.

"It will sound stupid, but it's given me the willies, the heebie-jeebies, a nasty vague sense of danger."

"Oh, God. New Age angst. Next you'll tell you're channeling Midnight Louie."

"Don't I wish," Matt said. "The Once and Forever King is back."

"Arthur?"

"Elvis."

After five beats of silence, she burst into deep contralto laughter.

Matt shrugged. "He's calling in on *The Midnight Hour* again. The listeners and other callers went crazy to recognize his voice. Our mutual friend in the FBI had the voice recordings analyzed the last—first time. They couldn't explain it. It was Elvis's voice."

"And they brought back the *The X-Files* for a limited run on TV too." Molina leaned in again, all vivid blue skepticism. "Look here, Mulder. There are no reruns in real life."

"Look here, Skully. There's Frank Bucek and the FBI. Send him the audiotape of my show tonight."

"What does this have to do with your alibi?"

"What can I say? The vocal reappearance of Elvis Presley got me all shook up. The show ran overtime. The last time this happened it presaged some very strange events at the Crystal Phoenix. I didn't want to go through anything weird again."

Molina sat back again. "Well, think of this, Marty McFly. The deceased shows signs of physical assault not attributable to gunshots or a fall. He's a low-level thug from an old Vegas family of muscle-headed muscle. Word is he was involved in an altercation a couple of nights ago at a nudie bar. You weren't on the air at *that* time. I don't think an imminent bridegroom went rogue to visit a nudie bar, not even Fontana brothers, but who knows what passes for a bachelor party today? That D.B. at the Circle Ritz was sure there. There's a hidden planet behind this sudden crime wave at the Ritz."

Matt felt, had to think the cliché was dead-on true, because his blood ran cold. His hands grew instantly icy. His heart pounded, pumping all his energy into physical defense. Yet he had to sit there and appear calm and certainly not somebody who had started the brawl at Lucky Stars nudie bar *before* he had to be at *The Midnight Hour.*

"Speaking of old mobsters possibly associated with Effinger," Molina said, innocently this time. "Are you getting anything useful out of that retired cop I sent you to, Wetherly?"

"Uh. Rapid change of topic."

"I'm through scaring you straight for now. That Elvis thing is too weird to be invented. Well?"

"I think old Woodrow is looking for someone to tell his stories to. He takes *The Midnight Hour* for one of those true-crime shows."

Molina laughed. She finally shifted her hip off the desk edge and moved from being in his face to a less confrontational stance.

"Watch yourself," she told him. "I'm beginning to think there's something serious to your quest to solve the sleazy doings and strange death of the late Clifford Effinger."

Matt stepped out of the towering new police headquarters building, gazing back at its central swooping T-shape of glass.

It reminded him of the illuminated red, purple, and blue neon-lit fifty-story "winged" shapes on the side or the Rio Hotel, which in turn echoed the immense concrete-and-stone statue of the white-robed Christ of the Andes near Rio de Janeiro, with arms and sleeves stretched as wide as the crossbar on the Cross.

Three similar images and architectural mimics, he mused, one holy, one secular and one legal. The Brazilian landmark represented God, the Vegas Rio represented Mammon and here, the sweep of a robe represented judges and justice.

Matt turned away to see Electra waiting by the parked cars, looking like a tourist in her brightly colored muumuu and flip-flop slippers. Two pink foam curlers still clung to her snow-white hair and the tall Fontana brother standing beside her for once wore an expensive suit coat that looked wrinkled and hung slightly askew.

It was a shock to see a Fontana either disheveled or less than smiling and gracious. Then he wondered what he looked like after sweating through his interrogation with Molina.

"Is it, um—" Matt said as he held his hand out.

"Armando." The man offered a firm, fast handshake. "We were told you had an appointment, so waited around."

Matt looked around for what fantastic custom limo Armando had found appropriate for a drive to the clinker. He knew he visibly started to spot Electra's blue Elvis-edition VW Beetle, a car Matt had won and given to Electra to replace her old Probe, the car he had recently wrecked beyond repair driving up two sets of stairs and through strong double doors to save Electra and her kidnapped cat, Karma, from imminent harm. Score: Probe Dead. Elvis Undead, and back in vocal *and* automotive forms.

"Matt!" She rushed to hug him. "You came to my rescue again."

"Temple sent me, but they released you before I could plead your case. In fact, I got a grilling of my own."

They began walking toward the Beetle, which had good headroom for two tall men with Electra in the back.

Bending considerably to assist Electra inside, Armando explained over his shoulder to Matt. "Ernesto thought seeing her own vehicle here would cheer up Mrs. Lark."

"Oh," she said, "I always smile when I drive this car, especially if I have to park it. So easy. Matt, dear, I meant to tell you. It was so nice of dear, sweet Elvis to give your radio show ratings a boost last night, now that he maintains a permanent residence in Vegas."

Oh, no, Matt thought. That was right. The new Elvis Experience made The King a permanent near neighbor.

He'd found Frank Bucek vague about why he'd been stationed in Vegas for now. Surely it couldn't be in hopes of hearing a new "Elvis tape".

Maybe it was time for a friendly chat.

6
Midnight Prowler

Temple almost felt the low growl of an expensive, powerful idling car before she heard it.

She sat up in bed, checking the red LED clock numbers. 1:00 a.m.

Her condo was two floors above the parking lot. The car was either right under her balcony, or a figment of an interrupted dream.

Couldn't be Matt's Jaguar, because he was still live on the air. She sincerely hoped.

Since an intruder had breeched the locked French doors off her bedroom only a couple weeks before that, she reached for the bedside table and her cell phone.

Temple had investigated self-defense two years ago when she'd been beaten up by two honest-to-God thugs in the Goliath hotel's guest parking ramp. Since she needed a pulley to reach five-foot-one barefoot, she'd invested in some shooting gallery training.

One of the instructors said a gun would look huge in her tiny hands and psych out a male intruder.

The plug-in night-light in the form of an acrylic crystal cat cast enough illumination to show that the plus-size cell phone also looked, and felt, huge in her tiny hand. But, she couldn't wield a cell phone and pistol simultaneously. Besides, she'd lost interest and the unloaded gun was languishing in her scarf drawer. She wasn't any good at wearing scarves either.

Midnight Louie was a shadowy presence pacing in front of the French doors to the balcony patio, answering with soft growls.

The low vibrating growling sound moved slowly along the exterior bedroom wall. Golly, the "live two stories up" advice to single women, even a soon-not-to-be-single girl, was not high enough. And something like the landlady's fifth floor penthouse was no better, except that intruder had not survived, unlike Temple's previous one.

Who had made the Circle Ritz Break-in Site of the Month? She was afraid she knew the Why. Somehow someone bad knew what she and Matt and Max had been hunting for.

Her eyes were adapting to the low light and focused on the repaired French doors. Fate wouldn't be so unkind as to break them again… Almost five hundred dollars gone.

The growl went more basso, on the move. Black smoke seemed to be eeling under the faintly illuminated balcony doors.

Then the automotive growl stopped. Louie's growls paused, then escalated into a shrill battle cry. Three feet of outstretched twenty-pound black feline fury hurled itself at the doors' matched levered handles.

The doors sprang outward to reveal the dead-solid black of night.

Midnight Louie overshot something dark that leaped aside. His forepaws ricocheted off the railing. Caught in the parking lot lights' green-tinged security beams with his green eyes blazing, he executed a four-point landing back on the patio.

Both hunks of blackness entered the room, but only one turned to shut the doors after them.

Temple lowered the cell phone. Her voice sounded as metallic and cool as the device in her hands. "The repair to the locks will run four-hundred and seventy dollars."

"No repairs," the intruder said. "I undid the lock a second before your resident black panther made his move."

"Too bad." Temple lowered her defensive mechanisms quite literally as Midnight Louie bounded onto the foot of the California King-size bed bought for Max Kinsella's six-foot-four frame. "I would have enjoyed taking you to the people's court. So, Max. You're back from Ireland. Kathleen O'Connor *didn't* kill you."

"And I didn't have to kill her," he said.

"Mission accomplished, and your cue to disappear from my life again, maybe wondering what happened to you forever. So why the midnight break-in? Drama? You're wearing cat burglar-black again from head to foot."

"Why the cell phone-fisted greeting? You weren't supposed to wake up."

"Midnight Louie has the hearing of an attack dog and he's on alert since the first break-in. And you're driving serious, obvious horsepower again." Temple put the phone on the bedside table as Max went to sit on the delicate chair Temple used to put her shoes on. He'd always looked ridiculous sitting there.

"I'd rather if nobody knew I'm back in town," he said.

"So I'm not anybody?"

He smiled. "You're somebody to a lot of people. That's your gift." His expression hardened. "What's this about a break-in?"

"Some fool burglar who tripped on the extra-long foot of the bed, thanks to your former occupancy. We figure the visible bathroom light on the other side of the unit I keep on for Louie convinced the intruder the occupants were awake over there. He hoped he could loot this side with no fuss. Instead he tripped, I yelled, '*Fire!*', and Electra came pounding at the door with gun and passkey in hand."

"Fast thinking. Don't you have a firearm? If you weren't a pistol-packing mama, how'd the idiot exit?"

"Matt jumped down from his balcony above and threw him over the railing."

Max's eyebrows raised. Temple didn't know whether he was more surprised by the elderly landlady dressed in full living color bearing a weapon...or Matt handily bouncing the intruder.

Ex-roomies, ex-lovers calling after hours were hard to read, especially if they were professional magicians and spies.

"I lead an interesting life," Temple said, more to herself. "Why must No one Know You're in Town? If Kitty the Cutter is declawed and content to stay in Ireland now that she can't hold the fate of your cousin Sean over you.... She *is* declawed?"

"Decidedly," Max said.

"So you've come to discuss your crazy plan to import me to Wisconsin to negotiate the Kinsella and—"

"—and the Kelly clans' reunion with their prodigal sons. Yes. Kelly is Sean's surname."

Temple shuddered delicately. "Just saying that reminds me of leaping hip-deep into emotional quicksand."

"But that intervention can wait." Max tented his long fingers in a sage-like manner.

Temple raised her eyebrows. She'd thought Max bringing his presumed dead cousin home would be Job One. Magicians always adore producing unbelievable effects, and resurrecting the dead was certainly a major one.

Max leaned back on the fragile chair. Its creak brought Midnight Louie over to investigate. Or intimidate. He sniffed Max's shoe, then sat to gaze intently up at him.

It was impossible to ruffle Max.

He smiled down at Louie and said, "Now that I hear you were broken into while I was gone, I'm even more convinced that until we find the bloody booty Kathleen and her dead cohort Santiago hid somewhere in Vegas, nobody in our cozy little treasure hunting club will be safe."

"That would be, you, Matt and me."

"And innocent bystanders."

"I doubt Matt is up to collaborating with you on anything at the moment." She eyed the clock. "You picked a dicey time to climb my balcony, ex-Romeo, when Matt is still tied up at the radio station for another hour or so."

"I said the fewer people who know I'm in town, the better. You have the best puzzle-solving talents of us three. You know Vegas inside out, even more than I do. This needs to be a two-man operation."

When Temple remained silent, he added, "Has it occurred to you someone or some entity in Vegas also knows about the hoard of IRA donations Kathleen gathered over the years in North and

South America from Irish loyalists and wants it at any cost? What if the inept burglar was after the Effinger drawing of the man fighting a giant serpent you and Devine brought back from Chicago? That representation of the Ophiuchus constellation ties into the magicians' cabal who owned the Neon Nightmare. They're dead or scattered, but what if someone found your ingenious sketch of the main Ophiuchus stars overlaid on the Las Vegas Strip?"

"I'm losing faith in this quest," Temple said. "Why are some bearer bonds—granted they're highly portable and international currency—and old weapons that are probably not half as lethal or expensive as the average assault rifle you can open carry in some states, worth that much?"

"Because, my fine red-feathered friend," Max said, his eyes sparkling with the anticipation of revelation, "of *one* thing I learned from Kathleen in Ireland. The bearer bonds are only a mere ten percent of the trove. The money came in a dozen currencies, and was converted to more easily smuggled forms."

"Gold coins?"

"Yo, ho, ho. Like pirates of old, matey?" Max cackled.

"So Effinger's slow death by drowning in a pirate ship attraction fits the booty? He must have known the location and refused to tell. Nasty."

"Still, coins are traceable."

"Gold bars!" Temple said.

"Heavy, but Santiago's international media entertainment installations would mean shipping heavy machinery, and gold bars would be easily concealable then. Still, something even smaller would have been better, and South America is known for exporting…?"

"Bananas!"

"I wasn't asking for an opinion. Yes, bananas number one, but something more valuable, besides oil and exotic lumber."

"And gemstones!" Temple realized. "Then…our assumption that the hoard was destined for a paramilitary group and heavy on weapons, may be wrong. We're not looking for a huge underground safe like the empty one found in the tunnels between Gangsters and the Crystal Phoenix hotels. And the Ophiuchus constellation's significant stars may not be dispersed on a landscape scale but on...."

"A much smaller, more human one," Max said.

"Oh." Temple's mind was reeling with possibilities. "The map and sketches are in Matt's unit. We have to bring him in on it."

"I can extract them."

"From his safe?"

"What's an honest ex-priest and media sensation doing with a private safe?"

"Danny Dove installed it when he did over Matt's monk cave into a hip bachelor pad. And added a TV that rises up from the foot of the bed."

She caught a gleam in the dark as Max rolled his eyes. "I could say so many politically incorrect things about that but I'll leave it to your imagination."

Temple was glad the room was dark. She felt herself blushing.

"Okay, Max. One last time around the merry-go-round."

He nodded quickly.

"And you can forget the idea of me going to Wisconsin to help you handle the Kinsella and Kelly generational two-step intervention."

His next nod was not so quick.

"Matt can do that for you, Max. If he's feeling generous, and if he doesn't find out I'm collaborating with the enemy."

"At least you're not cohabitating with the enemy anymore," Max quipped. "When's the happy day?"

"Unset, but soon. I've got the e-vite guest list. We'll marry the minute the issue of Matt's moving to a TV talk show in Chicago is resolved. He's...been distracted from pushing hard on that."

"Maybe he knows you can take the girl out of Las Vegas, but you can't take Las Vegas out of the girl. Your Crystal Phoenix PR position plays to all your creative strengths. I saw you during that Black & White band reunion debut. You're part diplomat, producer, on-site shrink, and detective."

Temple was really blushing now. She could have turned an eggnog glass into hot milk by pressing it to one of her cheeks at the moment, flushed from praise. Recognition. Max was a master impresario. She thought back to their early days, imagining her joining his act as the magician's assistant in glitter hose and satin bustier. She was petite and limber enough.

But Max worked alone, except for droves of doves for the finale, and she was not willing to be an accessory. Nor did she want to doll herself up like the dated *Playboy* Bunny. Even *Playboy* was out of the Bunny business, now that much racier fare was wallpapering the Internet. At ninety, Hugh Hefner was living on until death in the pre-sold notorious Mansion in L.A.

"You need to add 'talent agent' to my résumé," she said.

She didn't often confound Max, and explained. "Mariah Molina is an aspiring pop diva. She's joined the backup group for Black & White lead singer French Vanilla on weekends."

"Quite a big gig for a little tween girl like Molina Junior."

"Not so little, Max. She's been taller than me for a while now."

"Looking after her in the rock 'n' roll business should keep Mama Molina distracted from our quest. Too bad Mama never had a show biz break like that."

"She almost did, I've learned. That's why French Vanilla gave Mariah that to-die-for weekend spot."

"*Hmmph.*" Max shook his head. "I've been on the run too long. Kids grow up, friends die, My best girl moves on. It must not seem that long to you since we moved into this place, probably with a whacky expectation of fair winds and sunny weather."

Temple could have harked back to those few months they'd lived like newlyweds before his past forced him to perform the ultimate magical illusion and disappear without notice. But, no she couldn't. Not anymore.

"You're just growing old and sentimental," she told him, "now that your cousin is more than a nameless headstone in Ireland. It must have been so joyful *and* agonizing to realize Sean had been alive all these years."

"He's a war hero," Max said simply. "Married to a heroine. That woman put the fear of St. Patrick in me. Deirdre had to drag Sean out of that pub before he'd believe I wasn't coming back. A strong, determined woman. He wouldn't leave until I returned."

"Oh, Max."

"Yes, 'oh, Max'. How was I to know crazy, damaged Kathleen was seducing me away to save my life, and also lose my self-respect when I found how I'd been scammed. Sean was out of his head after the impact. Deirdre even caught the shrapnel edge of it, but she told the IRA boyos Sean was an American sympathizer, which he… we…were in our simplistic youth, so the IRA accepted him as a wounded one of their own."

"How badly was he—?"

"Enough that people are…tempted to look away, but then his eyes and spirit catch you and you forget about pity and look to your own soul and spirit."

Temple kept silent, nodding.

She sighed. "And you've brought all this back to the USA, expecting me—or Matt—or the both of us to change rain and pain to acceptance and reunion."

"Both of you have the magic touch with people, don't you?"

"You're the professional magician."

"I can manipulate and surprise people. Make them forget their troubles. Fight for them. But I seem to keep them at a distance and never cure them. Or myself."

"It seems to me, that if you have the guts to take Kathleen *and* Sean home again, and come back and ask Matt and me to assist—"

"I've quite a nerve on me," Max said, smiling ruefully, "as Kathleen put it."

He rose to leave.

"Wait! Where are you going?"

"To rob your fiancé's safe. I should keep custody of the puzzle pieces, given the break-ins. Meanwhile, I have some ideas about where in Vegas would be a good hiding place for a portable prize hidden by magicians."

"Since you are one," Temple pointed out.

"*Hmm.* Not feeling it so much lately. We'll see."

As soon as Max left, Louie lofted atop the bed to take his place.

"Pretty sharp defensive moves," Temple told him as he settled down beside her hip and began to tongue-bathe his shoulder. "Now everything you heard here is between you and me, right?"

7
Being Frank

"Wedding plans? Congratulations, Matt."

Frank Bucek's voice boomed out over the phone as much as it had commanded a class of seminarians seventeen years ago.

A lot of ex-priests ended up working in counseling, as Matt had, or law enforcement. It figured. Seminarians and priests knew about keeping vows and rules and contending with good and evil on a daily basis.

"May I assume I know the spirited young lady in question?"

"Yes, it's Temple, Frank. I know it's early in the day, but I'm wondering if you could join me for brunch at a little place near the Circle Ritz. The Magic Muffin."

Frank's laugh boomed out. "Magic Muffin, huh? Sounds like a clever concept. Sure."

Matt watched his cell phone whisk Frank's contact off the screen. As usual, Matt had two missions in seeing Frank.

Number one was finding out if he had indeed glimpsed Frank Bucek outside the Lucky Stars nudie bar when Matt has first been taken into the ugly world of retired cop Woodrow Wetherly. The other was, what could Frank Bucek do for him now, besides playing Best Man.

Matt had never patronized the Magic Muffin restaurant. It occupied a free-standing building near Electra Lark's cluster of commercial properties. The gone-under chain there before it used A-frame buildings as an instant recognition factor, but the trick had failed, and the entire exposed roof and exterior had been painted over like a classic hippie van with psychedelic lettering and images, the Franchise That Time Forgot.

Inside, Matt found a blackboard with neon-colored chalk descriptions of super-sized muffin meals from Meatballs to Vegan and sweet to sweet-and-sour. The muffins were as big as a pot pie and did come in that variety.

Matt got there first. He was the favor-asker. He was surprised to see that Frank had gained a paunch since they last met a couple months ago. He hadn't lost energy, though.

He strode over to greet Matt with a crushing handshake and a back slap.

"Marriage is a great institution, as long as you're not locked up in it," he said while seating himself, laughing. "I can't read that darn blackboard writing."

"Here's the printed menu, on the table. I think they have a steady clientele that doesn't need to read."

Frank laughed. His luxuriously haired graying eyebrows lifted as he scanned the menu.

"Two Meatloaf, Cheese, and Pepperoni-Olive muffins. I'm set."

Matt went with one Whole Wheat Breakfast Scramble, feeling like a wimp. But that disadvantage had always been Frank Bucek's personal magic.

Over the two-fisted-size muffins and huge mugs of potent coffee, Matt made his first pitch.

"I'd like to ask you to be my best man. We don't have a date yet, but it'll be soon. Probably not much notice."

"Matt, I would swim a piranha-infested Lake Mead, what's left of it, to stand up for you. Anytime. Anywhere."

"Thanks for the ringing endorsement. I'm also wondering… Why do I think I saw you someplace off-Strip that was…well, way more sleazy than anywhere two ex-priests should ever be?"

"My job takes me into situations beyond sleaze to human trafficking tragedy." Frank set down his coffee mug, empty, and stuffed his second muffin and napkin in his suit coat pocket.

"If you did think you saw me in someplace sleazy, maybe you shouldn't have been there. Guy about to get married. I gotta run. These muffins are sure portable. Thanks."

"Frank—"

"Just saying. Think about it. We'll be here."

"*We'll?*"

"Hey, this place as has every variety of Magic Muffin you can dream of. So does Life. Always order wisely."

Matt, his mind churning with unease after Frank had been so brusque and tight-lipped, was driving the Jaguar toward the entry into the Circle Ritz parking lot.

Then he recognized the ugly rear of the huge seventies junker he'd last seen parked in front of Electra's inherited building. It was idling by the curb just a short stroll away.

Why was Woody Wetherly's mysterious henchman parked on the street outside the Circle Ritz?

Besides lounging low in the driver's seat, gimme cap bill pulled down over his eyes, staring fixedly at the building's rear...where both Matt and Temple, and Electra on the penthouse level, had visible balconies overlooking the pool and parking lot.

Where an intruder had breached Temple's French doors recently, and more recently, another intruder had fallen to his death from the penthouse level he'd broken into. That left Matt's unit in-between untouched. So far. Good thing he had the treasure hunt maps in a hidden safe.

Matt understood the phrase "cold sweat" for the first time. Not that he hadn't sweated out some dangerous situations since following his no-good stepfather to Las Vegas, but now he actually saw someone watching and probably wishing Temple nothing good.

After the sweat came the defensive adrenaline rush, almost blinding him with icy-hot murderous intent.

Jesus, Mary, and Joseph. Not swearing, a brief prayer from his Catholic grade-school youth, calling on their protection. The interruption of his speculations and worries instantly calmed him.

He drove slowly past the car, the same one he had followed from Woody's place into the desert on a quickie digging expedition days ago. He willed himself not to be seen by the driver. That car gave him the creeps. It had returned from the desert with a bloody jackhammer in its trunk.

His own junker, a 2001 gray Chevy Impala, freshly purchased, sat parked around the block.

He'd have to park the Jag on the other side of the building, on the street. It was expendable. He locked it after pulling to the curb behind the Impala, and slipped the second set of keys out of his pants pocket, his hands shaking with excitement.

He realized Temple had mentioned seeing this guy around when she was out, scraggly looks and loping gait. Woody knew about and had clearly threatened Temple during his call-in to *WCOO*. Since then Matt had steered clear of the supposedly "retired" cop, who either wanted to discourage or goad him into some action. Over eighty or not, Wetherly was involved in current criminal schemes. Evil and greed had no expiration date.

Now, Matt needed to follow this unappetizing lurker and figure out what he was up to. Or choke it out of him. That was why his hands were shaking. Not fear, fury. The man was several years older than he. Closer to forty than to thirty. Prematurely stooped and lazy-looking, but that kind could be wire-strong.

And he had that frequent offender look. Beat-up billed cap, stingy soul-patch under his lower lip, straggly ponytail disappearing into the collar his lightweight Eisenhower jacket.

Matt struggled into a worn jean jacket while getting behind the Impala's wheel, picked up the greasy billed cap from a used clothing store from the passenger seat, mussed his choir-boy blond hair and donned it at a laid-back angle. He lowered the driver's window all the way, the air-conditioning off as if broken, and rested his crooked left arm on the window opening.

A lit cigarette in his fingers would be a crowning touch, but smoking was too foreign to mess with. He started the car and drove around the block as fast as he dared, then slowed to make the right turn onto the street where the jackhammer-toter had parked.

The car was gone.

8
Ring Around the Ritz

I stand with Midnight Louise watching Mr. Matt drive off in his "new" old car, leaving us ride-less in mid-tail.

"I told you," Miss Midnight Louise says, "we should have slipped into the Impala on the other side of the block while Mr. Matt was occupied into downsizing his look."

"You mean while he was changing into scruffy, probably stinky clothes to match the driver of the junker car he found so fascinating. What a loser that guy is, ponytail *and* soul patch."

"Whatever…"

For the moment, Louise sounds like little Miss Mariah in a teenage snit. "At least, Pops, the clothes would have made it easier to follow him if he left the Impala, which we cannot do now."

"If you would have listened to me," I tell her, "we would have slipped into the Jaguar right off, and not have had to race back and forth from that very unsatisfying breakfast rendezvous at the Magic Muffin."

I am huffing quite a bit from proving to Miss Midnight Louise I can still keep up with a car for a four-block round trip.

She shakes her head. "Only you would stop for a Dumpster inspection on a tailing assignment."

"There might have been evidence."

"The only evidence you found on this expedition is the bacon crumbs on your whiskers."

"It is of interest that Miss Electra has a popular breakfast joint near the Circle Ritz. Good for business."

"*Her* business, not ours. What has been the point of this runaround while Mr. Matt changes looks and cars? We have lost him."

"But we have gained information?"

"What?"

"Night before last, in the aftermath of Miss Electra's penthouse invasion, Ma Barker told me that tall, dark-coated men from here—men, plural—and one yellow-haired one, were showing up recently on the bad side of town. I have seen Mr. Matt's breakfast partner before."

"You have me there, Popster. I have not. And what is Ma Barker doing visiting you at the Circle Ritz when you could bop over to her headquarters at the police substation?"

"Family business, Louise," I say loftily. "Mother and son bonding. You would not know about that, since you are fixed."

"*Hmmph.* So who is this tall, dark-haired man who is so busy he has to run off with the extra breakfast muffin in his pocket?"

"They *are* super-large. I wonder if there is a dumpling-shrimp version."

"Daddy Greedy-gut!"

I choose not to take offense. "He is not a frequent player on the scene, but has been assigned back to Las Vegas only recently. Interesting. Mr. Frank Bucek, Mr. Matt's mentor from years ago in the seminary and now an FBI agent. And Mr. Frank did not seem to share much information with Mr. Matt, or have time to waste."

"Neither do we," she says as I wander over to sniff where the junker car of interest to Mr. Matt had been parked.

Hmm. Traces of leaking motor oil with an attar of crushed cactus flowers. The car had been in the desert, but where was it going now?

Only Mr. Matt would know for sure, and he was not talking.

"What will we do next?" Miss Midnight Louie inquires in an exasperated tone.

"At my favorite listening post two nights ago—"

"Under the bed like a chamber pot, no doubt!" she spits. "That is low, Daddy-o. Also an invasion of privacy, so there were *two* home invasions at the Circle Ritz that night."

I am not concerned about privacy when so many secrets are circulating among my nearest and dearest.

"I heard a familiar location discussed. That is what I will investigate next."

I look at the ugly oil spot the junker has left on the asphalt, like a very big bug died under its wheel.

"I think Ma is right. A sinister conspiracy is spreading into our territory."

"If it turns out as well as our tailing operation this morning, Pops, you had better pack a lunch!"

9
Serpentine Schemes

Matt cruised the Circle Ritz neighborhood almost blindly, his mind churning, trapped behind the wrong vehicles, looking ahead through their windshields for a glimpse of that bare-metal green paint finish version of psoriasis. Madly impatient to wait in line for a red light to turn.

Then, looming in Matt's rearview mirror, fast and furious, like a squad car that had burped its siren and pulled him over, only there had been no sound, was the driver of the junker glaring at him.

Matt had three vehicles ahead of him, including an SUV that blocked the sight of anyone crossing the intersection. The light was changing and the guy behind Matt laid on his horn as if he had died on it.

Matt looked left, right, ahead. Undecided. Traffic was moving. The car behind jerked ahead enough to tap his bumper. That was a common tactic of someone wanting to claim an accident and then bully a driver into paying him off to go away, or, worse, assaulting and robbing the poor soul.

The gap ahead of the old Impala was growing.

Matt wrenched the wheel, screeching, hard right into the side parking lot of a closed-down dry cleaning store, and put the car in Park.

He charged out of the idling car, slamming the door behind him as the other car followed him into the lot and stopped.

"What the *Hell* are you doing tailgating me?" Matt demanded. "I'm not falling for any scratch-and-dent scam. Get off my tail, buddy."

The man got out, slowly, not expecting this. "*You* were following *me*."

Matt snorted. "Like I'd want to look up your tailpipe. Your junker is worse than mine."

"What's your game, buddy?" He squinted at Matt. "I've seen you somewhere. You look familiar. Somewhere poor dead Ox was. Wait! At the Lucky Stars nudie bar. Word is a new guy was with Woody... That was you, all cleaned up. I didn't think much about it, 'cuz you looked so familiar in a funny way I can't put my trigger finger on it. Yet."

Not good. Had the guy spotted him at Woody's house too? Matt hadn't expected to encounter his prey face-to-face, standing up.

"Woody? You his errand boy?" Matt asked, aware his khaki slacks and beige leather loafers didn't match the shabby jacket and cap. He'd have to hope his dishonest face would look different enough under mussy hair to throw the guy off.

The man suddenly leaned against his diseased fender. The arms on his faded denim jacket had been torn off, a tough blue-collar look, and common in the Vegas heat. The arms folded over his chest displayed unimpressive muscle, but a ton of tattoos.

Matt had maybe twenty-five pounds on him, but figured this guy wasn't anybody's muscle. He looked and acted like a born sneak who'd be useful for sleazy jobs, like following and threatening women. And...digging up dead bodies...and moving corpses...or even fifty-year-old murder weapons.

The sleeves of ink on both arms crawled to his neck, ending with a fat spider in a web under his left ear.

Why did so many dispossessed people, convicts or depressed teens, wear tattoos as armor nowadays? A sign they could endure some pain? A third finger stuck up at the world? Tattoos were too chic now to be seen as threatening.

This guy's skin art was a crude and uninspired patchwork—except for his forearms. Snakes seemed a favored subject. The right arm showed the blue waves lapping and a set of serial blue-green humps of the Loch Ness monster in its most famous, and never duplicated, photograph. A small human figure with a headdress stood next to it. A fully seen serpent wound around his left arm in lurid colors, fighting some comic book hero with bulging muscles, ridiculously oversized, but…nude. What comic book superhero wrestled nude?

"You starin' at something?"

"Uh, yeah. Righteous arm tats."

"What would a Mr. Clean like you know about it?" The man lifted and turned his left forearm to acknowledge his major and prize tattoo. "Yeah, a beaut. Nothing canned. No one has a tat like this."

Matt watched the arm rotate as he'd watch a cobra coiling for a strike. Another blood-run-cold moment, not welcome on even a hot day. The naked man entoiled by a large snake seemed to move with the guy's rotating elbow, the point of having it on the forearm.

Man and serpent entwined, the exact image of the contested thirteenth (unlucky for him) sign of the Zodiac. Located in the constellation named Ophiuchus.

This same image had been discovered in his mother's Chicago apartment, in a fireproof box along with other memorabilia of Matt's late, most unlamented abusive stepfather, Clifford Effinger.

"Yeah," the tattooed man was saying, "my old man traced it out of some book in grade school. It was a kind of banner with him, I guess. Didn't go to school much past eighth grade. Had to work. But it's like based on some classic nudie sculpture. Famous."

Matt knew the sculpture well, the prize of the Vatican museums. "Laocoön and His Sons." A man and his two sons in mortal agony under attack by venomous biting and constricting sea serpents, probably sent by some miffed Greek god.

Matt felt an empathetic shiver from the ironic fact that Effinger had two sons as well, but the tattoo had been simplified to man and snake only.

The guy was still admiring his arm art. "When I was a kid, it was on the refrigerator door with a magnet, you know? That's when my uncle promised me I could get it tattooed on when I was eighteen."

"It was your uncle's refrigerator?"

The guy shrugged. "Them was still mob days. An Outfit *capo* needed my dad in Chicago. I never knew why. Anyway, he married some rich woman with a house and a snotty kid there. And bye-bye, Chuckie. So it was always me and my uncle here in Vegas."

"Your mother?"

"Never knew her. OD'ed on drugs, I guess." The guy's Mississippi-mud-colored eyes sharpened. "Why are you asking all these questions?"

"Why are you answering them?"

"That's because I was trying to figure it out, why you're passing the time of day admiring my tattoos, and where I remembered you from."

"That Lucky Stars fracas? I ducked out of there early."

"So you were the new guy with Woody?"

Matt nodded, hoping the guy remembered his worn jeans, scuffed motorcycle boots, and faded Grateful Dead T-shirt topped with a plaid long-sleeved work shirt. "I have Chicago connections too."

The guy started laughing, a humorless wheezing sound that ended in a cough. "You're telling me? I've finally remembered what else was under a magnet on that refrigerator door, with a Chicago phone number. A photo of some sad, but not bad-looking woman, and this perfect little blond kid leaning against her.

"My stepmom and stepbrother I never saw, but who kept my dad away from me for over twelve years. That kid didn't look too happy either, just the way you're looking now."

Matt knew he'd been "made", but he needed to know more, everything.

"Cliff Effinger had a son in Las Vegas? You?"

"And a not-real son in Chicago. Matt, they called him."

"And Cliff had a brother?"

"Well, he did, but Uncle Joe died too. I should say, was killed too. Nobody copped to either hit."

Gold mine, Matt thought. *Gold mine. How do I win over this guy?*

"What's your name?" he asked.

"Chuck."

"For Charles."

"Naw, just Chuck. Chuck Effinger."

"We should go somewhere and talk."

"And what game are you playing, little Matt, with your fancy shoes and down-low cap? Yeah, I noticed. I'm not as dumb as I look. Lucky Stars okay?"

"No, not anywhere near that crowd, where someone could overhear. I think we've both been had."

The nearest hamburger joint had a dated look involving lots of the color orange, Burgers 'n' Beers.

The tabletop juke-box music was loud, but there was an empty corner booth at the back.

"Two things we have to talk about," Matt said, sliding into the vinyl-covered booth as his pants caught on some taped-over cuts in the upholstery. "The first and the last."

Over greasy hamburgers and draft beer, Matt and Effinger's son compared past and present grievances.

First.

"I hated your father for hitting my mother," Matt said.

"And hitting you too, I bet. He knocked me around some before he left for so long. But he was my dad. And I don't think he wanted to be in Chicago. He had to go, like someone here was after him, or he was sent away by the mob for knowing too much. Where was your dad?"

"He disappeared, never knew about me."

Chuck nodded, lighting a cigarette. "At least my dad used to send me stuff. Comic books and toys. Even when I was getting too old for them. He'd come back from Chicago more often later."

"I wanted to kill your dad."

"But you didn't do that drowned-alive operation. That was planned, I think to send a message and shut my uncle up. Someone will pay for offing my dad like that. But it's hard to find who. Lots of people wanted to kill my dad. It wasn't just because they didn't like him or he bounced them around some. That was kinda his job, to do things for the mob."

"I had a chance to kill him, though."

"What stopped you?"

"Some parts of your life are just over, and you are what you *are* because of them. That won't change, but you can. So you walk away from the bad and move forward into the good."

"Golly, little Matt. That should be in a book. I won't walk away until I get my revenge."

"Let's call it justice."

"I've got a double dose of it coming, 'cuz they got my Uncle Joe into something bad too, and he ended up dead on a craps table at the Crystal Phoenix."

Matt's heart almost stopped. That sentence solved a cold case and maybe a big part of the puzzle that made this chronic loser a key piece. The body had initially been IDed as Cliff, but no records showed and no one had known Clifford Effinger had a brother. Meanwhile, Chuck was droning into his beer.

"Uncle Joe'd never go into a hoighty-toighty place like that, not willingly, and besides, it's crawling with Fontana Family muscle, who are more deadly than they look."

"So his death was meant as a distraction, to muddy the waters," Matt said. "What role would a retired cop like Woody play in this scenario?"

"He's always got some scheme going on. He's telling me to do the kind of things my dad did. Handle this schnook, look up that or this made man from the old days, if they're still alive. I can't figure what he's working up to."

"A cop retired since the nineties hanging out with ex-mob guys and sending people to burglarize the Circle Ritz? That'd be another unlikely place for aging mobsters to show up."

"Ouch, Poor Ochs," Chuck said around a ketchup-bloody handful of French fries.

It wasn't, "Alas, poor Yorick" from *Hamlet*, Matt thought, but it had a rough-and-ready eloquence.

"He wasn't a bad egg,." Chuck mumbled.

"Why'd they call him 'Ox', his size?"

"Nah, his size, maybe, but his last name was Ochsenhoffer or something that makes Effinger sound like a cool name. Woody could be putting a burglary ring in operation."

Matt nodded to encourage Chuck to continue.

"See, Woody is so old he goes back to the time when the mob ran this town in the seventies," Chuck said. "He was a green young cop, but they back and forthed with the mob then."

Matt got it. "That's why it took the FBI to come into Vegas in the eighties to get the mob out."

"Out, but not down. My dad used to laugh with my uncle about it being the 'same old, same old', with one big difference. And then they'd get to laughing so hard. They'd say 'if the dumb cops then and the dumb cops now only knew...'"

"And now both Effinger brothers are dead. Murdered."

Chuck's slack features grew taut. "Old Woody Wetherly is the only cop left now who might know what they meant. Anyway, he sure knows who to call on for major dirty work, and for small-timers like me as errand boys."

"And for something more?"

"I dunno who big-time is left that would engineer a mob-days, right-out-there gig of tying a gagged guy to a sinking ship in a nighttime show and letting him drown with a...what'd you call the bare-breasted ladies they had carved on sailing ship's fronts?"

"Figurehead."

"Yeah. Those ship ladies were more boobs than heads, if you ask me. And now the show is closed down and dead in the water too, and you can only see one anchored lit-up ship from the Strip. Did you know they did weddings on that ship for years?"

"No," Matt said, not liking the topic of weddings coming up with an enemy. But Chuck was still wrapped up in his "Wayback Machine".

"It's funny. My dad sent me a kit once. A put-a-ship-together kit. Too many pieces. I threw it away. Who'd ever dream he'd die on one? I'm going to find one of those kits and make whoever did that to him eat it."

Matt didn't know what to say. The monster had a kid who loved him, in his way.

"I'm sorry, Chuck."

"Are you, little-perfect-photograph Matt?"

"For you."

"What are you going to do with all this info? You're not the law. You're just some D.J. I know that."

Disk Jockey. Matt chuckled. He'd hardly touched his burger, but threw two twenties on the table. To reward the waitress who'd been derelict in coming around, which perfectly suited his mission.

"So?" Chuck pushed away his plate of massacred leavings, dead cow crumbs and cold fries buried in ketchup.

"So, I think the police will finally get a lead on who killed your dad and your uncle, and why. I don't know who or when, but it will happen. And you'll have your revenge."

"You mean 'justice'," Chuck mocked. He actually had a sense of humor. "I get the 'first' thing and all that stuff, but what's the 'last' thing you were talking about?"

Matt leaned in on Chuck, hands braced on the table rim, eyes and voice on the same jagged edge as broken glass.

"You will forget any instructions from anybody to follow, threaten, or harass with even a glance Miss Temple Barr at the Circle Ritz or anywhere in Vegas or the universe, or I will hunt you down and this time I *will* kill an Effinger. The last of the Effingers."

10
The Tony Awards

"Matt," said the man on the phone. "I have serious news for you."

He flashed back to his conversations with Frank Bucek and Chuck Effinger earlier that day. So what new crime figure was haunting him, because the caller sure wasn't Woody Wetherly. Yet the voice was vaguely familiar....

Then Matt recognized the caller, and wondered, *What next today?*

Caught by his personal appearance agent, Tony Valentine, a great guy he'd been avoiding, he turned to face Temple's balcony.

With his amateur sleuthing turning up deadly suspicions, his supposed career jump to going live on air in Chicago was a distracting issue he wished would go away. He'd have to be honest with Tony, but not just yet.

"'Serious' news," Matt repeated. "Usually, agents only have good or bad news."

Darn. By now the sound of his voice had drawn Temple from the kitchen, where she'd been tossing one of her "everything" salads.

"Matt," Tony was going on, gently but firmly. "We must talk. You and I know you haven't been acting wildly enthusiastic about this opportunity for some time."

"I'm sorry, Tony. With the wedding in the offing and...some personal matters involving relatives—"

"No serious family illness, I hope? I can certainly explain that."

"No. Complications, but not that."

"Then I hope you and the 'little woman' can still come by my office today." Tony was chuckling. "I'd like to see Temple reacting to my using that descriptive phrase."

Matt looked over his shoulder at Temple, who'd lurked there since he used the words "serious" and "Tony", trying to interpret the trend of the conversation.

"Couldn't resist," Tony said. "She's so earnest when she's angry."

"Ah, you want us to come in today?"

Temple was nodding vigorously.

"I think that would be best."

"Of course," he told Tony. "We're daytime people. About 4 p.m.?"

"Very good. See you then."

Temple was jumping up and down, her shoulder-length fiery waves bouncing, looking like a twelve-year-old who'd just gotten tickets to the rock band of the day. *Her* mind wasn't dwelling on the possible resurrection of the long-dead Jackhammer Killer. Or at least his jackhammer.

"Tony!" she screamed after the phone went off. "Needs to see us? Finally!"

"But for 'serious' news. I don't think it's good, Temple. He mentioned my putting Chicago off for so long. First, I'll need to give the Jaguar back, which is fine." In fact, Matt wanted the whole deal and every trace of it to disappear.

"Don't be so negative," Temple urged.

"Look. It's obvious he wants to break the bad news in person. He's a really decent man. I was lucky to end up as his client."

"Well, if that's the case, we'll just deal with it."

"But oh," she said, crossing fingers on both hands and her arms and shutting her eyes. "I hope, I hope, I hope."

Matt was glad she couldn't see the anguish on his face.

"Come in," Tony said as he stepped into the outer office to escort them past his young assistant's desk. Danielle had deluged them with offers of exotic-flavored espresso, but they were both too nervous to tote liquids at the moment.

Matt suddenly saw the tall, white-haired and distinguished Tony Valentine as the solicitous funeral director. Tony escorted Temple, businesslike in an aqua-colored linen suit and closed-toed red high-heeled pumps that did not convey a mourning mood, to a high-backed upholstered chair in front of his desk.

Matt took the matching chair, wishing it was the creepy vanishing one from old forties movie comedies that would drop him through the floor and flip back into place empty.

When they were seated, Tony put his elbows on his immaculately empty but impressive mahogany desk.

"I know you both have had a lot on your minds lately, especially Miss Barr's cat getting a commercial contract. I should get the paperwork on that in a couple weeks. And your upcoming marriage, when—?"

"Very soon," Temple said, glancing at Matt.

"Ah, yes, this is Las Vegas, capital of quick, inventive nuptials, even at The Mob Museum. I hope I'm invited."

"You're on my e-vite list."

"Excellent." Tony cleared his throat and looked at Matt. "I wonder if you know you've been my most recalcitrant client. If it were a marriage we were discussing rather than a talk-show host spot, I'm afraid the network wooers would all be retiring or dead before you'd make up your mind."

"I apologize. Sincerely. We've been dealing with long-term and recalcitrant family issues."

Temple nodded to back him up.

"You know, my dear young people, you must grab the golden goose at the first opportunity or it flies away?"

"I know, I know," Matt said. "I'm sorry to have disappointed you all." His glance at Tony ricocheted to Temple, who was sitting forward in her seat in suspense, her hands clasped on her red patent-leather tote bag, her shoulders back and her chin tilted high to take the bad news. *His* bad news. He took her hand.

"So," Tony said, "the network, being out of time and patience..."

Temple sighed.

"...finally realized that your reluctance was actually a sign."

"A sign?" Matt was not superstitious. "Like an omen?"

"That you obviously do not wish to leave Las Vegas."

"Ah…" Matt said.

"And they decided that was brilliant. Vegas was where to film the show."

"Oh, Matt!" Temple said, turning to him, her eyes shining… happy-tear eyes.

"And," Tony went on, beaming, "they decided that this daytime TV talk show should have *two* hosts. That you *and* Temple are naturals, like Kelly and Regis, and Kelly and, ahem, Michael Strahan, until recently…only New Generation. Even that darn crime-solving Disneysque cat could appear via film clips. The commercial sponsors would love it."

Temple gaped at Matt. "It's genius. It's perfect. I used to interview people as a TV news reporter. Matt, you're 'radio'. It'd be so much *fun*. And no more working nights. Isn't this the most wonderful outcome in the world?"

And, yes, he caught the firefly magic of it. Them, working together, inventing together. The couple who grows and works together stays together. He was flabbergasted, won over, excited by the possibilities. Temple was more outgoing than he was. She'd loosen him up. He was the cream in her coffee. They'd have a ball.

If he and Temple would live to enjoy a new media partnership.

Tony was right. This was serious business.

Tony saw them out personally. Advised them to "sleep on it" and "let it all sink in".

"Can you believe it"? Temple whispered almost before Tony's office suite door had closed. "Everything you did, all the putting off and delaying, worked like an insanely clever plan.

"I feel like we're Judy Garland and Mickey Rooney in those old forties movies, two crazy kids who are 'going to put on a show' to save the farm.

"Oh, I'm getting so many ideas—we could do 'flash' street interviews in cool Vegas locations. Maybe a Louie spot through his cat's-eye-view with voice-overs, and the scenes are in neon-color, or noir black-and-white, or mixed."

"Temple, I'm sure the producers will have plenty of must-do ideas for building audiences."

"And it's such great timing that I decided on our Lady of Guadalupe. We can get married right away, and ask Electra about okaying uniting our two residences as well as ourselves. She's been cleared of any charges in the intruder's fatal fall. And now, more good news! I'm so happy to have this uncertainty gone too and that we can forecast smooth sailing full steam ahead from now on. Oh, I guess that's a mixed metaphor, but you know what I mean. Can you tell me you aren't thrilled by this chance, this amazing turn of events."

Matt had to laugh and share her joy. Temple's giddy relief told him how much his secret worries had been weighing them both down.

And even as Temple hung on his neck, laughing and kissing and shaking off those tears of joy like a demented water spaniel fresh out of a lake, Matt felt a thrill at the rightness of the idea, like their marriage.

Yes, it was amazing they could work together, yes they could stay in Vegas at the Circle Ritz, yes they could get married right away. Putting the brakes on all that lovely karma, would be impossible.

So he would have to fix it all, right away, and if he had to ask for help from whomever he could—God, Elvis, or Chuck Effinger—he would. It was him versus manipulative Woody Wetherly and his schemes and the seemingly immortal Jack the Hammer and his brutal weapon of choice.

11
The Mysteries of Molina

"I'm glad you could stop by, Matt," she said after opening the front door, her left thumb nervously twisting the bulky but loose college graduation ring on her left ring finger.

Matt had never seen any other ring on Lieutenant C. R. Molina's hands. Was it a single mother's substitute for a wedding ring? Or valued in its own right?

That made him wonder why Molina had hung on to Temple's ring from Matt Kinsella for so long, calling it evidence. Had even Molina fallen under the irresistible spell the magician seemed to cast on women, from psychopath Kathleen O'Connor to sensible Temple?

"I must admit I'm curious as heck," he said, "but I'm not about to stand up my favorite homicide lieutenant when she calls me at home last night and invites me over for a 'talk.'" Matt smiled as she stepped aside so he could enter. "After all we've been through together."

"And after all you've been through with your irrepressible redheaded fiancée recently that you two *haven't* told me about."

"You've been pretty irrepressible yourself in saying how little you value amateur detectives, until lately."

"The Circle Ritz Munchkin does have a knack for letting trouble find her. And now she's even got you chasing your family skeletons."

She stopped and turned before letting him enter farther, turning sober. "Matt, I do understand your gut-deep determination to find out the whys and wherefores of your wicked stepfather's gruesome death. Do you take some satisfaction in his last torments?"

"No. Maybe when I was a kid under Effinger's heavy fist I might have. Real adults don't need revenge. So. I'm not still under suspicion?"

"Real cops don't need far-fetched suspects. Whoever gagged and tied your stepfather to the sinking ship attraction is a practiced killer, a pro who likes to sign his work with a sadistic flourish."

"I'm amazed you'd let an amateur like me look into that."

"Your recent drive to the rescue at Electra Lark's abandoned warehouse was pretty spectacular. Besides, you knew the victim. I want that creepy cold case solved myself and can't afford to put shoe leather on it. It's admirable you're keeping your better half out of your hunt for step-daddy's killer or killers. Has Woodrow been a help? The oldest uniforms still here said Detective Wetherly had confidential informants in the mob as far back as the seventies."

Matt hesitated. Was this his chance to call in reinforcements? Molina seemed a bit distracted, maybe not yet. "Yeah, Woody's stories from the old days would grow hair on a cantaloupe. I hope The Mob Museum founders interviewed him."

"Maybe not," Molina said. "Mobsters go viral and virtual, but retired cops fade away. Old-fashioned footwork is now lost behind a mountain of modern forensics and keyboard magic."

By then Matt had followed her into the comfortable living room, with the curled-up cat dents in the sofa pillows and unopened junk mail still tossed on the coffee table.

Molina swept the mail aside in a messy pile, perhaps expressing the level of her regard for Vegas's infatuation with The Mob Museum.

"Take a seat." She gestured to two roomy upholstered chairs opposite the couch. "Can I get you some lemonade? A cold beer?"

"I have a feeling this is a sober occasion. Coffee, if you've got it. Black."

"Does the Pope have encyclicals?"

Matt watched her disappear around the other side of the breakfast bar. Her kitchen rattlings sounded like the backbeat of percussion instruments against the steady hum of the air-conditioner.

He sat back to take stock, brushing a tuft of silken cat undercoat off his bare forearm.

Midafternoon on a hot summer Saturday. Molina at her least lethal, wearing boot-cut jeans, not tight, a loose black gauze top, and moccasins. And that universally familiar class ring no one ever wore unless it advertised an elite Eastern school. It stood out when she wasn't wearing matching blazers and trousers and packing a badge and gun on her belt.

Matt tried to read the ring's engraved design as she returned to set his mug down on a woven coaster on the coffee table.

"Drinking coffee in the summer," she commented, setting her tall glass of lemonade on a matching coaster. "That's what the night shift will do to you. And that slightly tense look around your eyes. That daytime TV job in Chicago ever coming through?"

Matt almost choked on his first swallow of high-octane caffeine. "That's supposed to be hush-hush. How do you—?"

"I have my sources."

"Yeah. Usually one of us civilians."

She squinted her spectacularly blue eyes as she probed his mood. "Or am I seeing fatigue from playing Dale Earnhardt and revving Electra Lark's old white Probe up the stairs of an abandoned building? Usually a white knight uses a horse instead of horsepower. How did you know there was any urgency to interrupt the doings inside that place?"

"Neither Temple nor Electra were where they were supposed to be. Vandals had been defacing Electra's wedding chapel and threatening her Circle Ritz residents." Matt took another swallow of coffee, smaller this time. "The place had recently been a murder scene, and…lights were on inside."

"Yup. Any passing citizen would have driven somebody else's car right up the exterior concrete steps and through the double doors and halfway up the stairway to the second floor. And why were you driving her car anyway? You have a sweet ride of your own. Although I'd never use a Jaguar as a battering ram, but maybe you have money to burn in your future."

"This invitation to drop by is beginning to sound like entrapment, Lieutenant."

"What?" She spread her arms in an innocent gesture. "I'm unarmed and unbadged, Matt. It's just that the Circle Ritz crowd always seems to spawn a miasma of questionable activity around it. You'd better marry Miss Temple and get her out of there before Max Kinsella shows up again and does it himself."

"No comment," he said.

Nor was he about to confess to acquiring an older cheap car for tailing possible mob killers, or mentioning that Rafi Nadir had already helped him buy that replacement for the Probe. Rafi was acting like Matt's bodyguard. Had Molina given her old flame the assignment. Still…why let Matt blunder around in very old and dirty mob business if he needed a keeper?

The coffee was cooling along with his patience, so Matt got to the point. "What is this meeting about besides pumping me on my laughable amateur Effinger investigation?"

Was Molina stalling for time? She seemed nervous, one foot tapping the area rug under the furniture. Something was up.

She shrugged. "Maybe you should forget it. Like God, the mob is dead and now enshrined in what passes for places of worship in Vegas, the new mob and old neon museums."

"You directed me to a source."

"An aging gossip, apparently."

"Woody Wetherly is older than Spanish Moss, all right, and about as attractive. Almost makes me appreciate Temple's harping on my wearing sunscreen."

"Don't be manly and forego it," she said. "Vegas sun is not kind to redheads and blonds. Think of the children."

Matt quashed a flush, finished his coffee and put the mug down on its coaster. "If that's the message of this meeting. Dump Woody Weatherly and use sunscreen? Consider me warned."

"Wait." She put out a spread-fingered hand. "You're right. I've been backpedaling on getting to the real issue."

Matt leaned into his cushy chair as Molina unconsciously took a singer's deep breath and said, "It's about Mariah."

"Anything wrong? Temple said she had an amazing chance to sing onstage weekends."

"Yes. That's going fine. In fact, she's working with her coach right now."

Matt chuckled. "Kids today. All junior high school Miley Cyruses and would-be viral Justin Biebers, hankering for instant YouTube fame and maybe fortunes."

"Yes, Mariah is about to enter the dreaded junior high school. That's what I wanted to talk to you about."

Matt put on his best puzzled face. He thought she'd be fuming about her daughter being in the running for Twisted Teen of the Year. Not that Mariah would...would she?

Molina twisted her class ring with both fingers. "It's about the Dad-Daughter Dance coming up in a few weeks."

Molina? Not only finger-twisting, but tongue-tied? All's wrong with the world, but how? Why?

Matt sat there blinking.

He usually morphed into the position of advisor and confident as easily as any ex-priest who'd heard thousands of what was now called the Sacrament of Reconciliation.

If this supremely self-possessed policewoman was this rattled, he didn't want to speculate what her—upcoming confession, put it in plain language—would be.

12
Strapless in Sin City

"Oh my favorite Cinderella slippers," Temple's aunt Kit Carlson Fontana said over the phone when she heard Temple's shocking proposal. "We need to go to a very cool cocktail lounge, my dear. My nerves are not what they were."

"I would think that being married to Aldo Fontana would do a lot for your nerves, Auntie," Temple said.

"Him I can handle. Your impetuous lives and times I cannot."

Smoke and mirrors. Las Vegas was the home of the absurdly glittering cocktail lounge and Temple loved every overblown one of them, although none was a smoke-free zone. For the short time she visited, she chose to think of the airborne eddies as produced by dry ice from a misty horror movie.

In the reflections all around them, providing film-splice glimpses of their images, Temple saw she and her aunt could be taken for mother and daughter, perhaps more than her own mother. Kit was a sophisticate who'd lived most of her life single in Manhattan. Her sister Karen had reared four strapping sons and one petite girl in suburban Minneapolis.

Once each had been served with the elaborate cocktail of her choice in a stemmed glass, Kit lifted her glass for a toast. "I congratulate you on not waiting as long as I did to tie the knot. A bride at sixty-something." Kit rolled her eyes. Her hair was a softer, faded peachy red than Temple's vivid red-gold, but they were both five-foot-zero.

"You were a gorgeous bride," Temple assured Kit. "And irresistible. Think about it. Aldo stayed single for almost fifty years."

"Well, I assume we can count from when he attained the age of majority at twenty-one, so he only had to deny himself matrimony for twenty-five years. Your mother in Minnesota would strangle me if she knew I was the first to hear details of your wedding."

Temple lifted and sipped in time with her aunt. "That's just it," she said after savoring. "Everything must be hush-hush. Just between us. I need the preliminaries in place."

"When is the big date?"

"Ah, not sure yet."

"So, niece. I am to stage-manage a formal wedding with out-of-town guests in four-four time. Sometime. Soon?"

"Not alone. Danny Dove will help."

Kit fanned her face with the table's specialty cocktails menu. "Oh, my further shattering nerves. I am to assist the foremost and fussiest producer-director in Las Vegas."

"Quite the contrary. He has promised to assist *you*," Temple said. Then she frowned. "Although the Ladies Altar and Flower Society at Our Lady of Guadalupe might be a challenge. I gather they're rather proprietary."

"You're not planning on a Crystal Phoenix wedding, like Aldo and I had? The Phoenix would roll out the red carpet for you. You're living in 'Vegas, Baby' and getting married in a parish *church*?"

"Las Vegas has long been noted for its variety and abundances of churches, Aunt," Temple said demurely. Cocktails tended to make her demure, which was why she didn't drink too many of them.

"Las Vegas is also noted for its variety and abundance of amazing, fantastic, sumptuous, luxurious wedding chapels too," Kit said. "Not to mention your landlady's uniquely charming Lover's Knot chapel where Matt's mother remarried for a first shot at real happiness."

"Oh, I know there are so many people who'd like a say in the ceremony, so many people to please."

Kit's warm hand clenched Temple's cold one. "When it involves your wedding, the only person to please is the bride. Truly. Otherwise you'll be honeymooning in a nuthouse."

"Thank you, Kit. That's the kind of advice I asked you here to provide."

"I'll do anything I can, whenever *it* happens, but why so vague?"

"Matt's agent's negotiations with the network producers on that talk show job are ongoing. We don't want to tip anything off. You know media people, Kit. You were an actress and then a novelist in New York City. These negotiations are delicate."

And, Temple didn't add, although she was dying to tell Kit all the fabulous news from Tony, *we can't marry until Max and I find the hidden IRA hoard of money and guns, and I find out what Matt's secretly involved in with Molina, who, if she's nice to me, can sing at my Our Lady of Guadalupe wedding with her daughter. If she is messing with Matt's head, she won't be allowed to sweep out the confessionals.*

"I do understand media nosiness," Kit said. "My lips are sealed with long-lasting 'Scarlet O'Hara Woman' ravishing red gloss. What do you need from me now?"

"Say yes to the dress."

"Shopping? For your bridal gown? First, curtains are out, despite my lip color. Oh, what fun!! You're so young. You can do anything. Princess Diana with clouds of skirts and shoulder ruffles. Not Kate Middleton, that was lovely, but a bit *too* demure, Kim Kardashian…"

"Nothing Kim Kardashian. I only require a train exactly my height, but I do require a train. One of La Kardashian's gowns had a train long enough to wrap the groom several times around, like a mummy."

"I'm sure her husbands felt like flies in a spider's cocoon. She seems to regard weddings as investment growth operations."

Temple was thinking. "I've wanted to wear a dress with a train since I realized I was never going to grow any taller than I was in junior high."

"Poor traumatized child." Kit patted her hand. "You do realize that sad lack of stature automatically enrolls us in the EHHCC.

"EHHCC?"

"The Endless High Heel Collection Club."

"And that's another thing. The front hem must be high enough to show the Midnight Louie shoes."

"This is beginning to sound like a custom tailoring job."

"No time for that. Off the rack is fine with me. Oh, and nothing strapless."

"Oh, my Great Granny's Garters! *Not* strapless. That makes it an impossible quest. Every bride today goes for a strapless wedding dress."

"You and Matt's mother didn't."

"We were *mature* brides," Kit said with pursed lips.

"I think following the crowd is *im*mature." Temple finished her cocktail. "Come on, take up your tote bag and walk to the parking garage and my car. I've found a bridal shop on Rainbow Boulevard that sounds promising."

"Probably why it's located there. Good marketing."

"Since marketing's my game, I figure they might have good taste too."

And tons and tons of lace, satin, and beaded chiffon white strapless wedding gowns.

"Oh," Temple said when she and Kit walked in the door and then stopped.

Two towering mannequins wearing strapless gowns greeted them, along with a bridesmaid and flower girl. And so did a tall brunette Temple's age who might bring to mind Lieutenant C.R. Molina if she'd ever wear leggings and kitten heels and a smart cold-shoulder top. Dream on.

Temple's heart sank. She and Kit suddenly seemed like Munchkins overwhelmed by a wedding party of six-foot-tall mannequins.

"Mother and daughter?" their greeter chirped, the chickadee voice odd coming from such a rangy woman.

They nodded mutely. It was better than explaining their relationship at length, which was the one thing they could both do, explain at length. Best not to start.

"Please sit." The woman gestured to a pair of expensive tufted leather boudoir chairs. "I'm Courtney."

"Temple Barr."

"I'm Kit. Kit Carlson Fontana."

A ghost of recognition materialized between Courtney's beautifully plucked eyebrows and floated away. Kit *Carson* had been an Old West pony express rider and Fontana was an old but ambiguously law-abiding Vegas name. Or maybe long, tall Courtney had dated one of the boys.

The clients' difference in surnames wasn't an issue. So many women kept maiden names or remarried like a Kardashian these days, all to the good of bridal shops' bottom line,

Behind the wedding consultant stretched rows and rows of bridal gowns shrouded in plastic like captive clouds. Or ghosts, all about seven feet tall. Temple glanced at Kit, intimidated for the first time in a long while.

Courtney's eye glanced, and then stayed glued on Temple's ruby-and-diamond vintage engagement ring from Matt...and The Bellagio Hotel's fabulous vintage jeweler shop, Fred Leighton, which accessorized Red Carpet women. It was not only gorgeous and Temple knew she'd faint if she knew what it cost, but she could endlessly daydream about the tragic life of some nineteen-thirties woman forced to give up the ring decades ago because of the Depression and her husband had jumped off a building. Or perhaps it had been a heroic gesture during the second World War to help family members escape Hitler...

Reality intruded.

"Something from Vera would suit a petite bride well," Courtney suggested, upping her estimation of Temple's means.

Something from the phenomenal designer suited Temple very well when it was Simply Vera from Kohl's department store. In the bridal department, they were talking thousands of dollars. Of course, there was that TV ad work for Louie and her coming up. Nothing signed yet, alas. She was sure Louie would kick in his advance share for a wonderful wedding dress, especially if he could have the wedding veil afterward as a very large tulle toy.

Courtney took a new tack. "Why don't we see what we can rule out."

She turned and led them between the intimidating rows. Given the voluminous skirts and trailing trains, the hangers hung on a six-foot-high rod. No wonder it took a giraffe like Courtney to sweep these heavy protective bags out of the row so she and Kit could stare through the plastic at a dazzling blizzard of billowing satin and lace and tulle Temple would look like a pygmy wearing. Besides, Temple was sure she'd soon go snow-blind.

"Is that a mermaid skirt" she asked about one candidate.

"Don't you like mermaid skirts?"

"I adore mermaid skirts, but wearing a tight sheath to mid-thigh and then having a ballerina tutu billowing out to the floor is death to a short woman. Not to mention impossible to sit in."

"The bride doesn't sit much at a wedding reception," Courtney pointed out.

"No, I don't suppose so." Temple hadn't thought beyond the church ceremony. "Anyway, strong horizontals must be avoided or I'll look like an albino mushroom."

"Don't tell me that rules out a strapless gown?" Courtney looked ready to burst into sobs.

"Well, yeah."

"Everyone wants a strapless gown, except—" Courtney caught herself before she said something uncomplimentary.

Temple had even seen a *Catholic* bride in a strapless gown illustrating the Pre-Cana website Matt had directed her to view after she decided on Our Lady of Guadalupe for the wedding site. Temple found she had some differences with dogma, but if the Catholics—stern advocates of the two-inch-wide "spaghetti" strap, according to hearsay—were finally okay with strapless, why wasn't she?

She told Courtney, never having deceived herself about her literal shortcomings.

"Flat-chested women. Short women. We need a strong central vertical, not to be chopped up with horizontal lines at the bust and thighs."

"We have some gowns with sleeves, but sleeves are so…"

"Matronly," Kit said brightly, with a brittle smile that no one in her right mind would challenge.

Courtney had a comeback. "Many brides do work out for several months before the wedding to correct that universal flabby little upper arm problem we women have…"

"That's like cutting the corpse to fit the coffin," Temple objected. There was a pause.

"Off the shoulder," Courtney suggested. "Very sexy. You have good shoulders and no upper arm issue."

"Are you kidding?" Temple was indignant. "Another strong horizontal, right above where I am not so sufficient and do not want to try to hold up a strapless gown. "

"A boat neckline."

"Ditto. And *that's* matronly."

"Vee."

"Better with cleavage, as are all those ill-fitting strapless gowns I see in the newspaper announcements. With so many of these horizontal slashes in the wedding gown styles, I might as well use a serial killer as a seamstress."

"I assure you, Miss Barr. Temple." Courtney was pleading. "We can find a gown to enhance all your lacks and conceal your awkwardness. We simply have to try some on."

She eyed Temple's footwear, a sprightly multi-color Ferragamo seventies sandal.

"What pretty feet and shoes. I see you're wearing only three-inch heels. We'll need to find some four-and-a-half-heel-inch sample shoes near your size. That will assist the verticality problem."

She gazed horrified at Temple's size five sandal in her hand. "We only carry that size shoe for flower girls."

During this dialogue and the shoe-doffing incident, Kit had vanished, Temple realized.

"But," said the adaptable and oh-so-amenable Courtney, who was likely four or five years younger than Temple's thirty-one and who sported a wedding-engagement ring combo on her left hand, "buying a wedding gown is not an off-the-rack proposition."

In the most understanding, gracious way, Temple was instructed that bridal gowns were special-ordered and could take weeks at the least and maybe months to arrive and then had to be fitted.

Or, if the bride needed to marry in haste, they could be rented at the *(sniff)* wedding chapels.

Temple shook her head, avoiding that unfortunate literary human movement known as "bridling".

"I'm afraid I need something sooner. A returned gown, perhaps, that could be refitted."

Temple had by now realized that Matt's mother and Kit had been married in off-the-rack dresses that didn't require fitting. She envisioned herself in an off-the-shoulder gown with a sash across the waist and another above the mermaid skirt, which was bordered with a wide satin hem. She would look like Queen Victoria or Mary Todd Lincoln at their most mushroomy.

Kit appeared from nowhere.

"Courtney, my dear," she said. "I just visited the fitting room."

"Ah, you're not supposed to go there. All those gowns are sold."

"Courtney, my dear." Kit took her arm even though it looked like a child reaching up to a mother. "I noticed a gown on a dressmaker's dummy that looks rather interesting."

Temple opened her mouth. A dressmaker's dummy could be wearing a suitable candidate for her wedding dress, which she was now thinking of looking for online under "white nightgowns"?

"I found the neckline rather intriguing." Kit raised her eyebrows.

No one could resist her Aunt Kit's raised eyebrows, especially Aldo Fontana, the second of his ten brothers, except for the youngest and most impressionable, to leave the bachelor life to marry.

"Well, if you saw something that might prove to be an inspiration." Courtney followed along after Kit like a stage hypnotist's victim plucked from the audience.

Temple did likewise.

She came face-to-face with a headless dressmaker's dummy, a black jersey-clad torso on a wheeled base wearing a white gown.

Temple moved around it, her eyes on the same level as the missing head. She circled left, then right in a silent flamenco dance.

"About the right length, I think," Kit said, definitely not "thinking" at all, but selling.

"And the neckline is…unique," Kit added.

"Genius," Temple agreed. "The only thing long about me is my neck."

"A swan's neck," Courtney added.

"And the bodice is bare in one way, yet not. I love it," Temple said.

"With opera-length gloves," Courtney suggested meekly, hopefully.

"Yes." Temple nodded. "So very *My Fair Lady*."

"Ah—" Courtney wisely remained silent after that.

"Hair half up," Kit said, "Princess Di's knock-off lover's knot coronet…"

"Electra will recognize that design and love it!" Temple said.

"…fingertip veil and lace-edged overskirt train, five feet long but flowing out."

Temple nodded.

Kit turned to Courtney, all business, all icy command. "Whose is this and how can we get it?" She could have been a mobster ordering a hit.

"It's…abandoned." Courtney again appeared on the verge of tears. "It's rather legendary. It was ordered by a magician's assistant on the Strip, several years ago. We use it as an example for flower girls, very feminine but…petite."

"A *magician's* assistant?" Temple asked.

Courtney was on firm ground here. She turned to Temple and looked down on her without appearing to tower. "Magician's assistants must often be tiny and agile. You know, to be credibly sawn into two pieces in a box. I'm told this one said she was leaving the business to marry. And as for the magicians, they come and go in Vegas, even the iconic institution of Siegfried and Roy, tragically not performing anymore. I believe this magician had retired, and his assistant therefore also. We tried our best, having such a petite woman as a client and designed this especially for her. But. It's Vegas. She disappeared."

"So we can buy it?" Kit asked.

Courtney laid a large hand on the dummy's small shoulder. "Can you buy a mystery? It's strange. I'm a veteran employee, but I never thought of this gown for you, Miss Barr. It's been a fixture. The staff had really liked the client, and then it was like someone in the family vanished. Not stood up at the altar, but never came in for the final fittings. We do weddings. This is a happy business, despite occasional silly spats over the details. I'll talk to the owner, but if someone loves our Lost Lady's gown, I'm sure she'll be happy to give it a new home."

"May I try it on?" Temple suggested, already realizing the very front of the hem would be ankle-length on her, when wearing the Midnight Louie Austrian-crystal pavé Stuart Weitzman pumps.

"Certainly. You and your mother can have a seat in our dressing room while I unpin it from the model."

Then they were alone, seated on slipper chairs in front of a narrow platform with three steps up, three steps down and a nine-foot train-flaunting "aisle" between them.

Kit took Temple's hand, leaned across the space between their chairs, and whispered, "Karen would have a fit if she knew I was playing Mama for a Day. I'm loving it. I'm way past my own children, and you're my favorite niece."

"I'm your only niece."

Kit shrugged. Her hand tightened on Temple's. "One thing. You don't think the vanished magician's assistant was from Max's act when he folded up his show in Vegas and hared off? That might be a little too weird in the 'something old' department."

Temple laughed "Kit. Max worked alone. He was the whole show. I might have fantasized being one briefly, but he never had a female assistant, except for a flock of doves, fifty percent of whom might be female."

"Max worked alone." Kit shook her head at herself. "I should have known."

"I'm really excited," Temple said. "That neckline is so different. The gathers and lines are graceful and there's the train, a slim yet sweeping train. Not a nuisance, not a pregnant peacock's tail with a bow on the butt."

Courtney knocked, swept in when invited, a long limpid column of white silk lifted high and trailing fabric. Now Temple understood that Courtney's height was a job requirement.

She dangled the confection from another hang-'em-high hook. Temple thought of Western movies.

"You'll need the correct undergarment, of course. But for now, I think *au natural* will work."

Temple turned her back to the mirrors, unhooked her 32-A bra and let it drop to the floor as Courtney wafted the gown over her bare shoulders.

Courtney plucked and twisted and hooked. Apparently these things must be done, as according to the Wicked Witch of the West, *del-i-cate-ly*. Temple looked over her bared shoulders at Kit.

Courtney turned to her too. "Mrs. Barr, I think you've called the size to an A-plus." She turned Temple to face her.

It was so strange to Temple, the tug of all that fabric on her twisting torso. She straightened her shoulders and lifted her chin.

"Voila." Courtney stepped back. "Wedding portrait pose already."

Kit had her smart phone stretched out and clicking away.

"The fabric is so light and airy," Temple said, taking a tentative step toward the runway.

Courtney and Kit were conferring on the slipper chairs in quick, low tones about "drape, accessories, head piece and veil".

The gown followed Temple as naturally as a breath. She finally peeked at herself in the huge three-way mirror. Definitely not your Photoshopped bridal site sight. She put a tentative high heel on a step. A bridal shoe bearing the black Austrian-crystal image of Midnight Louie should not be tentative.

She marched to the middle, turned around and swept offstage to face herself flushed and happy again in the intimidating three-way mirror. She knew she could never step wrong with Midnight Louie by her side and on her feet.

13
Mother Confessor

Molina unfolded and rose to her impressive five-ten inches of height, bending to swoop up his coffee mug and her almost full lemonade glass.

"I have a confession to make. Better get you a beer." And then she left the room.

Matt had little time to speculate, and decided to put on his counseling hat, a deerstalker in this case.

"*Hmm,*" Matt intoned as Molina returned to put the open beer bottle down in front of him, "Dos Equis. '*Dos*' is 'two' in Spanish. Two horses. You must be facing at least a two-pipe problem."

He smiled and answered her puzzled frown. "That's what Sherlock Holmes told Watson when the great detective was handling a particularly troubling case. It was a three pipe problem. So I'm playing Watson here? At least I don't smoke."

I regret to inform you," she said with that utterly deadpan Molina the homicide lieutenant face, "that you're facing a pretty nasty rejection."

"Rejection?"

All Matt could think was, *Oh, God, Molina had been keeping tabs on Kinsella and he was back in town...seeing Temple?* No. Temple wouldn't put up with his now-you-see-him, now-you-don't act anymore.

Still, his head was buzzing so wildly he almost didn't take in her next sentence.

"This is no mystery. You are no longer required as escort for the annual Fall Dad-Daughter Dance at the junior high."

"What? Mariah? She doesn't want to go now?"

"She doesn't want to go with *you*. I'm sure it breaks your heart. She's changed her mind, Matt. Mariah has decided to ask Rafi Nadir to escort her to the Dad-Daughter dance this fall."

"*Whew*," Matt said, just happy not to have heard the word, "Max", then taking a pull on the Dos Equis. "Would you be insulted if I said I'm relieved? That's a really mature decision on Mariah's part. Rafi Nadir has truly helped her fulfill her aspirations without betraying your confidence. He's playing a Dad-type role he never had a chance at earlier. So what's the problem?"

"Rafi Nadir is an Arab-American name," Molina said absently. "Think Ralph Nader, the long-time political activist, who has Lebanese roots. These days a Mideast ancestry can be as targeted as a Hispanic one."

Now she was twisting the condensation-dewed beer bottle in her hand.

"Look, Carmen." He nodded at her hands. "You never fidget. It's against your professional and personal code. You've been fidgeting since I got here. What's really going on?"

"Mariah and Rafi are coming back from a rehearsal session at a studio. Seems everything musical today involves digital manipulation." Her apologetic crooked smile and shrug were out of character too.

"Carmen, do you regret Mariah favoring him over me? I'm not insulted, if that's what you're thinking."

"It's not that."

"So he *is* her father and you guys can admit it now," Matt said. "Mariah's solved the problem herself. The Dad-Daughter Dance is the perfect coming-out party. It'll be a smooth transition. She's debuting in her first year in junior high and no one will know you kept it quiet when she was in grade school. Please don't tell me his ethnicity wasn't why you kept it secret. I know people are paranoid these days and your police connection—"

Molina exploded. "Yes, his ethnicity played a part in it. So did mine. And the paranoia was mostly mine. But that was fifteen years ago in L.A. How do I bring you up to date on fifteen years of lies?"

Matt stared at her troubled features. Time to back off. He spoke solemnly, but softly, confidentially, with a tone of wry humor. "You say, 'Bless me, Father. It has been fifteen years since my last confession.'"

He glanced at the LED clock visible on the kitchen's microwave oven. "And make it snappy. A lot of elderly folks are waiting in line, leaning on their canes and walkers, to spend their half hour in the dark little booth enumerating a supermarket cart of venial sins when you've got a Dumpster of big league ones to unload."

The kicker made her laugh. "A pity you and the confessional booths didn't stay in the priesthood. You would be a huge improvement over Father Hernandez's brusque, businesslike manner with penitents. So would the anonymity of a dark booth."

"The booths are still used for oldsters at Our Lady of Guadalupe, and me."

"*You?*" Then she took a deep breath and told him.

She'd been the "illegitimate" eldest bi-cultural daughter in the large traditional Hispanic family that followed when her Latina mother married a Latino man.

"How many younger siblings?" Matt asked.

"Now you sound like a sociologist. Six."

"So your magnificent blue eyes…."

"Came from a Daddy unnamed, a best-forgotten Gringo, seducer of my seventeen-year-old mother."

"It's hard to grow up in a minority community with such a visible badge of difference."

"You seem to like them."

"I do. So Mariah has her dad's dark eyes, and your Hispanic heritage. Did not knowing your real father haunt you?"

"No. I was too busy babysitting my half-sisters and brothers."

"More of a nanny than a daughter?"

"I never thought of it that way."

"Now you see what I do on the radio advice show. So you were a never-ending Act of Contrition on your mother's part," he added.

"That's harsh."

"I think it *was* harsh."

"We have time for another beer." Molina stood and disappeared into the kitchen.

Matt frowned at his interlaced fingers and shook off the gesture he recognized was one of old *Monsignor* Janoski's back during his own "illegitimate" Chicago childhood. Now he understood Molina's iron self-control and utter professionalism, obviously needed working in a macho man's field, but also to survive a family in which her very presence was a rebuke.

He was even beginning to understand better why his mother had fought so hard to grab a veneer of respectability, even if it was marriage to a loser like Effinger. At least she was married and Matt grew up as a kid with an identifiable father, however lousy.

No wonder Carmen Regina Molina was unraveling at having to confront her only daughter with her lies and evasions and self-shame. The daughter she had denied a father, as her own mother had done before her.

Matt shivered to his soul. Families came with long-standing PR as the social core of stability and future promise and safety. Maintaining that illusion took such a toll. Growing up was maybe realizing nobody was perfect, including yourself.

Molina slammed the beer bottles down on the low table.

"Short form on my family life. I had to get out of there. Worked my way through four years of college, then applied for the police force."

"Why the police?"

"I don't know. I'd been mocked for being a big girl, a tall girl in that culture of shorter people. I think my father may have been Swedish. Something really alien."

Matt smiled to himself. Coming from a Chicago full of blond Polish and Nordic people, he knew one person's "alien" was another person's relatives.

"Anyway," Molina said, "I thought I could make the physical. And— You're right. I had some crazy idea that I might be able to track down my real father."

"What did you find on the police force?"

"An administrative eagerness to employ women and minorities accompanied by deep distrust and dislike of both among all the ranks."

"You beat that. Look at you. A tower of authority. A commander of men. A damn good torch singer, and the only woman who can make my girlfriend secretly shake in her Stuart Weitzman heels."

"Really? Kinda like Dorothy in the Haunted Wood and I'm the Wicked Witch?"

"Naw. You're the Iron Maiden of the Metro Police."

"I know they call me that."

"That's a grudging compliment, but you know that. It wasn't always like that."

"God, no!" She glanced at him. "Sorry."

"God likes to be included in the conversation, especially when you're being honest. I'm as far from the priesthood—if that means you're thinking of me as a judge and excommunicator—as you are from the LAPD. What happened there?"

"We made it into the force. Women and Hispanics, Afro-Americans and Asians and even Arab-Americans."

"Ah," Matt said, sinking like Sherlock Holmes deep into the easy chair and the two metaphorical pipes and the unfolding mysteries of Molina. "Enter Rafi Nadir."

"He was even more alien than I was."

"You…bonded. How?"

"What is it always? What we had in common, being minority officers. Then, when he found out that I sang in the police choir, he said I should be a soloist. He pushed me into working up an act. We trolled L.A. vintage stores for my retro blues singer nineteen-forties wardrobe. What they sold then for mere dollars." Molina's smile was nostalgic. "Temple Barr would have died and gone to heaven in blue silk velvet."

"Those long, spare gowns in your singing wardrobe aren't right for Temple. More something frilly from the thirties and fifties. You're straight bobs or upsweeps. She's waves and ponytails."

"My, haven't you become the expert." She shook her head. "You remind me of Rafi. He's quite a pop culture marketer, you know."

"And adaptable. Do you realize Mariah is in the pop singer sweepstakes? If he was so supportive of your aspirations and a child was on the way, why did you split up?"

This new Mellow Molina vanished in a millisecond. "*Because* there was a child on the way!"

Matt flinched at her frustration.

"On the police force," she explained, "Rafi and I weren't just fighting prejudice from the white male officers and a lot of the public. If any staff cuts came, it would be among us minorities. While we were united against in-unit sabotage, we were also competing with each other."

She sat back to sip some beer. "I guess you need to know the intimate details if you're going to help me, us, with Mariah. Are you going to do that?"

"I'm stuck," Matt said, "but how intimate?"

"I didn't want to get pregnant. I wanted to establish my career, despite the odds. I like odds. I especially didn't want to leap into motherhood after years of helping to rear half siblings. Rafi was on board with that."

"I get it. The young Catholic Latina woman used birth control, even if it was against the Church's position."

"Well, the woman had to do it then, didn't she? Nothing really effective for men, no little pink pills for girls then. Men were pill-allergic until Viagra and the little blue-for-boys pill came along. Medical insurance would cover Viagra for men, but not contraception for women. They were making single mothers. How crazy is that?"

"Whatever, something didn't work for you."

"I doubt this is your area of expertise and way too much information for you. It will be graphic. The pill didn't agree with my system. Diaphragm and foam, together, that was pretty effective.

Then, a period didn't come. That was shocking. Even more shocking was finding a pinprick in my diaphragm. Not a manufacturer's flaw or the material thinning, but a big fat pinprick I could see with my naked eye under the medicine chest's top fluorescent light."

"You thought Rafi had—"

"To get me out of the running. He's from a religious and ethnic tradition where women's place is in the home, having babies."

"And your conscience was in a bear trap," Matt said. "Barrier contraception is one thing. Abortion is quite another."

"He'd said he wanted kids someday. I figured it for a two-with-one-blow."

"You're off the career fast track on maternity leave."

"It wasn't even a fast track, Matt. It was survival. I had school loans only a steady job could pay off."

"And you immediately suspected him, not some manufacturing issue?"

"We all were edgy and paranoid. And manufacturing issues aren't perfectly round pinpricks."

"Some malcontent in the manufacturing process could have done it as a prank."

Molina blinked her Isle-of-Capri-blue eyes. "You? Mr. Optimism? Coming up with a sick scenario like that? Product-tampering. Could be. And if I'd been the woman I am today, I might have come up with some benefit-of-the-doubt options too. But I didn't. I panicked. I left. I ran."

"Like Max Kinsella did to protect Temple from *his* past."

"Don't compare me to him! I was protecting my baby's future. I'd never let my child become a pawn, or a bone of contention."

"You're the woman you are today because you did that. You chose to become a single mother and have done an admirable job. But your trust issues are higher than the Eiffel Tower on the Strip."

She swallowed. Not beer. Just the bad taste in her mouth. "I was wrong. I made a rush to judgment, as the phrase goes. I underestimated Rafi. All my own baggage buried him. I can't explain it now myself. Only… I know, I see, disappearing so utterly without a word, was the worst thing I could have done to him. Because, and we've talked about this, he was innocent.

"He thought I'd been kidnapped, killed. He thought he'd been powerless as a cop and a partner, the worst thing to do to a man. He almost sank after that. Did sink. Didn't care, drifted, lost touch with family and friends. He made the department cut him. And always, he was looking for me, maybe dead, but looking for me."

"Gosh," Matt said, "you two are made to order for my new talk show. Dr. Phil would kill for you."

She half-lurched up. "You even *think* that…if that oily Oprah hanger-on ever got near me and mine—"

Matt started laughing. "Angst is not going to get you and Rafi past the tremendous hurdle that is Mariah, Mama Bear. Humble pie is."

"What does that old expression even mean?"

"Forget your own regret and guilt, and play district attorney. Make the best and most honest case you and Rafi can before the judge and jury that is your daughter. *Look.* She's a teen. Conflict with her mother is cool. *Listen.* Rafi has eased into her life and done the same mentoring he did for your singing talent. He's won her respect all by himself. That's what you don't want to sabotage at any expense. You're the villain of the piece. All you can do is repent."

"Grovel, you mean."

"Prepare for the shock and betrayal she'll feel toward both of you."

"And you'll be…?"

"Refereeing, I hope. Rafi *does* know you're planning to do this intervention?"

Molina swooped up the beer bottles and headed for the kitchen. "Yes, but not when."

"So when's when?"

She poked her head around the barrier wall. "He and Mariah should be back from rehearsing any minute now. I think we'll switch to Dr Pepper."

Matt stood. "Carmen Molina, you have got to be kidding me."

"Pulling off scabs is best done quickly. Glass or bottle?"

"Er, bottle. Better not to have contents easily thrown."

"How do we start?" Molina wiped her palms on her jeans.

"We put Mariah on the defensive. Have her tell me about her switch in escorts."

"Isn't that a bit manipulative?"

"Aren't you trying to defend yourself against years of major lies?"

14
The Skype Hype

After she dropped Kit off at the Crystal Phoenix, Temple returned to the Circle Ritz, singing in the elevator and dancing down the hall. "I'm in love with a wonderful guy" from some musical soon morphed into "I'm in love with a wonderful dress". Call her elated. She was just exuberant enough to commit to a bold move she'd planned to put in motion.

Waltzing from the living room into her office, she noticed Louie wasn't in there either. He must be out and about via the neighboring bathroom's partly open window.

Her business card lay near the desktop computer in her office It read *Temple Barr, P.R.,* as in Public Relations. Friends, and even Matt when they'd first met, had joked she really should put "P.I." as in Private Investigator on that card. She did have a knack for crime-solving.

Ordinarily, she worked casually around all the rooms, slouching on a chair or sofa or bed with her tablet or smart phone, but this was a delicate situation.

So she sat at her rarely used desktop, staring into the dark computer screen, sobering up fast. She was about to attempt the most dishonest, manipulative, necessary, and desperate "public relations" campaign of her career. Right now she was calling on every "knack" in her large tote bag of tricks and taking full, lavish advantage of an offer she couldn't refuse.

Her top clients, Van and Nicky Fontana of the Crystal Phoenix hotel-casino, had called Temple into Van's office as soon as they heard she had wedding plans waiting on Matt's Chicago career options. Van was the executive. Nicky was the mob family white sheep who'd made a go of a "legit" enterprise in a Vegas gone (relatively) straight.

"Listen," Nicky had said. "You're one of our most valuable employees, even if we may lose you to Chicago. Your family wedding is our Family wedding. Tut." He held up a well-manicured hand. Only Fontana brothers could make manicured fingernails sexy rather than an affectation. "My brothers tell me there may be flies in the ointment." He glanced at his cool, contained blonde wife, Van von Rhyne, who nodded.

"There always are in this town," Van said, rolling her baby-blues.

Nicky nodded. "That's your business, Temple, and my bros' business, yet I cannot help but think nine Fontana brothers will be useful as more than groomsmen for your nuptials if there are any bumps in the road.

"As for the costs of all involved, it's on the house. Our house. Whomsoever you want to import for the occasion to stay in a private suite, for the reception and before and after parties, etcetera, etcetera. We will even tolerate random government agents, and local fuzz," he said with a wink. "We are as clean as a toothpick at the Crystal Phoenix. Bring 'em on, all the conventional and unconventional guests. Just don't get hurt. *Capiche*? And I hope you will include Van and I in the festivities, or riots, as it may be."

Who could carp at that ungrammatical "whomsoever" and "I"? Nicky Fontana was a prince and Van his perfect princess partner. Words were Temple's business, but elegant hospitality was theirs, and she was lucky to have the use of it.

"Yes, sir," Temple said. "With pleasure."

So since Temple had means, she had opportunity. She was going to be nervy and pitch some Very Important People to attend not only her and Matt's wedding, but a surprise family get-together afterward. She figured it would only work if she contacted them in person. Enter Skype, the free video call computer face-to-face program, which Temple didn't use much herself and which would be outright foreign to an older generation.

To do this, Temple felt she needed to sit upright in her desk chair and play a pilot at the controls. Her fingers had tapped a paper list of names and phone numbers on the desk's right surface. Everything had to be concrete, firmly at hand.

She'd always been a tad leery of the digital. That was why she wore a round watch face as large as her slender left wrist, with a Big Hand and a Small Hand ticking off the exact second. It flashed some Austrian crystals, as did her big round sunglasses. As a tiny woman she wasn't afraid to accessorize big. People remembered that, and remembered her. And trusted her to Think Big too.

Before she pressed the starter, engaged the ignition, and took off into the wild blue Internet, she skimmed the list once last time. She had to keep an eye on who was who and who was where. She could not afford to make a mistake.

She'd confronted a murderer or four, and a psychopath or two, but this head-to-head was even worse. It was Family. And even worse, OPF, not other people's *money*, but *families*. That wasn't public relations, but private relations.

She took a deep breath, dialed the first number, and lifted her chin, remembering this was going to be Skype and computer cameras always shot upward to provide the best double-chin angle, like at the police booking room or the driver's license photo renewal set-up.

Not that she had a double chin.

Before she could take a second deep breath, she was looking at Max Kinsella, thirty years older, on the screen, full head of black hair graying in dramatic white swaths, but the eyes still piercing and demanding accounting.

This was the most delicate and volatile contact. Survive this and it just got easier.

"Miss Barr," the older Max said, "I presume. This is a bizarre… method of contact and communication, but you say it involves our son."

The woman beside him seemed petite, like her (*oh, cra...ah, crepuscular moon!*). Temple tried to swear, even to herself, as she did everything else, creatively. *Don't even* think *you reminded Max of his mother!*

The man went on. "If this is some Internet scam, I assure you, young woman, we will prosecute you to the full extent of the—"

"Cat!" the woman exclaimed.

Temple gritted her teeth while maintaining her friendly smile, a PR professional necessity.

Midnight Louie's big head had pushed over her shoulder, either recognizing a certain "Max" timbre in the man's voice or a verbal threat from the screen.

"Louie," Temple tried to shrug him out of view. "Butt out, there's nothing to eat here."

The woman advised her husband. "A con artist wouldn't bring a cat along."

He was not soothed. "We've heard very little from our son lately, scanty communication for years, in fact. That's the only reason we agreed to this mad meeting over the ethernet."

"I'm so glad you knew someone acquainted with Skype. I know you need to see me for myself, if *not* my cat. I work at home. Are the Kellys with you, as requested, Mr. Kinsella?"

Husband and wife exchanged consulting glances.

"Who hired you?" Kevin Kinsella barked.

"Nobody hired me. Your son would be very unhappy to know I'd contacted you and the Kellys."

"Unhappy?" That one word from Max's mother was a cry from the heart. "Is it something we did wrong all those years ago?"

It was something you failed to do right, Temple thought, but an ace PR woman couldn't say that.

"It's something you can do very right," she said. "I'm a friend of...Michael's, and he suffered a serious fall some time ago, during his magic act. It caused traumatic memory loss." True. "His pride has taken a body blow from the accident. He was always so self-sufficient."

Mrs. Kinsella reached for her husband's arm off-camera, and his grimace showed the full force of her grip. "He's mobile, he can communicate," she begged. "He's recovered?"

"All recovered, except for pieces of his memory of you and your husband and his best friend and cousin, brother really, Sean, whom he deeply mourns, and his aunt and uncle. The Kellys are there, as I so I hoped they would be?"

"Here, but dubious, as we are," Max's father said.

"May I speak to them?"

The couple parted sheepishly and a pair of very different features pushed through to stare at her, with hair red and curly as opposed to black and straight.

Temple could sense the couples' discomfited body language at being forced to crowd together around a tiny screen, but they all were eager for more news. Finally.

"You don't know me," Temple said. "I hesitated to contact you, but I think it would help Michael's memory so much, and help you to understand the long silence, perhaps between you all on your side of the generations too."

Silence.

"I've contacted you because I'm getting married soon."

"To Michael?" Eileen Kelly had spoken sharply. Temple understood why. Michael was getting married? Her dead son, Sean, never would.

"Oh, no," Temple said. "I'm marrying another wonderful man, a man named Matt." She appeared to think a moment. "But Michael will attend the wedding. We both think so highly of him, and thought that if you all could attend, it might break him loose from the prison of his amnesia."

"Catholic, are you?" Patrick Kelly asked.

"I've been known to attend Our Lady of Guadalupe in Las Vegas." True.

"Las Vegas!" Maura Kinsella was taken aback.

"Michael had performed here under another name until forced to take a sudden leave of absence." True. "This amnesia has gone on for a long time." Well, a few months.

"Hey, people. I would be the happiest bride on the planet if your families could come to my wedding. It might break the veil of Michael's memory. I represent the Crystal Phoenix Hotel, the most tasteful boutique hotel in Las Vegas. The management will fly in anybody I think essential to my dream wedding, and include paid-for luxury suites and the reception."

"Smells like one of those time-share vacation schemes," Kevin Kinsella grumbled in the background.

"Got it on Google," whispered a loud young male voice, presumably the nephew acquainted with Skype. "Hot Kardashian sundae, that place rocks!" A lad after Temple's heart. "Five stars. On Yelp. That's golden. Quit angsting, oldsters, and go for it."

"I assure you," Temple said, "it's a five-star wedding gift to me, like Michael and his folks," Temple said.

Temple didn't need to say another word. She merely stared hopefully in a starry-eyed bride way, into the screen.

The saying went, "Never let them see you sweat."

With Skype, that was possible.

Temple wiped her palms on her poplin capri-clad thighs and dialed again.

"Temple! This is such a treat. I can see you perfectly." Matt's mother's welcoming face on the screen made Temple's tensed shoulders loosen.

"That the mighty mite from Vegas?" Matt's crushing young cousin popped her Goth post-punk face into the Skype view. Krys considered herself as an also-ran for the bride role.

"Kyrstyna," Mira said, "is the only one I know who can get my computer to do this face-to-face trick. So we're talking from Krys's apartment, that we shared before I remarried. You remember it from your visit? It's very warm in Las Vegas now, isn't it? Not so much in Chicago."

It was very warm on Skype with Temple about to invite Mira and her new husband and his brother and long-time wife to the wedding.

"What is so important that we have to Skype?" Mira asked.

"Matt and my wedding plans are on speed-drive all of a sudden," Temple said. "Your new side of the family are invited, but it's coming up fast. You'll be flown in by the Crystal Phoenix, with luxury suites and the best wedding reception ever."

"Am I a side of the family?" Krys stuck her face into camera range to ask.

Just the beefy one, Temple was tempted to answer.

Krys was all right. Not fat, but a "strapping" Polish girl who was hiding being twenty and awkward behind an aggressively hip look, and lots of lip. She'd had her heart set on cousin Matt since she turned teen. More so because he had been a priest then, which made him safely out of reach. Temple could understand, but not cater to, that.

Even nosy, possessive Krys didn't know that Mira's new-brother-in-law had been Matt's father.

Temple wanted Matt's unacknowledged father at their wedding in the worst way. This was not a duty call for Max, as she'd just done. This was trying to maneuver a secret duet from the heart, for his mother, Mira, and Matt to have a genuine entire "family" for one day, Temple's wedding day, even if nobody knew it except the four of them.

Maybe it wasn't strange that Matt had grown up wanting to be a priest. After all, his teenaged Polish mother and father from a privileged family had met at a Catholic church, lighting a candle to the Virgin Mary. Mira was a sensitive girl from a boisterous, large family. Jonathan was defying his family to enter the armed forces, and couldn't admit to being frightened of a foreign war zone. It was love at first fragility. And Christmas, when lonely people longed for comfort.

The result was they never saw each other again, and Mira had Matt, named for the Disciple, Matthias. The boy's family knew, and bought Mira a two-flat so she'd have a home and an income property and make no claims on the wealthy Winslows. Being an unwed mother in her Catholic milieu carried immense shame. Desperate to give Matt a father, she married Cliff Effinger, who'd coveted her income property.

Jonathan Winslow was never told Matt existed. Until Matt tracked him down and did the job.

Mira, by sheer stupid coincidence met his widowed brother at her restaurant hostess job, and did marry Philip Winslow. So the secret family farrago remained operative in Chicago.

For one day, Temple wanted Matt's biological mother and father to share in his happiness, his success, secretly together in one big shared happy ending.

Secrets can be toxic, but secrets kept without rancor can heal.

This last Skype appointment would be a piece of wedding cake, Temple was sure.

"Hi, Mom! Guess what? The wedding's on. I've got the date, the place and, of course, the man. Now I just have to settle a few details."

"What?" her mother asked. "You're doing this without me?"

"No, it's just that circumstances, good circumstances I can't announce yet, call for—"

"A quickie wedding in Las Vegas! Oh, Temple!"

"It's in a church."

"*Whoopdedoo.* I don't care where it is, I want to know when-where so I can come down to help pick out the gown, the flowers, the reception menu… Surely there'll be a groom's dinner. Matt's parents should plan that."

"Uh, we're kinda blending all that into one super-duper mega event. But you don't have to worry about a thing, Mom. The Crystal Phoenix is handling all that. You're all on vacation on their tab, including flying my four brothers and their wives and kids down. I'm their favorite employee."

"And *you're* my only daughter. What were you thinking?"

"That a surprise would be really cool for you?"

"Wrong. The surprise is for the guests, not the mother of the bride. How often am I going to get this chance? Once. I want to weigh in on the placement of every last spray of baby's breath."

Temple felt her buoyant Happy Balloon trickle air and develop worry lines.

"The Ladies' Altar Society will take care of that. They're used to that."

"What am I? Chopped liver? And 'Altar Society'! What church?"

"Our Lady of Guadalupe."

"Of course it would be, with Matt. He's a lovely young man, Temple. You're thoughtful to honor his past priesthood, and I have no trouble doing that, but Catholics are very persnickety about their dogma and sacraments and ceremonials. They want to control everything."

So, apparently, did mothers of the bride.

Temple rallied her most diplomatic tone and arguments. "I'm sure Father Hernandez will make major concessions."

"On what?"

"You know, about a UU marrying a Catholic."

"Your UU credentials are long lapsed." Her mother was looking stern and frowning.

"Then I guess I qualify as a pagan," Temple quipped, "but they're okay with that."

"Well, they're always sending missionaries far and wide to get converts."

"Mom, I don't want to argue. I wanted to tell you the good news and get us all together down here for my wedding."

"Temple." Her mother folded her lips. "I guess I'm just shocked you'd leave me out of this. You know how I loved finding you the most beautiful little outfits as a baby."

"And all through grade and high school. Did you know, Mom, when I was real young, that the boys would lie in wait to get me in a tussle and get my clothes torn and dirty."

"No! My sons?"

"There's a lot you wouldn't know about your sons, unless you were their only baby sister."

"So, that's why…"

"They wanted to make me tougher, Mom. And they did. Inside, if not out. So you won both ways." She didn't go into the Mean Girls in high school.

"Temple. I never thought that treating you like the little doll you were was a…negative."

"It wasn't. I *love* being a clothes chameleon. You know I wanted to be a fashion or costume designer in high school. And I'm going to love doing that for my wedding. You gave me dreams, Mom. I'm going to dazzle everyone with them."

Karen looked away from the screen. "Well, yes. I did give you a non-girly name at least. Much better than Tessa, which I first thought of."

Temple quashed a wince.

"Okay Temple. Just tell me that you don't want to marry in dungarees."

"Promise. Van and Nicky, my bosses, you remember them?"

"Of course I do. Your father and I flew in and stayed overnight for Kit's marriage. Another sweeping example of the generosity of the Crystal Phoenix and Fontana family. That's the first time we met Matt and saw his stunning engagement ring on your finger."

"Well, they're sponsoring a private fashion show and fitting for our out-of-town bridal party members in the bridal suite for two days before the wedding. Including tux fittings for all the men."

"Fittings?"

"Yes, for keeps. Dad will *never* again be able to say he can't go to a formal outing you want to attend because he doesn't own a tux."

"My goodness, they must be fond of you. Am I going to be meeting any more of Nicky Fontana's Italian gigolo brothers?"

"Aunt Kit's husband, Aldo, recovering bachelor. And, yes, assorted tones and flavors of Fontana brothers. All yummy."

"Oh." She looked pleased. "That Kit, snatching up a confirmed bachelor at her age in life. I'm glad she's no longer living alone and single in Manhattan."

Karen made it sound like a spinster's circle of Hell.

Temple thought *Fun, fun, fun!*

"Temple. You didn't forget Kit. Is she coming?"

"Fontana brothers assemble in a flock. So I thought Kit could be Matron of Honor."

"*Matron.*" Karen hooted. Sisterly rivalry showed its acerbic head. "She wouldn't like that description."

Temple didn't know about that personally. "I'm thinking of lilac for her. But for your Mother of the Bride dress, there's a shade of exquisite medium green that goes with our hair color."

"Well, my and Kit's hair color has faded."

"Nothing about you is faded, Mom. The color I'm thinking of is close to jade green and is socko with the shade of the famous Tiffany blue gift box, a sort of soft turquoise, if you know what I mean?"

"I have seen a Tiffany gift box or two in my time, dear."

Temple smiled. Matt's mother would certainly be wearing the Virgin Mary blue topaz earrings he gave her. The women would recognize a tonal bond before they knew it. The subconscious was an awesome uniter.

"Now," Karen mused, her eyes cast up, while Temple fidgeted and the Roman church burned. "I think you must ask one of your nephews to be ring bearer. Todd is six and adorable."

"Louie is eight or so, and experienced."

"None of your brothers have sons named Louis."

"Louie is Midnight Louie. My roommate of the feline persuasion. He served as Ring Bearer when Matt's widowed mother remarried here in Vegas."

"But, Temple dear, using a cat as a Ring Bearer is just a joke."

"So I should use a fidgeting six-year-old who is scratching his bum through the entire ceremony?"

"Well, at least Todd would not be switching his tail."

"Speaking of that, I could use a flower girl."

"*Oh, oh, oh.* Crescent, Tom's girl, is seven and just precious, blonde curls, adorable in yellow with violet accents. Perhaps a dotted Swiss. No, organdy."

"Oh, would you, Mom? Would you do her dress and a matching basket for petals? I'll be wearing white, of course. You jade green, like leaves, and little Crescent's yellow and Kit's lilac will be the flower tones. Yellow goes so well with the gray tails and white tie the groom and groomsmen will wear, and Dad's new designer black tux."

"Well, of course." Her mother's eyes were already speculative, envisioning details. "I will do my best."

"You're always the best, Mom. After we sign off I can send you an image of my gown."

Temple did as she'd promised and sat back with a sigh.

She did feel bad about leaving her mother out of this necessarily speedy wedding, but that was a Vegas specialty and seemed normal to Temple now.

Her computer tinged her.

Oh, my goodness, Temple, her mother's email read. *That is absolutely and uniquely "you", and I now know my daughter is utterly grown up and her own self I could have never dreamed of when I held her as the tiniest of babies and for some reason named you Temple rather than Jane or Sue or Tessa, something ordinary.*

Now, I would like to make one little suggestion. Ruffle-topped, white satin elbow gloves would be the perfect complement to the gown.

Temple glanced to the glove box on her desk. Ruffle-topped white satin elbow gloves.

That is the perfect last touch, Mom, she emailed back. *You are the perfect Mom. See you soon. Love you!*

15
Dumped by a Diva

Matt tried to think himself into the comfortable upholstered swivel chair at *WCOO* radio, the muffling earphones on his head, the glass walls of the booth a black, blanked-out image reflecting him, only the voices riding the airwaves, one on one, he and a caller, like Elvis, he'd never meet.

He felt a faint moisture at his hairline, realizing this moment was more important than any TV talk show gig, and maybe performing "live" and on camera wasn't for him.

This would be the toughest audition for his vaunted step-up job, and nobody who counted in the network would see it. But he would know if he let any one of the major players down. He was like a judge. He had to be honest and fair, and make each and every one of them follow that path.

"That was so cool," Mariah was saying as the front door opened and footsteps sounded in the hallway. "That wiggly effect on the soundboard," Mariah's voice continued. It had a pleasant mellow tone he hadn't noticed when he both saw and heard her.

"The mic is your first and best friend," Rafi's signature baritone voice answered.

Right there Matt pegged why Mariah's singing voice was so mature. She'd inherited it from both sides. There was nothing light and girlish about her singing already.

"Oh." Now she was directing that slightly dismayed remark at Matt. "I didn't know you'd be here."

Rafi frowned behind her, not at Matt. "I thought your mother had errands to do this afternoon, or the session wouldn't have run so long." Rafi checked his cell phone screen, looking ready to bow out right now.

Matt now understood why Rafi, who had, only a week ago, physically extracted him from a mob nudie bar brawl with swift aplomb, was visibly itching to escape present company. To Rafi and Carmen, The Lie was always the invisible party pooper in the room and now Matt was in on it.

"Errands done," Molina said, coming out from the kitchen. "Don't run off, Rafi. Have some Dr Pepper. Good for the throat after a long vocal session, right?"

Nadir regarded Molina as if she were crazy, but took the offered bottle, as did Mariah, and Molina again ducked into the kitchen.

For once, the self-involved teen looked as ill at ease as her parents.

Her parents. Matt contemplated getting Mariah to make that leap in the course of an afternoon and felt like he was atop the Lake Mead dam attached to a bungee cord. Bungee cord. A doctored one had almost killed Max Kinsella. Matt decided he'd have to take the plunge too.

"Mariah—"

"She told you, didn't she?" Mariah blurted. "I can tell. This is a setup."

"What?" asked Rafi, pausing in sitting on the other chair flanking the couch.

Matt's quick head shake "no" diverted him to the other side of the couch, next to Molina's now empty place. Rafi, already well trained to house rules, leaned forward to put the Dr Pepper bottle on a coffee table coaster.

Matt and Mariah were now positioned in chairs opposite "the parents" sitting on the couch. A classic family confrontation arrangement.

Mariah was ignoring the adults to drink from the Dr Pepper bottle while slipping Matt nervous looks. She put the bottle on the coaster on the small end table between their two chairs. Matt mirrored the move.

He noticed Mariah's fingernails were the short, rounded style he'd seen in TV ads, painted in the popular Goth-dark gel polishes He'd once described himself to Temple as "sixteen going on thirty". Mariah was thirteen going on thirty.

"Mom told you, didn't she," Mariah whispered while Molina was still in the kitchen.

"Told me what? That you have an even better gig than backing up French Vanilla of Black & White?"

"No, silly. Oh." She sighed as her mother came in and seated herself on the sofa with Rafi. "I'm sorry. It just seemed right."

"Whatever it is," Matt whispered back, "if it seems right at the time, you have to do it."

"Even if someone might have their feelings hurt?"

"Hurt feelings aren't pleasant, but you have to face up to them."

"That's what you get all that radio money telling people?"

"Depending."

Molina spoke up, trying to sound jovial and only managing to sound suspicious. Cop talk was hard to moderate. "What are you and Matt whispering about?"

"Oh, Mom. I need to tell him…you know."

Matt jumped in, sounding as suspicious as Mariah's mom. "Mariah, what haven't you been telling me?"

Carmen tried to soften the blow, even though Matt knew what was coming. "I don't want you to feel slighted, Matt—there's been a change in plans."

Mariah overrode her. "You said I had to tell him personally." She turned to Matt. "I'm sorry, Mr. Devine. I know I promised you forever and forever you could take me to the Dad-Daughter Dance."

Matt smiled at how she interpreted "pestered" as "promised".

"Well, yes. I thought it was a done deal," he said.

"I can't."

"Can't go?" he asked.

"Oh, I have to go. Just not with you."

Matt raised his eyebrows.

"It's not that you're not cute or anything else, like that ex-priest thing. But…you're moving out of town and are doing things like getting married and even though you're sort of famous, I really, really think I need to ask Rafi because he's been so cool and is teaching me all sorts of really hot singing stuff to follow up on my Black & White gig with a Justin-Beiber-level breakout music video—we promise, Mom, no Miley Cyrus stuff. I'm still too young for that."

"What a relief," Molina said, electric-blue fire in her eyes.

Mariah missed the sarcasm.

Rafi pointed a finger at Mariah. "Disney Clean. That's where the film breaks are."

Matt couldn't believe they were discussing teen career choices.

Mariah turned to him. "See. Rafi knows music business stuff. I'm going to premiere a line-dance song at the D-D-D. I saw you dancing with, uh, Miss Barr, at the club after the B&W show opening, and, sorry, that's not what's happening. And, like, she's way too not the prime age group anymore. Even that Zoe Chloe Ozone shtick is so over..."

Her childish pseudo-sophisticated chatter had shocked her mother almost much as Matt. "Mariah! You're sounding like a brat."

Not the way to win over a kid you're going to knock off her platform shoes any minute now. Matt cleared his throat to intervene, but Rafi beat him to the punch, as he'd done outside the nudie bar not long before.

"Your mom and me are even older than those people." He took Mariah's hands and pulled her to stand before him. "What's bugging you, kid? Everything you want is going great."

She shrugged, looking down at her purple-painted toenails in their peep-toe platform sandals. Matt smiled at what he'd learned from Temple's shoe collection.

"I have to do school and all that stupid stuff Disney kid stars don't have to waste time doing. I'll be too old to be interesting pretty soon. I guess you're all so old you don't get that." She eyed everyone desperately. "I'm losing time to be discovered."

"Is that what you think your singing is for?" Rafi asked. "Not for the joy of learning and doing it, but for getting somewhere, anywhere? Anyhow? Your mother never had those selfish dreams that made no one around her good enough."

"That was *ages* ago, Rafi. She was never going anywhere. I mean, she was a cop."

"She's not 'a cop,'" Rafi said. "She's a lieutenant, and a damn good one. I used to be a cop too. Are we both not good enough?"

"No, no! You've been great. It's just that you're not, like, on the *brink* of something. Like I am. You've brinked out."

"You're on the brink of a good kick in the pants of reality." Rafi's face was grim. He was speaking generalities, Matt knew, but he'd accidentally nailed the imminent reality for his daughter.

"I've gotta do what I've got to do," she was saying. "You're just too old to understand and maybe I need a more hip manager, anyway."

Matt found his fists clenching. "Brat" was too kind.

Mariah tossed her product-rich curled and blow-dried mane of hair. "I bet Nilla knows somebody who isn't just…a, an amateur. If Mom's your only track record, it doesn't look good. Nilla says my voice is special. She likes me."

"Well, we don't," Molina said, standing. "Forget me, which you apparently have. You will stop dissing your father like that after all he's done for you!"

Carmen registered that she was using a trite parental line only after she realized she'd given away the game. She and Rafi locked gazes, each surprised at defending the other, then mutually dismayed.

"Adults always gang up on kids," Mariah ranted, not even absorbing her mother's slip.

Matt had forgotten the deep fears and the conflicting overconfidence leavened by self-doubt that drives teens, and he ought to know. He'd seriously wanted to kill someone at that stage.

The household tabby cats, spooked by overwrought emotions, picked that time to race through the living room, bounding over Carmen's and Rafi's laps on the couch and using the armrest as a springboard to dig into Matt's khaki-covered knees.

Amid the diversion and exclamations, including *ouch*! Mariah's stormy expression cleared. "Father?" she said, plucking out the word from the current sound and fury. "Are you talking about Matt? Mr. Devine? He's an ex-father."

All three adults eyed each other, obviously eager to use that misconception as an excuse. Molina had simply gotten rattled and referred to Matt by his former title.

"She means me, kid," Rafi said, rubbing at his black denim-protected knees. "Those cats come armed with switchblades."

Mariah bent to pick up one of the lean striped cats, now calm. "You've got to be kidding me." It was half order and half hope. She looked back and forth at the couple on the couch.

"I was surprised when I first figured it out too," Rafi said.

Molina bit her lip and kept silent, wisely not making it a mother-daughter blow-up.

"You? Surprised?" Mariah looked from Rafi to Matt next.

"It's true," Matt said.

"Then there's a whole lot of things that *aren't* true!" Mariah looked around wildly, clutching the cat that was about to use its flailing claws to escape her grip.

"What about my dead hero cop father, who died when I was two?" She stared at her mother. "You have that old clipping from a Los Angeles newspaper with the lousy-quality photo. You kept your maiden name because your married name would always remind you of what you'd lost."

And you!" She whirled to face Rafi. "Why'd you show up so late? Why didn't you tell me?"

"I didn't know when I first saw you at the teen reality show. We hit it off, remember? Without me even knowing you were my daughter."

"But you must have found out, oh, not before long. You didn't tell me for a long time."

"No…I wanted to, Mariah, I did, but I'd been, not my best self, and when we started working together, I really enjoyed it and—"

"And," came Carmen's voice, strong and certain. "I wouldn't let Rafi continue to tutor you unless he swore not to tell you. That was my job."

"Well, it's a big fat fail, isn't it? *You* not good at your job? Big freaking too bad." Mariah turned a bitter, angry face on her mother. "You know what's best for everybody, but it's all lies with you. I don't ever want to see either of you again. You should have stayed lost," she yelled to Rafi as she charged down the hall to the bedrooms, the two cats fleeing from her clomping platform shoes.

A door slammed, then slammed again.

"I need to talk to her privately," Matt said. "Someplace away from you two, out of the house. In the yard?"

"There's a swinging bench on the back porch. In the shade."

"A swinging bench, Carmen? Really?" Matt asked. "You don't strike me as the type."

"I'm not. It came with the house."

Matt eyed each of them in turn. "Both of you two settle down, drink a little beer, exchange some low-key recriminations and realize you only did what you thought best at the time and Mariah is going to have to grow up fast to see that. I'll do my best to get her there."

"Why did you drag me out of the house?" Mariah lounged almost off one end of the double-seated swing set, as if Matt had rabies.

Matt was amazed to think how fast a guy could go from hot to not with a teen girl.

"The one thing you don't want to do now, Mariah," Matt told her, "because it is so clichéd and a Disney heroine would die before doing it, is to throw yourself across your bed, sob your heart out, and call all your BFFs to B&M."

Her eyes widened in the dark, owl-like makeup outline of what he'd seen advertised as "the smoky eye".

"Can a priest even *say* those initials?"

"Ex-priest. I assume you're referring to Bitch and Moan. I just did. And I can also tell you that Best Friends aren't Forever and last about six minutes at your age. You've already got a cool singing gig going and the green eyes in school are out there looking for you. Envy is a Cardinal Sin and it runs wild among tween and teen girls."

"Why should I believe you?"

"I spent eight years at a parish school that went from kindergarten to senior high school and I would rather fight Isis than Mean Girls, who are shortly going to gang up on you in junior high because you've got 'too much.'"

Mariah did not look enviable, though. She was a mess. Her hair was tangled and looked "over" everything. Her red-rimmed dark eyes had a horror movie poster rawness and any makeup she used had smeared.

"Am I wrong?" Matt prodded.

"Everybody lies to me. Did you know about Them before?"

"Yes, but I didn't know *why* until your mom 'fessed up to me this afternoon."

Mariah's ridiculously high platform shoes easily reached the concrete patio floor and pushed the swing into gentle motion.

Las Vegas was hot in the summer, but not very windy. Dry desert air pressed down with the sensation of ironing, although Matt knew Mariah wouldn't know the clean, sharp smell of it. His mother had always had an ancient steam iron swathed in its electric cord at the back of a shelf in a closet.

It was a pity some hearts and minds were sometimes consigned to the back of shelves and wouldn't ever be smoothed into a wrinkleless state.

Matt's shoe toe scuffed the concrete to keep the swing's soothing maternal rhythm going. "Your mom didn't know her own father. Hasn't. Ever," Matt said.

"You're kidding."

"I didn't know my birth father until I found him several months ago."

"And you're a priest!"

"Was a priest. That's part of the reason I became a priest. My mom was ashamed of getting pregnant out of wedlock, so she married the only creep who'd have a woman with a kid."

"My mom didn't marry anyone."

Matt nodded. "My mom's quite a bit older than yours. She didn't have a way to make a living and support a child. So she married an abusive man."

"That's awful."

"Yes, it was. I try hard not to blame her for her decision."

"He hurt you too."

Matt nodded. "People didn't talk about domestic violence then. I know, Mariah, girls get told the facts of life early nowadays, so you know that girls and women can get 'caught' without 'protection'. A lot of single mothers now are wary of letting men live with their children."

"But Rafi is my father!"

"It's complicated. It was a tragic case of miscommunication. Each one was trying to do the best thing, but they were young and under pressure. Your mom will tell you it's her fault. I know she was acting on the most instinctive motive women have: to save and protect her child."

"Rafi was abusive?"

"What do you think?"

"Well, nooo. I mean he's been really standing up for my singing with my mom…oh. Because she *lied*, she was afraid to have him around. How did that happen? He said he didn't know who I was at first."

"I'll say it plain and simple. They'd been thinking of getting married, but their jobs were shaky because they were both minorities. They wanted to postpone kids. Your mom got pregnant, and thought she saw evidence Rafi had sabotaged the birth control so she'd have to quit her job."

"So he *wanted* me."

"But for the wrong reason, she thought. So she ran, Disappeared. He didn't know why. She could have been killed. He was devastated and left the L.A. police force, drifting until he ran into you and found a reason to pull himself together again."

"Wow. That's a *Lifetime* movie. And *I* brought them back together again. Do you think they'll get married? That would be even cooler. I could star in the movie."

"They've both been through whole *Lifetime* movies separately. It's hard to say what they'd want to do now. What would really be cool is you giving them a chance to make peace with each other and you."

She nodded, her distant eyes envisioning the autobio pic.

"And you can start, Mariah, by dropping the diva act. You're a smart, pretty, talented girl, on the way to wise, if you understand you now have what your mom and my mom and I never had, real parents trying to do the best for you."

Mariah regarded him sideways. "I think you're leaving something out."

"No. What?"

She gave him a small smile. "I think you think I was being pretty dumb and spoiled and that all the rest of those good things don't matter if I go that way."

"A-plus."

They did a high five.

"I'm sorry I dumped you for the Dad-Daughter Dance, especially since you and your mom had a hard time early on. You really are pretty cool and cute, but I think it's better if I go with my father."

"I do too," Matt said.

"Did you like your real father?"

"Yes. He's a great guy. My mom remarried. She married his brother."

"No! That is so *Lifetime* movie un-be-lieve-able."

"Anything can happen with those crazy adults."

"I guess," said Mariah. "We just have to understand they're going through a stage."

When Matt took Mariah back to the living room, Rafi and Carmen were lounging in separate chairs, looking away from each other.

Matt had no idea how to start the conversation back here in the common yet emotionally claustrophobic living room.

"Do you have any questions, Mariah?" Rafi asked. He looked at Carmen, desperate for a clue.

Mariah shifted her weight on the tippy platform shoes, uneasy for once at being the focus of everyone's attention.

Then she ventured a response.

"Is there anybody I know who isn't a, you know, bastard?"

The stunned silence was answered with Rafi's bellow of laughter.

"Me," Rafi said. "I have a large Greek Orthodox Christian family. Our roots go back to the Phoenicians. They've been unhappy I've been so distant. They'd love to meet you. You have many cousins."

"Oodles of half cousins on my mother's side," Molina added, "if you want to go to a family reunion."

"Well, maybe we can try that out in not too long," Mariah said, "because I have a secret too."

"And what's that?" Matt asked because the parents were afraid, very afraid. He was too, but he hid it better.

"Your fiancée has asked me to sing at your wedding," she told Matt.

"I thought she was 'over,'" Matt said while Carmen and Rafi stared in shock.

"Doesn't mean she doesn't have good taste."

"D-I-V-A," Matt warned.

"Just kidding. What? I *am* still a kid, you keep telling me."

16
Bless Us, Father

As a public relations expert, Temple was used to plunging into new settings and situations as a five-foot-zero bundle of energy on spike heels that dug into any assignment like mountain-climbing pitons.

She'd learned long before that small girls and women have to be dynamic not to be overlooked and underestimated. Or stepped on, physically or metaphorically.

So when Matt knocked on her door to collect her for their errand, he couldn't hide the confusion on his face.

Temple wore a classic beige summer suit, short-sleeved but long-skirted, and carried a slim navy-blue envelope bag on a thin shoulder strap, not her signature large, jazzy tote bag. He stepped back to view her shoes, navy pumps.

"That's not a three-inch heel," he said.

"Two-and-half."

"That's not a summer sandal style."

"Classic closed-toe pump."

"No hat?"

Temple shook her abundant red-gold curls. "I only wear one when driving the Miata with the top down. I assume we'll be taking your car."

"Well," Matt said, "I suppose the only thing you're missing is the black lace doily on your head and you'd be the perfect model of a nineteen-fifties Catholic churchgoer. We're only going to the

OLG Rectory, not the church. How did you know that navy is the inevitable color of Catholic school girl uniforms?"

"Is it really?"

Matt nodded, then shook his head. "Are you actually nervous?"

"Yeah. Father Hernandez is...imposing."

"That's the *man's* temperament, Temple, not the priest's. He's just a humble parish priest who's not so humble."

Temple stepped very close. "Now, if I were going to see *you*, I'd wear my new resale shop Manolo Blahnik heels and a thigh-high slit skirt with a cocktail hat tilted over my right eyebrow."

Matt pulled her close, as close as close could be, by her elbows and kissed her the way a dame dressed like that should be kissed. "Shall we stand up Father Hernandez?"

She teetered back as he steadied her. "No. I don't see a man about a wedding every day. Now I'm thinking I ought to."

Matt stroked the linen lapel of her suit. "The prim Save a Soul Mission lady from *Guys and Dolls* is an inviting look too."

"Hopefully not for Father Hernandez," Temple said, well, primly.

The Rectory resembled a grander, bigger house left over from an earlier era, red-brick, two-story, eight stone steps in a neighborhood of established one-story older bungalows. It was not only Father Hernandez Temple dressed to please. She didn't want to run into parishioner Lieutenant C. R. Molina looking like a frump. Not that Molina, as a professional woman committed to neutral-color pantsuits suitable for covering a gun holster, cared about what Temple would call a "wardrobe".

At five-ten with the attitude of a mother superior and stern dark eyebrows Temple itched to pluck into a more flattering arch, the two of them were oil and water in all respects. She'd have traded her wishy-washy blue-gray eyes for Molina's electric blue any day, though.

And now, with a gazillion wedding chapels in Vegas, Temple was going to be married in a family church in Molina's backyard.

Matt held Temple's elbow as he rang the doorbell. The housekeeper came at once, an overweight, beaming woman with natural silver highlights in her thick dark hair. "Miss Barr, Mr. Devine, Father is waiting for you in his study."

"Thank you, Pilar," Matt said.

Temple checked her analog watch to make sure they weren't late. Father Hernandez seemed a man you would not want to keep waiting.

To Temple, the "study" was out of a vintage English mystery. Dark paneling, bookcase-lined walls blinking gold from hardcover title spines, a huge old desk, and, behind it, in a broad Golden Oak swivel chair, the neat contained figure of Father Hernandez, with his Old-World bearing and piercing black eyes.

By God, if you were married by Father Hernandez, you would feel "married". For eternity.

Temple, from her family's membership in the Unitarian Universalists, an inclusive multi-faith church with humanist and social justice concerns, not dogma, wanted to know what Matt had grown up with, wanted to glimpse the renounced priest side of him. Wanted to see every side of what had made him the man she had to love.

She was startled to find Father Hernandez's dark eyes regarding her with a shy twinkle. "Miss Barr. How could I miss you that first time in the congregation at Mass with Matt? Quickly grasping the ups and downs, when to stand and when to kneel, and the responses of the Holy Mass, your fiery head of hair shouting you were an outsider in this Hispanic neighborhood, but you would not be caught napping, eh?"

"You're only as much of an outsider as you choose to be, Father Hernandez."

He nodded. "Very wise. I made an outsider of myself for a certain bad time, for which I owe Matt, and you, many thanks. I admit I felt disappointed that such a promising young man left our brotherhood, which is sometimes lonely." He sighed. "But the vocations we are called to may change as we face ourselves, and I am happy to be asked to marry you here at Our Lady of Guadalupe."

"It's a beautiful church."

"My family in Chicago," Matt added, "wanted the Polish Cathedral."

"Certainly a majestic site, and honoring your ancestry," Father Hernandez said diplomatically, for him.

"But it's so echoing and huge," Temple said. "Who could hear the vows? My family in Minneapolis would have chosen a parklike outdoor site or a historic mansion. That would have been more intimate but not...personally significant."

"So we figured," Matt said, "our families can come to Vegas. My Polish Catholic relatives will love OLG as a site."

"My family would be all right with a wedding chapel in Vegas or a cathedral somewhere else, so they'd be getting a bit of both."

"An excellent compromise. I see you've thought this out. Families can fly from both cities, meet here, and share the Las Vegas tourist opportunities."

"We'll be disappointing our beloved landlady, " Temple said, "who takes credit for providing the place that we met, the Circle Ritz. She also operates the Lover's Knot Wedding Chapel."

"Ah, Las Vegas," mused Father Hernandez. "Commerce is king. Now for the wedding date." He pulled out a calendar the size of a college annual, paging forward rapidly. "And of course we must book the pre-Cana classes, and announce the banns."

"Ah..." said Temple.

"A Christmas wedding would be nice," Father Hernandez said, twinkling again, which was most disconcerting. "Your red hair would be right in season."

"Father," Matt interrupted. "Her red hair is always in season with me." Matt sounded quite definite. "We've decided to get married now because—this is quite confidential—Temple and I are embarking on a whole new career together, right here in Vegas, and we'll have no time to get married that late in the year."

"Oh, but these things can't be rushed. Our Lady of Guadalupe is not a twenty-four-hour wedding chapel."

"Certainly not," Temple said, "We're thinking of an evening ceremony so no regular church services are affected. And with my Crystal Phoenix connections, I can pull together a family influx and a gala reception in no time."

"'In no time'? But the Church advises—"

"I've done pre-Cana counseling for years, Father," Matt said. "And Temple's a very quick study, as you note. If you like, we can do the eight-hour online course."

"Online course," the priest echoed, dazed.

"You know," Matt continued, "how much heart and heroism Temple has, when she almost died helping your elderly parishioner and when the convent nuns were being stalked by a profane anonymous caller and poor Peter, the convent cat, was almost crucified like the Disciple he was named for.

"Yes," Matt went on relentlessly, "our religious backgrounds are a world apart, but the sense of ethics we learned from our families and faiths jibe like the pieces of a jigsaw puzzle."

Father Hernandez cleared his throat and looked at Temple. "UU, Unitarian Universalist, you say. Uh, of course no extreme sectarian atrocities have ever been committed by that, er, sort of…non-faith."

"I must admit," Temple said in a small voice quite atypical for her. "I'm something of a fallen-away UU."

While Father Hernandez contemplated how one could be "fallen-away" from a faith that did not even require acknowledgement there was a God, Matt again intervened.

"So there's still hope, Father."

The priest threw up his hands. "My failure to keep up with my times before caused a lamentable lapse on my part in the recent past. Who am I to judge, as our Pope Francis has said with commendable humility."

He glanced at Temple with a smile. "I first remember you bringing your black cat to the blessing of the animals here. St. Francis was a joyous saint, the patron of all living things. When I heard the new pope had taken that name I knew a new era was upon us. A badly needed era.

"Go in peace and in your own time, my children. OLG and I are at your service. We will schedule for your needs and I will try to live up to your faith in each other and me."

"Wow," Temple said as they walked down the stone steps on the way out, "a quickie church wedding. His conversion to our cause almost made me cry. We kind of ran roughshod over him."

"That's the way the future goes. Are you sure can pull off a wedding by next Friday?" Matt asked.

"You'd be surprised. I've got the Crystal Phoenix's crack wedding team behind me. The groom just has to show up there to be fitted for your tux in the next four days. How does a honeymoon in San Diego sound?"

"Great. I'll notify Letitia." Matt liked the idea that keeping Temple busy and dealing with other people and them getting out of town for a while would cool down the Woody stalking situation. Temple and her impetuosity train were gearing up to full speed and he was ready to stop worrying and enjoy the ride.

"Oh, do you have the rings?" she asked.

"I bought them at the same time I bought your engagement ring. You have two guard rings and I have the usual tasteful but boring gold band."

"Really! You were *that* sure of me!"

"I was in an agony of doubt, even about the appropriateness of rubies," he said, taking her hand and watching the rubies and diamonds flash in the sunlight. "The three rings were a wedding set, so I decided to be optimistic."

"I can't wait to see them. At the ceremony. Just get me to the church in time."

Matt grabbed her hand and they ran down the last four steps, breathless and laughing at the bottom.

"You know," Temple said, gazing around the quiet neighborhood. "Let's peek in at the church again. It's been a while since I've been a customer."

"What a way to put it! This way, ma'am."

When they stood before the brick-and-stone façade, Temple tilted her head back. "The church building seems smaller than I remembered, but there are more steps to climb."

"And to run down to our waiting Gangsters limo," Matt said.

"I wonder which model they'll choose for us?"

"You're not ordering a certain one?"

"No. I want to be surprised," Temple said, extending a hand to lead him up the steps.

Going through the heavy wooden front doors immersed them in a cool, dim silent, soaring space. Their footsteps broke the skin of that silence and yet also empowered it.

Matt noticed that Temple dropped her voice to a whisper without thinking. "Look. I'd forgotten how the sunlight shattered the stained glass windows into a multi-color kaleidoscope effect on the floor and pews. like tiny jewels dissolving on the tiles."

"You UUs miss out on a lot of special effects," Matt teased her.

"Did I ever miss out. I see I am Goldilocks. Our Lady of Guadalupe is not too big or too small, but just my size. Like the amazing gown I've found, which will be *your* surprise."

"I've never been surprised by the amazing things you accomplish," Matt said.

They approached the altar on the center aisle.

Said Temple, slowing down to play the part. "I have to make the long, slow approach in perfect time to the music while you slink onstage with a few steps from the sidelines."

"At least I'm not going to be imported by a Fontana Brother in a pet carrier, like our esteemed Ring Bearer."

"Poor Louie. He so hates that collar! Still, he looks so handsome in white bow-tie and tails, as you will."

Temple studied the sanctuary as she would a stage set, which amused Matt.

"Four steps up to the altar," she muttered. "Lots of space for our small wedding party to stand. And there's Our Lady of Guadalupe at the back behind and above everything, with her image framed in a fretwork of gold leaf."

Temple turned to Matt as if he were a docent. "She's a darker skinned Central American native interpretation of the Virgin Mary, isn't she?"

Matt nodded. "The legend and the image's seventeenth-century origins have been controversial, but she appeared to a poor peasant, first speaking an Aztec language, it was said, so she bridged the native Indians and conquering Spaniards. That's why her Mexico City church is the third most visited sacred site in the world."

"I love her serene face and star-spangled blue-green cloak. So that's why the travertine of the altar has inset designs of carnelian and turquoise, really common in Mexican jewelry to this day. And the hanging red light above?"

"The sanctuary lamp," he explained. "It burns forever, showing that a consecrated host is housed in the tabernacle behind the altar. Listen, I'm sure Father Hernandez would be ecstatic to have me explain Catholicism 101 to you, but I'm also sure that busy brain of yours has many secular details to attend to."

And he had his own underlying worries that were in danger of ruining the happiest time of his life.

"Yes, we should go," Temple said. "This will be a small and intimate wedding, but it will have a stunning After Party." She took Matt's hand. "I've invited both Winslow brothers and their wives, so both your parents will be there, known only to us four, of course."

"Temple!" Matt turned away.

"Matt?" Temple sounded panicked. Was she thinking he'd be angry?

His fingers tightened on hers. When he turned back, his eyes stung, from the bright sunlight, of course.

"Temple, you're incredible. We've talked about that, but you've made the best wedding gift for me in the world come true, that I could never dream of doing myself. When I say *these* vows, not even eternity will end them."

"Really? I'd hoped, but it was…presumptuous of me."

"If you weren't a presumptuous PR hussy, I wouldn't love you as much."

"So. Then. You won't be upset if I confess that I also invited Mr. and Mrs. Patrick Kelly—"

He frowned, trying to place the unknown name.

Temple gulped. "…and Mr. and Mrs. Kevin Kinsella."

He couldn't help looking shocked.

"Too," she added.

"Incredible." He blinked again. "Instead of us going to Racine, you brought the shattered family to *us*. We're going to do an intervention at the reception."

"Privately."

"That means Mr. Max Kinsella is lurking somewhere in the neighborhood."

"Hunting the IRA treasure with my maps. I think it's a matter of life and death, but, of course, he wouldn't say that."

"So how did you manage to invite two couples we don't know to our wedding?"

"I lured them onto Skype and made a pitch about poor Max's memory loss and how he's a friend of ours, and seeing them all here might help him. Quite true."

"You convinced, conned, complete strangers, *they think*, to fly to *our* wedding to reunite with *their* lost black-sheep son and nephew?"

"Of course the Crystal Phoenix is footing the bill for all flights and suites. It's Van and Nicky's wedding present to me. Us."

Temple paused. "And I also invited Mr. and Mrs. Sean Kelly from Northern Ireland."

"Ah," Matt said. "'Sean of the Dead', back again. Now I understand. You made those three couples an offer they couldn't refuse and have designed a situation I can't refuse, nor can Max. It's fiendish, Temple. Simply fiendish. And I'm the designated driver."

"It's good practice for our new TV show."

"Could turn into an 'After Party' from Hell."

"I hope it turns out to be a Happily Ever After Party for everyone," Temple said. "I—

Oh, that reminds me! I want to drop in on the convent and invite the nuns personally. I have an e-vite list, but they probably don't do email or texting."

"You may be right. I'll check the church again and meet you outside in a bit."

"While you're here, thank the Virgin for getting you to me."

He nodded.

Her short but brisk high-heeled departing steps clattered like hail on the tiles. For the wedding, a carpet would make her step as silent as a ghost's.

Inside the church again, Matt shivered in the cool silence. He genuflected out of habit and then approached the altar with new eyes. Yes, the Virgin of Guadalupe watched over everything with her prayerful, maternal gaze. Including the altar.

Matt kneeled in front of it, as he had kneeled once to become a priest. Yes, he was right. The central design, carved in low relief from an impressive chunk of turquoise, was the humped serpent symbol of the Aztec god Quetzalcoatl.

And the signature of Clifford Effinger's work for the mob.

It was lucky Temple had given her groom a simple suit-fitting to accomplish in the next four days. He would have ample time to find out why investigating the Effinger clan, both then and now, was proving so dangerous.

17
Holy Cats

"I think we need to go to church," I tell Miss Midnight Louise, intending to shock her.

We of the cat persuasion are not notable pew occupiers. They are usually made of uncushioned wood and hard on the back (and also the soft underbelly).

And some of us remain faithful to the ancient goddess of our kind, Bast, who lent her noble feline head and fancy headdress to a slinky Egyptian woman attired during a time of an apparent linen shortage in the Nile delta and standing twenty feet tall. The younger generation are not so observant of the old ways.

"I applaud the idea," Miss Midnight Louise says, shocking me. "I assume you have a Catholic Church in mind, since you can confess all your many sins there."

"So much for your assumptions. It is not called Confession anymore, but the Sacrament of Reconciliation."

"Sounds like a mealy-mouthed substitute. How do you know all this churchy stuff?"

"My Miss Temple brought me to a Blessing the Animals ceremony at Our Lady of Guadalupe shortly after we first hooked up together."

"I also was there and blessed, but as 'Caviar', a Humane Society cat. Thankfully, I did not notice you there at the Big Moment. But your Miss Temple quipped I could be 'Midnight Louise'. And so they sadly named me after you when I became the Crystal Phoenix unofficial house detective. How could you forsake the Las Vegas Strip and the run of the entire Crystal Phoenix hotel and grounds to share a second-story flat with a nosy Nelly who cannot even decide which high heel shoe to wear, much less which man to marry."

"At least *she* has a choice. Females of our kind are at the mercy of their hormones."

"Exactly why I was thrilled to be 'fixed'."

I just shake my head. "I too am 'fixed', but by a fancy human procedure that leaves my anatomy intact in all its original glory, yet unable to sire unwanted kits."

"Yes, you have a smidge of political correctness. Not voluntarily, though. I assume you wish to visit the scene of the forthcoming crime."

"By 'forthcoming crime', I assume you are referring to the wedding." I hiss out a sigh. "Yes, I heard at home a few nights ago it is a done deal. Miss Temple will marry Mr. Matt at Our Lady of Guadalupe. They will honeymoon in San Diego and stay at the Crystal Phoenix afterward while their respective rooms at the Circle Ritz are combined into one larger unit."

Miss Midnight Louise's golden eyes squint at me sideways. "And where do you plan to live after all this ceremony and during reconstruction? In the Circle Ritz parking lot? Do not expect to move in on my territory. Your day as unofficial house detective at the Crystal Phoenix is done. You abdicated the job to me. Looks like you are homeless again, Pop. That is human loyalty for you. Maybe Ma Barker will let you sleep in the basement of her favorite abandoned house."

"Tut, tut, Louise," I manage to mutter in a calm tone. "It will all work out. Meanwhile, we both know unsavory individuals are circling our human friends. Time to hie our hides to Our Lady of Guadalupe."

"Lucky," says Miss Midnight Louise as we watch from behind an oleander bush while the white van zooms away on to its next stop, "that the church linen service truck happened to be passing so we could slip inside during the next delivery. It will take a week to get the odor of starch out of my sensitive nostrils."

"Luck, my rabbit's foot. I have been staking out the place. I calculated the routine."

"And we dropped off at the convent. The church is around the corner."

"Ironic," say I, "that a laundry service provided us transportation, given that those hateful laundry asylums for fallen women and girls unleashed Miss Kathleen O'Connor on all our friends."

"'Miss' Kathleen is it now? She does not deserve the courtesy, but she did deserve the four-shiv right-cross to the face you marked her with when she tried to shoot Mr. Matt. That was a righteous move."

"Why, thank you, Louise. You are mellowing in your full young adulthood, like our Miss Mariah."

"At least I remember where I am going. Where are you going? The church is that way."

I look over my shoulder. "I am heading to the convent garden. I am a nature lover. I am also here to see a cat about a surveillance job. He owes me one."

"One what?"

"One of his nine lives."

Louise looks shocked at last.

So I am first to bound over the concrete fence. By the time she has followed me to a blazing sunny spot on a bench beside the convent's back door, two well-fed middle-aged cats, plain yellow tabbies, spotless white paws, but other than formal gloves no marks of distinction, like my white whiskers on formal black. Nevertheless, these guys are swarming me like their long-lost littermate.

"Come on, boys." I shrug them off. "It is too hot for the one-paw Hollywood littermate hug routine.

"Peter," I nod to one, "and Paul. This is a young apprentice of mine, Miss Midnight Louise."

"Wow. Is this trim little number any relation to you?" Paul asks. Unfortunately. The boys direct their greeting sniffs and sideswipes to her.

"No," I say.

"Not acknowledged," Louise hisses back.

"Oh, you poor dear girl." Peter casts rebuking yellow eyes at me. "I am named for one Simon Peter, who denied a storied relationship in the Garden of Gethsemane. I cannot in all good conscience recommend doing that."

"Now you get a conscience, Peter," I point out with my first shiv waggling. "Miss Midnight Louise was named after *me* by humans who thought it would be 'cute'. There is no genetic proof."

"Ah," Paul says. "She is the fruit of one of those impulsive back-alley alliances and now she has renounced such irresponsibility. When we entered the order of nuns here from the Humane Society, we too took vows of chastity."

"Abetted by a good vet," Louise says sourly.

I must say that she does not take moonshine from anybody. I enjoy being not the sole object of her scorn.

"What can we do for you, Louie?" Paul exchanges a glance with Peter. "We have seen you stalking about the property."

"Evil-doers may lurk."

"We too have observed strangers on the grounds. We are cats of peace, and since the brutal attack on Peter, we keep close to the convent."

"Attack?" Louise perks her ears straight up.

Both boys shift their eyes to the side at the memory.

"Yes, it was when we first joined the convent, some time ago. Someone tried to crucify Peter to that back door."

"A crazy man who hated godliness." Peter hunkered down on his haunches. "I fought, but he had bagged me first and I was knifed."

Louise gives a short, angry growl.

Paul nods. "The act was discovered soon after and Louie's human, er, cohabiter happened to be visiting the convent. Not from any intention to join, I must add. Peter was rushed to the Lord High Veterinarian."

"Who was a female," I point out, to win favor with Louise.

"Louie saved me," Peter mutters into his whiskers. "I had lost too much blood. Louie donated his. He is a hero."

"Him confined in what carrier under what tranquilizer shot?" Louise demands skeptically.

"Louise," Paul says with a stern brush of what I would consider my second-most-valuable member, although his first is now pretty useless to him. "You are a cynical young female. We will never forget the bravery Midnight Louie showed here at the convent and church when we were besieged by a killer. He did nothing under duress, but was a heroic and kind volunteer."

What can I add to that? I give a Mr. Spock eyebrow-hair lift— there was something very catlike about that beloved character— and fastidiously preen my shiny black hair. I must look farther into the Vulcan nerve pinch. I believe it is a variation of the firm way a mother cat will gather her kitten's nape into her mouth for discipline and transportation.

Transportation! Another parallel universe conjunction.

Indeed, I believe all felines have a bit of the Vulcan in them. And do not forget the slinky, ebony feline fatale in the Gary Seven episode of Classic *Star Trek." Wowsa!* I would put the remote control on permanent pause for her!

"Well," Louise says with one of those damned Vulcan eyebrow-hair lifts. "Not to fear. We are here. Midnight Investigations, Inc. will inspect the grounds and the major buildings for traces of intruders. Totally gratis to you, dear boys. Is that not right, Louie?"

I was hoping for payment in custom-minced delicacies from the convent cook, Sister Mary Deli, named for Saint Delicius, virgin and martyr, but so heavenly manna slips away.

Lucky it did.

Miss Midnight Louise and I are heading to the parking lot, hoping to hop a ride, when I signal an urgent halt by curling my shiv-tips into her shoulder.

"Cut the unwelcome paternalistic guidance, Pops. I know where I am going."

"Sssst!" I nod to the sleek familiar silver car. Of course, a renowned automotive model would be named after a cat.

"Mr. Matt's Jaguar," she whispers.

I look around the lot. "And over there, in the Juniper shadows. That low-brow guy's junker. Now *he* is following Mr. Matt, and my Miss Temple. They must be seeing Father Hernandez, so the wedding is not only on, but imminent."

"Why would the wedding be of interest to shady characters like that guy?"

"I do not know, but steps must be taken, Louise."

"But what? How?"

Recalling the dozens of felines from The Case of the Cat Hoarder, an early investigation I assisted Miss Temple on before Louise's day, I realize they still inhabit the neighborhood and have a churchly turn of mind and meow. That gives me an idea, but I cannot share it with anyone.

One thing I do know. No shady criminals will make mincemeat out of the happiest day of my Miss Temple's life if I am around to make mincemeat out of them.

18
Bloody Mary Morning

What does the average bridegroom need besides a rented tux and a ring? Matt had that nailed. What he desperately needed was a reliable source.

This time he couldn't consult Temple, Internet researcher extraordinaire. He owned a small laptop, but digital wasn't his instrument. The church organ was, and he was smiling as he contemplated the music for their wedding. It would be impromptu, but Temple was insistent on one piece and one only for the walk down the aisle, their perfect song, however offbeat.

But first he had to survive for the ceremony.

He wanted to, but couldn't consult Lieutenant Molina. She owed him help, but she'd blow the game because she had to, as a representative of the law.

He suspected Max Kinsella was out there somewhere, following his own star, but Max had his own problems, as always. Matt knew from Temple that loner Max realized he needed help patching his family fissures together and pinned his hopes, for the first time, on someone other than himself. Temple and/or him. Rewarding as that concession was, Matt had bigger sharks to fend off.

He needed to figure out Woody's game, to explore those seventies local crime connections neither Max Kinsella nor Carmen Molina would have a clue about. He needed slightly shady savvy and major muscle.

So. Matt showed up at Gangsters custom limo rides and signed up for a solitary tour to Red Rock Canyon.

Of course, there wasn't a Fontana brother who didn't know who he was.

Ralph was on booking duty, single earring, probably a green garnet, winking at him. "Certainly, Mr. Devine. Will that be a party of two?"

"One."

Surprised at the imminent bridegroom's solitary order, Ralph, (the clan had apparently run out of Italian first names at one point) asked, "Custom limo style?"

"Something…Al Capone. But not with a snub-nosed, midnight-black Chicago aggressiveness. I'd like a softly lethal desert vibe."

Ralph cleared his throat. "Platinum Gray Ghost. And the preferred driver?"

"Aldo."

Ralph paused.

"I realize he's finally married and semi-retired."

"Mr. Devine," Ralph rebuked him. "One can never retire from being a Fontana brother. We are Family, and you are soon to become so too."

Matt nodded. Mob types are not over talkative.

A cell phone was used. A back-turned, hushed tone employed.

"When would be convenient?" Ralph asked over his shoulder.

"This is serious," Matt said. "Now."

Ralph pulled on his pierced ear and again muttered into his cell phone. Then he excused himself to go into the front office.

He emerged a couple minutes later to offer Matt a tall glass with silver rings embedded around the top half and a crimson Bloody Mary inside. Matt accepted it gratefully.

The Gray Ghost was a beauty, as pristine as in her nineteen-thirties heyday. The long, high vehicle pulled up before Matt had sipped down to the second silver ring.

Aldo stepped out of the driver's side, tall and tailored and tan and lovely like the Guy from Ipanema as opposed to the girl on the beach in the old song. He opened the driver's seat passenger door.

"We're soon to be related," Aldo said, "in some fashion far more complicated than guys know how to calculate. My wife's niece is soon to become your wife. Women keep better track of that, or so my very precise wife, Kit, tells me. I assume this is a private conversation between us guys. Welcome to the Family. Hop in."

Matt breathed a deep sigh of relief.

Aldo flashed him an ice-pick-sharp look. "That bad."

"That bad."

Matt had Aldo drive out on County Road 215 West through Spring Valley, Summerlin South, and then empty desert toward Red Rock Canyon National Conservation Area. He savored the strong, spicy Bloody Mary as his eyes scoured the monotonous desert terrain of sand and sagebrush to the east as they neared the park's scenic drive turnoff.

Ironically, glancing west, he spotted the white gown and black-and-white formal attire of a bridal couple, who looked the size of a wedding cake topper, taking photographs against the magnificent rusty-red rock towers bristling on the western horizon.

He finally spotted the landmark he wanted, a biggish bland yellow rock southeast of the park entrance.

"I think this is the place," Matt said. "Can you pull over along here?"

"Done," said Aldo.

The Gray Ghost sat parked on the shoulder of an anonymous stretch of highway through the desert, a couple tour buses kicking up dust at it as they passed. No biggie. Gangsters' limos were well-waxed and washed daily, Matt was sure.

Aldo gazed toward the dull, faded eastern horizon. "We're far enough off the beaten track to be en route to some long-ago Vegas mob boss's 'Boot Hill.'"

"You mean where enemies were taken out to be killed and buried? I followed a guy here."

Aldo waited.

"The other night."

Aldo waited.

"So," Aldo finally said, "you trailed a guy out here without being seen?"

"I think so."

"If you weren't an ex-priest, I'd say you had a helluva lot of balls. Dangerous job for a former white-collar dude."

"Funny," Matt said.

"And what did you see him doing without being seen?"

"The guy parked and walked to that clump of rocks."

Aldo looked, and nodded.

"You left your vehicle to follow him on foot?"

"I parked a bit farther down the highway, put my hazard lights on like the car was disabled. I backtracked. I figured he'd turn around and eventually head back to Vegas."

"Smart. Welcome to the Family," Aldo said with a slap on the shoulder. "Hey. You're not carrying. No holster."

"I'm not a member of the Family yet."

"Sounds like you should be. That took guts."

"Desperation."

Matt put his empty glass in a front seat cup holder. "Can you drive a bit onto the desert floor? My guy did."

"Not if I value the wax job on this long, lovely lady."

"Maybe you value the wax job on *my* not-so-long lovely lady."

Matt's oblique mention of Temple won a swift steering wheel turn and more than a limo's length of ugly jolting onto the desert floor. Aldo opened his winced-shut eyes to survey the bleak cactus-punctuated landscape before he diagnosed their location.

"More sand and scrub and stones closer up. And, uh," Aldo scratched his noble Italian nose with a forefinger. "This is what a bridegroom-to-be does getting ready for his wedding?"

"This is what a bridegroom-to-be does to live long enough for the ceremony."

Aldo took a deep breath, reclined the limo seat and put calming classical strings music on the system. "You watched him from behind this big rock?"

Matt nodded. "The night was dark, but the moon was yellow. He dug up something big and bulky and put it in the trunk of his seventies sedan. Whatever he unearthed was heavy enough to weigh down the massive junker trunk when he heaved it in inside.

"He drove back to Vegas," Matt finished.

"You were inclined to think he dug up a body."

"Yes. But it was far worse."

Aldo's mind was distracted. "Errand boy's job. But why *unearth* it?" he muttered.

"*Errant* errand boy maybe," Matt said.

Talking about this under the pulsing midday sun, listening to throbbing violins, the nighttime scene sounded stupid.

Aldo pushed himself off the cradle of his spine. "Now I like that news. We know this guy?"

"Unfortunately, I do, although I didn't know who he was then."

"So. You were in a great position to follow him again."

Matt nodded. "I ended up at the parking lot of that old building near the Circle Ritz that Electra Lark just inherited."

"Holy moly! You were driving her old white Probe. On a tailing operation. White? Man, you might as well have painted 'Moby Dick' on it. *That's* the night you drove up two sets of stairs to interrupt a nasty situation inside the abandoned building. We Fontanas were most jealous you beat us there."

"Yeah, but before I took that route, I followed that car to the parking lot and managed to jimmy open that old trunk lock and see what was inside."

"Dead guy."

"In a way," Matt said.

"Huh? If not a corpse, what did your guy dig up?"

"A decades-old jackhammer, with rust on its bit."

"Rust makes sense," Aldo conceded. "Dried blood makes even more sense. No wonder The Mob Museum isn't featuring this lost artifact in a Jack the Hammer exhibit."

"Are you agreeing with me that someone is reviving the ghost of Jack the Hammer?"

"Looks like it. Looks like someone who knew him and his ways back in the day plans to use the legend to intimidate."

Woody, Matt thought. *He's sniffed out the IRA bonanza, thanks to me dropping the hint of a treasure in his lap, and is planning to Jack the Hammer his way to finding it. The retired cop must have found and saved Giacco's signature deadly weapon all these years.*

"Don't worry, Matt, my man. Fontana, Inc. is keen on finding anyone who is stirring up old venues and vendettas in Vegas. Meanwhile, you just lie back in the weeds, keep Miss Temple happy, and anticipate the wedding reception we've got brewing."

"No way. That's too disturbing to forget, and why I need to talk with your uncle."

"My uncle? I'm told I'm gonna become Miss Temple Barr's uncle by marriage, but what do you need to do with *my* uncle? Besides, Macho Mario enjoys everyone having forgotten about his old, cold salad days in the seventies. He's in his own eighties now, wants to clock grandkid time, not sentimental journeys to the mayhem of the mob era."

"He'd better," Matt said. "Because I think seventies elements in Vegas are planning on bringing the bad old days back. Rock 'n' roll never forgets."

"I have to say the old man remembers the dead gangsters in The Mob Museum better than most of his nephews."

Aldo sighed and hit a speed-dial number on his cell phone. "Hey, Nicky. Assemble the clan. I got a feeling we're in for a bumpy ride on the wedding carousel." He hit another number. "Nurse Rachel, incoming." He checked the rose-gold Rolex that (of course) matched his rose-gold iPhone, and then the Gray Ghost did a whip-neck Uey heading back south on the highway.

Matt felt his spine impact the back of his seat.

19
Don of the Dead

Matt had glimpsed Macho Mario Fontana once. From a distance, at Aldo's and Temple's Aunt Kit's wedding at the Crystal Phoenix Hotel.

Matt had been most impressed that Macho Mario had all his hair at his age. And half of it was impressively silvered. He almost resembled the most Interesting Man in the World, recently replaced by a younger actor in the Dos Equis TV ads. Or the more professionally preserved Anthony Bennedetto, a.k.a. Tony Bennett.

Since Mario's sister, Mama Fontana, had founded an empire on pasta sauce, most people, including Matt, considered Macho Mario an aging Don, quaint, colorful, and a harmless throwback, even respectable.

The new Mob Museum in the renovated 1933-built post office and courts building downtown treated former mob kingpins like any other Vegas icon from Frank Sinatra and the Rat Pack to Elvis and Liberace, Phyllis Diller and Celine Dion, David Copperfield and Siegfried and Roy.

And Macho Mario also had his own personal high-profile exhibit at the Fontana Family hotel-casino, Gangsters. His personality seemed lavish on peccadilloes and light on lawlessness, but he definitely had been an up-and-coming young player in the bad old days of the seventies.

So when Aldo gingerly escorted Matt into the plush, secluded penthouse of Gangsters Hotel, Matt was prepared to tread lightly.

He'd been suckered by one old man and he wasn't about to do likewise with another.

"Aldo, Aldo, Aldo." A portly man wearing a quilted maroon satin robe rose out of his easi-lift chair to kiss his eldest nephew on each cheek. "You are here to tell me of times gone by." Macho Mario turned to Matt. "And I hear we are to have a priest marrying into the Family. What a weird world, but our own. *Bene, bene,*" he added in the manner of a Papal blessing.

"*Ex*-priest," Matt emphasized. "And I didn't just walk away like some. I was officially laicized when I left. I honored my vows until then."

"Yes, yes, yes." Macho Mario waved his left hand bearing a heavy gold signet ring as he sat again. "You are a real rules respecter. And we of a certain brotherhood respect that loyalty to be demonstrated to the letter. Most impressive, my boy. But now you marry, eh? I recommend it, having done it three times, not all blessed by the Holy See. So, even better for you, my son. You have less time to sin like me."

Mario kissed his fingers in Matt's uneasy direction. "You are like a seasoned Mama Fontana sauce. Sautéed in Holy Orders and a blessed man for it, but now graduated into the sadly human world we all live in. What can I do for you? Aldo said you needed my counsel."

Matt guessed it had been many, many years since Macho Mario's counsel had been seriously sought.

"Sit," Mario offered, or ordered. The only nearby option at a conversational level opposite the senior booster model Mario occupied was a wheeled and closed potty chair. This situation was surreal, but Matt sat.

"I need your help," Matt said. Baldly.

Mario tented his fingers and nodded. "Direct. That is good. I have it to give. I admire a man humble enough to seek."

Matt was already chaffing at having to kowtow to a notorious *capo*. He should be referring the old man to Hell for his sins. Yet Macho Mario was so obviously pleased to exercise his long-gone powers... He was old and not what he had been, unlike something sinister Matt had glimpsed still stirring like a Jurassic beast on the Las Vegas scene.

"I'm interested," Matt said, bracing his elbows on his knees as he leaned forward and concentrated all his attention on Macho Mario, "to know the dirt on a really bad man active from the seventies, and probably before as a punk, to the nineties. Someone who would tie a man to the prow of the Goliath's sinking ship attraction and let him die slowly in the dark just out of sight of a hooting audience of tipsy tourists there for the midnight show."

Even as he said it, Matt realized that he was now broadcasting in Vegas at the same hour as Cliff Effinger had probably died, only he hadn't hosted a talk radio show then. Not yet.

"*Hmm,*" Macho Mario hummed as he sank back into his own chair. "You said 'active' into the nineties. How about just up to the nineties? I have a cork-popper for you, my boy."

The old man beckoned Aldo near. Aldo went on one knee to be level with his uncle's seated, shrunken frame. "Some lubricant for my aging vocal cords, nephew. This will be a long story for me to tell and my future—?" His small black pupils flicked to Matt.

"Nephew-in-law, I believe," Aldo said, "but don't quote me. What are you drinking?"

"*We* will have Compari with Perrier water."

Aldo rose to rattle bottles and glasses behind the bar at the back of the shaded, sprawling bedroom that smelled of Vick's VapoRub.

Mario leaned forward and whispered to Matt, "Compari and Perrier water. The first drink James Bond ordered in his first book, *Casino Royale.* I like that "casino" is in the title. I ordered that same drink when *my* casino-hotel opened."

Mario rubbed his shiny lined palms together as Aldo set a stubby old-fashioned glass with an iceless blood-red drink on a swinging side table attached to Mario's chair and gave Matt a matching glass.

"*Grazie,*" the old man told Aldo. "Now step back. You may know much of this, but I have a feeling this young man needs to know it all. And I will tell all, young Matt, although you only are only a whisper of family, if you promise to come and tell me what comes of it, if anything."

Matt nodded. "*Grazie.*"

Aldo had retreated, like a discreet butler, to the room's far shadow. Mario glanced to his distant position.

"'*Grazie*,'" the old man repeated. "You have a not bad Italian accent for a blondie, but it will get better. All right. Have you heard of a man named Benny Binion?"

Matt nodded. The Binion name was notorious in Vegas history. "A lot. Owned the Horseshoe Casino Downtown. Didn't it used to have a million dollars embedded in a giant Plexiglas horseshoe in the lobby?"

"Yes. Benny founded the World Poker Championships at the Horseshoe. Where'd you grow up?"

"Chicago."

Mario cackled and sipped. "You're going to like this. Binion was a hanger-on of the Chicago Outfit that tried to take over Vegas. Almost did. Offed Bugsy Siegel. He was a killer hick out of Dallas and Fort Worth. Took over the numbers-running and gambling rackets there with a pistol and a sawed-off shotgun. Loved to be called 'Cowboy.'"

"He put on rodeos and cutting horse events, all that Western stuff, playing the fine generous citizen then.

"No finesse. We Fontanas had our eyes always on the future, the Strip. He dug his bootheels into the sawdust floors of Glitter Gulch downtown. The 'Horseshoe'. The name said it all."

Matt had a question. "Isn't that what they call the dealing mechanism that holds multiple decks for games of chance. The 'shoe'?"

Mario's upper lip curled. "Never thought of that, but 'Leslie' a.k.a. 'Benny' Binion didn't either, I bet. Despite his girly first name, he was a crude, murderous thug with a trail of dead men behind him even before he hooked up with the Chicago Outfit here, and you know how bad they were."

"No, I don't."

"*Hmmph.* Word was enforcer Tony Spilotro out of Chicago liked to get a guy alone in the desert and put his head in vice and crank until his eyeballs popped out."

Matt suddenly knew what a face going "a whiter shade of pale" felt like.

Old-time mobsters *were* as bloodthirsty as Genghis Khan and Dracul the Impaler, and yet such torture had happened in the last century. So Jack the Hammer hadn't been a Grimm Brothers' fairytale ogre, but the real thing, a thug of his time.

And someone was now taking that jackhammer of his out of cold storage in the desert.

There was only one reason for the storied violence of the mob. To threaten and intimidate to get money.

"Hey, kid. Suck a little Compari. From the old country. Put some blood back in your face."

Matt snapped out of his nightmarish speculations and did as he was told. One sip told him that Compari was a bitters, nothing sweet about it. Just like Matt's situation.

However, Uncle Mario was getting a little glow. "Arriving here just as the fifties were starting, Binion was a braggart, always buying up this property or that to get something going, whether the party wanted to sell or not."

Matt nodded. "I just heard of a case like that, um, today, involving a building my landlady inherited."

"Nothing evil's new." The old man leaned forward and Matt strained toward him to hear as his thin voice got lower. "Benny got more careful as he got more established, but I know for sure one unsolved murder he got away with. Ever hear about a jazz joint named the Zoot Suit Choo-Choo?"

Way too eerie to be a coincidence. Matt tossed off his Compari in one gulp while Mario winked approval at him.

"Ah…" Matt coughed. He tried to sound naive. "Wasn't that an all-black nightclub that got started in the fifties across the tracks from the Strip?"

"You're thinking of the Moulin Rouge. That was the first integrated hotel-casino, big-time operation. Chorus girls, acts, gambling. The Zoot Suit Choo-Choo was a low-rent joint, for kooks and the hip cats back then. Independent. Not mob. But the Strip was already clawing outward for land, and a crook like Binion always had his big ears to the ground."

Macho Mario's eyes lost themselves in rumpled bags of flesh as he searched his memory. "Black guy named Jumpin' Jack Robinson owned the place and starred there like he was Cab Callaway on a budget. Maybe he wasn't black, maybe Mexican, hell, maybe Giacco from southern Italy who had Americanized his name like a lot of them performers did then. Perry Como, Dean Martin."

Mario leaned closer, prompting Matt to perch on the edge of his squeaky, squishy "whoopee chair" seat so the old man didn't fall face-first on the floor. His breath smelled of garlic, false teeth adhesive and Compari. The name Giacco, pronounced "Jacko", shivered down Matt's spine.

"Yeah, the murder method harked back to Spilotro style," Mario whispered, going hoarse and a little "Marlon Brando" as *The Godfather*. "They were zoot suit wearers. You know, baggy pants, long jacket, pancake hat with a feather in it and a 'cat chain', an overgrown watch chain down to their ankles. Real clowns. I can't believe some of the dumb stuff I lived through. Some of those chains were twenty-four carat gold, and worth stealing. Some were steel toilet chains, you know, when the tanks were way up on the walls and you needed a pull chain as long as your you-know-what."

Matt almost choked again.

"Naw, a kid like you wouldn't know. Anyway, that's how Jumpin' Jack was found dead, hanging from his cat chain on an onstage light pole. Zoot Suit dancing king and Sin City wild card. Nineteen fifty-six. Never solved."

"And no suspects?" Matt had heard this story before and glanced over his shoulder to glimpse Aldo's pale suit, his undrunk glass of Compari blood red against it and positioned like a crimson pocket handkerchief. Aldo had *told* this story before, only days before.

Mario chuckled. "Cops wanted to finger a rogue mobster for it. A guy they called 'Jack the Hammer'. He was famous for taking guys out into the desert and using a jackhammer to encourage them to talk, or keep quiet forever. A real *paisano*, not a nobody out of Dallas. Name of Giaccomo Petrocelli. Giaccomo. Italian for 'James', but in English it shortens to just plain 'Jack'. Giacco the Hammer."

"What happened to this monster?"

"Somebody offed him back in the nineties. Most of his power was gone. He never adapted to Vegas going corporate. You had to be smoother than a jackhammer then. But I never made him for the

Robinson killing. I think it was Benny Binion having a last run at being the knee-jerk Cowboy killer he was before settling down to make real money from his enterprises.

"So. Talk about Binion in the seventies, nineteen-seventy-one, is when the really ugly action started. As far back as forty-nine Binion arranged a head-to-head poker tournament between Johnny Moss and 'Nick the Greek', who dropped two mill. Two mill in nineteen forty-nine! So twenty-one years later, Binion held a tournament for six high-rollers and Johnny Moss won again. Binion made it annual and anyone could buy in with ten thousand bucks. Benny hoped it would get as big as fifty players. Now there are thousands."

"So when did Binion's reign end? What did he die of?" Matt asked.

"Get this," Mario said with a ho-ho-ho chuckle. "Heart failure did in the 'Cowboy' killer from Dallas. I'll never forget the date because it was December 25, 1989. A Christmas present to Vegas as one of the most ruthless founders went down. He gave the rest of us a bad name. And he was immediately put into the Poker Hall of Fame in the New Year. And that's when the family fun began, when son Lonnie 'Ted' Binion began running things after Benny's death.

"Ted! A hopeless alki and drug-addict. Fifty-five the guy was. You'd think he'd make something of himself, like my sister's boys. Nicky, the youngest, owns the Crystal Phoenix, which is in a class of its own. Aldo here and his brothers run this hotel and their custom limo service and some other little things we won't mention." *Wink.*

"Ted had millions stashed all over Vegas, in his house and hotel and out there in the desert in Spilotro and Petrocelli country, including a huge underground vault holding a hoard of silver bullion and coins. The asshole only shared the location with the one guy he should have offed on completion of the job. Get this: the one who built the vault. Seriously stupid. And the guy was pronging his young stripper girlfriend at the time. Beyond stupid.

"Guess what?"

"Someone killed Ted for the money."

"Tried to make it look like a drug overdose, but it was faked. Nasty kinda death, drugged and then overdosed and then smothered."

"I remember news about excavating that huge desert vault," Matt said. "Who got the money?"

"Crazy. The scheming couple was convicted of murder, but went to a retrial on a technicality, where they were acquitted of murder, but convicted of burglary! Binion had changed his will two days before his death to exclude his girlfriend, but she got it all anyway, the house and the millions in its safe. There were millions in the hotel safe too, and still four or so million unaccounted for, and it has never been found. Presumed to be buried out on the Mojave."

Mario finished his Compari with a lip smack. "Fitting end for a bad outfit over six decades from Dallas to Chicago to Vegas. I love it when the legal system screws itself royally. Benny Binion was dumb not to have a bigger family. My nephews would never try to off me for my money, because there are too many of them. They can watch each other."

"They're also savvy businessmen who can make their own money, unlike what you say of the Binion clan."

Aldo came over and clapped Matt on the shoulders, raising him from the sinkhole of the potty chair at the same time. "Thanks for the great reference, Uncle, but I think our time has passed."

A woman in hospital scrubs covered in tiny penguins had materialized like a magician's assistant to take the still full Compari glass from Uncle Mario's hand.

Matt started to bid the old guy farewell when he realized Macho Mario Fontana was in lullaby land.

20
Intervention Convention

Aldo had reluctantly left Matt at his car in the Gangsters limo lot.

"I don't know what you're getting at, but it's getting at you, my man," Aldo had said in parting. "Time for a time out, maybe. I got some roles to play in your wedding, dude, and I don't want to lose the opportunity."

Matt bit his lip as hard as he thought driving home to the Circle Ritz. He turned in the parking lot on autopilot, surprised to find a black Chrysler speeding after him and cutting him off from turning fully into a parking space.

In the next moment a white SUV squealed around the corner to hem in both vehicles.

When a silent black Tesla followed, Matt got out of the Jaguar where he'd stopped it.

Frank Bucek got out of the Chrysler. Molina and Detective Morrie Alch jumped out of the SUV to join him.

"What's this?" Matt asked. "I'm being arrested?"

"You ought to be." Molina, dressed in a khaki pant suit with a badge gleaming on her belt, strode up to him. "Frank? Do you want to do this or should I?"

Behind them, Aldo and his rumpled ice cream suit lurked behind the authorities, shrugging.

"We were tailed," Aldo admitted. "It's been such a long time since any cops wanted to do so, I didn't look. Sorry. They caught up with me after you left Gangsters."

"I can't *drive* where I want?" Matt was stunned. "You've been having me followed, even Rafi that time?"

Molina smiled. "I wouldn't send a civilian on an assignment without having him checked from time to time. And you stumbled into some interesting criminals. We like where you drive. It's been very instructive, but now it's time for an 'intervention', as you might say."

"*You* are throwing that at me?" Matt was furious.

Frank stepped between him and Molina. "Matt, you are in over your head. It's not your fault. You should know even the ATF is involved as well as the locals and the FBI. It has an interest in any weapons at large in this country. The FBI put me in Las Vegas because of what you're tiptoeing around the edges of. You have no right to risk yourself like this when you've found the woman you love. If one of my sons—and mine are still pre-teens, thank God— was doing what you've been doing, I'd have been so proud I'd cry and then I'd confine him to home for a month.

"You've bulled your way into a crime of the century. But you've got to give it up. You can't go solo on this. You can't risk everyone around you. You've got to let us pros take the reins."

Matt stood still. In one way, he was relieved to shrug the suspicions and conclusions he'd been carrying off his back like a hiking pack. In another sense, he owned what he'd found out. He had earned his own conclusion.

Molina came around Bucek to face him. "Sometimes you've just got to let the past slide away. Sometimes you've got to let someone else show you the way. Isn't that right?"

Matt looked up at the Circle Ritz, at the people who lived there who needed to be safe from intruders and old crimes coming home to roost.

He nodded.

Molina looked over her shoulder at Detective Alch, who was already holding up some color computer printouts. She slammed the flimsy pages atop the Jaguar roof. "You know this man?"

"Yeah," Matt said. "Chuck Effinger. My…half-brother. My God." He paged through the three sheets. "What happened to him?"

"Nothing good. He has a long minor-crime rap sheet, but in this case, he's the assault victim."

"What did they use on his arms?"

"Not sure. Hydrochloric acid. Sander. Blowtorch. They wanted him to talk and we're sure he did. But not to us. He'd see us in Hell first."

She looked into his shocked eyes. "I'm sorry. You need to know this is serious. You need to know we're going to get these guys and are working on it even now, and you can *stay away* from these crooks and go and have your happy wedding, with Aldo and all the king's men on security."

She lowered her voice so only he could hear. "I'm sorry to blazes I referred you to such a compromised source. I'm putting security details on the Circle Ritz, the church, and the Crystal Phoenix. Nothing of this should touch you now. Okay?"

Matt nodded, still dazed. "Okay, Lieutenant. I did my job for you and I trust you to do your job for me. And mine."

"I promise to get you and yours safely to the wedding on time."

21
Midnight Louie's Dream Wedding

Many people joke about "wedlock". I suppose that is because the bride and bridegroom vow to be ever faithful and forego any romps of a romantic nature with someone else forever and ever.

Not a problem in the case of Mr. Matt, who is a proven celibate. That word is not to be confused with the ceremony's celeb*rant*, who is Father Hernandez and also one of these professional celibates.

But neither man was kidnapped and conveyed to the bottom of the altar steps of Our Lady of Guadalupe Catholic Church in a zebra-striped carrier!

(Although I understand that in olden days some brides were taken to the ceremony by force, hence the large number of groomsmen in weddings.) In our case, Fontana brothers.

I am royally annoyed by being confined, carried away, and treated like some human infant. Why? Am I not cooperative beyond all the usual behavior of my kind?

Do I not wear—again, when I was forewarned to fight it with every nail sheath?—the formal white tie around my neck. (On a breakaway band, so I cannot strangle if I get excited and try to run.) *Please.* Give me some credit. I know it is my job now to pose next to Mr. Matt's gray pant leg, immobile as a Buckingham Palace guard, during the interminable mumblings of the prayers and sermons and vows, and not move a muscle. I must admit I do have the impressive head of thick black fur for the job, if not the stature.

The small white box with the all-important wedding rings inside has not yet been affixed to my tie-band.

Why not? It is safer on my neck behind the formidable thorn bush of my ever-ready shivs.

But no. I have been "parked" in my conveyance on the end of the front pew overlooking the aisle and forgotten. All around me enough rustle and bustle to launch a major Broadway show opening is going on.

I hear Danny Dove's drill-sergeant basso voice projecting to the wooden beams high above, presumably representing Heaven itself.

"Places, people. *Please*. We do not have much time for the run-through before the actual-time rehearsal."

Well, I am not a "people", so I suppose sitting ignored is good enough for me. At least I have invited some of my own "guests", my nearest and dearest, which I blush to reveal includes my business partner and semi-honorary "daughter", Miss Midnight Louise.

We of Midnight Investigations, Inc. had a serious senior-junior talk before I allowed myself to be carted away from my Circle Ritz home, perhaps never to return again. (No one and nothing stops Midnight Louie from going where he pleases, but I may finally be too proud to come crawling back.)

"Louise," I say. "This is a very happy, yet sad day for me. I must let my Miss Temple follow her heart and go away with someone else."

"Jeez, Pop. Our Lady of Guadalupe is just a half hour's trot away."

"The road she follows from there goes ever on and on."

"And so do you sometimes." She sways a bit from side to side, considering. "You still have your PI business."

"Perhaps. But I only went into it to help Miss Temple after I found her first dead body at the convention center. I cannot be her sole bodyguard anymore."

"There are other bodies to guard."

"Louise, you have survived on the streets alone. You have never had a strong bond with a human. I understand. So, I am here to tell you, Louise, that it is possible, in some remote way probable, that you are…related to me. More than somewhat."

Her golden eyes widen. Definitely a bit of the Oasis Hotel's sizzling feline mascot Topaz there, or of Satin, the Sapphire Slipper bordello cat.

"Daddy Dearest!" she purrs. "Then I can get my name on the business as a Junior?"

"No. You are not a boy. Only boys are 'Juniors'."

"So what!" She gives me a friendly air-swipe on the cheek. "It can read, 'Midnight Louie, Sr. and Midnight Louise, Junior Miss'. I like that. Classy with a feminine touch. We can amp up the clientele for more female customers."

"Way too wordy, Louise, like you."

I sigh. Then…and now, coming back into the present with a mental lurch. I wonder where Louise is, given all this chaos.

I can only pass the time watching the flashing tuxedoed legs of multi Fontana brothers churning by, showing off their silver satin side stripes.

This is a wedding, folks, that may utterly and forever rearrange my happy home. You are lucky I am willing to participate in this folderol at all… I could very well go rogue and run off with the wedding rings.

But I am not heard or heeded, of course. I have always had a very bad feeling about the time and place of this wedding. And, luckily, I prepared well in advance.

The procession music sequence is about to begin. Distant voices from the choir loft at the back of the church are checking mic settings. I can only glimpse tall Miss Lt. C.R. Molina's dark hair in her persona of songstress Carmen.

I have nothing better to do now that I am once again confined to zebra-stripe quarters (is that not what convicts had to wear in the old days?) to hearken back to discussions the couple-to-be had within my hearing at the Circle Ritz only a week ago.

Well, actually, we all were in the privacy of my Miss Temple's bedroom, where I have been a planted listening device for more than two years.

When I occasionally flick an ear to fine-tune my built-in woofers and tweeters (not referencing dogs and birds), she sometimes wonders aloud if I have a flea in my ear and require a preventative treatment.

Please. No flea would dare to challenge the lightning justice of my super-sharp shivs, but I allow Miss Temple to monthly dab a little 'perfume' purported to ward off vermin on my neck. Rather like a vampire bite.

Frankly, warding off vermin—insect, or mammal, or human— has always been my job and I am very good at it without the assistance of applied substances, except for a bit of nip now and again.

Anyway, I am cleaning my toe hairs when I overhear the very discussion in question now, noxious as it is.

"Wedding-wise," Miss Temple says to Mr. Matt, "what are we going to do about your irregular family situation? My dad and mom can play their traditional roles, with dad walking me down the aisle, but nowadays the groom's parents may walk him down the aisle too, which is less sexist."

Mr. Matt mutes Jimmy Kimmel on the late-night TV. See, they are like an old married couple already. Disgusting! However, I have always wanted to mute Jimmy Kimmel, so I give Mr. Matt an invisible high-five and listen ever-so-much more intently, as the *Gossip Girls* do.

Mr. Matt considers with a sigh, "That would have to be my mother and her new husband."

"Who is genetically your uncle." Miss Temple frowns. "Wedding planning can get complex."

"The weddings I officiated at—" he begins.

Miss Temple threads her arm through his, rests her tousled red head on his shoulder and coos, "I would love to be married by you to you."

"Cannot happen," he says. "Anyway, the groom and his best man always lurked in the sacristy and appeared at the altar just in time to watch the wedding party coming down the aisle, starting with the mother of the bride and ending with the father of the bride. Simple enough."

"I invited both brothers *and* spouses, on the pretext that they are the sole brothers in the new step-family your mother has married into. You know how much being there would mean to your 'real' father. That man must be heartbroken to have been kept ignorant of your existence and not have been there for you from cradle to priesthood because of his parents' manipulations.

"If I had been the screenwriter on that situation," my Miss Temple adds indignantly, "I would have put the love-at-first-sight teen lovers back together in their middle years."

"You are a charming romantic, Temple. I know my father would have 'done the right thing' and acknowledged my mother and me, if he had known. But he went off to the military, against his family's wishes, anyway. And they 'handled the situation' without telling him."

"Was it because of their mondo money or were they just mean?"

"Parents back then expected to have authority over their children, 'for their own good'. Did not yours freak even now when you went off to Las Vegas with Max?"

"They were not happy. I was their only daughter and youngest child, but I was in my late twenties. Time to slash the cord." Miss Temple is quiet for a few moments. "Max helped me do it."

"Which is why, having been through several cord-slashings myself...my mom, the family, the church. the city of my birth, etcetera, I wish him well."

"That is so very noble of you. I see why you are such a star at advice-giving."

"In that mode, I am sure my father would have stood by my mother if he *had* known, because his family-approved wife has proven to be selfish and shallow."

"Really?"

"He does not love her, but he will never leave or divorce her, as a Catholic man, and for the sake of their children."

Miss Temple shakes her head. "He must see Mira often, with his brother at family events. It must be so painful."

"Yeah, but not unprecedented," Mr. Matt says. "There was a case in Chicago of two judges when I was on *The Amanda Show*. One married the other's divorced wife and, to retaliate, the other brother married his brother's longtime paralegal assistant."

"How weird."

"That is what people are. So no, on the gnawing pain factor," Matt said. "My genetic father is a realist. Love at first sight is a miracle, maybe, but real adults have to make compromises. My mother marrying my father's widowed brother, starting over, the two of them, at their age, has made her stronger than she has ever been. She knows the truth, and the truth is that you cannot go back thirty-some years to rewrite the present. And neither I, nor my 'real' father, would want to sacrifice seeing Mira strong and happy. And that is why I have come to peace with him and cherish him so much."

My Miss Temple swallows, and sniffles. "At least *we* have a happy ending, coming right up," she says.

I may have to relieve myself of a hairball right here on the zebra-print coverlet and gaze with loathing on the similarly patterned carrier against the bedroom wall. *You are next, you foul portable prison, and all your ilk!*

I freeze as my Miss Temple's fond glance falls upon me. "Louie has been flicking his ears back and forth all this time, and now he is hiccupping. Maybe that monthly omni-vermin application I use is not working."

Yes, there is *always an app for that* these days!

Mr. Matt shakes the sheets. "Maybe a vet should check him out before the wedding. We do not want our Ring Bearer to have a case of fleas."

I am so insulted I could spit, but then they would think I had rabies.

Whatever my human associates have decided to do about the fact that Mr. Matt has had three fathers of various stripes, I very well might have had brothers of different fathers. I sympathize with Mr. Matt's true father's lonely, isolated position. Among my kind, nature has decreed kitty litters commonly have multiple fathers. Yet I too have been tripped up in my past by secret patrimony.

I actually look around now to see if Midnight Louise has chosen to attend, although she was offered no position of importance, as I have been, like Ring Bearer. I suppose she could have been chosen Flower Girl, but I believe she would have sniffed at being offered such a childish role, not to mention the humiliation of wearing a collar and having some odiferous posy affixed to it. Me, my performing career has required costume bits, and I can adapt without having an existential personality breakdown.

Meanwhile, the show must go on. As the organ plays and Miss Carmen sings the processional song, various major players shuffle down the red-carpeted aisle, their order announced by Danny Dove from the church's rear. I am not required to perform until last, and my cue will be when I am released from the carrier. I see the flash of various Fontana brother legs as they escort various ladies forward, Mother of the Bride and Matron of Honor and Flower

Girl, as Best Man and Father of the Bride and Bride come in their ordained order. Ho-hum.

It seems I have nodded off during these deadly dull ceremonial preparations, and am awakened by a most rude method. I find myself swung out and up, my stomach mimicking the motion to an alarming degree. I burp up a bit of forbidden Fancy Feast.

"Ciao, Louie," a Fontana brother whispers into my suddenly liberated ear as the sweet sound of zippers parting ways on my carrier sends a shiver up my spine akin to claws on a back fence.

"Time to do your cameo soon, dude." Julio's nimble fingers affix a small white box to my white bow collar. Phfft. All that high-carat white gold is as light as an empty Temptations treat bag to my panther-like muscular neck and shoulders. Then…betrayed by a Brother. I am zipped into my prison again. At least I now have a better view.

First I sit there and scratch my neck.

That sissy white tie carries enough starch to float a barge.

I look around. Next up to the choir loft. Hmm. More activity than I expected. But I am ready, willing and absolutely able.

I look toward the altar to eye my future position between Best Man and Bridegroom, waiting to be relieved of the box affixed to my neck so the wedded couple can swear to be cuddlesome and clueless for eternity.

Pardon me. My view of married life.

But, lo, what light through yonder church front door breaks? It is the setting sun…and major felony is its name.

My claws seize in and out, sharpening themselves in vain on the tough nylon lining of my so-called "carrier". Peering through the black mesh sides, I am as handicapped as a film noir dame in a mourning veil.

I hear heavy boots rushing forward, grinding on the terra cotta tiles.

Silhouetted against the twilight, a crew of seven armed men advance with machine pistols, probably Uzis, one after another racking the slide on their firearms with ominous echoing metallic clicks.

I sit caged and ignored by the front pew, watching the wedding crashers advance on the royal red wedding aisle carpet chosen to accentuate my Miss Temple's pure-white five-foot-long-as-she-is tall wedding gown train.

"Do not move," the intruders bellow.

My Miss Temple certainly *cannot* move. That train makes for one mummifying cocoon, as she attempts to turn from the altar toward the thugs. The entire wedding party—all in white, some lurid pastels, and manly formal dude gray—freeze in their positions at the top of the altar steps.

My Miss Temple in her flowing white wedding finery resembles the famous "white marble" living statues at the Venetian hotel, models who move so subtly it is almost impossible to catch them in motion.

That waterfall of tulle veiling her from face to waist is doing my Miss Temple no favors in a crisis. If only, I think, the wedding party girls were bearing Beretta bouquets—*Viva Italia!*—and the boys were wearing ice pick boutonnières.

The invaders advance nearer, their weapons' black muzzles sweeping the pews right and left. I can only see vague outlines of the pew people against the lurid stained glass light, but they seem dumbstruck and obedient as well.

And who would not be dumbstruck by these bizarre wedding crashers. To conceal their faces, they are wearing white balaclavas!

Pause action.

Just what is a balaclava? It can be confusing, I agree. Is this foreign word the name of a Russian stringed instrument? Or is that word a *balalaika?* Or the name of a flaky Greek pastry? But I may be thinking of *baklava.* Normally, my kind does not eat sweets, but the Greeks, since even before the Trojan horse incident, were considered subtle and sneaky, and there is a lot of rich whipped cream cheese concealed between those flaky layers. Cheese is a protein, you know, suitable for carnivores. Ahem.

I have learned in my own home, after movie and TV show study, that balaclavas are a major accessory for bad guys. They are black stretchy ski masks, leaving holes for the eyes and mouth only.

Since no one can identify the wearers, they are worn by SWAT teams and criminals, like bank robbers and terrorists haughty enough to think that their ugly mugs are famous far and wide.

Okay. But these pure-white balaclavas are like Lady Godiva white-chocolate masks.

Wedding appropriate.

While I am marveling at the brutes' refined taste in headgear, someone steps up.

"Please," I hear proud Father Hernandez urge in a strained, almost unfamiliar voice of pleading, "do not sin on Holy ground, or hurt any of these worshippers. I have stepped away, see. I…we will not resist. All you see is yours, but know that our Holy Lord's vigil light burning twenty-four hours above sees the sins in your heart."

"Sorry, Padre," a basso voice growls insincerely. "We need to upset your ceremony until we get what we came for."

"Step back, Padre," another invader's voice orders. "Step back. You have been saying Mass for years over a fortune and your luck is about to run out."

The White Chocolate Balaclava Boys continue advancing, guns raised and at the ready, to the first altar step.

Okay. We have got a bead on the bride," another loud voice announces. "Everybody else, hands up and kept in sight. Move away from the altar."

One guy moves straight ahead, Uzi covering the bridal party.

I see the leader's ugly black wing-tip shoes approach the steps and the ladies' dainty heels and black-patent men's dress shoes parting to the right and left of the altar.

"That is right, priest to the far left with the fluffy ladies, bride and whatever. Dudes to the far right, remembering I would love to pick off a Fontana or two."

Then the invaders take a wide stance and make a demeaning demand.

"Wedding party, on your knees, bride, groom, do like the priest, and we will do a little holy excavation, Father, so you will live to genuflect another day."

"All of you. Drop on your knees."

Sorry. No can do. Not only do I kneel to no one, kneeling is not a default posture for my species.

I drop and hunch, thereby tipping my zebra-striped container over sideways on the floor. I can no longer see the action. I buck like a bronco to move my portable prison into better viewing position through the mesh sides.

A nudge (kick) from a Fontana size-eleven black patent-leather shoe in the carrier side is accompanied by a whispered, "Chill, dude" from a face leaning over my carrier zipper.

I glimpse gray pant leg. I have lived to sorta see a Fontana brother on his knees? Mama Fontana's Red Pepper Pasta Sauce forbid! The whisper continues. "Can the growling. Avoid attracting attention. You were supposed to be a stuffed stand-in here.

"Your real part was supposed to come much later."

I sincerely hope there is a "later" for my part, or parts.

The head guy says, "We have a bit of heavy lifting to do before any 'I do's' are said and *I do swear* to shoot anyone who looks sideways at our operation."

Shoes shuffle over tile, then I hear rough grunting and cursing, and the scraping of stone on stone, like a giant is using a mortar and pestle. If this were a horror movie, which I kinda think it is, somebody would be opening the tomb of The Mummy or Dracula. I prefer Dracula, because there would likely be bats on the scene, and I love chasing bats, almost as much as rats like the present company.

The grunts, curses, and scrapes get repetitive.

"Hey, bride," a guy shouts, "stop fussing with that bouquet. You throw it at any of us when we get close up, we will not be trying to catch it, and you will be left at the altar, dead."

That threat echoes in the silence. I can sense the stunned humans around me, frozen in horror. Maybe it *is* Dracula under that altar.

The growl low in my throat merits another toe-kick, but there is not a Fontana brother in the world who can shut up Midnight Louie when he is on the warpath. Besides, the people have moved too far aside to do anything. Me, I am not going anywhere.

"Temple," a thundering voice from above shouts, "You cannot do this. Thank God, I have reclaimed my memory. I have come to rescue you. Marry *me!*"

A caped human figure in black comes flying from the top of the nave like a huge raven on a bungee-cord pendulum, getting bigger. A rustling wind swishes, ruffling my already bristled coat, as the figure reaches the floor, dipping low enough to sweep my roommate and her trailing white train up, up and away to the other side of the nave.

"What or who the hell is up there?" a balaclava-masked guy shouts. "A vampire Tarzan bride-napper? *Shoot!*"

So there I am, struggling in the carrier, cursing the zipper tab that is resisting my insistent right incisor, a.k.a. fang, a.k.a. lock pick. I am basically Houdini doing an underwater escape from a locked shroud, losing-air-as-the-seconds-tick-by trick. Only without water.

Finally! Front fang connects with zipper tag hole and pulls down. I push my shoulders free. At last I shuffle off the hated portable immortal coil of my zebra-pattern carrier bag and leap out. Of course the exposure is dangerous, but I have been operating blind until now.

I see Miss Temple's beloved train ebbing away to my left as she disappears somewhere high and out of the action. The wedding party seems as stupefied as the invaders and guests in their pews. I bristle everything I have and run to center ground before the gaping hole in the floor to defend what is left of the wedding party.

"And somebody kick the cat with the stupid bow tie under his puss offstage while you are at it."

I can no longer contain the primeval feline warning that has rippled fear along human spines for millennia. It starts low in my belly, like a sports car engine, and escalates into a deep vibrating howl in my rib cage until it explodes from my throat in an ultra high-*C* shriek.

In perfect time, my personally auditioned Our Lady of Guadalupe cat choir pounces down from behind the red-velvet curtains in the organ loft hanging high behind everyone like a plague of the Red Death. Paws and claws pound down three sets of ivory keyboard, each key a gleaming "step" of sound, cats all the while howling a cappella. The resulting dissonance would wake the dead and promptly have even Dracula jumping back, cowering, into his coffin.

The human adrenaline high such unholy sound unleashes makes every heartbeat discernible, each throb a punch on a panicked jungle drum.

Hah! The wild shots into the distant ceiling have stopped. The ghost-faced interlopers are crouching, clamping hands to ears, with their weapons dropped against their legs.

The bridal party, however, leaps into frenzied action.

The missing, ahem, *new* bridal couple are swooping back down, a symphony in swinging black and white. Mr. Max sets the bride down on the altar steps and draws fire as he continues the swinging arc to vanish into the nave's blackest, highest shadows.

As soon as her white satin pumps touch tile, Miss Temple, with the piercing stare of a Medusa, her hair all crimson snakes lifted around her face by rapid motion, has slewed her precious train around to trip a falling intruder. Beside her, Mr. Matt has felled another man and knees him in the back as he bends to apply handcuffs to his wrists.

Who knew there were such kinky bridal accessories these days?

Father Hernandez raises his hands, but not for a blessing.

As I watch, he tosses the cape of his ceremonial satin chasuble over his shoulders and waves twin Glocks in his hands, covering faltering attackers, and ordering, "FBI, kiss floor and surrender."

The shifted altar stands askew, revealing a dark vault beneath the polished stone with its carved serpentine symbol.

I look for where more members of the wedding party might be, but the front pews are occupied by stoic onlookers, unmoved and oddly...inert. Has a poison gas been emitted? I gasp. Just the wrong move to make, if so.

Uniformed officers swarm from the side aisles to gather the confused thugs into custody.

Glancing up to the choir loft, I see Miss Lieutenant C. R. Molina bracing her Glock-full hands on the railing, wincing while my wonderful a cappella choir finishes running riot over the organ keys.

My improvised Katzenklavier diversion has worked wonders, but what the heck is really going on?

"Louie, Louie, Louie," my Miss Temple cries, rocketing out from the back of the church as the vanilla Balaclava Gang are marched out a side parking lot exit.

"They almost killed you. I was told *you* would be a stuffed cat in the Zebra carrier," she says, stroking me.

Well, I was "stuffed" in.

"So sorry, Miss Barr," this hovering FBI guy says. "He was sleeping so hard in this carrier at the Circle Ritz, we thought he was, well, stuffed."

"Louie naps in the hated carrier?"

I hang my head with shame. It does hold in body heat pretty well.

"So," she accuses, "he was grabbed and stowed right up here, by the altar. Forgotten," she says. "Released into the hail of gunfire. Would you like a bullet up your left nostril? I am so tempted."

"Ah, Agent Bucek," the guy says. "Come here, please. Um, civilian and cat coming unglued."

I am treated to the sight of silken priest's garb under an ex-priest FBI face. "*Mea culpa*," Agent Bucek mutters, "*mea maxima culpa*, Miss Barr.*"

"Okay, so long as he apologizes," my Miss Temple says.

"We wanted to make it look authentic," Mr. Frank Bucek says. "The planted gossip item in Crawford Buchanan's column said that a cat in a zebra-print carrier wearing a white bow-tie collar would be the Ring Bearer."

True, but I do not want these humiliating details bandied about. If I could get sleazy gossip-columnist Crawford Buchanan into my paws and claws, I would be giving his epidermis a custom tattoo. However, I have bigger guppies to fry right now.

Now that I am not looking at the world through black nylon mesh, I feel like Dorothy waking up back in Kansas again.

I can see clearly now that all the people at the front of the church are properly attired...imposters. Pews are filled with soft sculpture wedding guests imported from Miss Electra Lark's charming Lover's Knot wedding chapel. ("Every couple has a full house.") I wink at Elvis in his wedding-white jumpsuit, but he does not wink back.

Mr. Matt, I now see, sports a pale blond mustache, like an officer at our neighborhood substation that is such a reliable food source for Ma Barker and her Cat Pack. The best man is not Frank Bucek, but Molina's favorite detective, Morrie Alch.

And "Father Hernandez", now expertly divesting himself of the many layers of an officiating Catholic priest's robes, is really Mr. Matt's mentor from seminary days, now an FBI guy. A two-gun-toting FBI guy, Frank Bucek.

Then the bride all dressed in white and a mangled train pulls off her veil and red wig and turns out to be petite detective Merry Su, holstering the gun hidden in her bridal bouquet.

"And they rolled away the stone," intones an authoritative voice. The real Father Hernandez steps out from the sacristy and shakes his head to see the deep dark vault below the shifted altar.

The only person not unmasked and not now present is the bride-napping bungee cord jumper, Mr. Max Kinsella. I search the shadowy heights again. No trace.

Looking up at the choir loft, I see that any real civilians present are all now crowding to the safety rail, secure behind Molina and two uniformed officers. Mr. Matt, Miss Electra, Danny Dove, assorted Fontana Brothers...

Except for my Miss Temple, who is still embracing me...wait for it...the image of her racing down the red carpet toward me in slow motion, as if she could not be restrained from rushing to my side... perfect for our first commercial. Only she needs to be wearing her wedding gown and *I* am the dude in white tie and tails awaiting her at the altar.

It is a good thing I had my suspicions and employed the convent cats, Peter and Paul, to recruit local cats for me to train. They faithfully reported for duty at first sniff of any serious wedding action going down. Now they have run like rats from Hamlin down the two loft side staircases to the main floor and are even now vanishing into the neighborhood and back home.

Alas, I am caught alone in the limelight and a compromising position. Again.

As a final indignity, Miss Temple frees my bow-tie collar from the burden of the ring box and opens it.

Out pops the handful of Free-to-Be-Feline pellets the uniformed officer stuck inside.

She looks up at the guy in charge of my transport.

He shrugs. "I thought a little weight would give the ring box some verisimilitude."

"Are you an aspiring actor, Officer?" she asks.

He shrugs modestly. "I did do a couple of walk-ons for *CSI: Las Vegas.*"

Honestly. Amateurs.

22
There Goes the Groom

The "real" cast of *Wedding Rehearsal,* the Continuing Serial, packed the choir loft, laughing and hugging and milling.

Midnight Louie, back in his carrier and sporting a hang-dog look, had the organ bench for a pedestal. Fontana brothers were slipping him fishy-scented treats the agent assigned to bring him had purchased to lure him into the carrier, which had proved unnecessary.

"At least," Temple said, clinging to Matt, "we got a feel of how a real rehearsal would have gone. We'll have to do it cold tomorrow for the real thing."

"Naw." Danny Dove waved a phone over his angelic blond curls as if tipping a top hat in a some jazzy tap dance. "Got it all recorded on my cell phone. Plus the choir loft was already wired and set up for filming weddings, so the police will have more than one bird's-eye view to study. Their evidence team will be up all night emptying the hidden vault, but that altar should slip back into place with no problem."

"And, Danny," Electra added, "some of your chorus line dancers need to waltz my thirty soft-sculpture 'guests' back to their places in my wedding chapel."

"Enchanted," he said, with a bow. "We have the LeBron James edition extra-stretch limo for that."

"Electra," Matt asked, "will you be a real doll—" he winked and everyone laughed, "—and give Temple a ride back to the Circle Ritz? The groom-to-be must do a trifling but vital errand."

He answered Temple's inquiring look with a raised hand. "Top secret. Not for the bride-to-be's ears, eyes, or marvelously nosy nose."

Temple pulled him aside. "Now I understand what you've been secretly working on. Our wedding as a thief trap. I can't believe everyone was in on this, even Frank Bucek."

"Everyone except Louie."

"Apparently, he had a scheme of his own, but no, how could he have done anything? He was at home unaware an officer of the law would be coming to fetch him here to play his usual walk-on part."

"What about the cat oratorio?" Matt wondered.

"I've heard somewhere about that phenomenon. The area must be crawling with cats because many of the late Blandina Tyler's hoarded cats found new neighborhood homes. The church is always open, and the area behind the red velvet curtains must be a favorite hidden snoozing spot when the church isn't in use."

"It sure was this evening."

"You heard Louie yowl when the 'supposed me' was whisked away into thin air. That must have roused the sleeping cats. Homeless and feral cats are way more bonded than most people know."

Father Hernandez put a hand on each of their shoulders to join their tête-à-tête. "We have not one mouse or rat in the church or schools, thanks to Peter and Paul and the neighborhood cats. And you must remember, Miss Barr, that you brought your black cat to the Blessing of the Animals I performed. I must be a very effective priest."

"So you are," Matt said. "There might be some reclamation money due the church for the Binion stash."

"And that notorious, long-dead gangster is the source of the gold bullion I glimpsed?"

Matt nodded. "It should be the last of the millions he hid around Las Vegas. About four were missing."

"We remodeled the lower church in the mid-eighties," Father Hernandez said, "when the gangsters were supposed to have been banished. It's amazing some have remained to this day."

"Binion was still alive then," Matt pointed out.

"We created meeting rooms and a small chapel to St. Jude in the lower church, just below the main altar here."

"The Saint of the Impossible," Matt explained to Temple. "St. Jude sure came through for you, Father, and us today."

"The drive had raised extra funds, amazing for a poor parish, to commission a grand stone altar with the symbolic turquoise central image of Quetzalcoatl from the ancient Aztec tradition and the carnelian insets of the fish from the ancient Christian community on either side."

"The turquoise serpent portrays the endless coils of eternity," Temple said, "and the carnelian fish the enduring faith of the present worshipers."

"Not a bad interpretation for a UU," Matt said.

Once Father Hernandez had laughed, patted their shoulders, and advised rest until the "real" ceremony twenty-four hours hence, Temple returned to her cross-examination of Matt.

"One last thing you have to tell me right now. You okayed Max's special appearance?"

"Reluctantly, believe me. I didn't know he was going to *say* anything. Bucek and Molina needed something to distract the intruders' attention upwards and away from the bridal party hostages on the ground as their peripheral armed forces slipped in through the side aisles to get behind the action. *The Graduate* film's iconic wedding crasher scene with Dustin Hoffman running off with the bride came to mind."

"Max is hardly Dustin Hoffman, and he's communing with Molina these days?"

"Who doesn't?" he said good-naturedly. "It was all I could do to get Molina to let you and me and a few others into the choir loft behind police bodyguards."

"I nearly had a heart attack. Detective Su could have been killed."

"Or Max," Matt said. "It's not every bride who gets another marriage proposal at the altar," he noted shrewdly. "How does that feel? Do you think that it's true?"

"What?"

"That Max has regained his memories."

"I hope so," Temple said, "but I have more to make, with you. Golly, this was close. You're going to have a lot more to explain to me."

"I do, I do," he promised. "But my work here is not done. My last task won't take long. And then you'll know all."

Matt galloped down the loft steps.

He clicked off the alarm on the Jag at a run. Nobody was going to do an "intervention" on him this time.

The main parking lot held cop cars and evidence vans, but the bush-shrouded side parking area that concealed the wedding participants' and stagers' vehicles had been church-lot peaceful until his "blip" disturbed the evening air. Taking his low-profile old car from the Circle Ritz would be better for where he was going, but Matt didn't want to lose time.

As he'd expected, when all those creepy white balaclavas were stripped off, the heads beneath them were white, gray or bald. The masks were camouflage, not a quaint bow to the wedding rehearsal the wearers disrupted.

Matt was missing the only two persons he'd expected to be among the treasure-hunting thugs from the long-dead past, and one he'd be deeply glad to see among the guilty.

The Jag made the trip smooth and fast. Matt parked three houses down from his target. A low-rider with throbbing exhaust pipes gargled its way past as Matt got out and thumbed on the alarm, the driver rubber-necking backward. If it weren't not quite dark yet…

But it was, though Matt didn't have time for worrying about his wheels' security.

He loped down the uneven sidewalk toward the familiar sagging front porch, passing a curbside mattress wearing a map of tears and blood that sagged even more than the porch, waiting for a garbage pick up or a passing dog to piss it deader.

No car was parked in front of Woodrow Wetherly's house or in its crumbling driveway.

Matt eyed the front door. Closed like an indifferent eye.

He peered down the cluttered five feet holding litter and one ancient lawn mower between the house and the freestanding garage, unusual in Vegas, where carports had been king until the housing booms, and busts, of recent decades.

He bent to grab the garage door's hot metal handle, jerking upward fast and hard, so he could pull back before his palm burned.

The rattling mechanism could have been announcing a train outward bound at high speed.

In the quiet, derelict neighborhood, it was as loud as a five-alarm alert.

Yet nothing happened, nobody reacted.

Matt felt the heat wetting the underarms of his borrowed blazer, suitable for church, for a wedding rehearsal.

He should have borrowed a Beretta from a passing Fontana brother, maybe Julio, back at the church instead of a jacket. Not even Molina would have called them on their firearms there and then. Maybe especially not Molina. The brothers were the only civilians who had risked their skins to be on call during that charade. Temple's aunt had married one of them. Matt smiled. Maybe the "Iron Maiden of the Metro Police" would be the next to do so.

The whisper of that smile lasted until Matt jimmied the feeble wire fastening on the old Chevy's trunk open for the second time. Empty except for an oil-stained piece of canvas and several dented and spent Dos Equis cans.

Matt walked around the car and found a side door garage entrance. A skinny door on painted-out hinges. He pushed it ajar, saw some broken-down steps and a side door to the house. Tight. Getting between the garage and the house felt like squeezing through a mystery pipe. You didn't know where it began, or ended. He heard the faint whine of a power tool.

Far away, or nearer than you think?

He retraced his steps sideways, alongside the behemoth of a car, its raw ruined body paint scraping on his clothes. What did this proudly junker car say about its driver? Driven? Perverse? Hiding behind ordinary poverty and powerlessness?

Hey, midnight shrink, your instincts had better be as good as advertised now. You're going to be bawled out by law and order, and mostly your nearest and dearest, of whom you have way more than you deserve, for this solo jaunt into the heart of darkness.

Matt reached down, into his deepest dark place, the moment he had Cliff Effinger in his bare hands and could have killed him. And didn't. Did the God of the universe give credit for paths not taken as much as those embraced? What was a person's best weapon, justice or mercy? Paraphrasing Ecclesiastes…

There is a time for every season. A time to be foolish, a time to be wise.

A time to confront, a time to evade. A time to stand, and a time to fall fallow.

Like Leonard Cohen's "Hallelujah" song, thirty years in the making, the verses could go on forever. So the maker must cut to the exultant chorus at exactly the right time. And then stop the music.

Matt was now up the rickety porch stairs, quiet as a TV-show shamus.

The screen door was too conveniently agape, the wooden side door too artistically cracked.

He felt like the protagonist in a *Twilight Zone* rerun, wondering and then losing all certainty and hope of where or when he was, and knowing the outcome would always be dire.

There is a time to risk it all, and a time to run the table.

Tell me where is justice bred, in the heart or in the head?

In an old garage, he thought. Not the ordinary Las Vegas construction. In the hidden vault carved from under a church renovation. Not the usual Las Vegas method. Vaults. Underneath. Benny Binion buying so much property. The building near the Circle Ritz, used by the Zoot Suit Choo-Choo Club. In a basement. Not the ordinary Las Vegas venue. And its founder, Jumpin' Jack Robinson, hanged there on a zoot suit cat chain. Likely another Binion casualty.

Did someone harbor an obsession with *underneath*, the desert, the city, with vaults, not basements. Not middle-western basements for canned beets and fruits, but for illegal things, like alcohol, drugs, guns, skimmed money. The underworld, the Chicago Outfit, so powerful.

Underneath the Irish rebellion. The millions. Under a church basement, for Christ's sake. And the old building Matt had stormed with Electra's Probe car. Its basement was pockmarked with holes in the concrete, keeping the desert sandstone out. Desert storm.

Matt heard the whine of power tools, shaking the scarred and lusterless wood floor beneath his feet.

He charged the swinging door to the kitchen, onto a floor covered with a splotchy sixties-pattern of blemished linoleum.

Woody had lived here for a long time because its covered garage and the oddity of a basement suited him. And his work.

He'd lived here for decades.

But maybe not much longer.

Matt had always hated basements. His mother's two-flat in Chicago had one. Dank, dark, damp. Out of a serial killer movie. She soon married Cliff Effinger in hopes of giving Matt a "normal" childhood. From the first, Matt had hated Cliff Effinger, who soon became lazy and sour and abusive for reasons of his own and maybe a little because Matt despised him.

Matt began to see Effinger's point of view, as unjustified as it was. After Effinger was dead and gone, murdered horribly, and as much as Matt had relished his absence, he saw they had, and he may still have, common enemies.

And only by going down the basement stairs, where in his childhood a hidden monster pursued him up the stairs every time he ventured down there, would he stop the fear.

Bob Dylan sang that dreams were *only* in your head. Classic understatement of all time. No wonder Matt had wanted to march down the aisle to the guy's words and melody. He was an anti-social genius who named and banished lies.

Now, if Matt was going to do that, he would have to confront, and conquer, his dreams and nightmares.

The worst part of the basement steps was that they were usually freestanding, each step open to anything. Anything or anyone could be lurking down below to snake a fist or tentacles through a riser space and catch your ankle from behind. Any black-and-white movie monster.

And yet a kid could be sent down there time and time again to fetch a jar of pickled onions.

Do parents ever remember those horrors? See "AB Normal" brains floating in a jar labeled "Cauliflowers", a.k.a. Frankenstein's Monster in the making?

No. They had forgotten their own childhood fears.

Matt stepped sideways down the basement stairs, hearing voices from dozens of scary movies in his head. And maybe from down here.

"All right. *Rat-a-tat, you rat.*"

A machine whined, drilled, shut out sound, made vibration torture.

"You're crazy, kid."

Matt, on solid if lumpy ground at last, stepped into the cool fetid air. "He's not the only crazy one," he said.

The strobe light flash of black-and-white in his mind illuminated Woody Wetherly gagged with T-shirt material and bound by clothesline to a three-generations-back recliner chair covered in cracked turquoise vinyl upholstery.

A jackhammer bit was poised between his legs like a ballerina's toe shoe *en pointe.*

Chunks of concrete lay piled around the bit. Woody's bunion-distorted toes strained against their worn Reebok uppers.

"Matt, my man," Chuck hailed him. *What had he done?* "Aren't you always where you shouldn't be? You should be in church, man. Having a life. A *Life with Father.* Old-time family sitcom. Get it? Don't say I can't be funny."

"I think you're a scream." Matt eyed Woody, struggling to free his hands and whimpering through his saliva-wet gag.

"This Devine guy is not what he says he is," Woody managed to mumble.

Chuck nodded. Slowly. "You shouldn't have come, Chicago boy. I hate your guts too."

"But I didn't know anything," Matt said. "Woody did."

Chuck was rocking back and forth slightly, the jackhammer handle swaying with him. His face was bruised and cut, but his arms were raw, red, the tattoos sanded halfway off. Matt winced for his pain, both outer and inner.

"My dad," Chuck said, shaking his head. "Maybe he was just a dream, but he was mine. I didn't need being farmed out to my Uncle Joe. Dad knew too much and they hounded him out of Vegas to live all those years in Chicago, to keep an eye on him. He knew he knew too much of what-was-what back here. He knew he'd been sold out."

"Banished," Matt suggested.

Chuck eyed him with an appreciative glint. "Yeah. Big word. Banished. Gotten rid of while this piece of crapola was hunting the big payoff. Benny Binion's Last Las Vegas Big Cash Dump."

"And you've been sold out, in turn," Matt said. "What did he do to you?"

"He's got a sixth sense, Woody. Always has. He knew I knew something that might lead to the Binion money and went about getting it out of me and my past, my ink, my skin. Now I'm getting it back out of him."

Chuck pressed down. The jackhammer whined and then machine-gunned into the concrete floor, spattering Woody's legs, arms, and face with freckles of blood from impacting concrete spray. He screamed into the gag.

"Chuck."

"Yeah, perfect little Matt, what?" Chuck wouldn't take his eyes from Woody's bizarre figure.

"You had to get real close to that altar to see your father's mark, to know he'd worked there. Why? You didn't have to follow me inside."

Chuck wouldn't look at him. "I don't believe in that holy stuff."

Matt kept quiet.

"I got to wondering, that's all."

"Wondering what?"

Chuck's eyes—Matt noticed that they were a pale hazel in a pale, freckled-by-nature face—finally met his.

"I got to wondering why I wasn't you. So I went in and saw the altar."

He tore his gaze away to Woody. "Did he get it? Did Woody's years of favors and confidential informants pay off? He get his payoff over at the church?"

"No. The cops got it. And the FBI. And they're coming to get him pretty soon."

"*Oh-ho-ho-ho-ho,* old man!" Chuck eyed Matt again after taunting Woody. "Bet that feels good to you."

"Yes, it does."

"You're supposed to be super-holy and forgiving."

"Well, I'm not. But...*you,* you could be smart and on the move and read all about it in the newspapers. You could vanish and I could call Metro Police to pick up Woody, in one piece mostly, and, presto, you could be a vanished mystery man."

"You came here. From there. The money was at the church, under the altar?"

"Yeah. How'd you know?"

"This piece of scum had me follow you. After we, um, met, you could say. I was curious too."

"I led you to Our Lady of Guadalupe."

"Led me there, but I stayed to go in."

"Why?"

"Used to. Once. Go to church. Back when they made you go."

"You saw the altar. You had to get up close. You had to care about something you can't see, or steal, or hate, or beat."

"My dad." Chuck flexed his abused left arm. "This tattoo. Man fighting snake. Here's the real snake in front of us. All along."

"The constellation Ophiuchus."

"Huh. No. Not that crazy mouthful in the sky. This is. This guy. Ole Woody Wetherly, retired cop. My dad did mention Lucky Stars, like the nudie bar, if that's the stars you're referring to. This second tat I got is Quetzalcóatl. The plumed serpent the ancient Indians worshiped. My dad liked that image too. But this was his favorite."

He traced the faint tattoo of a mighty serpent entwined with a mighty muscled man on the other arm. "My dad lived by that ink."

Matt looked at the jackhammer still balanced on its bit, ready to bite into Woody's feet and ankles, legs, flesh and bone, and spew blood on them all.

"Chuck. You've already got your revenge, from the evidence of Woody's pissed pants. He's old. He's done. I can speed dial the cops and FBI to come get this guy and that damning weapon ten minutes after you and your scabrous junker are gone."

"What's scabrous? Nothing good, I bet. Hey, that's a seventy-seven Chrysler. It's got a lot of fond memories and a lot of buried glory and mileage on that six-figure odometer."

"Haven't we all?" Matt said.

"You'd let me go? Just like that."

"Hey, I'd give you credit, but it's best to skip that. We all saw what greed and cunning did for the Binions, father and son." Matt nodded at Woody. "I now see your dad was harsh at my house because he'd been kicked out of his—what'd you say, clan?—that this crooked cop put together and ran like a mob while playing the harmless old gent. So, Woody will get nothing but the justice your father would have wanted, and *you*'ll get a free run on that amazing odometer."

Chuck's smoldering look lifted upwards and became cagey. "I heard that Jag motor coming, vibrating these rotten floor posts."

Matt nodded. "Not the best surveillance vehicle, even I know that."

"You didn't waste any time racing over to save this sorry piece of naugahyde."

"Nope. Needed to nail a master criminal."

"Say I swap you out the junker for the Jag," Chuck proposed.

Matt sighed. "Just go far, far away, change the license plates, trash the VIN number, and get yourself a better grade of jacket on the way. As far as I'm concerned, you weren't here."

Chuck hesitated, gazing longingly at the jackhammer.

"Here. You'll match the car better." Matt shrugged out of his Fontana suit jacket, and paused when Chuck's weight on the jackhammer pressed down to produce a spray of concrete gravel. Matt turned his face away from the blow-back. Wetherly wriggled and whimpered.

Holding both hands up, Matt hooked the jacket on one forefinger and dangled it in view of Chuck Effinger.

Without a word, Chuck cut the air supply from the compressor and lowered the top of the jackhammer to the floor. Matt pitched the jacket to him, and it was over.

"Hey." Chuck paused three steps up the basement stairs, as his forefinger massaged his sorry soul patch. "Have a nice wedding for real, step-bro."

"Thanks. I will."

Chuck's work boots banged up the rickety stairs, then stomped through the house above. He let the front door bang on the way out.

Wetherly mouthed something through the greasy rag.

"Yes, you're right, Mr. Wetherly. I don't look like the type to torture you with a jackhammer." Matt used another dirty rag to wipe the jackhammer free of prints. "I'm glad he's gone. This is an old model and I don't think he used the proper safety precautions. Of course, Chuck is a 'known associate', I think they call it in law enforcement circles. His prints would be expected around your place, as anyone at the Lucky Stars could testify, not that they'd be that believable.

"How I got here is this. I'll say that I suddenly realized that some information you had given me was important. Say how I was referred to you for my radio show by a local homicide lieutenant. Yup, that's true. That's your despised, relocated LAPD woman cop. Anyway, the cops knew I was interviewing you about cold cases. So I realized something was relevant and rushed to confront you, only to interrupt some of your other big bad buddies intent on nabbing the hidden stash from *your* henchmen when they came back. I had to grab the jackhammer out of one's hands, my own prints blurring whatever was left of *his* fingerprints."

Matt folded his hands around the handles. "I didn't know who they were and I didn't want to disturb 'the crime scene', being an amateur. So I just phoned the police and asked them to please take you off my hands. Who are they going to believe, me or you?

"No, don't say anything. I need no thanks for saving you from a fate worse than death.

"Hammer toes."

23
Who's Who of Crooks

"And your other jacket?" Molina asked Matt on Friday morning, her eyes dark blue slits of suspicion. "The one you grabbed from a Fontana brother at the mock wedding rehearsal. It's gone...how?"

He and Temple were holding hands while sitting on the two smart new chairs in the new police headquarters building. Temple was not about to let him "dash off" again before the evening wedding.

But the jacket. Temple was so glad to have Matt back and safe from that crazy house and under official grilling she'd only noticed his jacket was missing now.

Molina didn't miss anything, blast her.

Seeking to provide a distraction, an old public relations ploy, Temple took an aggrieved tone. "Oh, Matt, it was your first Ermenegildo sports coat, a groomsman gift from the Fontana bothers. It's gone?"

"That's what the lieutenant is asking," Matt said. "I was in such a hurry, I tossed it into the Jag's backseat."

Enter Molina, on topic. "Which you left unlocked at the front curb of a house in a dangerous part of town. Might as well stake out a diamond-studded Cartier leopard on Cannery Row," she snarled.

Molina didn't exactly snarl, but Temple thought she came uncharitably close. And here her fiancé sat minus an expensive car and blazer. Whom did the law protect now?

"I'm sorry, Lieutenant," Matt said. "You directed me to Woodrow Wetherly. I thought he was trustworthy."

Molina leaned back in her new adjustable chair. "So, bereft of car and wearing apparel, you found Wetherly tethered and helpless and immediately called the police, *idly jack hammering the concrete between his feet* until they arrived? I didn't know you had experience in construction."

"Summer jobs during seminary. I was trying to turn the dang thing off."

"Sure. Play the ex-priest card. Miss Barr, are you still convinced you want to marry this unfrocked prevaricator?"

"Are you sure you're not jealous?"

"*Et tu*, amateur." Molina shrugged. "I will make up for my justified skepticism by singing at your wedding for real, not just as a substitute for Mariah at a faux wedding. There. Are you happy now?"

Temple gaped at Matt. "Do we want this?"

He laughed. "Anyone who wants to participate in our wedding who isn't a major felon plotting to use it as the occasion for an illegal treasure hunt is fine by me. That old man not only killed a major mobster way back when, he buried the guy's gruesome signature 'weapon' in the desert. His big mistake was digging it up. Maybe he was getting senile. Or sentimental over his illegal coup decades ago.

"But, Carmen, uh, Lieutenant," Matt turned to ask her, "why did you send me to a major crooked cop, when I just wanted to be sure that local criminal elements weren't still after Temple?"

"You never mentioned fears for Miss Barr's safety, only to investigate Cliff Effinger. I also simply wanted you out of my hair, all right? I'm relatively new to the Metro Las Vegas police. I had no idea who or what Woody was. He was recommended as an old-timer who knew the score. I *do* know he'll be key in clearing up a lot of cold cases from our books now, and we won't need a jackhammer to get that out of him."

"Clearing cold cases with Woody?" Matt was incredulous. "He was an out-of-date bonanza hunter, maybe, and a tool for some bad people decades ago. But…mostly a go-between. Look at how badly that Our Lady of Guadalupe caper went."

Temple plucked on Matt's replacement Emenegildo Zegma sports coat sleeve, courtesy of Aldo Fontana, fresh off his back with a deep bow when he had dropped them off at police headquarters.

"I know it was stupid of me to run off like that," Matt told Temple, "but no harm done. Darling."

She tugged again.

"Dear," he said, "you're going to get Aldo's Emperio Armani underwear in a wad if you distort the tailoring by jerking away at it."

"*Oops.*"

"After all, we'll be seeing Aldo tonight at the real wedding and reception and he'll want a full accounting of your and the sports jacket's adventures—"

Temple heaved a dramatic sigh and turned to Molina. "What you're not saying is that my dear, overprotective, mad-as-hell fiancé nailed Jack the Hammer thirty-some years after his 'death', didn't he?"

"Nicely done, Miss Barr, sweet deduction, despite having wedding cake and trip-worthy trains on the brain. There may be hope for you yet."

"What?" Matt was indignant. "The old cop was the murderer of the criminal, not the criminal."

"Miss Barr?" Molina tossed the ball.

"Oh, call me Temple. Anyone who sings as well as you do and volunteers for my wedding should be on a first-name basis." Temple leaned forward in her chair. "It's obvious. Giacco Petrocelli was aging and out of favor with the mob bosses, and off his game, just as his dogged pursuer, Woodrow Weatherly, was facing putting in his thirty years and retiring. The Mojave desert is no country for old men. Giacco lured Wetherly out there, and buried him with his famous namesake weapon nearby in no man's land."

"What?" Matt was stunned.

"And…" Temple loved her scenario as it blossomed in her mind, "since age makes most men lose their hair, their waistlines, and swap their twenty-twenty vision for glasses, what was to distinguish one absent, aging, liver-spotted sixty-year-old fading from potency in both crime and law enforcement from another?"

Molina laughed. She'd been watching Matt. She could hardly stop, a first occasion of unbridled public mirth from the Iron Maiden of the LV Metro Police.

When Molina could finally talk again, she addressed Matt, who looked like he'd been slugged with a jackhammer. "She certainly makes men's vows of eternal loyalty and fidelity sound unattractive thirty years on."

Temple glanced at Matt. He did look confused. She hastened to reassure her white knight, who had gone charging out after the wrong man entirely.

"You see how cleverly it happened," she explained. "'Missing' Giacco Petrocelli killed Woodrow Wetherly, then 'disappeared' by taking over his victim's house and identity. He had the driver's license, and you know how bad those photos are even with young people. He became a post-retirement Wetherly, bitter and ready to float a lot of schemes with a new generation of would-be mobsters, principally aimed at finding the last of Benny Binion's buried fortune."

Molina wiped her eyes. The laughter flush was almost as becoming as Urban Decay cheek tint. Temple resolved to get Danny to improve Molina's makeup for the wedding tonight. Meanwhile, they needed to get out of there and finish reception arrangements.

Meanwhile, Matt was puzzling out his own scenario.

"So I was dallying with Jack the Hammer? Why would he have or keep the jackhammer buried in the desert and then import it to his basement?"

Molina shrugged. "A lot of cops, when they retire, are allowed to buy their service weapon. K-nine cop retirees can often purchase their partner dogs at a very reasonable price."

"A jackhammer is not a pet," Matt said. "And Petrocelli was no cop."

"A K-nine dog is also a deadly weapon," Molina reminded him. "Cops and crooks can get strange attachments to their tools." Molina smiled and glanced at Temple. "The animal-partner bond is the most understandable one. These creatures have extraordinary instincts that have saved lives."

Temple nodded, accepting the unspoken accolade for Midnight Louie. When it came down to it, a cat "walks by himself", as Kipling put it, and is more suited for subtle investigative work. A canine, with its pack loyalty, tracking gifts and noisy bravado, does the advance scouting and takedown work.

"And don't forget Louie's key role in luring Wetherly's gang to the faux wedding. Electra Lark, the target of your suspicions twice, Lieutenant," Temple said sternly, "had a photo of Louie as Ring Bearer in white-tie collar and ring box. She 'leaked' it and the place and date of our 'faux' wedding to gossip columnist Crawford Buchanan. The piece went viral and Giacco couldn't have missed it."

"Good thing Buchanan didn't show up," Molina said.

"He ran into a Fontana brother and had car trouble," Temple said. "I would never want that oozy, oily sexist to attend even my fake wedding."

Matt was still processing a total turnaround of dead bad cop and live crook. "So no one ever found poor old Woody's body and IDed it?" Matt asked.

"No. Presumably buried in the desert. Miss Barr must have a theory."

She did. "I'm remembering the 'pre-buried' dried-out body found on the site of Mr. Farnum's futuristic 'invisible' attraction recently. Later, Santiago, who seemed to be on a treasure hunt of his own, died there. Could that first body have been the real Woody's mummy? Can DNA be done on it?"

Molina knitted her wooly dark eyebrows. That Brooke Shields look was decades out of date. Temple so itched to give them a wax job. Or sponsor a bachelorette party ice-cube, eye-brow plucking marathon. Maybe, in Molina's case, for past snubs…without the ice cube to dull the pain. Too bad there wasn't time.

Temple's thought must not have shown on her face.

"What did that phony environmental art huckster Santiago have to do with any of this?" Molina asked.

Matt gently removed Temple's hand from its clutch on his sleeve. She'd been seriously unnerved by his artless confrontation with a notorious monster and his favorite jackhammer in a creepy basement. Knowing about Chuck right now would freak Temple out and would do nobody good.

The lost IRA money and guns Kathleen O'Connor and Santiago had amassed in the Americas over the years seemed as legendary an object of obsession as the seven lost cities of gold known as Cibola to the Conquistadors, unlike the post-modern Ted Binion stash.

"Santiago?" Matt asked. "Caught in the middle, maybe. Being the kind of arty showman he was, he was probably just investigating Temple's client and his use of a genuine light-bending technique to make objects 'invisible'. Figuring it out and using it would boost his reputation."

Molina shook her head. "This is Las Vegas and, yes, this Cirque du Surveillance scenario you describe fits right in. There may be almost as many pretenders to the under-church vault contents as the thousands of remaining claimants to Howard Hughes' land in Summerlin. What time is your real wedding? I've already helped Mariah for her solo and need to coordinate our vocals with Danny Dove."

Molina struck a palm to her forehead. "Lord, I never thought I'd live to say such a thing."

"Cirque du Surveillance?" Temple asked, surprised.

"No, working with Danny Dove. You two are going to have the biggest, small church wedding in Las Vegas history, a good kickoff to your new media careers, God help us."

Molina smiled. "I do hope my opening solo during the procession fetches a five-second clip on your new show."

"You're coming out as Carmen." Matt was surprised.

"This is Vegas, baby. Gotta keep up with the budding teen sensation daughter. Mariah and I will do our first duet on the recessional."

"But you'll be armed, just in case?" Temple asked.

"This is Vegas, baby. No one is going to mess with your precious tablecloth train while I'm in that choir loft."

"It seems Midnight Louie handled that choir loft 'mews-icale' direction job pretty well during the mock rehearsal," Temple noted.

"And every darn note off-key."

"That being the point of a distraction."

Molina held firm. "No armed and aurally dangerous cats invited this time without wearing white tie."

24
Altared Circumstances

Here I sit, a Member of the Wedding, but the lowest, literally, and the last.

I again am confined in a zebra-print carrier. Out of sight behind a pot of chrysanthemums that make me sneeze. On the floor in front of the reinstated altar, only this time everything is for real.

My neck is again circled by a black collar sporting a white bow tie.

I deserve more respect. I am bearing a lot of gold and diamonds today. You would think they could spare a few diamond collar studs for the occasion, after I have saved the day, *this* day, in two fashions.

First, I am still fuming over sacrificing myself to be an object of ridicule by the terminally annoying Crawford Buchanan, whose piece of Yellow Journalism mocked my Ring Bearer role so successfully that a gang of nearly deaf and blind and media-moronic, heavily armed crooks got the idea to try to knock over the faux wedding rehearsal, *and* the church altar, and got caught.

In addition, anticipating possible criminal matters, I organized (in the literal sense of the word) an unexpected performance in the organ loft by my personally picked cat chorus, which was pitch perfect in assaulting human ears.

Granted, all persons present were equally driven a bit squirrelly by the sounds, but my friends were expecting some sort of invasion and were better prepared to press on despite the ear-piercing diversion. And hard-of-hearing thieves require a full operatic assault.

Anyway, if I were not indignant I might succumb to something worse, sentiment. My kind has to be strong enough to walk the mean streets from an early age, to prepare for a sudden sundering from family and clowder at the swipe of a speeding car or the jaws of rogue canine or capture and a long, fruitless stay in a shelter cage. The lucky ones will find a loyal and considerate human partner. I have done that, but am feeling a bit crotchety over a possible changing of the guard.

My Miss Temple's father is not the only dude here giving away the bride.

I reserve my right to pout, and never undertake such a traumatic role again.

Something black and fluffy sideswipes the black mesh side of my container.

"Do not worry, Pop," says Miss Midnight Louise. "I will never leave you."

I do not know whether to be consoled, or horrified.

I hear my roommate's voice echoing from underneath the organ loft's projection.

"It will be fine, Mom. Electra will arrange my train after everyone is seated and then run down the side aisle to her chosen pew on the central aisle, so she can still get photos.

"And the Phoenix wedding photographer will cover the entire ceremony from every angle. Once the Fontana brothers have seated you all, Dad and I will nod to cue the wedding march and will move slowly forward."

"You have chosen an oddly named song, Temple. 'Love Minus Zero-No Limit.' What does that even mean?"

"Unconditional love. You will hear it in the words during the procession. You know, by the famous Minnesotan, Bob Dylan. His words sing and the melodies are grand."

"Not to worry, Mrs. B," comes Danny Dove's assuring stage director's voice. "Every step will proceed with the precision of a cuckoo clock Maypole dance, I guarantee it."

"But, as Mother of the Bride, I am to go first," Karen objects. Like her daughter, she is tiny, red-headed, and stubborn.

"Not to worry," Danny repeats as I hear his quick steps waltzing her into place. "That is why I have given you the most reliable and suave Fontana brother as an escort, Julio."

"Oh," Miss Mrs. Karen says with a pleased lilt in her voice. Fontana brothers tend to have that effect on females of any species, age, and state in life." She adds, sounding relieved. "That was most thoughtful of you to keep it in the family, Danny. We are privileged to have such a Las Vegas star managing our little wedding."

"We are all family at the Crystal Phoenix, my dear Karen. For a Mother of the Bride who looks like the bride's sister today, I would do anything."

Miss Mrs. Karen sighs. I cannot tell whether she is impatient or flattered.

Danny goes on. "Then the order is the Matron of Honor alone, Miss Kit. Flower Girl, Miss Crescent. The Ring Bearer will be borne to join the party at the altar."

"So then," I hear Miss Temple's voice. "Last but not least, Dad and I march down the aisle and then Dad peels off my left side—"

That sounds a bit gory to my ears.

"—to sit beside you, Mom, on the first pew allocated on 'our' side. Alone, I mount the four shallow steps to the altar and make my Vanna White train-whipping turn. Every fold will fall into place perfectly, with Aunt Kit, my most 'un' matronly Matron of Honor already waiting on my right side, and Crescent joining her. Matt and his Best Man, Frank Bucek, having come from the right side of the altar, are waiting for me. Father Hernandez holds the middle ground."

"It sounds like a football play," Roger Barr grumbles, "with my little girl in the middle of a scrimmage. If I do not trip on that foolish train I deserve a Most Valuable Player award."

"Gosh, Dad," my Miss Temple says, "everything goes out over the mic. Remember, we are being taped."

"It is my ribs that will be taped if you do not wrangle that five feet of train well. All that filmy white stuff kinda looks like you stepped on a roll of toilet tissue That Time Forgot."

"*Dad!*" But she is laughing. "Play nice. This is your only time at bat."

Oddly, those are sobering words to me. If I were inclined to think I was on anybody's mind right now, this is my only and last time "at bat" too. It was one thing to act as Ring Bearer for Mr. Matt's sadly mistreated Mama after she found true love in midlife, but now I am doing it for my own fate-chosen roommate.

Ah, the times we have had together, when I ripped the face off an assailant and she cradled me and praised my sharp claws and velvety little ears. The times when my place of pride on her zebra-stripped coverlet with the red piping so reminiscent of my best dueling scars was shifted aside for an interloper of her species.

Luckily, there were not many such of those occasions. At least she is choosier than Ma Barker before her recent involuntary celestial conversion.

And now my Miss Temple has committed the terminal human sin against my kind. She has chosen a dude of her kind over me, forever and ever, amen.

Hmmph. Forget zebra-striped anything. I get custody of the faux goat hair area rug and the TV remote.

Watch me and weep.

25
Here Comes the Bride

Temple stood at the back of the church, her right arm hooked onto her father's left one clad in a his new tuxedo jacket.

He winked at her.

Behind her, her mother, Karen, and Matt's mother, Mira, fluttered in tandem at the fringes of Temple's ankle-length hem, then her fluid filmy train, then the "fingertip" length Illusion lace veil that arched like a thunderhead cloud from the crown of her head, giving her—*hallelujah!*—that so deeply desired attribute, height.

As did the diamond dazzle of the Midnight Louie Stuart Weitzman Austrian crystal-studded pumps on her feet.

Aunt Kit, Matron of Honor, flitted in front of her, fingernails fluffing the mounded red-gold curls atop her head, teased into giving her *height*. She last fluffed the longer side curls framing Temple's face and shoulders.

Kit sighed. "You are so perfectly Audrey Hepburn in *Breakfast at Tiffany's,* my dear. If she'd been a redhead. Or worn a wedding dress."

The real Audrey Hepburn had worn such a gown in her real life, Balmain in the fifties. High neck, long tight sleeves. She'd starved as a child in Europe during World War Two, this elfin actress. She probably hated her bony frame, even as it became ultra fashionable and thrived when the post-War fashion world went to emaciated models, like Audrey and Twiggy and Kate Moss.

Temple, always the cultural cataloguer, was happy to celebrate and share Audrey's forever girlish style. Little women, the title of an iconic girl's book by Louisa May Alcott for almost two centuries, could grow up to do very big good things. Audrey and her charity work for UNICEF, being one example.

The organist began an introduction.

Temple checked the three wrist buttons of her elbow-length white satin ruffle-topped gloves. She would have to undo them during the ceremony so Matt could slip the wedding rings, diamond guards and the engagement ring, on her finger and she put his gold band on in turn.

She liked that the process involved legerdemain. Some silly hidden tradition. She was beginning to appreciate church ritual.

"Oh, if only I could get married again," her Matron of Honor whispered.

"That was just months ago, Kit."

"I'd waited almost a lifetime for Aldo."

Temple took a deep breath. A bride knows when she has embarked on the right lifetime. She knows when she has found the exact ritual gown for the journey.

Aunt Kit knew too.

The gown was a halter-style, cut away at the shoulders, but demurely filled in over the chest. The stunner was a high elegant neck ruffle to the chin, too frilly to be Victorian and framing Temple's face and hair. The fabric lines gathered tight at the breastbone in front and under the bare shoulder blades in back, and then flared with the grace of a Greek statue to the ankle-length in front like a ballerina's skirt. The back pooled into a loose liquid cataract of embroidered and crystal-studded silk ending in a long, airy white train.

The style was girlish, yet subtle and elegant. Not pretentious, but pure of line. It was perfect for a short woman, it was perfect for a sincere woman. It was perfect for her.

"If I'd had a daughter," Kit whispered. "I could not be more proud. Thank you for sharing your wedding moments with me. My sister Karen behind you is so choked up with Minnesota stoicism she can't say this herself, but I'm sure she's as blown away as your bridegroom will be."

Wow. Temple looked down the long crimson carpet and along all the pew-ends draped in flowers, candelabra, and white silk falls of petals, and the backs of familiar heads to the small, all-masculine group waiting at the end of her march. Father Hernandez in shining satin vestments, the men in silver-gray white tie and tails, the edge of a zebra-print carrier visible behind Eduardo's shiny black-patent formal slipper, stationed at the first pew on the right.

Matt's blond head blazed like a candle flame in the dark-of-evening nave of the stained glass-crowned church.

A Fontana brother, princely in mien…but Temple was suddenly too throbbing with stage fight to identify him specifically, darn it… offered her mother his arm.

Practical Karen was a vision in a jade-green silk suit topped, for the first and probably last time in her life, by a totally frivolous veiled hat that tilted over her crown of silver-and-red curls, marched down the aisle for real.

Beside Temple, her father sighed to observe Karen's dainty erect figure. Temple glanced over to see his own wedding replaying with pride in his eyes.

Kit pranced solo down the aisle, sizzling as always in an orange organza ballerina-length gown that thumbed its nose at her well-maintained red hair. No envisioned lilac for her, but Totally Kit.

Little blonde Crescent in yellow organdy frills and black patent leather Mary Jane shoes went last, scattering white rose petals on the red aisle runner.

And then the full-throated church organ played the song Temple had first heard Matt playing on the little Hammond organ in Electra's wedding chapel, "Love Minus Zero, No Limit". And she heard a mother and daughter in the choir loft singing counterpoint, entwining the lyrics from the organ melody in a way that spelled Harmony with a capital H.

She scanned so many familiar backs and heads in the pews—Electra had brought her soft-sculpture Elvis from her Lovers' Knot wedding chapel, she noticed. All of them blended through her loving gaze into a soft-focus blur. What terrific friends and relations she and Matt had, Temple thought.

She smiled at her father, slightly sweating brow and all, and stepped forward into the rest, and the best, of her life.

26
The Wedding Party Party

Well, somebody here must keep his eyes undimmed, his ears unstoppered and his powers of observation unsullied.

You will notice that there is only one captive observer in this candlelight and silver silk crowd.

It is not that I expect additional mayhem. No, now that the real wedding ceremony is finally in gear, I am panting in expectation of nauseatingly prolonged versions of what Hollywood has made famous. "After the Main Event parties."

For weddings, these are called receptions and will include the wedding party and all the invited guests here in the church. Nicky and Van will surely make the red carpet installed on the church aisle look like an amateur operation when it comes to the "Red Carpet" treatment at their Crystal Phoenix.

For days, I have been an unwilling confident on all the details of The Dress, The Wedding Procession, The Vows, The Kisses, The Reception, The Going-Away.

Amazingly, there is not a Coming Back celebration. That is the status I am really interested in.

So nothing here can surprise me...except a little something I glimpsed among the empty pews as I was carted up to the altar by a Fontana brother in advance of anyone else involved in the main event. No processions for me. Just a crude, caged presence in place, and then left last to be carried out.

I have sacrificed much of my dignity and free will, not to mention a bathroom break, to stand up for and beside my roommate on her day. I have had to crouch in this silly zebra-striped carrier wearing a white bow tie with a small white box affixed to it by a red ribbon. (I must admit that white and red are my best colors, at least.)

I hunker down and prepare for unbridled droning. At least the Jackhammer mob wedding crashers offered some fresh "optics" to the rehearsal and commanded a lot of buzz at the rehearsal dinner, to which I was not invited, much to my relief.

Once Eduardo released me while he did most of the work: opening the ring box and passing up the rings, he lifted me up for photo and filming ops. I held my head extra high for a full view of the white formal bow-tie and so no regrettable double chins should show. I gazed serenely on my subjects. I accepted Miss Temple's cheek-to-cheek pose with Mr. Matt hovering above.

I did not break a sweat. This was the matter of a minute or two and earned a bit of applause among the congregation, which Father Hernandez frowned upon.

At last I am forgotten and returned to my cat cave at Best Man Frank Bucek's feet, where I hear the vows, etcetera, while thoroughly grooming my face, mitts, chest hairs and everything else I can reach that has been ruffled by the formalities. I am longing for free rein.

So has the audience, evidently…I mean congregation, I guess. Suddenly, they have been liberated.

Everyone penned into the pews stands and crowds to the aisle to take pictures. Flashes twinkle in the interior twilight. Most people hold their cell phones at arm's length, but I recognize some expensive cameras and camcorders. A hired professional photographer darts like a madwoman on the fringes.

I finally see my Miss Temple's precious train as she marches out on Mr. Matt's arm to the organ and a rousing solo by Miss Carmen. Why is it called a "train" rather than a "tail"? That is so misleading. I envisioned something like a clacking chain of those cans one sees tied behind honeymooners' getaway cars.

No. This train is a sumptuous graceful plume of gleaming white silk, much like the terminal member of my lost love, the Divine Yvette. I *knew* my Miss Temple would have been a dainty purebred shaded-silver Persian, had she been fortunate enough to be born a cat.

I am lost in reminiscence, regret, and admiration. I am so fixated, I notice when Mr. Matt hesitates and whispers to my Miss Temple who looks at a side aisle.

In that moment, I remember that "some little *thing*" I spotted in the back pews as I was carried in, that I was not free to investigate… until now.

A bright flash from that very location has my hackles bristling. The bridal party members at the altar are moving into the aisle to follow the couple, so I lose sight of my erstwhile roommate's divine new tail anyway. I dig my pitons into crimson carpet and rocket out ahead of the procession. Flashes triple in number as people *ooh* and *aah* and laugh and blink at my rushing to the head of the queue. It is a long, long way. I am a rocket cat…

I dive into a pew, all sixteen shivs and four dew-claw scythes out and into the body crouching there.

"YEEEOWWW!"

That is not *my* battle cry, it is what my prey hollers. Something springs up into full view…and the immediate custody of a deuce of Fontana brothers that appears as if beamed there by the Starship *Enterprise* just as the wedded couple march up.

"Crawford Buchanan," my outraged Miss Temple IDs the lurker. "You crashed my wedding. I knew you were low, but I did not know you were that low."

Between two Fontana boys, Crawfish Pukecannon, looks punier than ever, and he is now wearing his graying hair in that trendy Asian topknot you see on men appearing on TV martial arts and celebrity dance TV shows. The ubiquitous man bun! I hope Mr. Matt will not have to affect such a hairdo on his new talk show!

My hair is always impeccably clean and buzz-cut and timelessly elegant in the manner of black velveteen.

My Miss Temple's new Mister glowers down at the guy. "So you are the rival PR guy. I have heard plenty about the dirty tricks you played on my wife. You are leaving here now, quietly, without any recording device on your person."

Meanwhile, the organist has amped up the music to cover the conversation. Mr. Matt nods at the brothers and swoops his bride back into a graceful departing pace, everyone following.

I remain to enjoy the sight of the brothers turning Crawford upside down and shaking until his wallet, cell phone, car keys, nail clipper, mascara wand, allergy inhaler…*mascara*? Duh. Well, he *is* noted for his deep radio-deejay voice and long silky Daddy Longlegs eyelashes.

A third Fontana brother bends to sweep his belongings into a shallow woven collection basket. The three Fontana brothers hustle Buchanan out, discreetly, to the parking lot.

I am not about to make a scene at my roommate's wedding— any more, that is—and amble unnoted outside to the church steps.

I am just in time to weave my way to the first row of assembled ankles and find everyone looking up.

The wedded couple pause and do likewise to see what I see... two matched white doves spiraling up and up over the gaping crowd.

Oh, sure, they look graceful and lovely-dovey, all right, but I would not gaze upward without my mouth shut. Birds do manufacture something called "droppings". I have heard these ceremonial birds are really white carrier pigeons and that makes sense, because they fly away home to shock and awe another day. But pigeons are the most notorious droppers of all.

Several more white birds of bridal paradise join the first pair, to a concerted *aaaah*, their fluttering wings producing the sound of paper caught in a fan. Me, I would only drop my jaw in this instance to make a heroic leap at dinner.

It is not lost on me that this display may be a last good wish from Mr. Max Kinsella.

As I am musing on the quaint ways of humans when it comes to winning and losing the mating game, I sense a sudden impending doom.

A fourth Fontana brother out of nowhere bends down from behind to sweep me into the open maw of the zebra-striped carrier.

So with a parting hiss at the vanished Crawford Buchanan, I gently go into that dark night. I am sure such a prominent member of the wedding as the Ring Bearer will be feted at the Crystal Phoenix reception.

27
Lofty Endings

The church was empty and silent. The choir loft organ was silenced. The organist en route to the reception. Only one person lingered in front of the huge organ, brushing the keys as if debating playing.

"You can come out now," the hesitant organist said. The sing-song tone used in kiddie games of Hide and Seek sounded come-hither in Lieutenant C. R. Molina's rich contralto voice.

Max swept a red velvet curtain aside as if tossing off a cloak and let it fall back behind him.

"All in black," Molina observed. "For a funeral, not a wedding? You look like a cat burglar matador. I've been wondering whether you're the 'something old' or 'something blue' for our recent bride."

"I'm not singing the blues like you do, believe me."

"I seldom do believe you."

She, meanwhile, finished hiking up her long crimson velvet skirt to pull a compact pistol from her ankle holster, clasped above a forties-style magenta platform sandal.

Max owed his shoe sense to living with Temple, so he felt like he was eyeing the cover of a dime pulp detective novel, except the gun was a sleek modern Walther.

The ankle wasn't bad either, escaping its usual prison of navy or khaki boot-cut slacks.

Eyebrows could use plucking, according to Temple as well.

"Your voice on the wedding march was in even better form the second time," Max said, stepping away from the convenient red velvet curtains bracketing the church organ, now no longer the stage for a feline love-in howl. "You have the alto undercurrent to make that Dylan song rock."

He ran a hand over the curve of the organ's side as he came around it into view. "What a magnificent instrument," he said. "Phenomenal wood-carving and brass pipes to die for, speaking of your voice as well."

"And speaking of *your* 'brass'..." She slipped the weapon into her sequined envelop purse from the forties. "Going next to the reception, are we?"

"You think I should?"

"It was a shame I was stuck up here in the choir loft when you pulled your bride-napping stunt up at the altar at the fake rehearsal yesterday. Frank Bucek neglected to forewarn me. You almost had me fooled. It flashed through my mind that I should plug you for Matt Devine's sake. It's risky to leave the one person always armed out of the loop."

"That *was* a risk," he admitted. "A last-minute distraction I suggested to Bucek."

Max grinned. "The way you rushed the loft railing, braced your hands on it, aimed at me and shouted, 'This is not happening on my watch' was so authentic, the attending bad guys fell for my bride-swiping act at once."

"Only on TV." She looked at the deserted scene of decorous ceremony below, a candlelit still life. "I believed you'd do it. Swing down like Tarzan and then swing the bride up and away, Quasimodo whisking Esmeralda the Gypsy girl to the top tower of Notre Dame. You always had that corny movie swashbuckler air."

"Thank you." Max gave a small, mannered European bow.

"And shouting that you'd recovered your memory, that Temple mustn't marry Matt. Really Vegas Strip encore quality."

"Rather riveting, if I say so myself."

"The faux Temple seemed actually stunned, stunned into inaction as you'd planned, as you swooped her away from the oncoming thieves on a hope and a bungee cord. The famous *The Graduate* movie climax all over again. 'Cli*max*', get it?"

"Sadly, yes. Dustin Hoffman snatching bride Katherine Ross from the altar. They used a bus, though."

"Definitely too pedestrian. Too bad Merry Su wasn't Temple Barr, but I bet you could get a date with Detective Su now. You knew Temple would hear it up here, of course."

"I'd promised Temple that if I ever recovered my memory, *our* memories, I'd tell her at once."

"So have you?"

"Told her anything more or recovered my memories? No. And I was too busy with thugs after getting her safely into your ex-squeeze's arms off stage. Rafi's a good man in a pinch. You should be nicer to him."

"Don't distract me."

"Distract you?" Max stepped closer. "I never thought of that. You might have a concealed holster elsewhere under that floor-length gown."

"And no desire to arrest you now. For what? To ruin so many decent people's sense of ordinary happiness?"

She slapped lightly at his shoulder. He was six-four. She was maybe five-ten and now wearing vintage five-inch platform heels to be visible in the choir loft. They were well matched for wrestling. And she was maybe enjoying playing the femme fatale off the nightclub stage for once. For real.

Max stepped away, suddenly. "If I had anything to report for reasons other than a desperate ruse, it would be for me to tell Temple and only Temple. And I'd be a cad to do that even if I did recover my memories of our relationship. So…that's for me to know and you to find out, as they say, in whatever way you can use. Lieutenant. Or Carmen."

She laughed, then clapped a hand over her mouth, remembering the serious vows recently said below.

"If you don't want to be the ghost at the real wedding, Mr. Kinsella, I suggest you've seen enough, and should leave before somebody lingering from the happy departing wedding party spots you."

"Just wanted to recognize your stunning vocal performance." He looked one last time over the railing, as if to memorize the scene. "The perfect preface to a wedding, a hidden treasure found under the altar. Symbolic somehow."

"Could be Fool's Gold. It will take a while to total how much is there. I don't know how long. I'm just a humble wedding singer."

"It was generous to do that for Temple and Matt. And just think, from what I hear, your enormously talented daughter is growing up and getting ready to sing at *your* wedding."

"Life moves on," she said, tilting her head.

He nodded. "We all have to leave our pasts like a train of flowers and tears trailing behind us. Best to gather up the petals and leave the rest behind."

And then Max Kinsella was gone, just as she'd opened her mouth to reply, because his words, unintentionally, reminded her she'd never had a wedding of her own, nor ever expected to—

And the pang of that realization cut deeper than she'd ever dreamed, and she heard the microphone-magnified vows drift up again. *I, Temple, take thee, Matthias....* Father Hernandez *would* use the full formal disciple's name, Old Latin-mass-saying stick-in-the-mud. Perhaps, sooner than she'd think, she'd be here like this for Mariah.

And, sadly, it had felt like Molina was losing a welcome thorn in her side, and gaining another daughter as her eyes became a wavering screen.

It was a wedding, dammit, and people, even cops, were entitled to get mushy.

"Mom?"

Mariah, sweetly attired in a violet dress halfway between teen and Grammy fashion maven, stood at the top of the choir loft stairs. "Rafi's waiting to drive us home."

She would never call him "Dad", thanks to the past and the limited role her mother had allowed him in their lives.

Carmen regretted that more than she could say.

But hey, Mariah accepted him as mentor and friend and the one person she was fiercely afraid to disappoint, and maybe that was even better.

"We sang well. I think," Mariah said. "You really knocked the recessional out of the roof."

"Thanks, *chica*." Carmen put an arm around her daughter's shoulders. Wowsa, Mariah was going to be tall like her mother and her undiscovered maternal grandfather, certainly.

It would be good to look ahead to standing shoulder to shoulder.

28
Purple Heart

The Crystal Phoenix had prepared a sparkling, extravagant reception area where everyone awaited the bride and groom. Temple held her breath at the sight. Matt's parents, all three, her parents. Her four brothers, wearing suits, could she believe? With kids in tow. Van and Nicky, her perfect bosses. And Tony Valentine and assistant Danielle. All the Circle Ritz residents and Electra. Carmen Molina, now wearing a snazzy black outfit with Mariah and Rafi. Letitia and Dave from *WCOO*. My gosh, Courtney!

Courtney dipped at the knees to embrace Temple. "I'm so proud I was able to help you be so beautiful. Perhaps we could have a copy of the formal portrait for the shop?"

Kit whisked Temple to a private room to divest her of the train and fountain of veiling, leaving only the Lover's Knot headpiece.

"And the gloves," Temple said. "They're so elegant."

"Ah, you look so lovely pared down, m'dear. Audrey Hepburn revisited. You'll tire of those gloves. They're a pain to eat and drink in."

"Well…maybe I shouldn't risk them getting dirty."

"Did you see? In the Church. During the recessional?" she whispered to Matt during the bridal couple's first dance alone on the floor.

"I didn't see much, except for you."

"Your mother. She met your father, Jonathon, at a side altar as the bridal party marched out. They lit a candle to Our Lady of Guadalupe together. I'm sure the pro photographer got the shot. She's good. Gets the unexpected moment."

"It'll be wonderful to have that in the wedding album," Matt agreed.

"And we'll send an album to all the older-generation attendees."

"So they'll each have a copy."

Temple nodded.

"You never stop making people more than they can be," he said, sweeping her into a swell of waltz music. "Are we doing this all right?"

"Are you kidding, Mr. Celebrity Dance contestant?"

"We've had a bad review." He glanced at Mariah in her Purple Rain finery.

"Teens, always so critical," Temple said. "Wait until Zoe Chloe Ozone shows up in TV clips."

They laughed and at that moment...cousin Krys came up to them.

"You made it," Temple said, startled.

"Yeah. They said an extra ticket would be okay."

"Better than okay," Matt said, embracing her and kissing her cheek. "So good to see you, Krys. You look great."

"You too," Krys said, a little too crushingly. She turned to Temple. "Good show. Some Ultra Violet gel nail polish for the ring thing would have been a major pop, but you really got your girl on."

"Thanks," Temple said, shaking her head as Krys moved on. "One dedicated fanatic already."

As the dance music stopped, everyone applauded, and Tony Valentine stepped onto the empty dance floor. Tall, crowned by dazzling white hair, patrician, he brought the happy buzz to absolute silence.

"My name is Tony Valentine, and I'm here to give out some valentines. I'm here to toast the future of this lovely couple." He raised a champagne flute as everyone present with one to flaunt mimicked his gesture. "And to announce that they will be staying in

Las Vegas, after a suitable honeymoon elsewhere, to head up their own syndicated television talk show."

Gasps. Buzz. Applause, applause. Smiles.

"The Crystal Phoenix will deeply miss Temple Barr," Nicky Fontana stepped forward to say, "but we have always been her fans and will follow her to assured triumph in her new career. And," he added, "I think Mr. Valentine has another heart up his sleeve."

Tony stepped back into the spotlight. "Also, I wish to announce that another beloved personality at the Crystal Phoenix is stepping into the limelight."

There was a pause. Two waiters carried a linen-clad dining table to the center of the dance floor.

A purple velvet pillow was imported to the table by Aldo Fontana, who fluffed it.

Eduardo carried in a zebra-stripe cat carrier and deposited it on a white velvet dining chair Ralph placed center stage.

Chef Song, the executive chef whose white cap was far higher than Tony Valentine's natural Lyle Lovett-style pompadour, placed a simple low bowl on the table.

Something savory was heaped therein.

Eduardo unzipped the carrier with a dramatic gesture.

Midnight Louie poked out his jet-black nose, surveyed the room left and right, up and down, sniffed the zipper edge and the tablecloth edge, wrinkled his nose and jumped onto the purple velvet pillow. Cameras and cell phones clicked and flashed.

Nicky Fontana stepped forward again. "From a humble start as a homeless stray on the Crystal Phoenix grounds, Midnight Louie has captured our regard for his transition from a canny yet perhaps desperate wanderer to a productive resident guardian welcome wherever he goes.

"He is small, but fierce."

Midnight Louie sat, leaned forward to inhale the aura of the single exquisite bowl, nodded, and proceeded to lap and chomp the contents. Right in front of Chef Song. It was not koi, but it was exquisite seafood. He would endorse nothing else.

"The first bowl of Á La Cat International Chef tidbits," Tony said to applause, "and there will be a ground-breaking commercial series featuring Crystal Phoenix favorites Miss Temple Barr and Mr. Midnight Louie, Esquire."

A roar went up from the crowd.

Miss Temple came to pose cheek to cheek again with Louie. She lifted her leg and ankle bearing Midnight Louie Austrian crystal pump to the center of the white velvet pillow on the chair as cameras and films captured every image and wolf-whistles abounded...

Midnight Louie burped. He opened a heavy-lidded eye. He seemed to be on the floor, in his carrier, behind an uninspired hotel convention tablecloth of burgundy linen.

Had he been dreaming?

29
Reception Deception

Matt and Temple, a bit worn from the festivities, had escaped the reception to stand in a small wood-paneled library with a bar so discreet no barman waited to serve them.

The "them" included Max's bewildered parents all the way from Racine. And another Racine couple, his aunt Eileen and her husband Patrick Kelly.

Temple took quick mental notes to match with her Skype impressions.

Kevin Kinsella was tall like his son, thick black hair dramatically streaked with white. Max's mother, petite Maura, had deep-mahogany red hair Temple envied. It gave her presence. Gravitas. No one would ever dare call her "carrot-top" or "cute". Her sister Eileen's similar color hair was feathered all over with white, like wedding cake frosting.

"You're a lovely young couple," Eileen Kelly said.

"And it was a fine Catholic wedding in a beautiful church," Maura added. "The Spanish style is stunning. But Eileen and I and our husbands, the Kinsellas and the Kellys, don't know why we're both here, except for an even more-than-usual rare and cryptic message with the wedding invitation that this 'Private Reception' is courtesy of our literally prodigal son, Michael."

Matt exchanged glances with Temple, both of them startled to hear Max's real first name used.

These sets of parents resided in a sixteen-year time warp. One pair had grudgingly accepted the puzzle of a long absent son, one had become long reconciled to having a dead son.

Matt cleared his throat. "Michael Aloysius Xavier Kinsella. We know him as 'Max.'"

The two sets of parents blinked for a moment to translate the string of given names to "MAX."

Kevin Kinsella answered. "Michael or Max, we thought this was some crazy 'surprise' and we'd end up really being at *his* wedding."

Temple felt a pang echoed by Matt's sudden pressure on her hand.

Once it could have been. For a few surreal, crazy moments yesterday it had been.

"I'm sorry," Temple said. "Yes, magicians love surprises, but that would have been cruel. This is as gentle as we could think to make it, since we know Max and you don't know us.

"You saw our names on Skype, on the wedding invitation. You know I'm Temple Barr, a public relations freelancer, and the Crystal Phoenix is my best and most prestigious client.

"My husband"—first such reference!—"Matt Devine is a syndicated radio show counselor and we're about to go national with a TV talk show."

"Most impressive, young woman." Kevin Kinsella leaned back into the goose down cushions. "But what do TV celebrities have to do with us or our AWOL son? We were deceived into hoping for a reunion."

"To have come all this way, no matter how lovely and festive the occasion…" Maura's voice began to shake.

"Oh," Temple pled, "we have such good news for you all. Please let us take our time with it. We don't want to shock you."

Eileen stepped forward. "And you have affixed these family matters of strangers to your own wedding? Why?"

"Simple," Temple said, stepping forward to meet her, "my and Matt's work, our hearts are committed to being good with people, and you, dear people, have been living under a cloud of well-meant misconception for almost two decades."

"You certainly are direct," Patrick Kelly said.

"I'll be more direct." Matt went behind the bar. "There's some world-class Irish Whiskey here. I understand your families' separate devastating losses have caused a breech between the sisters and their husbands. How about a toast to new understanding? Also, we have a toothsome nonalcoholic champagne for anyone, and especially Father Hernandez, when he comes along."

"He's—?"

"One of the finest and dedicated priests I've known. And I've known many. I used to be one."

Jaws dropped.

Keeping separate, but edging forward like newborn zombies, the couples approached opposite ends of the bar to accept the Irish "water of life", pronounced 'whiskey' in Gaelic, in glittering Baccarat glasses.

Kevin sipped the straight drink the color of his wife's hair. "Now *you* are *my* kind of 'Whiskey Priest'," he said, turning an insult into a compliment.

Matt smiled. "I'm afraid I'm Polish, but I do envy the Irish their humor, their heart, their dash."

"Are you Irish Catholic?" Eileen asked Temple, eyeing her red hair, which the Phoenix's beauty salon had styled into a dazzling sunset cloud. Temple never wanted to sleep on it again and lose the effect, but that would be rather counter-intuitive on a wedding night.

"I'm an Anglo-Celtic mutt, but am I Catholic? No."

"Not even *Lutheran*?" Maura asked.

"No. I'm not Lutheran, although I'm from Minnesota and realize the Catholics and the Lutherans are not fond of each other." These sixty-something couples would know that rivalry well.

"Episcopal then!" Eileen was sure. "She seemed at home with the liturgy," she told her husband Patrick.

"No." Temple was amused.

"What then?"

"Besides my wife?" Matt put in.

"I'm UU." Temple waited.

"UU? Is that for a Utah University?" Patrick wondered.

"Well, my parents are out at the reception, and are Unitarian Universalists, but I appear to have fallen away some."

"'Unitarian Universalists' are that all-of-everything equally church," Kevin said. "How can you fall away from nothing?"

Temple shrugged. "It avoided a lot of angst."

"UU," Maura mused. "That's why you wouldn't object to a Catholic wedding ceremony."

"No. My only ceremonial requirement was a train as long as I am tall, five feet."

"That was *indeed* an impressive train," Eileen agreed.

"And your gown was lovely and very modest, like a nice Catholic girl's." Maura beamed at Matt.

"Let's face it," Temple said, glancing down. "I haven't got much to be modest about."

"She has an Irish sense of humor," said Kevin.

Eileen sipped thoughtfully. "You two keep treating this occasion as a celebration. And it is, obviously, for you. But you keep trying to pull us into it. We're all strangers to you."

"I do want you all involved," Matt admitted, taking Temple a tall crystal flute of Father Hernandez's champagne. "I've married the love of my life, we've got the job offer of a lifetime, and I've been honored to be asked to officiate, by Michael/Max, as an ex-priest and a counselor who learns more than he informs, over the correction of a tragic family…disintegration."

He had poured another Jameson's and now went to the coffered door, balancing the precious Baccarat glass on his palm like a butler.

"Presenting the world-renowned Mystifying Max, magician, counterterrorism agent and prodigal son."

Max stepped through door on cue in his borrowed Fontana brother silver-gray tuxedo. It was always a performance with Max, Temple thought. A pose that kept him one step removed from that act of terrorist violence that had changed everything in his life.

"My God." Maura stepped toward him, her right hand reaching for what must have seemed a mirage. "You're the image of Kevin when I married him." She covered her mouth with the other hand as her eyes floated in sudden tears and she swallowed a sob.

Kevin quickly stepped between her and their son, partly to shield her emotional meltdown, partly in anger. "Explain yourself, Michael. Your mother always understood your grief at Sean's loss, but you didn't understand the depth of hers, with you growing so distant, almost the same as dead, from the family. An occasional postcard from Europe with a performance venue pictured on it. We understood survivor's guilt, but not the lengths you took."

Max took the drink from Matt's hand. "They told me," he nodded at Matt and Temple, "that telling you would be my moment of penance. If I only had to explain just my seventeen-year-old self. I'll start there."

He looked at Eileen and Patrick apologetically and sighed.

"You were so right to worry. Sean and I were stupid kids who did exactly what you four 'stuffy' parents warned us not to do on our high school graduation trip to the old country. We scooted right up to Northern Ireland to view the Troubles firsthand. And drink even more beer without being carded."

As the parents stirred and prepared to condemn the risk, Max gestured them to be seated.

"Please sit down." Temple indicate two roomy loveseats set at right angles around a large travertine coffee table equipped with crystal coasters. Each couple took a sofa as Max's narrative continued.

"Yes, we promised that we, with our good grades and love of family history, would benefit from seeing the Old Country before we moved on to college. They call it a 'Gap' year now.

"It was all innocent stupidity." Max advanced into the room, looking at his mother. "It's such a strange thing, Mom. America is a melting pot, yet we all still cling to our ethnic origins." He looked around, "Irish being a common one, but Polish as well." He nodded at Matt.

"To be seventeen having your first look at an another country, an island, among people who look exactly like you, speak with the same lilt, drink the same ale, laugh at the same jokes...to feel at home so far away from home. It was inebriating. We courted the colleens. The black Irish and the red-haired girls who seemed so exotic and yet familiar at the same time. Far more interesting than our American high school girls. Besides, we'd gone to all-boys' high school with the Christian Brothers.

"We competed to drink ourselves under the table, we competed to spirit a girl away from the pub to…wherever. We met one stunner of a Black Irish rose. Older, early twenties, but so much the better. We wanted to win her to ourselves to sample whatever undescribed bliss that had been cruelly hidden from us."

Max shrugged. "I won. A hollow victory. The pub bomb exploded while I was 'off-campus'. But that was not the only bomb that day. The other bomb that exploded my life was one Kathleen O'Connor, as damaged a young woman as had lived through the hell of Magdalene laundries called "asylums", where young pregnant girls were overworked and abused for being victims of institutionalized ignorance and family assault."

"Oh," Eileen breathed rather than said. "That Judi Dench movie *Philomena*." She rose and went to sit beside Maura on the Kinsella-occupied couch. They looked at each other for a long moment before Maura reached out for Eileen's hands.

"Philomena?" Patrick asked. "I had a nun named that in eighth grade. We never saw any such movie, Eileen." He glanced at the sisters' twined hands. "And you two haven't been so cozy since— He eyed Kevin with a question in his eyes.

"We went to the movie theater on our own. Together. Last year." Maura spoke defiantly, smiling through her tears.

"It was a true story, about a young unwed mother named Philomena. Her toddler son was adopted out to America, for money, from one of those merciless homes named after Saint Mary Magdalene. Not a newborn, a two-year-old! Can you imagine the lasting severed bond? Remembering each other, lies to both kept them apart for decades, never again meeting. At least Philomena finally learned her son's fate. He'd died in the prime of life and had asked to be buried at the Magdalene institution graveyard, in case his mother ever came looking for him. So she did find him at last."

Of course, Temple thought, they would go to see *Philomena* together alone, almost furtively, women who had lost sons at the same time from the same brutal event. Sisters who had carried on with guarded emotions and doubt and self-doubt and subtle estrangement.

Temple knew the movie's plot and wasn't watching the women. She was watching Max. He downed the remaining three fingers of whiskey in his glass in one heroic go. Set the expensive crystal down with a thump on the long table behind the couch, and came around it to kneel in front of the weeping women, covering their entwined hands with his large ones. Head bowed, voice raw, he whispered, "Bless me, Mothers, for I have sinned."

During the long silence punctuated by the women's sobs, everyone kept stone-still. Matt caught Temple's glance returning to him, and pulled her closer.

"I know," she whispered. "You've heard that beginning sentence in a lot of Confessions. 'Bless me, Father, for I have sinned'. Would you have ever dreamed you'd hear it paraphrased by Max?"

Matt shook his head. "It will do him good. And it's the perfect way to apologize to this crowd."

"And sinned again." Max went on, sitting back on his heels.

"What is this?" Kevin sounded uneasily gruff. "An Irish wake? More whisky and less tears. What's done is done." He eyed his son. "So what more are we to learn, Michael, that we have an unsuspected grandchild somewhere?"

Max was able to discharge his deep emotion in a shaky laugh. "Not that. No. Sorry." He rose and sat on the huge square coffee table's edge. "There's still a lot more story to come, though. We Irish love telling and hearing stories."

Temple retrieved his glass and went to Matt, already holding the Jamison's bottle. He cocked his eyebrows as he refilled it and eyed the others.

"As a humble radio counselor, I'd advise a topping off," he said as he made the rounds. "What is the famous line from that old movie you love?" he asked Temple.

"Bette Davis in superb sardonic form. 'Fasten your seat belts. It's going to be a bumpy ride.'"

Temple took her champagne glass, sat on the coffee table beside Max, and set the glass down on the nearest coaster. Matt settled into Eileen's place on the sofa after offering her husband Patrick an inquiring look.

"There'll be no more waterworks, I hope," Patrick muttered.

Max sipped from his glass and gave Temple a wry smile before continuing. "You were all quite right after the bombing. I underwent paroxysms of guilt on all fronts. It took a while for the authorities to sort out the crime scene and separate the wounded from the dead, or pieces of them. I knew Sean had gone missing." Max shut his eyes for a moment. "I had to provide his toothbrush for DNA testing, which was quite new then.

"No one was there to stop me. I became a vengeance machine. I told the IRA men that Sean and I had come over hoping to join the movement to free Northern Ireland from the British…yes, what we now call 'young naive foreign fighters' for ISIS. I'd always done magic tricks as a hobby and that makes you very observant, very able to *be* unobserved. I was a perfect spy, really, and I found the two men who'd planted the bomb and gave their names to the British. I never heard what happened to them, but a swift, secret killing was fine with me then. Many people were badly wounded, but Sean was the only one dead.

"Of course, in my guilt and fury I had no time for colleens whose eyes 'shined like the diamonds', as in the old song. I didn't know that Kathleen's savage early life had made her psychotic about being abandoned. She couldn't understand that my bond with Sean made avenging him my only priority. And I didn't know then she was an IRA agent, a champion fund-raiser well-known to the scattered Irish abroad.

"So," Max said, "when I came home for the closed casket funeral, I saw that my lies to cover up why we were in Northern Ireland in that pub weren't credible. And I saw that the pressure of one cousin back from a pub bombing without a scratch—or visible ones, anyway, and the other cousin identified from fragments—would gall good people, one family happy but guilty, the other reminded daily of their loss, and guilty. And me guiltiest of all."

Matt shook his head. "Catholic guilt is built-in. We're asked to examine our consciences from the age of seven, and that situation was a perfect trifecta."

Maura just sat there, numb. "Our collective grief blinded us to the living. We thought of you still as a child. And here you'd been through war, through your own hell, and we didn't know it."

Max shook his head, to deny her need for guilt. "Then word came that the IRA realized I'd 'betrayed' them, probably alerted by Kathleen, and had a price on my head. In those days before the peace, IRA sympathizers were everywhere, especially in the U.S. I had to get as far away as possible or my family and friends could get caught in the cross-fire. By then, counterterrorist operations had heard of my exploits, so they both saved and recruited me and magic became my cover. It turned out I was quite a good magician, especially at disappearing acts."

Temple turned to face Max. "So you were already adept at it when my turn came."

"You?" Maura jerked her head toward the other couch where Matt was now sitting. "But you just married *him*." She stared at Temple again.

Temple smiled. "Yes, Maura, your son swept me off my feet in Minneapolis and directly to Las Vegas, where he had a year's engagement as The Mystifying Max. We planned on marrying soon. When he realized some shady characters had waylaid me to inquire about him, he left on the closing day of his act, without a word, the same night a dead man had been discovered on the hotel premises, which made him a suspect."

"He left without a word?"

"I followed him from my home city and family and a good job." Temple linked arms with Max. "And, to ensure my safety, he left me here for the police and other less honest people to harass. Still...I love my freelance public relations work, and Vegas is the place to be for that. Then Matt moved into my apartment building. And Max did finally come back to face the music."

The moment of astonishment hovered, a paused recorded *Lifetime* movie moment.

"And," Matt announced from behind them all, from the door through which Max had entered. "So, finally did Sean and his wife Deirdre of County Tyrone, Northern Ireland, come back."

30
In Sunshine or in Shadow

Everyone had automatically turned toward Matt's voice, beside the open door Max had used, now framing Sean and Deirdre Kelly standing together arm-in-arm like a life-size couple on a wedding cake.

The Kinsellas and Kellys stood as one, shocked to their feet to face the unexpected couple.

Except Max. He bounded over the Kinsella couch and ushered them into the room, his enthusiasm masking how tense and shy and wary the newcomers were.

Cries of "Oh, dear God" and "Glory Be" and "My darling Sean". "Our lost boyo, Sean."

Max and the couple were mobbed in an incoherent group hug.

Alone and marooned behind, Temple told Matt through a teary voice, "This is the greatest wedding present ever."

He hugged her and teased, "Are you sure you don't want to do the counseling part of our partnership?"

"You're over the moon about this reunion too."

"I talk to so many lost souls on the radio. Found souls are a rare reward. But there'll be a bit of hell to pay for Sean, just like Max. They both withdrew when they should have trusted and been open."

"Gobbledygook!" Temple's non-Irish was up. "Sean's family is so amazed to see him alive, they haven't even noticed the price he paid to survive. As Max did. They weren't ready to accept the truth, what, sixteen years ago? The guy's instincts were right. The families had ladled an ideal vision over the future of 'their boys' and had to grow up themselves to accept the truth."

"Pretty profound," Matt said, "we'll have to see if we can get them to appear on the Devine Temple show."

"Now I feel like a snooping reporter. Let's just be eavesdropping well-wishers going forward."

"A heck of a way to celebrate a wedding night."

"We're flying out tomorrow, alive and well, and will be alone, without even the Fontana brothers, for six wonderful nights."

"Even without Midnight Louie?"

"Oh. He *will* be miffed. I'm glad the Crystal Phoenix gave him the spotlight for his revived commercial career. And I know he'll enjoy supervising the renovations. Surely he'll even more relish having the California King to himself."

"We could leave now," Matt suggested.

"No way am I missing a sob in this saga."

So Sean went back to the beginning and told how Deirdre had suspected some scheme by Kathleen O'Connor and stayed with him when Kathleen lured Max away. Deirdre had wanted Sean to leave then, too, but he'd found Deirdre an enchanting colleen herself and wanted more time with her while he waited for Max.

She finally dragged him away just as the bomb exploded. Yes, she had some scarring, but Sean had a concussion and traumatic memory loss as well as shrapnel damage.

She nursed him back to health, with the blessing of the IRA, which believed Sean, recovering slowly, was an American boy wanting to fight in the cause. Eventually he was able to fight for the peace. The only peace on earth ever made in a bitter ethnic struggle of more than eight hundred years.

Perfect, no. But admirable.

Sean and Deirdre retreated to literal peace and quiet at their Bed and Breakfast in Northern Ireland's County Tyron. Sean had finally recovered much of his memory, but, sure, how would he explain taking so long to remember his own family? And how would he justify his youthful disobedience and risk-taking? All he needed now was Deirdre and a simple Irish cottage and a life of world-class sunsets on the edge of the Atlantic.

The families were all soothing murmurs and touches and tears and protestations that they would have understood, which is when Max and Sean exchanged a glance of perfect agreement. Your families always think that they are up to the job, but sometimes errant young souls must figure things out the hard way.

Temple yawned.

"Am I boring you?" Matt asked.

"Never. But...I think the Oscars are over and we're not invited to any of the After Parties."

They slipped away, unnoticed.

A wandering Fontana brother prowled the hall.

"Why, Ralph, it's nearly one a.m.," Temple said.

"You recognized me, Miss Temple."

"But, of course. It's the earring."

"You remembered."

"Yes, but I suggest signature individual lapel pins for more accurate identification."

"You would abuse and penetrate the exquisite weave of an Emenegildo Zegna suit with a pin? Heresy. Perhaps...cuff links are less cruel, Miss Temple. Mr. Matt, do you own an EZ suit?"

"Not that I know of."

"Oh, you would know. Then allow us to arrange a visit with our tailor for your debut TV show."

"That's a bit overwhelming. I'd like a honeymoon first."

"That is why I am here to drive you home." Ralph cocked an ear at a burst of simultaneous talking beyond the closed door. "Did I hear a woman crying?"

"Family reunion, Ralph," Temple said. "Tears of joy."

He nodded knowingly. "And tears of *vino*. You should hear us Fontanas at a family reunion. Surely you can join us next time; you are now family."

Temple linked arms with Matt, and then Ralph. "That sounds wonderful, Ralph, but now we'll all visit the full reception again, with everyone Fontana...and Tony and Courtney and all.

"Then we're off the see the Wizard, the Wonderful Wizard of Oz, who is somewhere out there smiling in the neon and glitter and fairy dust and fever of the Las Vegas Strip, family reunion capital of the world for a night."

31
Under Reconstruction

"How was San Diego?" the woman behind the nameplate reading *Lieutenant C. R. Molina* asked.

"Wonderful. The famous Hotel del Coronado lived up to its reputation, and the view was amazing too."

"*Hmm,*" Molina said. "You may wonder why I asked you to visit me at work here at police headquarters?"

"It isn't for another girly luncheon outing to the off-price mall nearby?"

"Sadly no. Although I do find Coldwater Creek intriguing."

Temple wrinkled her nose. "I think you should really do Express."

"Size would be an issue."

"Only for men."

"Aren't you the snarky TV hostess already? No, I asked you to stop by because I have a wedding present for you, Miss Barr."

"Oh. You and Mariah already sang."

"We appreciated your gifts of the, I'm told—" Molina rolled her eyes "—'adorable', I quote Mariah,—custom T-shirts, rhinestone-festooned, is that the word? With the image of the Midnight Louie Austrian crystal high-heeled pumps."

"First off the press for the commercials."

"I'm sure the podiatrists of America salute you. Mariah is asking for an additional model, black on white instead of white on black, for French Vanilla's backup singers, including my daughter on weekends. I'm sure the commercial ramifications of such exposure will suit your new talk show career."

"Oh, yes! Perfect."

"Enough of popular culture, Miss Barr."

"I thought, after the wedding, we were Temple and Carmen now?"

"We *were* Temple and Lieutenant Molina, but this is police business."

"Yes, sir." Temple restrained herself from saluting.

"I can assure you that the Department no longer has any intent of pursuing Michael Aloysius Xavier Kinsella, also performing as the Mystifying Max, as a person of interest in any suspicious deaths in Las Vegas. So far this year."

"He's off the hook for the cold cases? Why? And why are you telling *me*?"

"Mr. Jackhammer, firmly in custody while you were distracted getting married and having an X-rated honeymoon apparently, having been thoroughly terrified by the events at his house and by your new husband, has confessed to killing Cliff Effinger and his brother, Joseph R. Effinger, as well as assorted other victims, including his inside man at the Goliath Hotel casino ceiling, who coincidentally died the very night said Mystifying Max completed his run as featured magician and disappeared to leave us all in the lurch."

She concluded, "So you'll be happy to hear Max Kinsella is free to start over in Vegas with a clean slate."

"What do you mean, 'start over'? He never really left."

"Well, with his house burned down—"

Temple bit her tongue, annoyed that Molina knew that before she did. "He didn't say anything to me."

"Then you haven't been associating with him recently."

"Uh, not much." Temple paused. "I think we all know whodunnit. Kitty the Cutter turned firebug. That house was an historical treasure. Orson Welles had lived there."

"And, most relevant to the Mystifying Max, it was the home he shared with his late mentor, Garry Randolph. All their magic show paraphernalia burned as well, I imagine. I suppose his new gig as house magician at the Crystal Phoenix will be a welcome distraction."

"No. Max isn't doing that, after all. Which is a shame, since I can't represent the Phoenix in PR there any longer anyway. That would be a conflict of interest with my new job. Jobs."

"Really? I can't say I'm surprised you and Matt are about to become Vegas's new young media power couple, but 'jobs' plural?"

"And Louie. He—we—have the most exciting multi-commercial commitment. My feet, his feet, my voice, his voice. V.O.s, of course."

"V. O. The four-years-in-the-bottle designation for Cognac?"

"Oh. No."

"V. O.? Very Obnoxious?"

"Voice Overs."

Molina nodded and produced a smile. "A happy ending for all concerned."

Temple flashed her a Look. "You can be very Mean Girl sometimes, Carmen."

"Sometimes, Miss Barr, it's my job. Sometimes it isn't and is just for fun."

Temple put her front-seat "topper" on, a brimmed straw hat with a cloth scarf attached so her sun-vulnerable redhead's white skin was protected, and took down the convertible top on the Miata, letting the rushing wind blow past her.

In no time, she was at the Circle Ritz, peering with Electra Lark through the plastic curtains that enclosed construction.

"Before we explore, dear," Electra said, "I have a small token of my admiration and thanks for getting me out of hot water on the murder front, not once but twice."

"Oh, Electra, this second time was so bogus. Living here is thanks enough."

Electra produced a tote bag from behind her back made of a soft shimmering fabric.

"Hot pink! I don't have that color. Thank you!"

"There's something inside."

Temple rooted through a bouquet of pink tissue spangled with tiny silver stars to pull out a matching piece of fabric. A T-shirt as vividly colored.

"'And though she but little, she is fierce,'" Temple read aloud from the front type. "I love it! That line's about Hermia in Shakespeare's *Midsummer Night's Dream*. And the tee is hot pink too."

"Raspberry, they called it. And it came in extra small."

"Of course! It would be a crime if it didn't. And we know crime!"

"It's from your old employer."

"Old employer?" Temple was confused. The Crystal Phoenix? The TV talk show deal and commercial deals would take a while to launch, so she could continue to rep the Phoenix for a while.

"The Guthrie Theater in Minneapolis," Electra explained. "Since you moved in and told me about doing PR there, I looked it up on the Internet. And now *you're* going to be a performer. I thought this would be perfect for you and your new role."

Temple gathered the tee to her chest. "Yes! It's so perfectly thoughtful of you. I hadn't thought that way about everything. I'm gonna be a star, sort of. Thank you."

The T-shirt made it through an effusive hug and back into its bag.

Temple looked at her first "curtain" as a star, the plastic construction sheeting draping her longtime residence and the scaffolding extending up into the unit above.

"I'm so glad you're allowing our alterations, Electra."

"Allowing it? Temple, this will be the most charming, ultramodern vintage unit in Vegas," Electra said. She gazed up through what had been the floor of Matt's apartment. "Even if you should outgrow the space—"

"What do you mean 'outgrow'?"

"Well, you know." Electra winked. "Get another cat. The remodeled unit will be the most in-demand in Vegas."

"Speaking of cats…" Temple was frowning at Midnight Louie, reclining, whiskers down-turned, on her plastic-shrouded sleeper sofa. "I'm amazed he's sticking around here in all this construction mess. Louie is such a loyal, loving home-body big guy. I worry he might get hurt remaining on the premises under construction."

"Temple, he's safer here than anywhere else."

"What do you mean?"

"I mean that little black she-cat at the Crystal Phoenix is chasing him away from there. I went over to consult with Ernesto, who has been such a dear boy in supervising security here while we're open to the world on two floors, and she chased poor Louie all the way to the reserved spaces in the front driveway."

"Midnight Louise did that? She always seemed such a dainty sweet little cat."

"So did you, Temple. And look at how many crooks you have exposed."

"But Louie's staying here. Look! His Free-to-Be-Feline bowl is almost empty under that plastic sheet."

"I fill that bowl over and over again, Temple, and it's always empty in the morning."

"So you *are* applying tins of sardines, oysters, and shrimp over the top?"

"That's always gone too."

"Maybe he's lost some weight." Temple hoisted the cat up to her chest. "*Omppph.* Still at least twenty pounds. Maybe not."

"This has been quite an upheaval for Louie, Temple. His home is not the same. It will never be the same again."

"I know, I know. I feel horrible about it, but he's so adaptable. Such a survivor. I'm sure he understands, don't you, boy?" She chucked him under the chin. Was that a tiny spray of white hairs she spotted growing? Was Louie feeling abandoned? Depressed? *Gasp.* Middle-aged?

"Oh, Louie, Louie. Things are changing, but that's life. It will be better soon."

She pushed her face forward, but he turned his away, gazing up at the hanging plastic shroud covering the construction area, where a steady pounding made Temple want to run away and come back another day.

Maybe poor Louie was feeling that way too.

"Please, Louie," she entreated him. "Hang in there. Everything will be wonderful soon."

32
Gilt Trip

Speaking of the Guthrie Theater, my performance is, of course, a major Thespian moment.

Instilling guilt in humans is a delicate, but remarkably easy process.

I have been practicing for this role since a fuzz-bottom. That is how we train these people to perform.

First, one must cultivate a certain Continental ennui.

You suppose yourself French, and world-weary. Your eyelids can barely remain open, your gaze can barely reach for the ceiling, were even a menacing wasp circling.

You think yourself as heavy as you can be, the opposite of what a sane human would do, and your right front mitt and vibrissae, a.k.a. whiskers, may twitch minutely.

Humans sigh, but our breed yawns. Long and deeply. Life is all too empty, cheerless, woeful and not worth living without X-Tasy Bits-brand liver and kidney and a nice Chianti.

What? Your human victim wants to play kissy-face—whisker-crumpling, muzzle-smooching kissy-face? *Ugh.*

How off-putting. You twist your neck until avoiding all contact makes it plain you are barely managing to put up with this sadly enabling creature who wants only to make you safe, warm, dry, and overweight. And inside.

I hate to do this, but I realize that my journey with my Miss Temple will not be over until we both understand we have our parts to play and our peace to make and will always be together, come rain or shine or bloody murder.

For now, I let her put me down (thank Bast!). What is this obsession with picking up? I came with four on the floor, fully equipped from the factory, and will be leaving the *Daily Planet* obit pages the same way, many years from hence. I hope.

Meanwhile, as Miss Temple sets me back down with copious sniffles and tears, I plot how to get her where I want her, where it will do me and her the most good.

Mostly her.

Unlike Sam Spade, I am willing to play the sap for a dame.

If it suits me.

But only for so long.

33
A Peak Experience

When Temple returned from the work in progress at the Circle Ritz to her and Matt's lovely suite at the Crystal Phoenix, she sat and thought, and shuffled pieces of paper on the handsome desk meant usually for show.

The suite had a real safe, built into a wall, not the cheesy metal boxes on hotel closet shelves, and she'd brought out the maps of the Strip and its attractions.

She got up and went to the window-wall. Her twelfth-floor suite was at an ideal height. From up here she could still see the canyons of streets and highways between the towering buildings. The darkening mountains were notched against a cloudless sunset sky on her right and the Strip lights were gaining on the coming dark on her left.

She paced. Thought. Sighed. The delicious week in San Diego had soothed away tensions from the previous whirlwind sequence of two weddings, an armed robbery attempt, a fraught multi-family reunion, and a current renovation of home, sweet, home.

Temple's brain was now rested and revving up, getting ideas.

She still had Max on speed-dial. She felt a bit guilty for using it.

"Here comes the bride," he announced as he answered. "What a beautiful wedding, Temple."

"How do you know? You were invited, but you didn't accept."

"I was invited, but I didn't have the bad taste to show up at the actual ceremony and general reception and have to be explained."

"Always mystifying."

"Always practical."

"The doves were a nice final touch, but the Fontana boys got the credit."

"And they've earned it. Besides, I had to brace myself for my command performance at your so very delicate and emotional production of *A Family for All Seasons*. You will be magnificent on a talk show venturing into current issues. I have never been so masterfully manipulated to be honest."

"You know everyone in your families needed to reconcile the past."

"Yes, yes. Very sensitive, but back to what an absolute beauty of a bride you made. I may not have recovered my memories of me, of you, of us, but I confess I felt very sorry for the poor sod who missed out on you, whether you were coming down the aisle or managing a hell of a tricky family reconciliation."

"Catholic Confession is now called the Sacrament of Reconciliation, I'm told," Temple said demurely. "I may not be Catholic, but I'm pro reconciliation."

"Good for you. I may not have been apparent at the actual wedding, but that doesn't mean I missed most of the main event at the church."

"*Not*. I knew you couldn't resist being the ghost at the banquet. Did you like my train?"

"Train? Oh, yes…killer."

"Liar. You don't give a whit about trains. I thought so. You were concealed up in the choir loft. You crashed my wedding too, like that skunk, Crawford Buchanan. And *you* were invited."

"I appreciated that, but the best view in any theater is always from the balcony."

"True," Temple said, looking out at the Las Vegas view.

"We haven't talked since the family intervention."

"I know. It may seem crazy to call, but I've had a brainstorm about the puzzle of the late Effinger's drawing and the Ophiuchus constellation."

"As a practical man, I assume the Mister is hanging over your shoulder."

"He should be, but the TV show producers decided they wanted copies of the pro-shot wedding tapes. The producers are here on other business, so Matt's at the Bellagio, in their faces, discussing the limits of our public versus private lives. Get that established now or lose all control. Tony is with him."

"Such problems," Max teased. "Therefore you're home alone?"

"Yes, darn it. I really need to show you what I've found."

"You're in the mood for a scandal? So soon after the wedding cake?"

"I was hoping the Mystifying Max could still disappear and reappear without a soul knowing about it."

"Ah. A chance to use my rusty cat burglar skills. Excellent. Do unlock the balcony doors, I've had an emotionally fatiguing week because of an auld acquaintance not forgot. Sean and I flew to Racine before he and Deirdre flew back to Northern Ireland."

"Their B and B sounds like a great honeymoon locale."

Temple laughed at herself. She was planning on how she could be wicked and hook up Max and Molina. Seemed to be a bit of rivalry-attraction there.

Look at me! Temple thought. Married barely a week and already a matchmaker. Max and Molina…two tough, single, probably lonely people…what if? Then she imagined them walking down an aisle together, knew it would be at swords' point, and laughed at herself.

Max must have lurked in the choir loft, though. Which meant that wedding singer Molina must have been a tad complicit. At the least, she hadn't ratted him out, which would have ruined the dove bit.

Fifteen minutes later came a rapping, gently tapping on her glass balcony doors. 'Twas the raven-haired Max, and nothing more. Thank goodness.

"You climbed twelve stories?" Temple asked. "Impressive."

"Not really. I took the elevator to the eleventh floor and managed one story. Tell me," Max said as he closed the balcony doors behind him. "Your beloved will be understanding if he should find out about this?"

"He will. I'll tell him. He may huff and puff a bit, but ultimately he'll be okay with it, yes, because he's my beloved. He knows in his heart and his bones that you're no threat to him."

"As well he should. He brought down Jack the Hammer. I would never mess with a guy like that. He's really come into his own, hasn't he?" Max said seriously. "You have that effect on people, Temple. I have yet to say that about myself, but I'm working on it."

"Max, I was so sorry to hear you lost your house, and all your history. I loved that place." The thought of both Max and Louie feeling homeless nagged at Temple like a hangnail you keep picking at.

"You've obviously been talking to Molina. That home had been tainted already. Kathleen attacked us all in that place. Threatened you. Shot Matt. Gave my noggin another memory-blasting blow. At least I remember that."

"Are you really so…resigned?"

"No. The house being destroyed was a blow," Max said, sitting on the sofa arm. "Don't we all cringe when we hear the vast toll of innocent flesh ISIS takes and then it destroys the architectural legacy of all peoples of times gone by?"

Ordinarily, Max admitted to no vulnerabilities, but this was a new, more philosophical Max.

"Kathleen did it?" Temple asked, wincing.

"Who else? She never had any home, any history but a hidden and destroyed…and destroying…past. I guess she thought she was owed to do that to someone else."

"Not 'someone'. You. I hate her for what she did."

"Me too. But for her acts, not for the small stubborn part of humanity she clings to."

"That's generous."

"That's what I learned from you, and Matt did too. What can I do for you?"

"I've been working on the maze that is the Effinger murder, the IRA donations, the Synth magicians and the Ophiuchus constellation puzzle."

"All that and getting married too?"

"Matt's quest is ended."

Max's laugh was rich. "He's the accidental hero, isn't he? Uncovering a treasure hunt far more sinister than the mystery we've all been following. My God, he's got the angels on his side for having the guts to go up against the nastiest secret killer in Vegas. You do know he was on top of it at the end like mob-buster Elliott Ness, and isn't 'fessing up to that because it would be awkward for you and Molina?"

"Yes, all that. And I'm very proud. But my latest insight can't wait. I've moved the crude Cliff Effinger drawing of the hero fighting a giant serpent that supposedly represents the thirteenth Zodiac sign of Ophiuchus, and the "house" shape of the major stars in the Ophiuchus constellation over each other on tracing paper and have had a breakthrough."

"Can't this wait until we can summon our Round Table to discuss our Table of Crime Elements like we used to? Matt deserves to be in on the end of the puzzle if you've found it. As you say, he's way too secure to resent me anymore. Especially since I was diplomatically absent at your wedding."

"And you could spot any brewing trouble better from up there. Did Molina know she had hidden backup?"

"You must stop thinking she knows everything."

"She knows Kathleen burned your house down, and I didn't know about that." Temple frowned a little frown. "Have you been consorting with the enemy?"

"I wouldn't call it consorting." Max looked uneasy, not a Max Look Temple had seen before.

"Well, well, well," Temple said. "Did Kathleen pay dearly for erasing your history like you were ancient ruins and she was ISIS when you tracked her down in Ireland?"

"Ruins! I'm not so newly humble to admit to that. All I can say is that Kathleen is not to be found in Ireland anymore."

"You didn't find her? I don't believe that."

Max shrugged. "I couldn't say I found her peace of mind, but I found the daughter she gave up shortly after birth."

"Daughter? Born in the Magdalene institution? Taken away from her? Oh, Hoover Dam and double damn! The poor woman. No wonder she was a crazy witch."

"Poor *girl*. She escaped with her infant daughter while yet a girl herself and found a nice agnostic family to rear her. Not an easy thing to do in Ireland, believe me, to find people who are not undiluted true believers."

"She found a UU family!"

"What passes for that over there, yes."

"Maybe I'll have to reevaluate her."

"And that would be *your* reconciliation moment."

Temple nodded. "Don't judge until you walk in another woman's...Stuart Weitzman's."

"For you. For her, the way Kathleen walked was thorny beyond shoes."

"Darn it, Max. You're making me cry for Kathleen. She stole one shoe of my best pair of heels, yet she returned it. Everything was a taunt for her."

"Don't cry for Kathleen. She'd hate that, and you won't be able to show me what you found."

All right. I want to demonstrate another radically different imposition of the Ophiuchus stars on the Las Vegas map."

"And why not wait for your devoted spouse?"

"Because true inspiration strikes rarely and soon fades. I thought of you for that 3-D visualization a magician has. And for what I realized I saw on the marvelous altar front, and saw echoed in the nave of Our Lady of Guadalupe church."

"So your getting married got you a glimpse of a treasure buried for three generations and clued you in on the equally long-missing IRA funds? Ironic, but the loot in the church was Ted Binions', not IRA connected."

"I do realize that. And Matt will be happy to come home and collect his Giacco Petrocelli memorial jackhammer and come along with me to find out, if you don't want to."

"Actually," he admitted, "Binion's stash being unearthed gave *me* another idea on the IRA puzzle."

"That settles it. Max. We need one last rendezvous at the Neon Nightmare." She stood up. "I'm wearing my capris and deck shoes, and carrying my tote for the papers. So I'm ready for a treasure hunt in a pyramid."

His expression turned cautious, closed again. He obviously didn't want to go there. "That place is out of business."

"But I'm not."

"That's comforting, but it's a deserted venue."

"The best kind for kinky criminal doings. To be discreet, you can drive and meet me there."

"Is this town still big enough for the two of us?"

"The three of us. Don't forget Midnight Louie."

"The three of us."

"It's Vegas, baby."

34
Midnight Magic

Things have changed, changed utterly.

Along the Las Vegas Strip. Among my favorite people and places.

Yet some things will never change.

My Miss Temple—(forget Missus, an ugly word, totally not French, and Madam has connotations. In my book, ladies are always Miss, but I will grudgingly use Mrs. on occasion)—is a known vintage clothing lover.

I have long realized the addiction went beyond suits and shoes to such finds as the snazzy chrome nineteen-twenties toaster that holds any snail mail she still gets. Sadly, she buys cat carriers new; at least until I get my paws and claws to work on them.

The biggest objects of her vintage obsession are the cluster of modest motel-casinos in the nineteen-forties that grew into the dazzling skyline of higher and higher hotel-casinos...whose grandeur faded one by one as they became "gut jobs" and fell to make way for ever grander and higher replacements.

I find myself musing on how the Strip itself mirrors more than half the twentieth century and a bit of the twenty-first. And how change and rebirth is impossible without death, whether it is the death of the body or an idea or a vision.

That is why I retreat nowadays (when ripping and pounding at the Circle Ritz make even the zebra-print carrier no retreat), to the abandoned Neon Nightmare building to meditate, as my breed is wont. It seems a perfect metaphor for Vegas dreams and melodramas.

Las Vegas has so much flash and cash floating around in its neon stew that when a venue is slowly dying, it is an instantly detectable Black Hole amid the wheeling, glitzy galaxies of the Strip and even the night sky so often overpowered by the wattage below.

It had been that way for the Dunes and the Aladdin in the eighties as "new ownerships" appeared on the desert sands in the east horizon and quickly sank into the mountains in the west. Including The Sands itself. Such names, from the Stardust to the long-lasting Riviera, only recently imploded with pomp and ceremony.

We hip cats about Vegas mourn these losses, every one a prime Dumpster-diving location in its heyday, as well as the epitome of class and creativity for its time.

The implosion of the Grand Old Dames of the Strip kicked into high gear during the nineties, destruction becoming a massive stage show itself. First, the impeccably placed charges. The filmed countdown. The wide media coverage of a once-fabled building holding memories of once-fabled entertainment acts collapsing in seconds into itself, into nothing, melting like the Wicked Witch of the West in *The Wizard of Oz*. And all death throes available on YouTube now. Watch them and weep for the bygone glamour.

Only the dead neon remains, stocked in the Neon Graveyard museum, a past art fondly remembered, but too passé to revive on a large scale. I and my compadres often stroll there, and I nap under the giant Silver Slipper shoe in honor of Miss Temple. Passed down from generation to generation of my lineage have been the sumptuous seafood entrees at, say, the Dunes amid Art Deco grandeur. All gone, gone utterly, along with plenteous inexpensive buffets. Now tourists desiring seafood at a hotel buffet must have the tops of their hands stamped like at a cheap nightclub to be scanned to give them entry if they have paid for that option.

Yet desert flowers can lay dormant and then bloom spectacularly, even if only once in a blue-suede moon. And the media always loves a spectacular failure. And resurrection.

Like Elvis, who was the quintessential Vegas entertainer, larger than life, flawed and beloved for it, immortal for his sad mortality.

That is why Graceland in Memphis has created its first permanent outpost at the Westgate Las Vegas Resort and Casino.

I find that news very exciting. Fact is, Elvis and I share a certain simpatico spirit. I have seen his ghost out and about in Las Vegas and am expecting even more encounters now that so many of his beloved objects have landed here.

Some may pooh-pooh my "Elvis sightings". True, a lot of nut jobs have claimed that honor. But none of them can also claim a historically established heritage of nine lives. That is how I believe I can see Elvis. I can slip in and out of my past and present lives if I am in the right meditative mood. It is nothing like the psychic powers Miss Electra's overbearing companion, Karma, claims.

These are dude-to-dude moments when our psyches intersect. They did not call Elvis "the Memphis Cat" for nothing. In fact, he and I cleared up the cold case about who killed Jumpin' Jack Robinson at the Zoot Suit Choo-Choo to get the land it sat on, which still has a valuable, but lost, gambling license. He went there in person as a young first-time Vegas act and I went there in spirit, diving deep into my hep cat catalog of lives.

So I listen when Miss Temple is muttering to me while sopping up Internet trivia on Elvis's latest incarnation at a big off-Strip venue.

"Wow, Louie," she says, staring too long at the screen. "Elvis has finally, really never 'left the building'."

That is the announcement made after his concerts, when fans were hopping and shouting for encores, but the concert was over. "Elvis has left the building."

"Elvis is back almost where he began here," she says. "The attraction building is the real deal, not some ersatz pretender. Before it was the LVH-Las Vegas, then the Las Vegas Hilton. It was originally the International Hotel, where Elvis performed more than six hundred sold-out shows between his 1968 'comeback' and 1976 death."

I press nearer. Elvis's comeback had only lasted a short cat's life. Eight years. How old am I? It is none of your business, I would trumpet to anyone crass enough to ask.

"*Hmm.*" Miss Temple is sliding onto her spine on the chair. "When Priscilla Presley opened 'Graceland Presents ELVIS: The Exhibition-The Show-The Experience' last year on April 23rd (Shakespeare's birthday, Miss Temple and I know, but so few follow the Bard these days), she looked as gorgeous and young as only a seventy-year-old Hollywood celebrity can. Imagine going from child bride-in-waiting to ex-wife to savvy businesswoman and mother guarding the major legacy of Graceland."

That is very hard for me to imagine, especially the child bride-in-waiting part. I do not wait well.

I see the screen morph into Elvis and Priscilla's wedding photo.

Miss Temple frowns. "Not an inspiring wedding gown, Louie. One of those sixties waistless long sheaths. She does have a small train, though. Oh, well. Back to business."

Miss Temple is devouring the new attraction's details because she might use them in related press releases.

She often talks to herself by pretending to talk to me, and, face it, I am a world-class listener because I have chosen not to talk back. She has no idea that I, too, have a deep, abiding interest in my buddy, the King.

"The redone old International showroom opened on the 59th anniversary of Elvis Presley's first, ill-attended Las Vegas performance at the Venus Room of the New Frontier Hotel. Now the renamed 'Elvis Presley Theater', it has been restored to 'vintage perfection'. I gotta see that vintage perfection, Louie. Think Matt would go with me?"

I would, but I do not need a ticket to sneak into any show in town.

"And," she exclaims, "Some PR genius even dug up, excuse the expression, an aged cocktail waitress who had worked at the International then and remembered Elvis."

Miss Temple laughed uproariously at the computer when she read that.

"What a PR coup," she said. "Imagine a Vegas hotel keeping a cocktail waitress employed into her eighties. I suppose Elvis was her claim to continuing employment. Good for her!"

One forgot how young Elvis had been when he had died. Forty-two. When his life spirit has intersected occasionally with one of my lost early lives, he is in his mid-thirties prime, like the black leather he wore in his comeback TV show, sleek and dangerously sexy. Also like me when Miss Midnight Louise is not around to rain on my parade.

And like Miss Temple, I love every facet and era and trace of the 24/7 carnival fantasy show Vegas always has been and always will be. And I know Miss Temple and I both will always mourn a classic attraction gone dark.

35
An Attraction Gone Dark

The sun also fades fast in Las Vegas.

As she drove up to the Neon Nightmare, Temple could barely make out the support structure for the galloping neon horse that had given the nightclub its name. Neon Nightmare, the horse being the "mare" part. It had reminded her of Dallas's famous red neon flying "Pegasus", restored in both its nineteen-thirties original and a new version commissioned before the first horse had been miraculously found disassembled in a box and restored.

The parking lot lights were dark too, so Temple drove her red Miata with the convertible top down, as if that provided any security, right up to the main entry door.

The building was a black glass-clad pyramid, inside and out, a nightclub owned and also used as a private clubhouse by a cabal of magicians delighting in all the secret mystifying stage scenery, effects and props of their profession.

"Boo." Max's face appeared at her lowered driver's side window.

Temple started. With his black hair and trademark black turtleneck sweater and slacks, she hadn't noticed him leaning against the building. Magicians before and since before Houdini had used Men in Black against a black curtain onstage to create their illusions.

"Sorry," Max said when she blinked. "I forgot how spooky this place was." He opened the door and Temple handed him her tote bag while she locked the car.

"The place is closed," she said. "How do we get in?"

"No worries. I already 'cracked' it. I did perform here as the Phantom Mage for a while."

Temple took in the faint reflection of them as a couple in the dark door, cast by a distant street light, a dark attraction that had gone darker.

"You almost died here, Max. How can you stand seeing it again?"

"You're right. Standing is taxing. We should go in and sit down."

He produced a small but powerful flashlight and tapped the seamless black façade. A wide door clicked ajar. Faint light shone behind it.

"Temple, we have nothing to fear from the things that *almost* got us. It's the new ones that *might*."

"And your greatest enemy is out of the country for good? In Ireland. She'll stay put?"

"She's *very* not at liberty."

Temple ventured inside reluctantly. She was dying to ask more about Kathleen O'Connor, but Max had walked to the long black-glass bar and put her tote bag on it.

Where it went, she went, and vice versa. Temple followed him to determine the light source that lit up a wall of liquor bottles still in place.

"Hurricane lamps?" She laughed. "Your idea of housekeeping?"

Temple studied the empty space. The black glass floor effect was always edgy. When the dance floor and the black mirrored walls of the pyramid pulsed to piped-in music with neon colors and shapes zapping into the air above, and the dancers gyrated and the drinkers at their tables shouted at each other it had that Vegas Hell vibe, like the crazy-popular deejay-driven electronic music nightclubs mesmerizing young Vegas visitors nowadays and putting zillions into the Strip venues.

Temple looked up to the peak high above where a swirling universe of lighted constellations rotated. She looked down fast, dizzy.

Max took her elbow.

Temple shook her head. "How could you leap down from there on a bungee cord every night? I get chills thinking about the High Roller ride at LINQ entertainment center."

"You've always yearned to be taller."

"Not that way." She shuddered to think about that giant Ferris wheel of swaying cable cars.

"Let's sit at the bar and examine your Ophiuchus file."

Temple started laughing. "That's the worst pick-up line I've ever heard."

With that, Max picked her up and perched her on a high barstool.

"I need to get rid of these dangerously tippy things," Max said as he leaned easily into sitting on the adjoining stool. Nobody should have to hop up to a seat in a bar."

"The world should be more considerate of short people, but I don't think you can change that all on your own."

"No, but here I can."

"What? You're staking out an abandoned building like a homeless person? Which you are after that witch burned you out of house and home."

"Not exactly." He spun to lean back against the bar, spread out his long arms and surveyed the vast black satin space. "I own it."

"It almost killed you and you bought it? That is so...contrary and unpredictable. And yet 'Max,'" she said. "When did you buy it?"

"After it failed. I felt it had potential."

"Potential to be a rogue building and kill."

"I do need a home."

"So you've been living here. In all this gleaming, mocking, deceptive blackness?"

"No." He nodded at the opposite wall where a rail-less stairway and the balcony above it were barely discernible.

"You're living in the cozy, English-y clubrooms of those crazy magicians who called themselves the "Synth"! I spent one of the most heart-pounding moments of my life stumbling across that place and those people. Aren't they all dead now?"

"Ghosts won't hurt you, Temple, unless they're in your head. The only dead Synth member is the leader, Cosimo Sparks, knifed in underground tunnels connecting the Crystal Phoenix, Gangsters, and our old familiar venue here, the Neon Nightmare."

Temple hooked her high heels over the stool's lower rung, as she always had to in bars. She frowned, for a long time, as Max went back behind the bar to pour Bombay Sapphire into two crystal lowball glasses and place them before Temple.

He came around to reclaim his seat and one glass and stare into it as the hurricane lamps flickered, broadcasting a searing kerosene scent that unnerved Temple, but not Max, who was waxing contemplative without even a sip of liquor.

"I look at Sean and Deidre, and realize he recovered from that bomb and its scars long before I could. I had no right in Minneapolis to sweep you into my ungoverned, unsafe world, Temple."

"Then why did you?"

"I think I thought that you could save my soul. And you did." Max smiled. "It was selfish and self-pitying. I regret being an aggravating hiccup in your life."

"Oh, you Irish. Always the martyrs. I needed to be jerked loose from my lovingly smothering family and get a little excitement in *my* life."

Max lifted his glass. "A toast. To our separate but exciting futures."

The crystal was Baccarat and rang like a heavenly chime from above in this hellish place.

"And so," Temple said, "to work." She pulled her tote bag flat on the bar to shuffle a deck of white papers onto the black onyx glass.

"We've always thought the drawn representation of the Ophiuchus constellation, the naked hero twined by and fighting a giant serpent, was a representation of what the ancient Greeks or other cultures saw in the stars. And we were half right. Matt recently learned that image had grabbed his stepfather's pre-teen mind like a leech. He drew it constantly in class. The son he abandoned kept one drawing attached to his uncle's refrigerator with a magnet. He had only that one keepsake image and memory of its significance to his father, and he inked it on his arm when he came of age.

"After my fake wedding, when a long-ago renovation was used to conceal the lost Binion stash of millions in gold under the Our Lady of Guadalupe altar, Matt recognized the altar's central decoration, a turquoise carving of serial 'Ms' like the Loch Ness monster humps, with serpent heads at each end."

"Surely not Ophiuchus."

"No, but close. And not Ouroboros, the ancient eternity image of a serpent or dragon biting its own tail. After all the excitement, I looked it up. It represents the Central American god, Quetzalcóatl, the feathered serpent, often depicted with a semi-naked human avatar standing beside the giant snake. Christian conquerors would integrate native symbols into the 'new religion' they forced upon the native people. The original builders of Our Lady of Guadalupe were part of that tradition, almost subconsciously by now."

"So," Max said, "the altar bore another representation of Cliff Effinger's man-snake fetish, which is very Freudian, by the way—"

"I get it," Temple said. "And Cliff Effinger used it like a signature he put on all his mob jobs, including one more than twenty years ago to hide the Binion stash in the renovated church basement. Using the altar as a cover, which would have tickled a perverse sadist like Giacco Petrocelli."

"But Binion had no idea that the altar itself was marked by a maker during the construction?" Max asked.

"No," Temple said. "He was a rather dumb guy, to give the location of his hoarded millions to the man who built the concrete safe in the desert for him and who was, um, intimate with his wife."

Max laughed and sang, "I am I, Dumb Coyote—" It echoed many times against the glass walls. "*Man of La Mancha*," he explained.

"Oh, yeah, the old Broadway musical about Don Quixote. Come to think of it, 'Don Qui-ho-te' always did sound like "dumb coyote" when sung. I didn't know you could sing, and on key."

"No need for it," Max said.

"Well, I can't."

"You've got to give poor Carmen Molina *some* advantage over you."

"No, I don't," Temple said. "She persecuted you, and me, like Javert after poor Jean Valjean in *Les Misèrables*, another Broadway musical. Say, they were depressing for a while, weren't they?" Temple was adamant on that. "Anyway, it was that odious Woodrow

Wetherly Molina *sent* Matt to for information who was the dyed-in-the-woolly-white balaclava mask villain."

"The man fooled people for decades, it seems," Max said.

"He was clever. A mobster who killed and took the place of the cop trailing him decades ago, who kept running crooked schemes into his eighties. Giacco Petrocelli. Jack the Hammer and his bloody jackhammer."

Max's eyes narrowed. "A monster as well as a mobster."

"Exactly." Temple's ire would not die. "That man was willing to *kill* people, not only to ruin my wedding, if I were prone to get in a huff. He needed a guaranteed congregation with a small guest list and specific times so he could round up and neutralize everyone in the nave of the church while his gang uncovered and plundered the basement stash."

"'Neutralize.' Don't we sound like a task force?"

"We were. Electra even announced the phony wedding rehearsal at OLG by emailing a photo of Midnight Louie in his white bow-tie as Ring Bearer to Crawford Buchanan's fleazy gossip column. Louie went viral and it was an invitation the criminals couldn't refuse."

"Fleazy?" Max asked.

"It's my new word for unutterably low."

Max shook his head. "I've created mini-me monsters. Going undercover, tailing criminals, planting traps."

"Are you continuing that spy stuff, Max? You said Kathleen was no longer a threat."

"Not to us."

"Matt and I have our talk show and Midnight Louie and I have our national commercial gig, but what are you going to do?"

Max pulled the papers closer. "Solve where the IRA contributions have been hidden right now. If the mob can't fool Matt and Fontana Inc., can a cabal of rogue magicians and retired Irish rebels fool you and me?"

A thump atop the neighboring barstool made Temple jump. Max leapt up and clutched his shoulder like a Fontana brother who had misplaced his best friend. And he obviously wasn't even armed.

"Louie," Temple said. "What brought him here tonight? How'd he get in?"

"The building has been neglected and isn't as secure as it will be," Max said. "Apparently, just mentioning his name summons the demon."

Midnight Louie didn't seem to like Max's explanation for his coming when "called". He lashed his tail furiously against the stool seat. The big black cat's chin barely cleared the bar's lip, but he stuck it out. Pugnaciously.

Then he tilted his head as flirtaceously as a kitten's toward Temple.

She could hear him saying, if he would deign to talk to her, "Somebody mention *my* name? At last!"

"My apologies. Pull up a stool, Louie," Max said, drawing Louie's stool closer. "First you are sleeping in my California king-size bed at the Circle Ritz with my ex-girlfriend and now you are cadging a drink at *my* bar.

"Sorry, Louie, nothing you can drink," he added. "Liquor keeps, dairy products don't."

Temple couldn't help smiling. Males get so possessive at times.

Louie responded by jumping atop the bar and sitting on the papers.

"Louie!" It was a battle Temple had fought many times. Work in anything but a paperless industry and your cherished feline companion will be on every possible pile, all over them, digging down under them. *Sigh!*

"Wait a minute," Max said. "He's placed the dead-center of his, um, posterior on the 'house' image of the major stars in Ophiuchus."

"What? Divining by cat rear? The spirit of the Synth magicians survives. Look, Max. Cats are attracted by the scent of ink or toner. That's all."

"But that's exactly what I've been thinking about. You were saying you'd come to a new conclusion on the Ophiuchus constellation's major star outline."

"Only that we've been calculating it as referring to an area along the Strip. Look." Temple took the transparent tracing paper of the house image and spun it as if transfixed by a pin.

"It matches *all* of Las Vegas inside the five major highways," Max said. "That's a bigger canvas than we've been considering, not a smaller one."

"Well, maybe we've been looking small, rather than big."

"Or...maybe the opposite. Sorry, Louie." The cat grumbled with a smothered growl as Max pulled the "house' version of the Ophiuchus constellation drawing out from under him.

"This would be highway 159 or 589 just below it on the north," Temple said. "and that connects with Interstate 515 going southeast to Henderson. And you can get on Interstate 215 going directly west, for the bottom of the house, and 215 swings up north again to connect with 15 going parallel to the Las Vegas Strip to cross state routes 589/Sahara and 159/W. Charleston Avenue just south of downtown east and west. And there you have your rough 'house' shape in the stars."

"Very true." Max looked up and then down. Louie mimicked his motion.

"We're inside it," Temple realized. "We're east of the Strip toward the junction of state 589/Sahara with 515. Right where a major star in the Ophiuchus constellation is located."

"Rather, Temple, the Neon Nightmare is. Magicians are drawn to astrology too. Ophiuchus proved to be an unlucky star to the Synth members when they got greedy and schemed to get the IRA loot. Kathleen and Santiago wanted them to provide the cover of a magical diversion for a major last Vegas heist for the Irish cause. Only Santiago had gone rogue and Kathleen didn't know it."

"Everybody was duping everybody," Temple summed up.

Max looked up. "And the stars weren't aligned to let anyone profit. The Synth leader was murdered and cabal members scattered. Santiago was murdered. Kathleen returned to Ireland empty-handed, the reputed guns and loot lost."

Max smiled. "Maybe that's why it was a tough venue to make profitable. And cheap to buy."

"Cheap?" Temple was skeptical.

"Cheaper," Max said with a smile. "Remember *Star Trek*?" he asked Temple.

"The new movies?"

"No, *Star Trek* Classic from the sixties."

"Please. The women's costumes were so sexist, boldly going into *Playboy* territory. Not my kind of vintage."

Max smiled. "Always the consistent crusader. You've lived to see *Playboy* so over. Anyway, I wasn't thinking of the 3-D girls, but the 3-D chess game."

"I remember a still photo of that on a vintage nostalgia auction site."

"You're moving from vintage shops to online?"

"Most worthwhile vintage clothing *is* online now. I had a bid number registered for Debbie Reynolds' fabulous Hollywood costume auction a few years ago, and watched every second. The bidding for one of Judy Garland's simple Dorothy dresses going up and up to almost a million *dollars* was breathless. You wished she could have lived to see what an iconic character she created.

"But even trinkets I bid on went up into the hundreds…a swooping hat, some gloves, and so much of our cinematic history went to Asia. Call me xenophobic, but that kind of rankles. Debbie saved Old Hollywood by buying out *MGM*'s entire stock before anyone valued it. She was the only woman star with the guts to try to float a Vegas venue based around her career and costume collection, and it failed. She finally couldn't afford to maintain the collection."

"She made millions on the sale, didn't she?"

"That's for her heirs, and she knows she saved those things for posterity, but it hurt to let her lifelong passion go. I know."

"Temple. That must have been when I went 'missing'. Had I been there I'd have bought you a fabulous hat if I'd known. And one for Debbie to keep too."

"Which is why you will find the perfect woman for you, and I warn you, I've started shopping right now."

He laughed again. "Right now we need to decipher what Louie is sitting on."

Temple sighed. "If it's on a small scale, what is shaped like the child's drawing of a 'house'?"

Max spread his long fingers and twisted the traced image over the blow-up of central Las Vegas.

"Most shows on the Strip are mostly two-dimensional. We see that on TV, in films, we learn to think that way. When I appeared to be walking on air in my act, with all the doves landing on and flying around me, I was actually, thanks to fast-winking strobe lights, walking back and forth between the foreground and the background, like a zigzag sewing machine, although I appeared to be going on a straight, linear line."

"The depth was the distraction."

"Everything in magic, and too much in life, is a distraction, Temple."

"Too much *math* for me."

Midnight Louie looked up, intently and made those jaw-tremoring *chee-chee-chee* chirps cat make when spotting prey.

Max picked up a black remote control Temple hadn't noticed and aimed it at the interior apex of the Neon Nightmare.

Louie leaped to the lowest liquor shelf, then up to the top one, chirruping steadily.

"This place is a huge cat toy, isn't it?" Max said. "All those dancing shifting lights. Care to accompany me to the top?"

Temple took a deep, shaky breath. "No."

"The hidden scaffolding that continues up and behind the Synth's third-floor clubroom bird's-nest on the opposite wall, it's quite safe. You'd have to leave your heels behind, though."

"I hate heights."

"You wear high heels every day."

"That's on a small scale."

"Look at Louie."

His round, intent eyes moved with the circling images. The traditional signs of the Zodiac, crab, goat, scorpion, lion, along with the disputed thirteenth sign.

Max whispered, "A still central core is generating the illusion of movement and depth. Ophiuchus circles his attacking serpent continually. It's like a clockwork construction, and, like clockwork, has many parts. Game?"

Temple kicked off her heels, which hit the bar side and fell to the floor. "If you can replay your almost fatal fall, I can climb some pathetic…hidden, dark, secret scaffolding."

Oh yeah. Maybe.

Max was as sure as a mountain goat and he easily wafted Temple from level to level by a firm hand grip. Since his remote control handled the working lights, the backstage structure was well-lit and simple. And the scaffolding was three feet wide and solid, she was relieved to find.

At the building's pointed apex, a nest of spotlights dueled, creating crossing beams of colorful shimmer. That was when Temple began to lose confidence.

Max left her clinging to two cross bars and climbed higher. His black clothing was soon invisible against the dark, mirrored surfaces and dueling lights. She envisioned the four floors of empty space below, equally dark, and also reflecting crossed sabers of colored lights.

"Max," she whispered, ashamed of her cold feet.

Something warm and furry brushed her calves.

"Louie," she whispered again, reassured.

Then Louie's silhouette vaulted up past her, backlit by the light show. For a moment he seemed as huge as a leaping black panther.

The opposite wall flared with a yellow-lit image of the wrestling man and giant serpent.

Then the circling light show paused. Had Max made the apex of the pyramid go dark for an instant? And stop?

Another click. Only the yellow work lights were on and Temple had to squeeze her eyes shut against the sudden illumination.

She heard and felt Max and Louie leap down onto the lower scaffold, one large *thump* that vibrated the boards, followed by a smaller one. Temple teetered, spreading her bare toes for balance and looking down from a sideways squint. Up here the scaffolding was ten feet wide.

It could have accommodated a van.

Somehow, that didn't make her feel better. There was always getting down.

"Max Kinsella, why I let you talk me into climbing the inside of this magic mountain I will never know, but I am so over you."

He leapt down beside her. "I wanted you to be the first—and last in this country to see. Look."

Max's hands opened the magician's typical black silken square that produced white rabbits and doves.

Nothing white appeared. His cupped hands held a mini-universe of captive, eye-dazzling red, green, blue, and white…the colors of what she'd taken for gel-tinted theatrical spotlights, now boiled down into large, faceted gemstones.

Louie stretched himself three feet long along her leg, and Max did a knee-dip so he could see too.

Louie's paw automatically tensed to touch.

"Oh, no, boy," Max said, "this is a very different kind of kibble than you eat."

"He doesn't," said Temple. "Eat kibble. He just pretends to. He's in it for the toppings I ladle on it to get him to eat the healthful Free-to-Be-Feline. Which he doesn't."

"What a con that cat has going." Max laughed as the silk square shrunk in his hands and disappeared.

Temple looked around. "This entire building's lighting system is a spinning gigantic kaleidoscope in the sky," she realized. "Made from the IRA money Cosimo Sparks found, converted into jewels, and then secretly kept. He was the worst crook and hypocrite ever. He *murdered* people to maintain a phony scam about Strip-rejected magicians finding Kathleen O'Connor's stockpile of undelivered IRA support funds, and all along he'd found and converted them to diamonds and rubies and sapphires and emeralds to dazzle night-clubbing tourists right in front of his duped co-conspirators' eyes. Why?"

"It was a magician-conning-magician scheme, all right," Max said.

Temple looked down. Plain yellow-white spotlights raked the black mirror walls. The neon glamour was gone. The Plexiglas looked scratched and dull under the unrelenting light.

"How are we going to get back *do-o-o-o-own*?"

"No! No, Max, *no-o-o-o!*"

Not a bungee cord!

She was not suicidal.

Temple felt the air rush up and her stomach swoop down and then bounce back a tad as she gasped to a stop, hanging a couple inches above the black glass floor and her abandoned shoes.

"Exactly heel height, I believe, Madam."

Temple pushed her feet into the only kind of height she craved, her high-heeled shoes.

Stable again, she released her death grip on Max's arms. "Anyone who ever offers me a ride on the Rio's zip line is going to die the death of a thousand nail file jabs," she told him.

Turning and looking up to the dizzying apex, she saw Midnight Louie flitting down the scaffolding to the stairs with fluid skill.

She turned back to Max. "And what are *you* going to do with the jewels?"

He hefted the black silk scarf, now knotted into a jewelry bag. "Return it to those who suffered from not having it."

"The IRA widows and orphans fund."

Max's smile was somehow secret. "Yes, and for other devastated Irish lives."

"So it's Ireland again for you. And what will you do with this place afterward?"

He looked up. "The technical apex would make a fine penthouse. I could live here. Redeem the place. Redeem myself. Or—"

"Or?"

"Find another place, over the rainbow."

"You're holding a rainbow in your hands," she pointed out, "only you know you can't live there."

"And don't we all do that sometimes?" He bowed. To her and to the cat sitting beside her. "I give you the Irish wish that you live for your rainbows, not for the rain."

She did tear up a bit, for all the people she'd met who couldn't do that, and Irish wishes were always so…infectious.

Louie rubbed on her ankles and she looked down, imagining she was wearing the ruby-red slippers and she'd instantly be back at the Circle Ritz with Matt.

Of course Max was gone. She didn't have to look up and around to know that, and hoped he got to live his own wish. A trio of jewels—ruby, emerald and sapphire—remained on the black glass. A wedding present, she guessed.

She wondered if the Midnight Louie shoes would do anything other than shed Austrian crystals if she tried to knock the heels together three times.

She looked down at Louie and to the door.

On the dark floor on which they stood, the stilled, naked, no longer jewel-toned lights cast a path like a yellow brick road.

36
Command Performance

Molina felt like a green rookie on a stakeout.

She had plenty of reasons to be nervous.

She'd agreed to this "meet" without knowing the purpose.

She'd known the venue was fairly formal, so she'd worn the long black microfiber skirt with a discreet knee-length slit Mariah had whined for her to get for the Barr-Devine wedding reception.

In an act of rebellion against her fashion-obsessed daughter, she wore a bronze forties jacket with padded shoulders and black sequin cuffs and pointed collar. And her magenta suede platform forties shoes for when she moonlighted as the torch singer "Carmen".

Mariah had tagged it a "Goddess" look and approved, although disappointed that it wasn't Rafi she was dining with at the Paris Hotel Eiffel Tower restaurant. When she'd lied and said it was FBI agent Frank Bucek, Mariah made her *"Oh, Mother"* face. Frank was married. The man she was meeting was not.

Now Molina was shuffling forward toward the closed elevator door, as obviously unescorted as an inchworm on a maple leaf.

He appeared beside her just as she reached the brass pole end of the velvet rope and no one remained between her and the closed elevator door to the Paris Eiffel Tower restaurant and the valet who would usher her in. Her turn.

Suddenly "their" turn.

"Timing is everything," Max Kinsella commented.

Sure was. He'd let her feel the embarrassment of an imminent "left at the altar" position. What a manipulator.

No one behind them grumbled about the last minute line-hopper. It was as if Kinsella had been invisible. Hardly. She flashed on his black shirt, black tuxedo jacket. More Oscar Red Carpet than stage magician garb.

"You look very 'Midnight Louie,'" she said, as they turned together in the elevator to face the doors for an eleven-story ride to the elegant French restaurant.

"The highest of praise. I even filed my nails and washed behind my ears."

"I'm not checking," she said.

"Looks like you've done me one better; I've not glossed my lips. You've not been here before?"

"No. Tourist attraction. High-priced tourist attraction. Over high-priced tourist attraction."

Max shrugged. "And on me tonight. I can understand your viewpoint. It's hardly worth the cost unless you snag the one table at the very—point—the prow where the glass walls meet in a Vee." His long tented fingers demonstrated. "Each person at that table for two gets an exclusive view of the Bellagio Fountains when they come on at eight and nine p.m. Sad. The fountain show and music used to play every half hour from dusk until midnight."

"I wouldn't know," she said, "cost and conservation, I assume." Someone had indeed buffed his nails, even more discreetly than Julio's. To outdo a Fontana brother at being a Fontana brother was no small achievement.

He, meanwhile, was running his glance up from her shoes to her shoulders, where a large brandy-colored rhinestone pin perched on the shoulder pad of her vintage "Joan Crawford-style " power suit-jacket. It was the antithesis of anything Temple Barr could ever wear. Or maybe anyone other than Anjelica Huston or a cross-dressing football linebacker.

"Really high heels," he said, looking her straight in the eyes. "I like."

"I don't need to be unintimidating to you. You're already cowed."

He laughed, and she heard a new freedom in it. "Is that what they call it? I know a leader of men can't ever be too much of an Amazon."

"Not with some of the Neanderthals still on the force. The meteor has struck and they're fading away, and still don't know it. But let's not talk work."

"What else would we talk about, Lieutenant?"

"What you really want tonight."

"I'm not that kind, I assure you," he answered.

She laughed, skeptically. The hostess was heading their way. Molina had been scanning the room while they waited and chatted. "The corner table is taken," she noted, raising an eyebrow. "I thought for sure you'd swing it."

"Look again."

She jerked her head around so fast her short bob whipped cheekbone on one side.

Empty. Reset. The previous couple abducted into the Twilight Zone somewhere. He'd invited her to look without doing that himself, as if prescient. The magician always had to surprise, not that she showed she knew it. Molina had needed to develop a shell beyond showing surprise, facing the dirty, tragic details of an endless parade of crime scenes.

The hostess waited before them, large menus cradled on one arm like a baby, to lead them to the desired corner table.

Seated, facing a view of the fountains that intersected with his somewhere in the black overlit Vegas Strip night, she wondered what *she* really wanted from Max Kinsella.

"Relax," he said. "I can at last. You should try it."

"Really?" She shook out the large white napkin to cover her black lap, to avoid looking him in the eye. They'd been…antagonists for so long. She hated the artificial, the imitation, the slippery.

She *was* armed. The dainty pistol at the small of her back. You never knew. Somehow, she still felt naked. Was that "relaxation"?

"Let's just have dinner," he said. "I feel I owe you a grand one, for the headache I've been."

"I feel you're right."

She decided to go berserk. Appetizer for $28 Warm Lobster, Spring Onion Soubise, Basil Infused Peas.

"No Fois Gras?"

"The daughter is a member of PETA, no abused geese."

"Don't tell me! No caviar?"

She longed to make him pay the $290 price tag for a "Trilogy Osetra Caviar, Golden, Russian, Siberia", but fish eggs were probably another daughter-forbidden food.

No one should expect her to avoid magnificent beef. She ordered "The King" filet mignon at $69.

He raised her to $79 with the Rossini filet mignon Fois Gras with Truffle sauce.

She frowned. "Don't you know that 'fois gras' are force-fed geese livers. Brutal."

"Yet beef is a more politically correct food than some others? All right. Being politically correct costs." He topped her with $89 for a 22-ounce bone-in rib-eye with bone marrow.

"It's hard to renounce being a carnivore," she agreed, ordering a snappy peppercorn sauce while he stuck to lulling bordelaise. A steal at only 6$ each.

"Apparently," he said later over a second glass of the smoothest red wine she'd ever tasted and must be sky-high in cost, "you're intent on eating and drinking me out of house and home when that's already been done."

"You do owe me. I've dismissed all charges against you."

"You can't fool me. You can't be bought. Not even by this magnificent dinner." He looked beyond her. "Apparently the Strip is celebrating my innocence. The lighted fountains are flaring to life, right in time for dessert."

Once one looked at the glorious golden rise and fall of the Bellagio fountains, which performed on an automated evening schedule, it always made viewers breathless, like viewing Fourth of July fireworks through a precious topaz lens.

Yet through the glass walls of the restaurant, it was a silent symphony in your head.

"It always reminds me of Tchaikovsky's most popular work," Max said, "used for fireworks displays, the 1812 Overture, celebrating the Russians thrashing Napoleon."

"That's a bit bombastic," she said. "From the rhythm of the fountain highs and lows, it looks a lot more like popular music in this pantomime we see through the glass."

"You would know, of course. *Hmm.* I'm thinking it might be Frank Sinatra's 'Luck Be a Lady Tonight.'"

"Funny. I 'see' Gene Kelly's 'Singin' in the Rain.'"

"Apt, and you're the musician. I'm just a magician with a tin ear. Still, those explosive bursts remind me of the Overture's climactic volley of genuine cannon fire, ringing chimes, and the brass fanfare finale. Explosive, lethal. Defeating Napoleon doesn't happen every day. Not as smooth as dessert here, say, but most symbolic."

Also erotic, Molina thought, as she watched the plumes of gushing water play tag with the pulsing lights.

The waiter brought two white bags emblazoned with the Eiffel Tower restaurant name…

"Dessert to go," Max explained. "The famous Eiffel Tower sculpted in white chocolate."

Max held out his paper bag to her. "A souvenir for Mariah. Say it's from Rafi."

She nodded.

And the waiter left behind the black padded book concealing a bill on the table.

"Are you sure you can afford me?" she asked.

"My current magic wand." Max flipped a tightly rolled bill through his four fingers like a tap-dance cane. When he unfurled the bill, the number one had a train of zeros.

"My work here is done." He slipped the bill inside the small black book.

Mission accomplished; she must be the most expensive "date" ever. Molina concealed a smile as she bowed her head to examine the white chocolate Eiffel tower inside. Two made a mother and daughter pair. Mariah would love it. She looked up to an empty chair opposite her to say thank you.

Molina screwed herself around in her chair to rubberneck. Max Kinsella's black back had already passed the hostess station and disappeared into the line waiting for what was now her table and soon to be available again.

She turned back to the view one last time to imprint the image of the furiously flaring fountains, spotlighted against the Bellagio's Italian Lake Como façade. Fountains and lights were really soaring now. She recognized an unforgettable rhythm. Wasn't Whitney Houston's "The Star-Spangled Banner" on the roster of music? "O'er the rocket's red glare" maybe…

"Oh, my God," she muttered, checking inside the black book holding an over $600 charge and a bill with a one and three zeros on it. One grand. He'd promised her a "grand" dinner.

Who was the mustached man on its face? Didn't matter. She grabbed both bags and nodded appreciatively to the waiter aching to pounce on the tray on her way out. Eighteen-twelve overture, her left foot.

She was reaching for her cell phone. Her vintage suit coat— surprise!—had real pockets.

"Detective Alch, we have overtime to put in. And ask the Captain to use any pull he has with the Bellagio management from past arrests we've made there. Also WET, W-E-T, the design firm that handles the Bellagio fountains and the Mirage flaming volcanoes.

"I've got a notion where the IRA small arms to possible rocket-launcher weapons the Feds want are hidden. Down in the biggest set of plumbing tunnels in town. I think they use frogmen to clean it. Thank God the shows are down to only two an evening. Frank Bucek is going to be ecstatic. Well, maybe a little bit more mellow."

Molina eyed a dim reflection of herself in the elevator doors on the way down. Temple Barr had been right about one thing. She could pull together an awesome look if she tried, if she wanted to look chic while being led by the nose to the object of a quirky law enforcement quest.

37
Mad Max on the Run

"Long bumpy flight?" Liam asked. "You look like hell."

Max unzipped his black leather bomber jacket to reveal the airplane wear, a bespoke suit jacket underneath it. He had more than one stop this trip and had more than one role to play.

He examined the familiar IRA clubrooms, a dingy "below-stairs" pub with the street level a precious ten-second dash above them.

The clientele were the same ex-IRA men. Max was about to take it for a second home, with the remembered scents of yeasty ale and damp wool.

"How'd Sean take to the US of A?" Liam, the leader and spokesman, asked.

"It took to him, but he's back home in County Tyrone. He'll get a lot more American visitors at the B and B now."

"Newfound family. That was well done. Sean is a good man," Liam agreed, shutting his eyes as he pictured Max's cousin's bomb-marred face, Max supposed. "He deserved better than what you and Kathleen left him with."

Max shrugged. He couldn't change what had happened or these men's opinion of him, or her.

"You've got the ransom." Liam's sentence was not a question.

The boys in the bar had been giving Max's suit-jacketed form under the loose jacket the hard-eyed once-over since he'd clattered down the several steps from the street in his motorcycle boots.

He didn't look like his pockets were stuffed with American dollars or British pounds.

He'd kept his back to the wall near the stairwell as the men in billed caps sat ringed around their tables and the one long bar. Probably with an Uzi underneath it.

"I thought," Max said, "our business was not so crude and criminal as kidnapping and ransom…and revenge."

Work boots scraped their readiness for action under the tables and behind the bar.

"But," Max went on, "if you insist, I'll have to see Kathleen before you can see the color of my—excuse me, *your*—money."

Liam nodded to an underling to fetch her from beyond the same door she'd vanished behind, kicking and flailing, a couple weeks ago.

They dragged her out the same way, hollow-cheeked and hollow-eyed now, with the gaunt beauty of a martyr, and slammed her small frame into a chair.

"How have they treated you?"

"It's not been a stay at the Paris Ritz," she muttered so under her breath he didn't make out "Paris Ritz" at first.

"You've not been beaten or molested?" he asked.

"They've not gotten that close." Her voice was a rasp.

He expected that she'd not made it easy for them to be easy on her. Nothing to be done about that now.

Max turned again to Liam. "The money your agents long ago collected in the Americas was also long ago converted to a more compact, more easily smuggled form of currency." He stepped up to the empty table in front of him, reached into a side pocket and paused, smiling, at the scrape of metal on wooden tabletops around the room. Political rebels favored showing weapons that announced their presence, unlike secret agents and hired killers.

"If I may—?"

He eased a large jeweler's pale chamois bag into the light. "Small plastic bags are more usual," Max said, producing a magician's square black silk cloth out of thin air. Now there came the restless shuffles of shoes on damp-swollen wood. "This is more impressive."

He wafted the cloth. It settled without a wrinkle on the rough wooden tabletop.

Then he poured out the pouch's contents. Tiny crystalline clicks announced a tumbling cornucopia of white and rainbow-hued cut gemstones onto the dramatic black background.

"Holy Mother of God," Liam breathed.

Even Kathleen stood, weaving on her feet, forgotten by her guards. "Judas priest," she whispered, but she wasn't looking at Max.

He nodded at her "Yes, Santiago's work."

Liam looked from him to her, fearing a code.

"Santiago?" he asked.

"I mentioned him before. He partnered Kathleen in raising IRA funds, but got greedy when it was time to deliver the goods. He converted the North and South American IRA donations to gemstones in Brazil, where the dealing is good, and then concealed them in Las Vegas. I found them."

"Where? How?" Kathleen demanded. Max shook his head at her to stay silent as her captors gripped her arms again.

He spoke only to Liam. "How and where doesn't matter. I stopped in Antwerp en route here to establish their current value on the international market."

Max put a hand to his left breast pocket, eyeing the surrounding intent gazes and palms on pistols. "Pax. Only getting out a signed statement of value."

Liam nodded when he raised his eyebrows, so Max moved his hand farther inward to pull out a thick business-size envelope of heavy cream paper.

"This is a signed and witnessed appraisal on each stone, and estimation of the value, by Poirot Père et Fils of Antwerp, gem dealers since eighteen-eighteen. Cost me a bundle."

The men started rising to crowd around.

"Her by my side first." Nothing but stage presence and voice supported Max's command.

And a man keeping his word.

Liam nodded.

Kathleen straightened her shoulders and shrugged off her keepers' hands. Ten uncertain steps had her within two feet of

Max, gazing on the jeweled cache. "Santiago. He was never going to deliver the money," she muttered.

"How do I know," Liam asked Max, gesturing his men to fan out behind him, "if you didn't take a 'tip' from the pouch on the way here? How do I know this isn't a magician's illusion, or fakes."

"There comes a point," Max said, "when an Irishman has to take the word of another Irishman or what has all this bloody business been about for centuries and decades? Or the peace, for that matter. I made enough money as a performing magician to want to find this…prize, these funds, given by immigrant Irish folk and their descendants from street sweepers to self-made millionaires, to go to those women and children who suffered generation after generation. I believe that's what Kathleen wanted it to go for, although her partner was a true Judas and hid these dearly purchased gems from her as well.

"And, Liam, I trust you to do as you say. If you find me wanting, you know where to find me, or ask Sean, but he'll tell you go to hell."

"We do still have a hostage of sorts," Liam answered with a crooked smile. "So you swear by Sean's name and broken body?"

"I swear. And on the grave of my friend, Garry Randolph."

Liam looked away. Overzealous ex-IRA men had shot Garry dead in Max's passenger seat during a fruitless, damn foolish street chase through Belfast.

Max sighed, opened the envelope and unfolded the papers to the last page, to point out a karat weight figure to Liam.

"Holy Mother of God! That many? That much?" His men crowded closer to see.

Beside him, Max sensed Kathleen cringing at Liam's repeated ejaculation, for women sworn to the holy mother of God had abused her beyond breaking.

"You'd better put the jewels all back yourself," he cautioned Liam, who nodded and started to do so. No suspicion must fester among brethren.

Max reached without looking for Kathleen's left arm, a stick of itself, and dragged her almost-limp body up the stairs.

The night was chill and damp. The scent of rank fish-and-chips oil tainted the air. Only a few stars poked through a tiny skylight of unrelenting black night.

The air revived Kathleen a bit. Especially when Max slung her over the back of the motorcycle seat and yelled, "Hang on. You know you know how."

After twenty seconds, he felt her small hands making fists in the bomber jacket pockets, curling into the lining. He pulled in the clutch and opened the throttle into spurting speed and started the 'cycle waltzing along Belfast's ancient, war-torn streets.

"Where are you taking me?" Her voice against his shoulder came and went like a thread on the wind.

He smiled. Her will to live was not dead. You can't keep a bred-in-the-bone psychopath down.

"The Paris Ritz sounds like a good idea," he shouted back.

38
We'll Always Have Paris

"What's happening in Las Vegas?"

"Do you really want to know?"

Kathleen tilted her head over the lip of the wineglass she held in her saw tooth-nailed almost-to-the-quick grip. No manicurist could restore those cuticles and nails without a two-month grace period, at least. He pictured Kathleen clawing at every exit from her captivity minute after minute, like a wild thing with only raw desperate persistence on its side. It had been cruel to let them imprison her, but he'd had no choice. He'd had to win her ransom and settle affairs at home before going abroad again.

The candlelight glanced off the epee-thin white cat-claw scars on her left cheek. It was hard for a woman to claim they were four dueling scars contracted at Heidelberg University as a "badge of honor", as heroes did in operettas.

"Midnight Louie" was an intriguing name, but it didn't sound like one that belonged to an unmasked Zorro.

He was amazed to realize that Kathleen's eyes were really green, not vividly green, but a sad, fatigued, pale, old-grass green, without the lurid surprise of the blue-green contact lenses she had worn while wreaking chaos on everyone he knew in Las Vegas.

"Temple Barr has married Matt Devine," he finally told her, " and they're hosting a locally filmed national TV talk show together," he said.

"Married, are they? Happy, are they? Where does that leave you?"

"Not unhappy."

She started laughing low in her throat. The harsh merriment gradually got louder, until people turned around to see what was so horribly funny. "A wishy-washy state for you. Their joint new career sounds as improbable as us doing the same thing. What *will* you do now?"

"I don't know. Not a another show, per se."

"You still have the Max Kinsella magic. You took those Irishmen for a ride."

"A last gasp. With Garry gone—"

"Oh, Unholy Mother of God. I burned his...your house down, didn't I? I was crazy mad, wasn't I? Don't take that as an apology." But she looked uneasy.

"If you need to know you significantly impacted anyone's life, you can take credit for me."

"And you reward me with a stunning new black dress at the hotel boutique and dinner at the Paris Ritz. You must admit I made your life...interesting."

"And what have you made of your life?"

She lifted her hands as if washing them free of herself. "Revenge has kept me alive since I was a toddler. It's let me down. *You've* let me down. You won't be the motive for my manias any longer, you can't stop me from recognizing that I cannot fix what other people did to me. I thought if I could break you, or yours, it would justify my past, my failures. I just wasted everybody's time and you all go on, whole, while I continue to break apart. It isn't fair."

"No, it isn't. You're right. I was a little in love with you and it could have been a lot, if not for the IRA bomb and my missing cousin. What can *you* be, Kathleen? Besides what you are? Think about it."

He reached into his suit pocket and took out a small, square black-velvet box. He knew she'd conned many men into such a gesture for years since they'd met so long ago, but she'd never conned the boy he had been, or who had tried to be a man then. Like Molina, she was approaching forty, a dangerous age for a woman, a single woman. As a young woman, she'd underestimated her strength and saw only weaknesses. Hers. And his.

"It was an unforgettable moment, Kathleen, and still is." He opened the box to show two-karat diamond ear studs dangling emerald green shamrocks.

She gasped. "You swore to Liam."

"Ninety-nine-point-five percent true. I had to save something out for you."

"For me?"

"For what you suffered. 'Her eyes, they shone like the diamonds…'"

"'You'd think she was queen of the land,'" she continued. "'And her hair hung over her shoulders, tied up with a black velvet band.' That's how you always thought of me?"

"How could I not? You were a woman. I was a clumsy kid. I'm not a poor man, even with a burnt-down house, Kathleen. What do you want? Could you be a memoirist, a historian of the Magdalene asylums? Write your own *Philomena?* Join the Magdalene protesters trying to reunite severed mothers and children? An artist? I could send you to the Sorbonne. To any university."

"To psychiatrists?"

"Only if you wanted to frustrate them. Anyway, I 'liberated' something else." He produced a second black-velvet box, this one holding a pendant, a small but magnificent emerald teardrop edged by pavé diamonds.

"For your daughter Iris. From you."

She folded her hands at her breastbone, as amazed as any sixteen-year-old prom queen.

"Thank you for this, and for this." She looked around the grand, gilded restaurant and out onto glittering Paris. "Will you keep an eye on my daughter?"

"Of course. I found her. Iris will do fine, Kathleen. You did the right thing."

"Perhaps the only right thing in my life. I know you can manage to give my daughter my gift without letting her know it's from me."

"You're still young, and beautiful. You can have a life not caged by the past."

"You make me see there is only one thing that sets my heart and soul aflame, that has ever done so. Sadly, it is no longer you. I was that far successful in banishing my first obsession. I need to look elsewhere for a reason to live. So you're right. My hatred needs a new home. And it isn't Paris. And your self-hatred?"

Max shook his head, regretful. "What a terrible twist of fate that the few, possibly redemptive moments of our lives were so quickly followed by the worst years."

"*Hmm.*" Her eyes gazed into some bottomless sinkhole he'd never seen. "No. I'll never be normal. When hatred is the only thing keeping you alive and in one entire piece for so long, happiness seems like torture.

"The nuns hated our ruinous beauty, my mother's and mine," she mused. "That crazy cat did me a favor by marking my cheek. I feel I can no longer tart myself out for a cause gone by. So I'm a lost cause who needs another to pursue."

"Then," Max said, "I have someone I want you to meet. But first, a last, just dessert?"

She decided swiftly on chocolate.

39
Past Acts

Once they were bowed out of the Paris Ritz by an elderly doorman who might possibly have done the same for Princess Diana and the owner's beloved late son, Dodi—although the hotel had been massively renovated since then—Max took Kathleen's left arm and steered her away from the brightly lit tourist areas.

As in all major world cities, the distance between dazzling affluence and exclusivity was as thin as the gap between a five-star restaurant and the Dumpster behind its back entrance.

Max sensed the excitement in Kathleen's rigid frame as he pulled them down a narrow, filthy-smelling street to a tiny European Car with No Name.

Once inside, he handed her a black hoodie and donned a black leather jacket over his fine suit coat.

"I would have preferred a motorcycle," she said.

"Too unprotected. We're going into a No Go zone."

"Like Belfast was during the Troubles."

He nodded. "The French authorities do *not* want us going there and the residents do *not* want us going there."

"Defying both sides. I love it!"

"No swagger until we've found our connection."

She was gazing out the small windows. "Drug connection?"

As the streets narrowed, the stench of food and raw sewage deepened. Max's moving gaze flicked on idling teenage punks and drug dealers watching them pass with the eyes of starving wolves.

He twisted in the cramped driver's seat to pull the Beretta 92 FS pushed into the back of his belt out and into a side jacket pocket, feeling like a slumming Fontana brother.

Kathleen was scanning from left to right. "Men in skirts and women in head scarves. Oh, my. Reminds me of the priests and nuns in the Magdalene asylums."

Max ignored her. He had to spot a specific mid-rise building that had an open market in front. Under a striped awning, a mélange of scents and people and various languages roiled.

"Men in robes and caps, women in black, like me," Kathleen commented. "One with a white tote bag over her shrouded shoulder. Shades of Temple Barr. Excuse me, Temple Devine. Bet she loves that surname."

"Not much. She still works under her maiden name."

"Strange to view the world from an eye-slit in the fabric covering your head and face and neck, like a wimpy balaclava, or...a nun's wimple and veil among those orders who still wear habits."

Max sighed. "Speaking of that, put on this Hijab before you exit the car. The world is different, and the same."

He jerked the car to a stop near a brass monger's tables, and hustled Kathleen out of the car. Wearing the expensive flats he bought her and the long black gown and long-sleeved top with hoodie, which he jerked down over her scarf-covered head, she passed for a Burqa-clad woman.

Inside the carpet-hung doorway were dim, shawl-covered lights and another woman swathed in the ISIS-required full-face black Niqab to reveal only her hands and eyes.

Max nodded to the woman and indicated Kathleen. "Rebecca."

Kathleen flashed him an accusing glance. That was the name the Magdalene nuns had forced upon her when young.

"Sidra," Max said, "this is the woman I told you about."

"Her skin is pale, she is green-eyed, obviously a Westerner."

"She's a master of disguise, a skilled undercover agent, strong and clever," he said.

In acknowledgment, Sidra's lids closed over her beautiful black-brown eyes, framed by midnight-black kohl. "Woman from Ireland rebellion," she said, her English words thick and halting. "We need teachers for English, for girls. Brave teachers."

Kathleen's dark brows frowned. "I am not a teacher."

Max answered, "If you can't feel anything but hatred, what about feeling useful?"

She cocked her head. "Is that why you brought me here? To teach children whose language I'd have to learn? Who's the teacher? Why do they need an experienced agent in the schoolroom?"

Sidra followed their interchange. "I was student who would be a teacher in my time." She dropped the lower part of her Hijab. "I was lucky. The acid missed my eyes."

Kathleen stared expressionlessly at the ruin of the woman's cheeks, nose, lips, and neck, melted to the bone. No wonder her speech was altered.

She turned on Max, the shocked, savage, betrayed look she'd been deprived of doing for seventeen years. "You've brought me here against my will, deceived me."

In answer, he clipped out the familiar ISIS/ISUL "religious" credo: women as chattel, cattle, slaves. Sex slaves, from prepubescent girls to unbelievers' mothers, wives and daughters. Mothers of young girls spared long enough that their daughters would mature to become eight-year-old concubines and their sons turned into slaughtering machines.

"Your old cause is settled, Kathleen," he told her, "but you're needed in a new one."

Kathleen stroked her smooth pale cheek with the almost invisible pale scars. "I'll go with you," she told the woman, "but I am not merely a teacher of girls. I will be a teacher of men."

"They already have their schools."

"Mine would be different."

Sidra reinstalled her veil, looking at Max.

Kathleen interrupted any answer he would give. "I have an ear for languages. I can change my eye and skin color. I am a chameleon."

The beautiful eyes held a question.

Kathleen realized the comparison was unfamiliar. "Like a lizard whose scales turn color to blend into its background. These men like to bomb, torture, destroy, enslave, and behead. I wonder if there is something they would very much *not* like to have beheaded?"

The woman's eyes widened, then narrowed.

Kathleen continued. "What's good for the…she-goat, is even worse for the goat. An American saying. It would certainly put a crimp in recruitment."

The woman nodded. "You mean, we could…?"

"We always could, we just didn't. Us." She pounded her breast bone with a fist. "No more enslaved sisters and mothers and daughters."

Kathleen eyed Max and said under her breath. "I won't bother telling her that I hate men."

Sidra nodded. "Once we are in Afghanistan, we will pass unnoticed unless they wish to beat us for being seen on the streets. I envy Western women. They are so…inventive."

"I'll leave you then," Max said. "Remember, Sidra. She is small but fierce."

Kathleen put a clutching hand on his arm. "You've always had a nerve on you, Max Kinsella." She lowered her face veil. "And so have I."

He watched the two black-shrouded women leave the tented room to blend into the Parisian night. Black-shrouded ghosts, indistinguishable.

> *"Her eyes they shone like the diamonds,*
> *You'd think she was queen of the land,*

Only alternate closing lyrics resonated in his mind.

> *And her hair flowed back from her shoulders,*
> *unbound underneath a black linen band.*

40
Midnight Louie Rings Out the Old...

Alone at last.

As soon as my Miss Temple and her Mr. Matt have made their evening visit to console me on my temporary solo stint at the Circle Ritz and moved on to view the reconstruction above (I am secretly looking forward to stairs and a double balcony), I rush to the zebra-stripe carrier that has been left behind as my presumed sleeping quarters.

I duck my head into the open end, under the hated zippered top, and put my right foot in, my left foot in, and shake it all about in this hokey cat pokey.

As I had hoped, an errand-boy Fontana brother had brought the carrier "home" and done the same usual, tidy job as they would do on a Gangsters limo returning from a jaunt if a customer had left a nail file or a diamond ring behind.

My probing shivs snag something old that makes me blue, leftover from the wedding. I drag it into the concentrated illumination of a nightlight.

I have found a black velvet band.

I pull on the elastic break-away section until I view the white formal bow-tie that has survived two weddings.

Now that my role as Ring Bearer has been exposed to the entire viewing public by a weasel of a man who has been a thorn in my Miss Temple's side and other assorted places, I need to wash my mitts of the whole miserable, humiliating situation with a ritual of my own.

If I must wear costume bits in the future commercials, at least I will be well paid for it. These two Ring Bearer gigs for Mr. Matt's mother and now my new united roommates must be the last of their kind. The end.

I pick up the collar with a snarl of repulsion on my lips, crush it under my foot, and use my head to stretch it open enough to don.

Then I begin my long journey under cover of night to dispose of this unwanted souvenir for good.

Of course I am caught at the very outset by a hanger-on from Ma Barker's cat pack as I trot through the parking lot and into the shelter of the oleander hedge.

"Where are you going, Mr. Midnight?" pipes a small, wee voice.

"None of your business." I look down at what would be a dust bunny if it was inside. "What are you doing here alone? You are too young to be out without your mommy."

He takes offence, hisses more like a teapot than a snake, and produces a darling spiky little halo of yellow-orange baby fur. *Bast spare me!*

"I am four-and-a-half-months and twelve days old."

"Too young," I growl. "You need to eat your Free-to-be-Feline and grow up to be big and strong like me."

"That stuff is rank. I see you drag Free-to-Be-Feline out to the clowder, but I never see *you* eat it."

"Because I gobbled so much of it when I was your age." (And did not know better.)

I try to pass him, but he has those kitten reflexes, and bobs and dodges when I do.

"Look, Kit. I am on important business. Dangerous business. Life-threatening business."

"Goodie. I want to be your—"

I give him the mild brush-off with a side-bump. "Be my what?"

"Apprentice."

Now there is a dirty word if I ever heard one.

I nose him back into the light of the parking lot with a few gruff growls. "Look at you. Scrawny as a starving rat. What do they call that coat color?" I survey a mash-up of white paws and yellow and orange stripes and tufts sticking out any which way.

"Ma Barker calls me her little pumpkin."

"That is not an effective street name if you want to get out and about in the neighborhood and survive the bullies."

"What would be better?"

"I am not a walking Name-the-Baby book."

He sits down and hangs his head.

"Okay, fuzz-bottom. I got a better name. Punky. Why did you hang around when Ma put the kittlings to bed back at the police substation?"

His round kitten eyes, too muddy to tell their final color, narrow. "The substation is a low-level crime-fighting operation. I saw all the housebreaker and Fontana brothers action around this place and figured you would soon be beginning a new undercover assignment."

"Undercover assignment?"

"Under the cover of that sissy zebra-stripe carrier. I see they import you to crime scenes in that."

I like this kit. "Yeah, well, I had to go along with that low-profile approach to save a lot of people."

By "crime scene", I am not sure whether he means my formerly exclusive roommate's faux wedding-cum-armed robbery or her real-this-time wedding. In either case I witnessed me, myself, and I becoming a third wheel as well as a much put-upon Ring Bearer.

Okay, I did stage manage a masterful musical distraction at the first "wedding", and got revenge on Crawford Buchanan by exposing the pusillanimous wedding crasher at the second once-in-a-lifetime event.

(And it had better be, because I will not don the Collar of Shame again.)

I shudder to recall the many photos and videos taken of me wearing my formal white tie, and Buchanan's snarky references in his gossip column to my "cushy midsection, slightly askew whiskers, need of a manicure and a rubdown with a lint-remover".

While I seethe doing a fast rewind down memory lane, Punky's sharp little shivs are prodding my shoulder.

"Crime-fighting, that is what I want to learn about, Mr. Midnight. I was best in my litter at fly-catching, bug-biting, and free-style cactus-climbing."

"Climbing, huh?"

The kit dances around me, feinting with his tiny claws.

"It is going to be a long, confusing walk in the dark," I warn, "unless I can catch us a ride."

"Motor Vehicles of Death?" Punky nods. "Usually they catch us, I am told."

"An urban legend. It goes two ways with MVDs," I tell him. "Always a hard call for our kind. Black is beautiful, but invisible on dark streets. White is a flag for sadists who, sadly, go for road kill. Your coat color is almost fluorescent, which makes you a target. Life is hard, but death is harder, Punky."

"I will be all right. You know your way around."

"That I do. Can you tote this fancy neckpiece while I look for a quick ride?"

"Sure." He sits upright as I paw the thing off my neck and lower the white bow-tie around his. He takes a deep breath so his upright posture does not sink.

So I now have an unwanted tail. Can Bast make things any harder for me? I am pretty sure she can.

"A C-A-B," Punky asks, after we roll out of the backseat of one in perfect low-profile harmony with the feet of a somewhat smashed couple from Kankakee and onto the Las Vegas Strip. "What do those initials stand for?"

"Could Annihilate Babies," I snap.

"Ouch! Mr. Midnight, are you mad at me?"

"Better give me the ball and chain again," I say. "First, hang on to it real tight."

Punky braces his tiny feet and squeezes his eyes shut as I pull the elastic part taut and do a powerful head-duck and neck roll to suspend the black velvet collar and its abhorred attachment again around my neck.

"That white bow tie is very George Clooney on you," Punky says.

I am momentarily flattered. "What do you know about George Clooney and his taste in ties?"

"I saw him getting out of a limo once."

"You do get around for your age. Look. We are heading into stormy waters, lad. Best you follow and observe."

I take stock of the journey.

Once upon a time Las Vegas Boulevard was not known as "the Strip", but it was always wide. Now, with centerline boulevards and hotel-casino properties reaching for or renting space out right to the curbs, it is one big digesting-anaconda of a parking jam.

Everything designed to be seen from a majestic distance, like the Luxor's pyramid and Sphinx and even Leo the Lion at the MGM-Grand, are now crowded and seem kitschy, gigantic, gift shop gewgaws.

In one sense, that makes it easier for lower, in terms of stature, forms of life to mingle with the foot traffic unseen, and harder. I herd Punky through.

"Tails high and toes never still enough to smash," I hiss into one of his half-size ears as we head toward a mob of milling feet in tennies and sandals and flip-flops, all hot and sweaty.

We are heading north, passing the Paris hotel with its half-size Eiffel Tower opposite the Bellagio.

"Look, look, Mr. Midnight!" Punky goes up on tiptoes to snag a claw in my collar, "The Paris hotel's balloon is so pretty, and across from it the famous Bellagio fountains are starting to light up."

"Yeah, yeah, the fountains are one of the last free sidewalk spectaculars left on the Strip, my boy. You want to stay well back or your toes could be a canapé. Listen, I am on a quest. I do not need interruptions."

"Oh."

"Do you know what a quest is? A quest is a place you have to go and a, a—"

"You need a bathroom really bad and there is no sand close by?"

"Not really, no."

"Yes, yes. Have to go. These fountains are very helpful for tinkling."

I sigh. I cannot leave the pipsqueak unattended here and I have to go…keep on walking.

"Look, look, Mr. Midnight. There is a man in the fountain."

"Crazy drunk. They will wade in sometimes."

"He is a really big man."

Now that the lights are flashing on and the water is plashing and splashing, one of the programmed songs starts.

"Vi-va Las Ve-ay-e-gas."

I have already turned to march on, and would have preferred some Souza as walking music.

"Looky, looky!" Punky shrills, about as loud as a cricket, his needle-sharp nails pricking me on the hindquarters.

I turn with a hiss and a snarl. You have to keep these over-caffeinated young ones in their places.

And in the fountain spray I see Punky's "really big man".

Elvis in a white jumpsuit, jewels of all the colors of the rainbow sparkling on his belt. And collar. Hey, Elvis wore really big *collars*. You would think Orion had come down from the sky. Way better than Ophiuchus.

"You see that man?" I ask.

"Oh, yes."

I nod. I suspect the wizards who program these spectaculars can superimpose any image they want on pulsing water and light. A really great marketing tool to broadcast the singers of the current song likenesses. Still, it is not such a bad thing to see the King when one is on a quest. And the kit may have some ESP to make Karma's blue eyes green with jealousy.

"Okay, Punky. We are getting close to my goal. I can use a loyal Page."

"Page? Some of those are in the big blue carts that do not have good things to eat in them."

"Not the kind of pages that people recycle. A Page is a youngster who serves a Knight of the Realm…an apprentice."

"All-righty, Mr. Midnight!" He tries to high five me and misses my mitt entirely with his mini-me version.

"Okay. Here we go. On to Mount Doom."

"Ooh, this sounds scary."

The kit is right. Despite the distracting and bright sights and sounds, we are treading into the heart of darkness.

The first sign is the beginning of a distant, low thrum far beneath foot and paw, an inner-earth engine warming up, consuming heat to make motion.

Punky suddenly worms his way under my midsection. None of that mama stuff!

"What is that big monster purring, Mr. Midnight? Is it the Sphinx or Leo the Lion statues coming to life?" He looks around and up into a forest of hairy human legs blending into a ceiling of crowded-together Bermuda shorts hems.

"This way, follow me," I order.

Soon we have tickled ourselves into the first row of watchers at a roped-off barrier.

"That was hot work, Mr. Midnight." Punky is breathless, but still with me.

"We are facing the second last, free, spectacular attraction in Lost Vegas, son."

"Oh, my." He eyes the dark, humped barrier ahead of us. "Is it that very big fish I hear about in bedtime stories, a whale?"

I have no time to explain that a whale is not a fish, nor a fish story. I nudge him under a baby stroller so no one will step on him.

"Stay here and do not move unless an excited tourist tries to foxtrot over your toes. Watch toward the right, and, no matter what happens, stay where I can see you. That is your trial assignment."

Punky curls into what might pass at a casual glance for an orange tennis ball.

I look up into the impenetrable black sky above the two wings of the lighted hotel high above us. *The Mirage* is emblazoned in huge cursive letters on each wing.

"And if I do not come back—"

"Oh, no, Mr. Midnight!"

"Tell them that I competed my quest."

No worries about being seen haunt me as I slink down the long hairy-legged front line. The whale of a hump Punky spotted is an artificial but fully "live" flame-spewing volcano sitting in a huge lagoon of water. The volcano will erupt in moments, but first the drumbeats introducing the explosive musical score expand into an ominous rumble joined by tribal chants.

The ground trembles beneath feet human and feline. Fireballs on all levels shoot into the air high above the volcano's cauldron. The rocks in the lagoon pulse with red-hot lava, whisker-scorching close.

I could leap from stone to stone to the volcano top in a twinkle when the heat is off. Now, onlookers are feeling the glow even behind the safety rope line, their rapt faces reddened by the pyrotechnics exploding everywhere, even in the plunging waterfalls pelting the lagoon with lava and ash.

I must reach the cleansing sear of the very lip of the volcano. Moving quickly to keep my pads from burning by a wrong step, I climb the rocky incline of ultra-realistic faux rock, rather like Vegas itself.

I am high enough now to be a black moving silhouette against a fiery red curtain of shooting flames. The lagoon waters below are steaming into a smoky mist.

"Oh!" an onlooker shouts. "Something alive is on the volcano."

"Something alive. Look!" becomes a chorus.

I have climbed high enough. Now I need to leap twenty feet up to the top while programmed flumes of fire shoot twelve feet into the night air. Here is where I leave the over-heated lava rocks and bound onto the nearest trunk in the cluster of palm trees.

The trunk's ragged, dense network of stiff fibers rejects the first clutch of my shivs, and I slide down, down before I finally get a good hold.

"It is a cat," someone shouts. "Call the SPCA."

Too late now, folks. Computer programming is computer programming. I ratchet my way up so my back is almost level with the volcano sides where the palm tree trunk curves lower.

The graceful fronds sway above me like hula dancers' skirts. How peaceful. How disturbing. I have hit the moment of truth. I will have to release my bridging palm trunk, twist myself right side up, and manage to land on the only surface that is not erupting with fire and ashes like a hot plate popping corn.

I pause to hear a last onlooker wail, then absolute silence as they realize I may be making Midnight Louie's last leap.

Well, not by name. Although I am sure I will be identified by the loathsome white bow tie, if we both are not burned to cinders first. In some sense, I face a Viking warrior funeral, ruined by a frivolous bit of outdated twenty-first century wearing apparel. Oh, the horror.

In the silence I hear a piercing kitten shriek.

"You can do it, Mr. Midnight! You can do it!"

I give my spine a half-axel skater's twist while releasing my shivs.

Falling water and fire blur past my gaze.

My bones thump with a four-point landing on fake volcanic rock.

Do I hear cheers?

Not done yet.

I claw my way to the edge of the cauldron and gaze into real fire. I work a sensitive mitt pad under the breakaway collar. Breakaway for my safety, of course, so that is why I am clinging to a place where I can make a suicidal leap into a pet cemetery for one. Me.

I jerk my neck back, simultaneously push my front mitt forward, and the white bow-tie collar snaps like a slingshot. I watch a small white-and-black dot falling into ashen gray and sparking red flame, and then into nothingness. My work is done here.

No wonder men hate to wear ties.

The End.
(for now)

Afterword
Of Collars and Katzenklaviers

"Come gather around, cats and kits from all Las Vegas clowders."

I stand on an elevated rock to survey an impressive convocation of cats making a black and white, red and orange, and yellow and gray patchwork on the beige desert landscape west of Las Vegas. The sight resembles a giant calico cat reclining.

My audience is scattered, having to avoid settling their posteriors down on a member of the dominant desert species in this location, all varieties of thorny cactus. Still, we share certain spiked defensive attributes of our own, both the animal and the vegetable.

I have lowered my voice an octave and raised my high notes a trifle to reach the crowd of Vegas cat packs or gangs or clowders, to be technical.

"First," I say, "I must credit my faithful researcher and Internet magician, Miss Temple Barr, for whose nuptials some of you 'gangsters' turned into 'songsters'."

Shrieks and howls rise from each group as I call out their clowder colors.

"From the West side, the Jet-Blacks.

"From the East, the Koi-fighters.

"From the North, the White Blizzard.

"From the South, the Kudzu Nation."

"We came together, my friends, to plot a daring foray and provide a discordant distraction to foil armed robbers at a wedding.

We were successful, but we must also think back to a horrible time in our breeds' past.

"A cat may look at a queen, people say.

"They were speaking of human queens, like Queen Elizabeth of England, queens who sit upright on a throne and wear heavy glittering headdresses and remind me of Bast the cat goddess from ancient Egypt in her temple statue. Both human Queen Elizabeths have lived long and prospered in separate centuries.

"And then there is the fact that cat fancy breeders today call Mama cats "queens". How right they are."

Shaken paws and encouraging yowls.

"And that the veterinarians' device to keep a cat or dog from licking wounds and stitches is called an 'Elizabethan collar' from the stiff lace collars in Queen Elizabeth the First's sixteenth-century court.

"And there is the collar I wore to play the part of a human Ring Bearer at the ceremony where so many of you performed."

Now the growls and mewls are discontented. No cat likes a collar of any kind.

"Thankfully, it is employed more often with dogs (who would lick a cactus if they could), rather than our superior breed."

A huge vibrating purr shakes the sands under me.

I gauge my audience's mood and move on quickly. (Full disclosure: I have, on occasion, for commercial and publicity purposes, donned some odd bits of human attire.) "Now that we have had a history and wearing apparel lessons," I tell my eager audience, "I will proceed to a less glorious, but no less cruel fashion long gone (thank Bast!). All of you know and have heard at your fathers' and great-aunts' whiskers, of that fiendish invention...The Katzenklavier."

Angry growls make low thunder throughout the gathered hordes.

"Some may think I refer to the dreaded days of the witch hunts, during which cats of my color were burned along with our cherished human companions. For five hundred years, my friends!"

A hundred tigers seem to roar back at me.

"That is right. Our people—a loving, peace-loving population— was demonized and almost destroyed for being the color of 'evil' and the mythical 'Devil' humans hate and fear, black like me."

I raise a mitt with the shivs curled into my pads.

The answering roar makes me flatten my ears to my skull.

"Torture," howls the multitude.

Whew. Rabble-rousing is hard work.

"Now to these humans, who were so handy at torturing their own. Sometime in the 1500s they tired of their own limited antics and looked for entertainment toward tormenting their fellow creatures.

"I will not go into all the hideous sins of those days, some of which persist today, as this is a family audience, and I hear many kits squalling among you.

"A popular diversion, especially for bored royalty and, apparently, Germans, was playing the klavier. The word meant 'keyboard' in German, and it resembled the piano we see everywhere in Las Vegas on billboards and signs and on stage."

Heads nod in the dark, their reflective irises winking gold and green. A pervasive *Hmmm* indicates their rapt attention.

"So someone put cats selected for the tone of their mews into boxes with their heads and tails sticking out. Then they attached the boxes to a piano keyboard so that when a key was hit, a sharp spike speared the appropriate cat's tail to produce a full-bodied meow."

"And that is not all. Three hundred years later, in 1803, the German who invented the word 'Psychiatry' (could have used one, I think), prescribed that chronic daydreamers—who probably would be described as 'catatonic' today—'should hear a fugue played on a cat organ "so that the ill person cannot miss the expression on their faces, and the play of these animals—must bring Lot's wife herself from her fixed state into conscious awareness.'"

The patchwork in the moonlight shivers like one moving mass as yowls and screams and shrieks of sympathy and rage ascended to the small cold stars in the night sky.

When rage had exhausted itself, a mass sigh seemed to drift over the desert floor before every cat assembled went silent.

"Now," I say, "you saw that I reassembled this heinous 'cat organ'. Only here and now you were not confined or injured, but brave volunteers willing to surprise and bring down evil men."

I take a breath. Not all these feral cats have had the experience of seeing a piano keyboard or understanding the sequence of the centuries. Not many had begun life as a library cat as I had when very young and impressionable. But cats do not survive as ferals without being curious and clever and they certainly can channel each other's emotions.

"In conclusion," I say, "I salute your unique and amazing voices of varying range and timbre, and how you scared the evil humans out of their skins and into very long jail sentences. And for moving as quietly as church mice to arrive and depart and, especially, for not snacking on church mice on the job.

"Go forth as proudly as a pride of lions, and the appetizers are on me."

Tailpiece
Midnight Louie Sums up

I so hate doing math, even though I have many more toes to do it on than most people.

Sixteen toes and sixteen shivs, which is the number four squared, which is fifteen more razors on my person than "Big Bad Leroy Brown" had in his shoe. No wonder I am such a successful, and respected, private investigator. They do not call one variety of cactus "Cat Claw" for nothing.

Yet, no matter how tough a guy is there are some things he cannot say, or change.

I have come to a sad parting . My days as an "alphacat", as depicted in this sequence of twenty-eight mystery novels, are over.

Be warned, though. I am still an Alpha Cat in capital letters, and have not hung up my snap-brim fedora for good. That is a metaphor, folks. It means I still do not like wearing human hats unless very well paid. And it looks like I will be with my new TV commercial contract.

I have had quite a time shepherding my human crew on their way to a reasonably happy ending, or a dead end, in the case of the bad and the murderous. And they say cats are hard to herd.

I am expecting to see all of my friends and acquaintances around Las Vegas in the future, as you may do if you pay a visit to Chez Louie again.

Farewells should be short, but sweet.

I am short, but not sweet.

And that is one thing that will never change.

Very Best Fishes,

Midnight Louie, Esq.

Want Midnight Louie's print or e-scribe
Scratching Post-Intelligencer newsletter or
information on his custom T-shirt?
Contact Louie and Carole at PO BOX 33155
Fort Worth TX 76163-1555
Or sign up at www.carolenelsondouglas.com.
E-mail: cdouglas@catwriter.com

Tailpiece
Carole Nelson Douglas on
Getting There and Back Again

Well, who thought we'd all live this long?

This is the 28th and final title in Midnight Louie's alphabet mystery series.

Back in 1994, after writing the first two Midnight Louie mysteries, I knew I could not abandon this charming, swaggering, politically incorrect big guy of a stray cat.

So I committed to an "alphabet" title series that would eventually expand to 28 titles. What a rash leap of faith. There was no guarantee that publishers or sales would keep the series (or me) going that long, twenty-four years.

The thick and thin of the publishing industry is legendary, but Louie and I are both stubborn survivors, and I knew that Louie had "legs". And, thanks to the support of readers expressing love and support from the days of notes and letters to thousands of emails, we made it through.

I "met" Midnight Louie in a newspaper feature I wrote in 1973 about a homeless black motel cat a woman flew two thousand miles home to rescue. The lodgers called him Midnight Louie and he lived off the motel's expensive koi fish and the kindness of strangers. A trip from the fish pond to the pound's Death Row was imminent. As a newspaper reporter, I was intrigued when the woman wrote a three-inch-long Classified ad that cost $30 to give him to the "right" home for a dollar. I defied journalistic custom to let him tell his story in his own words.

And he paid me back when I decided to make him a self-appointed Las Vegas PI whose narrative first-furperson chapters framed an innovative four-book "miniseries" inside a category romance line. That started a miniseries trend for trilogies and linked books that spread like wildfire through the many romance lines then, propelling many superstar careers of this day.

Not Louie and me. The editor "gave" the idea to the "real" romance writers she was pushing and kept us from publication for four years, then drastically cut the four books to fit into two volumes and buried them on the publisher's list. Being done wrong only drove this twenty-pound, hard-boiled, alley-cat charmer into the mystery genre. That's why I call him "Muscle in Midnight Black". Louie's adventures account for 32 of my 63 published novels and he stars in several short stories to boot, including an appearance with Sherlock Holmes and Irene Adler.

As for Louie and me now, we're looking forward to exploring a reimagined world where the familiar remains in place, but fascinating new characters and cases enter stage left, and right. Even Louie can't reinvent himself single-handedly for such a long-lasting career. Only readers can do that. Thank you all for your support of the journey Louie and associates and I have made in the best of company, you.

ABOUT THE AUTHOR

www.carolenelsondouglas.com
www.wishlistpublishing.com

CAROLE NELSON DOUGLAS is the award-winning author of sixty-two novels in the mystery/thriller, women's fiction, and science fiction/fantasy genres.

She is noted for the long-running Midnight Louie, feline PI, cozy-noir mystery series (*Cat in an Alphabet Soup, Cat in an Aqua Storm, Cat on a Blue Monday,* etc.) and the Delilah Street, Paranormal Investigator, noir urban fantasy series (*Dancing with Werewolves,* etc.). Midnight Louie prowls the "slightly surreal" Vegas of today, narrating interlarded chapters in his alley-cat noir voice. Delilah walks the mean streets of a paranormally post-apocalyptic Sin City, fighting supernatural mobsters with Louie's wile, wit and grit.

Douglas was the first author to make a Sherlockian female character, Irene Adler, a series protagonist, with the *New York Times* Notable Book of the Year, *Good Night, Mr. Holmes,* and the first woman to write a Holmes spin-off series. Her award nominations run from the Agatha to the Nebula, including Lifetime Achievement Awards from *RT Book Reviews* for Mystery, Suspense, Versatility, and as a Pioneer of Publishing for her groundbreaking multi-genre work. She has won a clowder of Catwriters' Association first place Muse awards, and is a four-time finalist for the Romance Writers of America's Rita award in four different categories.

An award-winning daily newspaper reporter and editor in Minnesota, she moved south to write fiction full-time and was recently inducted into the Texas Literary Hall of Fame. She does a mean Marilyn Monroe impersonation, collects vintage clothing and homeless cats, and enjoys Zumba, but has never danced with werewolves. (That she knows of.)

CPSIA information can be obtained
at www.ICGtesting.com
Printed in the USA
LVOW12s1145181216
517753LV00001BA/8/P